... of grace and forgiveness

... most broken moments."

—*LIBRARY JOURNAL* FOR
UPON A SPRING BREEZE

"Irvin's novel is an engaging story about despair, postnatal depression, God's grace, and second chances."

—CBA *CHRISTIAN MARKET*

"A warm-hearted novel that is more than a romance, with lovable characters, including two innocent children caught in the red tape of government and two people willing to risk breaking both the Englisch and Amish law to help in whatever way they can. There are subplots that focus on the struggles of undocumented immigrants."

—*RT BOOK REVIEWS*, 4-STAR REVIEW
OF *THE SADDLE MAKER'S SON*

"Irvin has given her audience a continuation of *The Beekeeper's Son* with complicated young characters who must define themselves."

—*RT BOOK REVIEWS*, 4-STAR
REVIEW OF *THE BISHOP'S SON*

"Once I started reading *The Bishop's Son*, it was difficult for me to put it down! This story of struggle, faith, and hope will draw you in to the final page . . . I have read countless stories of Amish men or women doubting their faith. I have never read a storyline quite like this one though. It was narrated with such heart. I was full invested in Jesse's struggle. No doubt, what Jesse felt is often what modern-day Amish men and women must feel when they are at a crossroads in their faith. The story was brilliantly told and the struggle felt very real."

—DESTINATION AMISH

Beneath the Summer Sun

OTHER BOOKS BY KELLY IRVIN

EVERY AMISH SEASON NOVELS
Upon A Spring Breeze

Beneath the Summer Sun

Through the Autumn Air (available August 2018)

THE AMISH OF BEE COUNTY NOVELS
The Beekeeper's Son

The Bishop's Son

The Saddle Maker's Son

NOVELLAS BY KELLY IRVIN
A Christmas Visitor found in *An Amish Winter*

Sweeter than Honey found in *An Amish Market*

Snow Angels found in *An Amish Christmas Love*

One Sweet Kiss found in *An Amish Summer*

The Midwife's Dream found in *An Amish
Heirloom* (Available January 2018)

Beneath the Summer Sun

KELLY IRVIN

Library of Congress Cataloging-in-Publication Data

Names: Irvin, Kelly author.
Title: Beneath the summer sun / Kelly Irvin.
Description: Grand Rapids, Michigan : Zondervan, [2018] | Series: An every Amish season novel ; 2
Identifiers: LCCN 2017039622 | ISBN 9780310348085 (paperback)
Subjects: LCSH: Amish--Fiction. | Large type books. | GSAFD: Christian fiction. | Love stories.
Classification: LCC PS3609.R82 B46 2018 | DDC 813/.6--dc23 LC record available at https://lccn.loc.gov/2017039622

Printed in the United States of America

17 18 19 20 21 / LSC / 5 4 3 2 1

To Debby, Doug, Pam, and Larry Junior
(may he rest in peace). Love always.

See, I have refined you, though not as silver;
I have tested you in the furnace of affliction.

Isaiah 48:10

DEUTSCH VOCABULARY*

aenti: aunt

bopli(n): baby

botching: clapping game

bruder: brother

daed: father

danki: thank you

dawdy haus: grandparents' house

dochder: daughter

eck: married couple's corner table at a wedding reception

Englischer: English or Non-Amish

fraa: wife

Gmay: church district

Gott: God

groossdaadi: grandpa

groossmammi: grandma

guder mariye: good morning

gut: good

hund: dog

jah: yes

kinner: children

lieb: love

mann: husband

Meidung: avoidance, shunning

Mennischt: Mennonite

mudder: mother

nee: no

onkel: uncle

Ordnung: written and unwritten rules in an Amish district

rumspringa: period of running around

schweschder: sister

suh: son

wunderbarr: wonderful

*THE GERMAN DIALECT SPOKEN BY THE AMISH IS not a written language and varies depending on the location and origin of the settlement. These spellings are approximations. Most Amish children learn English after they start school. They also learn high German, which is used in their Sunday services.

JAMESPORT, MISSOURI, FEATURED FAMILIES

THE TROYERS:

Jennie (widow, husband was
  Atlee)

Matthew

Celia

Micah

Cynthia

Mark

Elizabeth

Francis

James and Olive (parents-in-
  law)

Darren and Bertha (brother-
  and sister-in-law)

Raymond (brother-in-law)

THE MILLERS:

Peter and Kate (Jennie's brother
  and sister-in-law)

Luke (brother)

Silas (brother)

THE GRABERS:

Leo (bachelor)

Aidan (Leo's cousin)

Henry (cousin, married with a
  son: Matthew)

Timothy (cousin) and Josie and
  their children: Samuel,
  Robert, Vera, and Nyla

Paul (cousin, bachelor)

THE ROPPS:

Mary Katherine (widow,
    husband was Moses)
(children still at home)
Barbara

THE KAUFFMANS:

Laura (widow, husband was Eli)
Children all grown

THE WEAVERS:

Solomon (widower)
Elijah
Luke and Jane (their son:
    William)
Ruth and Seth Byler
Sophie and Obediah Stultz
    and their children: Esther,
    Lewis, Martin, and Angela
Hazel and Isaac Plank and their
    children: Rachel, Sarah,
    Levi, Gracie, Jonah
Bess (daughter-in-law, her son:
    Joshua)

OTHER FAMILIES:

Freeman and Dorothy
    Borntrager (bishop)
Cyrus and Josephina Beachy
    (deacon)
Iris
Joseph
Rueben
Samuel
Carl
Louella
Abigail

ONE

THE SMACK OF THE BASEBALL AGAINST AN ALU-
minum bat sounded like summer. At thirty-seven, Jennie Troyer
hadn't been a student in many years, but the end-of-school picnic still
caused her spirits to soar as if she were ten and set free for the next
few months. She might be old, but she understood how her children
felt. That curious lightheartedness for this one afternoon on the last
day of April.

Smiling at the thought, Jennie clapped as Cynthia smacked a
blooper into what served as right field and scurried to the discarded
rug that did double duty as first base. Micah hurled the ball to Celia at
second base, and the chatter from the parents seated in lawn chairs on
the sidelines reached a crescendo. Jennie's children comprised almost
half the players on the field. Their cheeks were red, their hair sweaty,
and their clothes dirty, but they didn't seem to mind that summer
had arrived early in Missouri.

After all they'd been through—no matter how much time had
passed—they deserved a few hours of carefree, childish play. Despite
the heat Jennie shivered. She studied the rows of corn plants in nearby
fields and tried to recapture the happiness she'd felt only seconds

earlier. Raising her face to the sun, she begged it to burn away a pain that still barged into her day at odd, unexpected moments.

"Your *kinner* are on fire today, aren't they? I'm surprised Francis isn't out there too." Mary Katherine Ropp plopped her dumpling-shaped body into a sagging lawn chair next to Jennie's. Grasshoppers sprang in all directions in her wake. She smelled of charcoal and grilled hot dogs. "He's Elizabeth's little shadow these days."

Afraid her perceptive friend would read her face, Jennie sprang to her feet and did a head count with her index finger. Matthew, her graduate and oldest son at fourteen, stood at third base, his hands on his hips, his usual sullen look on his face. Followed at various places on and off the field by Celia, thirteen; Micah, eleven; Cynthia, ten; Mark, seven; and Elizabeth, six and just finishing her first year of school. No Francis. At four, her youngest had a mind of his own, a penchant for trouble, and sturdy little legs to carry him there.

"Mark was showing him how to swing the bat only a second ago." With so many mothers in the mix on picnic day, Jennie could count on family and friends to keep an eye on her youngest, but still she surveyed the crowd. Force of habit. Since Atlee's death four years earlier, she held both father and mother reins in tight fists that she didn't dare relax. "I better track him down before he decides to eat an entire pan of applesauce cake or feed a worm to one of the *boplin*."

"He's probably playing on the swings. Let's talk about the store while we have the chance." Mary Katherine crossed her ankles and sat still for what was most likely the first time that day. "Your help would mean so much to me and the others, but even more, it would be good for you. It's time."

Not time. The mere thought of talking to the English tourists and making change while they waited made Jennie's hands tremble and her mouth go dry. Several families had pooled their meager funds to open a new tourist store in Jamesport. Jennie loved sewing quilts and baby blankets, embroidering dresser scarves and pillowcases, making jams and jellies, and baking cookies for the store. Working there was another angry beehive altogether. "I better check on Francis. You know how much trouble that boy can stir up."

"We need to talk." Mary Katherine tempered her firm words with a sweet smile that didn't match the worry in her blue eyes. "Soon."

Her friend never worried about anything. Leastways not that it showed. Torn, Jennie paused. "What's wrong?"

"Nothing. Nothing new." Mary Katherine clapped for Mark's single into right field. Jennie automatically joined her and the other parents. "The store was my idea. Folks need the income. They're not making ends meet just farming. They haven't for a long time."

"It was a good idea."

"We're putting a lot of our precious savings into the monthly lease payments and the renovations." Turning the space from a butcher shop into Amish Treasures had been a major undertaking, but one they'd accomplished together. "So far there's only a trickle of customers."

"The tourist season is only just beginning." Jennie let her gaze wander across the crowd along the sideline. No Francis. "Give it time. Everyone thinks it's a good idea."

Mary Katherine frowned, her freckled nose wrinkled. "I don't know about Freeman and the other men."

"They would've said no if they didn't."

"I'm a widowed woman. They want me to make myself useful, I reckon."

"You worked at the bed and breakfast. You're our scribe for the newspaper. You've always been helpful. Your middle name is helpful."

"My middle name is Katherine."

She said it with such aggravation, Jennie giggled. Mary Katherine shook her head and grinned. "Go find Francis. Make sure he's not climbing on the roof. We'll talk later. We also need to finish Bess's quilt. They'll be publishing their announcement any day now, if I'm not mistaken. And I've never been mistaken."

Indeed, she rarely was. They needed to finish the blue-and-white Double Irish Chain quilt for Bess Weaver, who would leave her widowhood behind soon—as soon as she and Aidan Graber got around to telling the world they planned to marry. The Gmay elders were pleased with that, even though everyone pretended not to know. How could they miss the looks that passed between those two? The elders likely weren't so pleased with the remaining trio of widows—Jennie, Mary Katherine, and Laura Kauffman—who each had more than their share of years alone.

Some things couldn't be helped. Or were meant to be. Or some other such silly platitude. Jennie kept busy and chose not to think about the empty corners of her life. If she didn't have a husband, she certainly couldn't be trotting off to work in the store. Her children already lacked a father. They needed their mother at home where she ought to be.

Jennie tried to keep her tone conciliatory. "Come by the house later. Pick up Laura on the way and we'll get in a few hours of quilting tonight."

"Good plan. We'll talk while we sew. Bring me a glass of lemonade when you return, if you don't mind." Mary Katherine scratched with plump fingers at barbecue bean sauce that had dried on her apron. Catsup and mustard stains made for an abstract painting with the apron as an impromptu canvas. Her tone said the quilt would not be the only topic of conversation. "All that burning hot dogs on the charcoal grill has given me a heatstroke. I'll cheer on the team."

At fifty-five plus, Mary Katherine had the constitution of a much younger woman with vim and vigor that Jennie tried her hardest not to envy. Most days she felt much older than her age. Envy was a big, fat, slimy sin. "Of course. Lemonade and humongous slices of applesauce cake all around."

Mary Katherine acknowledged the veiled compliment—she'd baked the cake—with a small grin. She leaned back in the chair with a contented sigh. No doubt, in seconds the older woman would be snoozing.

Swatting at a cloud of gnats, Jennie threaded her way through the clusters of folks visiting and eating homemade vanilla ice cream that called her name even though she was stuffed with hot dog, chips, baked beans, and coleslaw. No Francis at the food tables. No curly brown-haired, dimple-cheeked little boy who looked like an angel and raced around like a dervish that reminded her all too much of Atlee.

Don't. Don't do it.

She forced herself to breathe, in and out, in and out.

A gaggle of girls cut in front of her, laughing, hands entwined, racing for the homemade ice cream station manned by Atlee's brother, Darren Troyer. Their gazes connected over the sea of white prayer *kapps*. He had that same dark, curly hair as his brother, but his was washed through with fine silver strands that stuck out from under his straw hat. His salt-and-pepper beard curled in just the same way as his brother's. The same steely blue eyes cut through her. Jennie swerved left.

A sudden chill ran through her despite the humid air that

warmed her damp face. She wrapped her arms around her middle and ducked her head. Her gaze landed on the bruise on her wrist. She'd hit it on the gate the day before, trying to corral the horses. The ugly black-and-blue mark mesmerized her.

Atlee grabbed her arm and jerked her around to face him. "You'll do as I say and you'll do it now, *fraa.*"

Pain ripped through her arm and shoulder. "I'm sorry. I didn't mean to disagree. I only meant—"

"You don't know your place. You never have." His fingers tightened in a painful grip. His other hand came up and wavered in the air overhead. It dropped. "Go on. Get in the house. The laundry won't do itself."

She stumbled back, afraid to look away, even though he rarely hit her. Not like that. He used words like fists. They hurt far more.

"What's going on, Ms. Jennie? You look perturbed."

Jennie flinched, jumped, and stifled a shriek. Her sisters-in-law—all three of them—looked up at the same time from a whispered conversation that surely involved a critique of her widow's life. Jennie shrugged and smiled. She turned to greet Nathan Walker, itinerant book salesman, who always managed to arrive at these gatherings while food still prevailed in abundance. "*Nee,* no, I'm not worried."

It had been four years, and still, those moments came. Not as often, but just as heart-stopping. She schooled her voice to halt the tremble. "I'm looking for Francis. It seems he's wandered off."

Nathan shoved his red St. Louis Cardinals baseball cap back on his head, revealing a tan line across his forehead. His damp auburn hair was plastered to his skin. He wore his usual white short-sleeve cotton shirt, khaki pants, and Nike sneakers. He dressed like a man who didn't worry too much about what he put on in the morning. "Want me to track him down for you?" His broad smile warmed blue eyes with a slight tinge of lilac in them. A color that bemused Jennie every time she saw him. What exactly did a person call it? Something outlandish like periwinkle? "He can't have gone too far on those little legs."

It was her job alone to keep Francis safe. It had been since he was six months old and Atlee had left her struggling to care for seven children. No matter how hard it was, she couldn't shake a sneaky feeling of relief.

It had been fifteen years of never knowing what might set him off, never knowing what angry load he would decide to dump upon her the second he set the buggy in motion after a lovely, yet egg-shell fragile day. Guilt married relief. He was gone.

No one knew her guilty secret. But God knew. God knew because He let it happen.

Her dream of being a wife and mother became an increasingly menacing nightmare with each passing year and each new baby. What kind of monster did it make her that she had longed for sweet release and it had come—in the form of her own husband's death?

Stop it. Stop it. Stop it.

"Jennie?"

She started.

Nathan stared, a puzzled look on his face.

"*Jah*, yes, I mean. You'd be surprised." She swallowed against the bitter taste of bile in the back of her throat and perused the yard where the men had set up a trampoline. Several children took turns bounding into the air.

Think. Think. She wouldn't put it past Francis to try to skinny up the pole. No, he wasn't there. Nor had he convinced one of the younger mothers to push him in the tree tire swing. "Last week, I found him beating a path down to the pond on his own when he was supposed to be helping in the vegetable garden. I'm not sure if he intended to go for a swim or fish. He has no fear."

Francis also didn't seem to find it necessary to tell her about his adventures. He might be the spitting image of his father, but he didn't share Atlee's affinity for endless proclamations and angry tirades. In fact, he barely spoke a word. Probably because he couldn't get one in edgewise with six older brothers and sisters.

"He's all boy, that's for certain." Nathan laid his ever-present backpack of books on a picnic table bench. Not that he would sell books at the picnic. These were books he read. The man always had one at the ready in case he had a free moment. He turned and strode toward the schoolhouse, his long legs pumping. "I'll check inside if you want to look in the outhouses."

The thought of the trouble a four-year-old could get into in an outhouse curdled the food in Jennie's stomach. She broke into a trot and headed first to the boys' building. Empty. Fighting the urge to pinch her nose against the odor of bodily functions heated by a brilliant sun, she called Francis's name. No answer. "Anyone there? Francis, are you in there?"

No answer. She did a quick peek. Empty. No one in the girls' outhouse, either.

Where had he gone? Two purple martins scolded her from their perch on the bird apartment house the boys had constructed. Neither seemed willing to share her son's whereabouts.

She whirled and tromped through overgrown dandelions and

scraggly grass to the school. Nathan bounded down the steps. "Empty except for Nellie and Sue Ann *botching*. I told them they should go outside and enjoy the day." He jerked his thumb toward the fence and the open field on the other side dotted with rows of corn stalks just breaking through the soil. Small leaves fluttered in the lackadaisical breeze. "Any chance he took off exploring on his own?"

Nathan's use of the German name for the clapping game made Jennie smile. He spent a lot of time playing games with the kids. "With Francis anything's possible."

Her blood pulsing in her ears, hands sweaty, Jennie gripped a fence post. Surely the gazes of her brothers, their wives, Atlee's family, and even Bishop Freeman were upon her. How did she get over the fence with its barbed wire without ripping her dress, or worse, falling?

Smiling, Nathan knelt and stretched apart the bottom wire and the second one. He smelled good. Like spicy aftershave. She tried not to notice, but a person couldn't help what her nose decided to do, could she?

She crawled through the space and straightened. Despite herself she looked back. Freeman frowned. The tribe of in-laws stared. His sisters had those same icy-blue eyes and the same black hair peeking around their kapps. It was as if Atlee peered at her wherever she went, following her, taunting her, accusing her.

"Are you all right? Aside from Francis taking the fun out of the picnic?" Nathan wiggled through the opening, an intricate feat given his six-foot frame, which appeared to be mostly legs. "You look..." He paused as if searching for the right word. "Tired." His expression said that wasn't the word he sought.

No one, besides Mary Katherine and Laura, ever commented

on how Jennie looked. She started forward, careful not to step on the plants. She let her gaze roam to the other side and the tree break that divided the field from another filled with sprouting rye. No sign of her son. "I'm fine. No reason to complain."

None whatsoever. Which didn't keep a body from doing it. It was human nature, Mary Katherine would say.

"If you need help with anything, I'm available."

This Mennonite traveling salesman wanted to help her? "How long will you be in Jamesport?" Not the proper response at all. She should've said *thank you* and let it go. "I mean, don't you have work to do?"

"Actually, that's what I wanted to tell you. I was looking for you—"

"Please don't do that." Fear thrilled through her. She quickened her step toward the heart of the field. "Francis, Francis! Are you out here? If you are, you better come back now." No answer. She didn't want Nathan thinking about her at all. She didn't want any man thinking about her.

She glanced over her shoulder again. In the distance, Leo Graber hitched his horse to his buggy. He probably intended to leave the picnic early. Not unusual for a man who wasn't much for socializing.

"Why would you be looking for me?"

"I didn't mean to offend you." Nathan's sunburned face turned a deeper, burnished red to match his hair. "I only wanted to say, well, nothing, I guess. I mean, just say hello, I guess."

His arm swept out, forcing Jennie to halt.

"What—?"

"Look." He whispered the word and then put a finger to his lips.

She followed his gaze. A sleeping Francis, his straw hat clasped in his dirty hands, his curly brown hair wet with sweat, lay sprawled under an inkberry bush sprouting below the farthest oak trees in the windbreak.

Just beyond him, curled up like a garden hose, lay a rattlesnake enjoying the shade on a soft cushion of weeds.

TWO

Jennie stopped breathing. Her lungs protested. She didn't want to move, not even to let them expand and contract. Silly snake facts spouted by her son Micah when he wanted to make her shiver presented themselves. Snakes can't sweat so they avoid the afternoon sun. They take naps during the day and come out when it's cooler and dark. This one would likely stretch at least four feet long, not including its rattle. Its skin glowed brown and golden with a darker stripe down the back.

Jennie's mouth went dry. Her stomach chose that moment to heave. The hot dog did not want to stay down. Purple spots dotted her vision.

"Cottonmouth?" Nathan whispered. He stood motionless at her side. "Poisonous?"

"Rattler." She tried to speak without moving her mouth. "Rare here, but you see them. Obviously."

"Don't move." His voice barely audible, he took one step, stopped. "I'll grab Francis and we can hightail it out of here."

"Nee. You'll startle him and he'll holler." Her fear of snakes might be big, but her fear of one of her children being hurt was greater. She searched the ground. Not a single rock big enough to dispatch the viper. "Don't. Move."

Leo could help. If anyone could help it would be Leo. He'd know what to do.

He was a man who never flinched. He'd been through the worst. Since that terrible day, he'd taken everything in silent stride.

She turned slowly, carefully, tiptoeing at first, ridiculous as it must look, and then ran.

Her sneakers sank into the rich, dark soil, impeding her progress. The scent of sweat and grass and dirt assailed her nose. She needed to run, faster, faster. *Gott, help me. I know we're not on the best of terms, but please, Gott, help me.*

Leo had the reins in his hands when she reached the fence. She slammed to a halt. "Help. Snake. Rattler. Francis."

He dropped the reins and reached behind the buggy seat. A long, lean, deadly looking brown rifle emerged.

Rifle in hand, he hurtled over the fence like a boy half his age. His straw hat plummeted to the ground. His legs were much longer than Jennie's, but fear and adrenaline that tasted like metal on her tongue propelled her in his wake.

Leo slowed, slowed some more, halted, then stepped forward with a balance and ease that spoke of a much smaller man. He raised the rifle, took aim, and sent the snake on its way in an explosion of sound that made Jennie jump even though she knew it was coming. The acrid smell of gunpowder filled the air and burned her nose.

With a blood-curdling scream Francis rolled over, hopped to his feet, and ran straight into Jennie's open arms. She scooped him up and hugged him hard, despite the urge to take him to the woodshed for a "talk."

"*Danki.*" She spoke the single trembling word to Leo but let her gaze encompass Nathan. He was willing to do more. He simply hadn't known what to do. "Francis thanks you too."

A spark of something indefinable in his amber eyes, Leo nodded and set off across the field, his rifle slung over his shoulder, his gait loose and easy. Taking it in silent stride, just the way she knew he would.

Francis wiggled, trying to break free. "Snake."

"Nee. That's a poisonous snake. Dead or not dead, stay away from snakes."

"*Gut.* Micah says."

"Your *bruder* knows I'm afraid of snakes and he likes to tease me. Besides he's talking about garden snakes, not rattlesnakes. Not to mention you've caused enough trouble already."

His expression perplexed, Nathan's gaze swung from Francis to Leo's receding figure. "He carries a rifle around in his buggy?"

"Turkey season opened last week."

"He didn't have much to say."

"It's rare he says anything." Jennie corralled Francis with a tight grip on his arm. He smelled of little boy sweat and cookies, an aroma like cologne to her discerning nose. Others might not understand Leo, but she did. He lost something valuable and he didn't know how to get it back. "He walks to his own beat."

"Any particular reason?"

"His *daed* dropped dead in front of him when he was young, and a few years later, his *mudder* passed. It hit him hard. He never quite got over it."

"He doesn't believe in God's plan?" Nathan looked pained. "Or he doesn't like the one God has for him?"

"He was baptized same as the rest of us, but it seems he skips out on church services more than most." Jennie would never dream of doing such a thing, but she understood the desire. How could God's plan include falling in love with a man who took her breath away with his romance before the wedding and took her breath away with his anger after it? How could God let a father die in front of his young son, leaving him to feel the guilt and pain of not being able to rescue him? "He has his reasons."

"I'm surprised the bishop allows it." Nathan made as if to pick up Francis. "He's heavy. Let me carry him for you."

"Nee, he's capable of walking." She held on tight to Francis's arm. For some reason she couldn't seem to let go. The bishop had been with Leo after his father died. He'd been there when Leo's mother followed. Freeman understood and made allowances. They all did, hoping Leo would be healed of his malaise. Jennie had prayed for it all those years ago, prayed Leo would see her and seek her out. She'd seen him looking at her in church or at frolics, a strange, pained look on his face. But he didn't. Atlee did. "Freeman and Solomon Weaver talk to him pretty regular, but his cousin Aidan's the only one who can really reach him."

Aidan Graber and his bride-to-be, Bess, who thought match-making between his cousin Leo and Jennie a good idea.

Not a good idea. If Leo had been interested, he would've come to the singings. He would've asked her out for a second buggy ride after that first, awkward one. But he hadn't. He'd disappeared into his own little world, leaving Atlee to step in.

"You can let people help you." Nathan's tone took on a tinge of defiance. "There's no shame in it, especially for someone who has seven kinner to raise on her own."

"I have all the help I need."

"You don't want my help you mean?" Nathan's arms went slack at his side. He glanced at the buggy receding in the distance. "Is it Leo?"

"I don't know what you're talking about." The man was a little too perceptive. She'd given up on Leo a long time ago. "You were kind to help me look for Francis today. I appreciate it."

"I always want to help." Nathan sighed and rubbed his big hand across his clean-shaven chin. "If you can't figure out why, I'm in deep doo-doo."

"Doo-doo." His face split in a grin, Francis slipped from Jennie's grasp and skipped around them in a widening circle. "Doo-doo!"

The boy rarely said a word. He picked this one to repeat?

Shaking his head, a rueful smile on his face, Nathan pivoted and walked away with a backward wave of his big hand.

"Not nice. We don't say words like doo-doo." Jennie propelled Francis forward on his dirty, bare feet as Nathan waded back into the picnic crowd. Aidan stopped him for conversation, then Solomon Weaver, followed by Freeman Borntrager. Bess handed Nathan a plate of cookies. He smiled and gestured. The man was well liked by everyone. "Besides, I think it might be me, not Nathan, in deep doo-doo."

THREE

TALK ABOUT CRASHING AND BURNING. THE SOUNDS
of folks enjoying the picnic loud in his ears, Nathan tried to concentrate on Freeman's words. Instead, the conversation with Jennie
continued to ring in his ears. He hadn't said what he meant to say.
What could he say that Leo-to-the-rescue's rifle blast obliterating a
rattlesnake wouldn't overshadow? Nathan had chickened out. More
hen than rooster, that was him. *Bawk, bawk, bawk.*

He hadn't told her his plan. Just as well. She was oblivious to his
feelings, that was apparent. *"I have all the help I need."* It didn't look that
way. Every time he visited her house with new books to sell—which
she invariably sighed over and then rejected as too expensive—she
looked exhausted. Pretty, but exhausted. She kept the house neat
and orderly, but it needed a coat of paint, the gutters needed cleaning and straightening, and the steps were about to collapse. Nathan
hammered with the best of them, and he knew his way around a
paintbrush. And he knew how to lead a pack of kids despite not having any of his own. It came from being a natural-born salesman.

"You got a pain in your side?"

Freeman sounded a bit peeved. Maybe it was the hot sun and a case of indigestion from the picnic foods. Or, more likely, as bishop he was used to having an attentive audience.

"I'm fine, just a little sunburned." Nathan was always sunburned. The fate of a redhead. "So you like the biography of Sitting Bull. Interesting."

And Freeman was off again. Nathan preferred fiction of all kinds—mysteries, historical, suspense, literary, commercial block-busters, poetry, short stories—but he didn't mind an occasional foray into nonfiction. Anything to keep from thinking about his future and what he should—or shouldn't—do.

Right now, however, he couldn't concentrate. He couldn't forget the look on Jennie's face when he said he wanted to help her out. She'd looked . . . terrified. What about him frightened her? After two years of stopping by her house every few months to share his wares and eat her fried chicken or baked pork chop casserole and playing endless games of Scum and Life on the Farm, she still didn't relax around him. She was wound tighter than a guitar string. She was unfailingly polite. She always offered to feed him, which a bachelor such as him-self, always on the road eating hot dogs from convenience stores and greasy fast-food hamburgers, appreciated. But they never got beyond the polite conversation. She saw to that.

No matter how much he tried.

Not that he would tell the bishop any of these things. It was quite possible Freeman already knew. He seemed to know everything. Nathan studied Freeman's face. It was lined with years of knowledge and wisdom in every wrinkle. The man was honest beyond measure, plain spoken, and he never seemed to lose his cool. However, he didn't have much of a sense of humor, and some might call his view of the world narrow.

"You don't like biographies?" Freeman frowned, his pale-blue eyes made huge by his coke-bottle, black-rimmed glasses. Fanning himself with a copy of *The Budget*, he settled into a lawn chair in the shade of the schoolhouse, his gaze on the noisy softball game that seemed to have gone into extra innings. "I find it interesting to know the rest of the story of folks you read about in the newspaper or in history books."

Nathan eased into a spindly, straight-backed chair with a sunken cane bottom that looked the worse for wear. "I like biographies. Especially of American historical figures. I just read a new biography of Mary Todd Lincoln. I'm still thinking about how close Francis got to that rattlesnake. He shouldn't be running around out there on his own."

"He's four." Borntrager waved his hand as if to sweep away Nathan's concern. "He's fine."

That was the way of the Amish. Their children were deeply loved but not coddled. They learned chores early, learned discipline early, finished school early, and usually married early. And enjoyed work as much as play. Nathan liked that about Plain folks—they dove into work with joy. He wanted joy, with work and with play. "All's well that ends well, I guess."

"A trip to the woodshed might teach the boy to stop his wandering ways."

"It's hard for me to imagine Jennie doing such a thing, but I suppose she has to do it, with no husband."

"I've not seen any evidence of it. Her oldest boy Matthew has had his troubles." Freeman's tone held a note of concern. "But that's neither here nor there for you."

Everything relating to Jennie interested Nathan, but Freeman wouldn't want to hear about it. One step at a time. "It's coming up on the busy time of year for farmers."

"Yep. Been busy planting all spring." Freeman tipped a Mason jar and took a long swig of homemade root beer. It had to be mighty warm by now with no ice and the sun pounding overhead. "Harvest time will roll around soon enough."

"I imagine there's plenty of work to go around."

Freeman frowned. "There's always work to be done for farmers."

"Especially Plain farmers who don't use machines. I reckon it takes them a lot longer to do the same job and it's more work."

"Hard work reaps many benefits." Freeman pushed his glasses back up his long nose. "I think you're getting to a point here, my friend, but you're taking the long way around."

"I'm tired of life on the road. I'm thinking about settling down." Nathan was tired of many things. He wanted a faith that didn't involve traveling the world showing it to others to get them to come along the way his parents had done. God might want something different for Nathan, but He had to know it wasn't a good fit. It simply wasn't. Nathan didn't want to tell people about his faith—he'd rather show them by his example. And that was exactly what Amish folks did. "For me, that means giving up selling books. I'm thinking maybe I could hire out as a farmhand, get some experience, and eventually start farming myself. What do you think folks around here would think of that idea?"

"Folks around here like you a lot." His face creased with an unapologetic grin, Freeman belched with gusto and slapped his chest. "They already know you. That's half the battle when it comes to getting hired. You're not a stranger. You have any experience?"

"No, but I grew up in farm country. I've been watching people farm all my life." He could see himself driving a hay loader drawn by a team of Percheron horses or driving a manure spreader. He could work a threshing machine or a hay baler. He knew enough about engines to work on even the gas-powered ones. He'd have time to burrow into the thoughts and faith of these folks who worked so hard to stay off the grid. "Besides, I'm a fast learner."

"Could be. Of course, it remains to be seen." Freeman didn't look convinced. He stood and stared out at the road. "How's that van of yours doing?"

What did the van have to do with Nathan wanting to be a farmhand? "She's never let me down yet. She only has a hundred thousand miles on her." Nathan had no trouble waxing eloquent over his mode of transportation. Bunny had been his closest friend for the last two and half years. "They'll go twice that."

His eyebrows raised, Freeman shook his head. "She?"

"It. It, I mean."

"Next you'll be telling me you named it, like we do our horses. Those are hard miles you put on that van." Freeman laughed a deep belly laugh. Maybe he did have a sense of humor. "The reason I ask is Bob is retiring from his taxi service. We're already short taxis around here. I was thinking you might consider that for a new vocation. 'Course you'd have to get rid of some of those books you carry around."

Nathan did tend to travel with his most valued possessions—his books. They gave him a sense of well-being. He was never alone. If a lull occurred in his schedule, he could always hole up in a motel and read. If the weather turned too ugly to be on the road, he read. If he got a cold and he didn't want to inflict his germs on his customers, he read. His books served as his friends through thick and thin—kind of like Bunny.

Freeman cleared his throat.

Nathan hastened to respond. "If I settle in one place, I won't have to lug my books around in my van. But the last thing I want to do is drive some more. I've had my fill of driving. I'm looking to settle down around here."

Freeman stroked his white beard, nodding, looking like Santa Claus out of uniform. "Why Jamesport? You could settle down anywhere on your route or back home—you're from Kansas, aren't you?"

"Arlington, Kansas. Originally. My family eventually moved into Hutchinson. My closest relatives are in Haven now."

"Why not Hutchinson?"

Now the conversation had gone to the edge of personal and beyond. Nathan squirmed in this chair. His parents left Hutchinson years ago to work for Amish Mennonite Aid as missionaries planting churches. Nathan had been a child. His sisters and brothers had similar callings, but in the states. Distant cousins were the only ones still in Kansas. All these years later, he still felt abandoned. And guilty for feeling that way. Spreading the word of God should be more important than one kid with a selfish streak.

God let Nathan know every day that it was. The message came in loud and clear. *When are you going to do your part?* "I don't really know anyone there anymore. Folks around here seem more like family than anyone back home."

"It's not any of my business, I reckon." Freeman took off his straw hat and wiped his forehead with his sleeve. "The important thing is whether you know enough about farming to earn your keep as a farmhand. You might be better off driving people around. You know how to drive and you have a van."

"So you don't think anyone will hire me to work on a farm?"

"I didn't say that. Folks are kind. They'll give a man a chance. Show up on time, work hard, mind your manners, take instruction, make them glad they hired you. They'll pass the word."

Nathan stood and stretched. With any luck Freeman would tell everyone Nathan was looking for a new job. "Thanks for giving me your thoughts on this."

He started across the yard toward the van.

"One more thing."

Nathan glanced back.

Freeman stood and lumbered toward him, leading with his potbelly. He waited until he was even with Nathan to speak again. He kept his voice low. "Being *Mennischt*–especially your kind–is not the same thing as being Amish like me. Or Jennie Troyer."

Technically his background was Beachy Amish Mennonite, but to folks like Borntrager that simply meant Nathan was not Plain. Close only counted in horseshoes. "My kind?"

"Whatever word you want to put on it. The kind who drives a van, uses a microwave, has a phone in his house or even in his pocket, the kind who wears clothes like yours."

All the trappings of being assimilated into the world. It was true, but being in the world did not mean being of the world. At least that's the way his kind of Mennonite saw it. His kind wanted the whole world to know about the gospel. The Amish chose to keep themselves separate. He respected that. He admired it. He needed that kind of distance more than Freeman could imagine. "You're right. I know the difference."

"Just making sure."

"Settling down in Jamesport isn't about any person in particular." More like a bunch of people–his family mostly. And then there was

God Himself. Nathan liked Jamesport. He liked the people—all the people. His feelings were complicated, too complicated to explain in the middle of a school picnic. "I need a change."

"You've been selling books here for years. It's not much of a change."

It could be. It could be a big change. He wanted it to be. If Nathan could be honest with anyone and get the answers he needed, it would be with Freeman. "And if I wanted to . . . find out more about becoming your kind of Amish, would you be open to that?"

A long silence filled with a steely gaze and pursed lips followed. Freeman sniffed. "Is that a belt you're wearing?"

Not sure where the bishop was going with this, Nathan nodded.

"And those are pockets and a zipper on those pants?"

"Yes."

"Do you have a cell phone?"

"I do."

"A computer and a TV?"

"A laptop but no TV. My room at the motel has one, though."

Freeman wrinkled his nose and shook his head. "Those are small things to you. You probably think they're insignificant when it comes to faith. If you feel that way, you don't understand us. You don't understand how we live or why. Being a Mennischt such as yourself doesn't mean much when it comes to converting. And that doesn't begin to cover the faith issues themselves."

"I was baptized as an adult. I know the articles of faith. I believe in them."

"As they pertain to your world and your church."

"It's a lot closer to your world and your church than most."

"Agreed, but still Mennischt."

"So, no chance?"

"I didn't say that. Think about what I've said and come see me next week. We'll talk."

It was better than *no* even though everything about the set of Freeman's shoulders and the frown on his thin lips said otherwise.

Nathan settled into his van. He sat there, not moving for several minutes, watching the kids play and the women chatter among themselves. Laughter floated in the air. A fragrance like peace enveloped him. He unbuckled his belt, slid it from his pant loops, and tossed it into the passenger-side foot well.

Small steps.

FOUR

BLESSED SILENCE. ENJOYING HIS RETURN TO SOLI-
tude, Leo Graber raised his face to the breeze lifted by the steady
movement of the buggy. It felt good after the clammy cold that had
invaded his body when Jennie slammed to a halt at the fence, her pretty
face contorted in fear. All he'd wanted to do was make a quick geta-
way from the picnic. *"Help. Snake. Rattler. Francis."* In that moment, he
hadn't had time to think about why she came to him. What made her
think he could help her? He hadn't helped his father. His heart began to
pound again. *Race through the field. Stop. Raise the rifle. Take aim.*

Don't miss. Don't miss. Don't miss.

The slight weight of the rifle in his hands. The heavy weight of
Francis's life on his shoulders.

A man didn't expect that at a school picnic.

Jennie trusted him. God knew why. He'd let her go once before.
He'd let her marry another man when she should've been with him.

Breathe. It was a long time ago. Breathe. The familiar chatter of
blue jays calmed him. He clung to the sound of the *clip-clop* of his new
Standardbred's hooves on the asphalt and the squeak of the buggy
wheels. *Live in this moment. Don't think.* Leo concentrated on the ripple

of the horse's massive muscles as he pulled the buggy. His previous owner called the horse Red. Red was a decent name for a horse whose coat glinted magenta in the sun.

A pickup truck belching black smoke and smelling of diesel fumes overtook him and whizzed by. The odor mingled with the scent of horse and newly poured asphalt. The farmer waved as he passed. Leo waved back. He cranked his head side to side. *It's okay. It's all right.* Now he could go back to his furniture and the quiet that came with it.

He had an order for an oak dresser waiting for him. He could forget about the past and lose himself in a present that involved no loss, no pain, no hurt. Mary Katherine Ropp wanted him to sell his furniture in her store. She wanted him to do what she called demonstrations in the store. She wasn't the first. Other stores in town, more established shops, sold furniture. They wanted his furniture. Instead, he kept to himself. Some said he punished himself. The less he talked, the less he felt.

The muscles between his shoulder blades knotted at the thought, and his mouth, already parched, went drier than Sahara sand.

His father's face, suffused with pain as he writhed in the snow-covered pasture where they'd been hunting because Leo had begged his dad to go, flitted across his mind, chased by his mother's. More pain. *Stop it.*

Work kept his mind occupied. He needed his work. He forced himself to whistle a tune. He'd build furniture whether people bought it or not. He'd stack it in the living room, the extra bedrooms, the kitchen if need be. He could line it up on the road with signs that said TAKE YOUR PICK and BEST OFFER. People could buy his furniture without coming to the door.

No. He'd still have to talk to them.

Why did it pain him so? He stopped whistling, lost in the question that buzzed around him like a vulture circling high overhead.

The sound of his father's voice, silenced all those years ago, echoed in his ears. "Suh, *you don't want to farm, don't. But you must earn your keep. You'll figure it out. Don't let others influence the path you decide upon. It's yours.*"

Seconds later, *Daed* sank to the ground. His beloved rifle slid from his grasp. His face contorted in pain. Leo stumbled forward in a deep snow that had come early that year, knelt, reaching. Daed's face went slack. His eyes stayed open but saw nothing. His heart, overworked from tromping through miles of snow in search of a buck, had given out.

Hunting had been Leo's idea. An innocent way of spending time with Daed doing something they both enjoyed outdoors.

Leo tried to talk to his father, tried to make him listen. He shook him with hands slick with sweat despite the cold. "*We don't have to hunt anymore. We can go back to the house. You can rest. Mudder will make hot cocoa.*" He pulled on Daed's jacket. "*Let's go. You're getting cold. Forget about the deer. Forget about it.*"

Daed's head lolled to one side.

Leo closed his eyes for him. Something a son should do for his father.

Red whinnied. His head bobbed. Leo's memories receded. "What's the matter, Red? Hungry?"

The horse plowed to a stop. The buggy shuddered and halted.

"Hey, we're not home yet." Leo snapped the reins with a gentle flick. "Come on, Red, there's still daylight. I have work to do."

Red whinnied, but he didn't move.

Leo snapped the reins again, harder this time. "Let's go. We've got work to do."

The horse didn't budge.

Any second a car would hurtle over the rolling hill and smash into them.

Leo leaped from the buggy. "What's the matter, buddy?" He slid his hand along Red's shoulders, withers, and back. The horse sidestepped and neighed. "Okay, okay, let's get off the road and then we'll talk."

Horses were much easier to talk to than people.

He led Red to the grassy shoulder and as far off the road as possible. Dandelions and purple prairie clover swished around him. Grasshoppers flung themselves out of reach. Clouds of gnats billowed. Leo waved them away with a gentle swoosh. The horse favored his front legs. He seemed to be shifting his weight back and then side to side, as if they hurt.

Not a good sign. "What's the matter, friend?" Red's head bobbed. Leo rubbed the velvety spot between his ears. They perked up. The horse's intelligent, sweet eyes seemed to beg for understanding. "Not feeling so hot? We'll figure it out. I promise."

Leo squatted and ran his hand over the left and then the right leg. The hooves felt hot to the touch. A pulse pounded in his legs. Red sidestepped. Leo ducked his head and sighed. The horse whinnied as if in agreement. Laminitis, most likely. "Sorry, buddy, I know how much that hurts."

He'd been afraid this might happen. The horse was heavier than he appeared in the photos sent by his previous owner. Standardbred horses tended to be at least seventy-five pounds lighter than the average horse. Not Red. The space between his shoulders and loin was hard and firm. He looked cresty with a lot of fat making his neck arch at the top. He'd apparently eaten too much of the lush spring grass that sprouted across the pasture after nice rains that preceded good crops. He might be taller than other horses, but he was also just plain fat.

Not to be mean. Leo simply didn't know how to dress up words. Another reason he kept his mouth shut.

Laminitis was a painful disease that took ages to treat and often returned. Worse, Red might never pull a buggy again. Leo leaned his forehead into Red's shoulder and ran his fingers along his back. "We're putting you on a diet. But first, we need to make you feel better."

That meant getting his friends involved. Todd Riker, who qualified as vet and friend, needed to examine Red as soon as possible. More bills loomed in Leo's future. He'd lost Jake last year to old age. The horse dropped dead—his heart gave out—one night while out to pasture. Strange how these things kept happening to Leo. At least he hadn't been present this time. Still, finding a magnificent creature, a member of his family, had perished during the night had left him numb with a sense of despair that had nothing to do with the expense of replacing him. Now replacing him would become even more expensive. It didn't matter. Red could not be allowed to suffer. Laminitis felt like standing on a throbbing toothache, according to Todd, who couldn't bear to see an animal suffer any more than Leo could.

He straightened and stared at the long road ahead. They were a good five miles from the turnoff to his home, just outside Jamesport. The walk would be into the blazing sun setting in the west. Sweat dripped in his eyes. "Well, we best get started." He patted Red's back and smoothed his dark mane. Red swung his head around. His nostrils quivered, his breath warm on Leo's arm. He neighed softly, a plaintive sound. Leo patted him again. "I know, but you can make it. We'll take it slow and easy. I got all the time in the world."

He leaned down to unhitch the buggy. He would come back for it later with one of his cousin Aidan's horses.

The familiar singsong of hooves clattered on the asphalt. He looked back. A wagon stuffed with the Troyer family approached. Matthew drove. Jennie, looking as sweet as ever, sat by her son's side.

Leo sighed. Red neighed in agreement. More talking seemed likely to ensue.

FIVE

THE CHATTER IN THE BACK OF THE BUGGY DID nothing to dispel the silence in the front. Jennie glanced at her oldest son. Matthew should be happy and carefree, now that he was done with school. He wanted it, so why had he been sitting on the wagon bench like a lump on a log looking like he'd just lost his best friend, wordless, since they left the picnic? She tried to remember if any of her brothers—all six of them older than her—had been this morose upon entering their teenage years. They teased her. They taunted her. They protected her. Between sixteen and their marrying days, they'd disappeared a lot. This nastiness? This she did not remember. Why did he keep snapping the reins as if the horse's pace didn't suit him?

"Are you in a hurry to get home?"

"I got chores to do."

"The others will help."

"They're more of a hindrance than a help."

An exaggeration if she'd ever heard one. If all her children went through this stage as teenagers, Jennie was in a heap of trouble. "What's the matter? You graduated. I thought you would be happy."

"Nothing's the matter."

"The softball game was fun. You made a good catch there in the last inning."

He shrugged. "They won."

No one was keeping score as far as Jennie knew.

Matthew had never been a cuddly child, but his dark moodiness had increased in the last year. Growing pains? Part of becoming an adult? It was hard to say since he refused to talk to her about it. He needed a man with whom he could talk. Maybe her brother or even her brother-in-law.

"If you have something on your mind, I reckon Peter might be able to help."

"Nothing's on my mind."

A chill ran through her despite the late-afternoon sun. His tone was all too reminiscent of his father's. "Being a graduate doesn't excuse you from respecting your elders."

His only response was to snap the reins and yell, "Giddyup!"

They topped the hill and began the descent. A buggy was parked on the highway shoulder. This was not a good sign. Jennie wiggled in her seat. Even if Leo stood next to the buggy, a person had to stop. He looked no gladder to see them than she was to see him. He'd helped her out earlier with the snake. Without hesitation, but also without comment. It looked as if she would have the opportunity to return the favor sooner rather than later.

The horse whinnied. Leo shushed him with a soft pat on the horse's ample neck. Wasn't the horse new? Her brother had said something about a new sorrel to replace the bay who keeled over in the pasture a few months earlier. She touched Matthew's arm. "Stop."

Frowning, he tugged away from her touch.

"Matthew, I said, stop."

Grunting, he obliged with a sharp tug on the reins.

Leo went back to unhitching a beautiful sorrel from his buggy. "Howdy."

"Do you need a ride?" Celia spoke when Jennie didn't. "We have room for one more."

"Can't leave Red."

Elizabeth hopped from the wagon, landed on her knees, and rolled to her feet, oblivious to the dirt on her apron. "Is he sick?"

"I'll help you doctor him." Cynthia followed her younger sister with an even less graceful plop. Her skinny arms flailed and her kapp slid back. "I know how to make a poultice. I can find some mud yonder by Marvin's pond."

Francis hurled himself over the side of the wagon without a word. His roly-poly body ended up at Cynthia's feet. She yanked him up without looking at him. His black pants were gray with dirt and one knee sported a hole. He hid his dirty face in her dress.

Soon all seven of them would be lined up along the road—all except Matthew, who stared ahead, the same surly expression etched on his face Jennie saw morning, noon, and night. "Stop. All of you." Jennie put up her hand even though not one of them looked at her. They milled around Leo. "Let the man speak. He may not need our help."

Leo grimaced. "He's gone lame. I'm walking him home."

"We can help," Elizabeth piped up. "We can sing. It'll make him feel better."

"You could tie him to the back of the wagon and ride with us." Micah volunteered. "Matthew can go slow, can't you, Bruder?"

Matthew grunted.

Leo's gaze connected with Jennie's. He seemed nonplussed by their peppering. Talking to people was harder for him than shooting a rattler. "Better to walk him. His legs hurt."

Jennie felt a flicker of relief. Followed by shame. Her children were kinder than she was. She didn't want Leo in the wagon. She had an open face. Her mother always said that. He would see her mixed-up feelings and know she couldn't understand why he had acted the way he had during their *rumspringa*. He'd been interested, she was sure of it. But he never lifted a finger to follow through.

Her children needed to see her set the example. Should Leo be in the back surrounded by them or in front holding the reins? She had no idea. Matthew was the man of her house now, let him drive. Let Leo sit next to him. She could sit in the back. The thoughts buzzed her brain like bees around a hive.

"Get up here with Matthew. I'll move to the back. We'll make sure your horse is fine. No sense in you walking all the way to your house."

"It's out of your way."

"We aren't in a hurry."

"Neither am I."

A person couldn't help a man who didn't want help, could she? "We don't mind."

"You have livestock at home waiting to be fed."

He worried about animals more than he did people. "They won't starve in another hour."

He stared at his boots as if contemplating how to get her to leave him alone. "The back works. Close to my horse."

And far from her. Also a good thing.

He started toward the back of the wagon, Red in tow. The horse whinnied. He tried to lie down. Leo coaxed him forward, whispering in his ears. He patted his long neck. "Let's get you home."

His voice was so soft and sweet, not one Jennie would've associated with a man who had massive shoulders and big meaty hands covered with fine black hair. The sheer force of his muscle caused a shiver to run through her. Ridiculous. This was Leo, not Atlee. She was a grown woman. She couldn't allow herself to be afraid of anyone or anything. "Poor thing. He's in pain."

"He is." Leo led him around to the back of the wagon.

The bellyache of an engine that had seen better days filled the air. Jennie peered beyond Leo and Red. A dusty white van loomed in the distance. It headed down the hill toward them. Red reared.

SIX

A WAGON IN THE MIDDLE OF THE HIGHWAY WASN'T unheard of in these parts. But coming up over the hill to find one surrounded by youngsters directly in a person's path took a man by surprise. Nathan slammed on the brakes.

Bunny shimmied and shook. The minivan's backend fishtailed.

He muttered a quick prayer and eased into the slide, then straightened. A cluster of Plain kids bolted toward the shoulder of the road. A woman—Jennie Troyer—leaped from the buggy. She stumbled and fell.

A horse collapsed. Leo Graber dropped to his knees next to the animal, one hand jutted in the air as if he could make the van stop with sheer force of will.

Nathan hit the brakes again. This time the van halted within inches of the horse, which made no attempt to rise. Nathan breathed, trying to still the hammering of his heart. Sweat dripped in his eyes. His shoulders and arms ached.

"Thank You, Jesus." He uncurled his fingers, one at a time, from the steering wheel. His knuckles throbbed. "You are a good God."

Even if he didn't always get the answer to his prayers he wanted.

Like a spoiled child he complained instead of accepting God's will for his life. *You are great, Lord. I'm the weak one.*

Feeling like an old man, he turned off the ignition and sat still, breathing. After a few seconds, he shoved open the door. He had to grab his leg, pull it from the foot well, and set his foot on the asphalt. His muscles shook. "Everyone all right?"

Leo looked up. "Jah."

"I didn't hit him, did I?" He'd never seen a horse lay down and stay down. "Why doesn't he get up?"

"His legs hurt." Leo's tone suggested he still didn't approve of Nathan's driving. Or of him. "Nothing to do with you."

Thank God for that.

On wet-noodle legs Nathan staggered past the other man to the kids, who clustered around Jennie, all talking at once. His pants sagged down around his hips. He hitched them up with one hand. Belts might be seen as vanity, but they also served a purpose. His shoe skidded under him. He glanced down. A big horse plop squished out around his Nike, the odor reaching his nose a split second later. Suppressing a groan, he wiped the sole on the grass and kept going.

Jennie stared at her palms, her face as white as his shirt. He waded through the kids, who parted at his approach. "You're bleeding."

"Just scratches." She hid her hands behind her back like a naughty child with a pilfered cookie. Dirt and leaves adorned her apron. Her kapp hung crooked to one side, revealing fine hair the color of ripe wheat. "I'm fine."

"Her hands are bleeding, and she has a scratch on her nose." Celia and Cynthia chorused. "She jumped. Did you see her jump?"

He had seen her. His heart still clamored for release from his chest. "I saw."

"I'm fine." Her gaze met his. She straightened her kapp and brushed the leaves from her apron, leaving behind a red stain. The scratches on her palms were deep. "I need to get home and get cleaned up."

"Let me take you into town to the emergency clinic."

"I'm fine."

She seemed to think if she kept saying it, the statement would become fact. "Let me see."

She shook her head. "I'll wash up at the house."

Her stubborn expression made her no less pretty. Nor did the scratch on her upturned nose. He ripped his gaze from her to the children. "What about the rest of you? Anyone hurt?"

Their heads shook simultaneously. Francis buried his head in his mother's apron. Fortunately, both were equally dirty. "Let me give you a ride to your house. Matthew can bring the wagon home."

"No need."

An impasse.

"I'll drive them." Leo spoke from behind Nathan.

Nathan turned. Leo's soft voice whispered in the horse's ear. Neighing, it scrambled to its feet.

"Good boy. Attaboy, Red. Attaboy." Leo's hand smoothed the horse's back. He patted its rump. "We'll get you home in no time."

He talked a lot more to horses than he did to people.

"Isn't it farther to their house than yours?" Nathan tried to keep the pique out of his voice. It was small minded. The goal here was to help Jennie and her kids, however possible. "If you need to get it home, I can help her—them."

"People first." Leo strode to the front of the wagon and climbed into the seat. "All aboard."

The kids didn't need to be told twice. Laughing and pushing, they clamored into the wagon.

Jennie lingered. She brushed the leaves from her apron. "Thank you for the offer." She ducked her head. "It's kind of you. We'll be fine."

"No problem." He forced a cheerfulness he didn't feel. She was fine. She didn't need his help. She couldn't see how he felt, but then he hadn't told her. He couldn't. Not with the gaping chasm of their differing faiths between them.

She nodded and trudged past him without making eye contact.

"Until then."

She glanced back, finally. "Until then."

He stood and watched Leo drive her and the kids away. She had called upon Leo to help her with the snake. Now she helped him with his horse.

Maybe that's why she didn't need Nathan's help. She already had someone.

SEVEN

TIME TO ADMIT IT. JENNIE NEEDED READING GLASSES. She peered at the quilt block stitching in the early evening sunlight that filtered through the open windows of her home. The flower petals, white thread on white material, might be slightly crooked. Of course the bandages on her fingers and palms might have something to do with it. Her shoulders ached from the jolt when she hit the ground on all fours. Surely, she'd looked like a clumsy girl catapulting out of the wagon that way. A van barreling over the hill straight at them—all her children—seemed to require nothing less at the time.

Still, she was glad for the company. Having Laura and Mary Katherine here kept her from reliving the scene earlier in the day with Nathan and then the ride home with Leo. Jennie craned her neck and stretched, all the while surreptitiously checking Mary Katherine's and Laura's work. The other two women wore their reading glasses without thought for vanity. Their work on the Double Irish Chain pattern with its blue-and-white squares and quilted flowers looked perfect.

Laura looked up and smiled. "Are you all right? If you need to rest after your adventures today, just say so and we'll get out of your hair."

"Nee. Just a cramp in my neck. And I didn't have any adventures." She adjusted the propane lamp she had lit on the table next to their quilt frame. Its heat vied with the cooler evening breeze that wafted through the open windows. "I'll get us some tea."

"Let me do it." Mary Katherine stood. "You've had quite the day, what with fending off snakes and getting run over by vans."

"I didn't get run over."

Her protest was lost on Mary Katherine. Her expression that of a woman on a mission, she trotted past Francis and Elizabeth, who were playing with wooden blocks strewn across the living room's pine floor, and headed for the kitchen.

Elizabeth scrambled to her feet and scooped up Indigo, the black-and-white kitten she carried around the house day and night. Rufus, the muddy-brown mutt who followed her everywhere, stood and stretched with a soft whine in the back of his throat. "Can I have one of the brownies Mary Kay brought? Her brownies are the best." Elizabeth held Indigo to her face, letting the kitten's fur brush against her cheek, her look of innocent pleasure so sweet. "Francis wants one too. So does Rufus."

"You can have one, but not your animals. Sweets are bad for them." Jennie assumed this to be the case. She couldn't afford a vet for her daughter's menagerie.

Francis, ever Elizabeth's shadow, disappeared through the doorway behind them.

"I hope they bring us some." Laura chuckled, a dry sound like tissue paper rustling. "Mary Kay is the pied piper of baked goods."

Jennie nodded, but the words barely registered. The look of concern on Nathan's face as she left him standing next to his van on the side of the road floated in her mind's eye. It had been a long ride to

Leo's place to drop off the horse and then on to her farm. The children peppered the man with questions, which he answered with the patience of Job but without elaboration. They were starved for a man in their lives. That was certain. Her own brothers tried. Especially Peter. Brother number six and closest to Jennie, Peter took Matthew and Micah on as farmhands, teaching them what they needed to know to be farmers, but he wasn't much for talk or affection. He did what he could. Atlee's brothers also helped when they could.

"You're certainly lost in thought this evening." Laura's needle moved with precision and quickness despite swollen, painful knuckles caused by her arthritis. Fueled by sheer determination, no doubt. "What's on your mind?"

"Like Mary Kay said, it's been a long day."

"It's more than that." Laura's shrewd features shone in the lamp light that softened the wrinkles around her mouth and the lines around her green eyes. "You look troubled."

In all the years since the three women—four until Bess started courting with Aidan in earnest—had gathered to can, cook, sew, quilt, and talk, Jennie had never told them. As much as they were like older sisters, she couldn't bring herself to tell them. She didn't lie. She simply kept her story to herself. "Nathan said something today."

"Are you going to tell me, or do I have to drag it out of you?"

"He said he was looking for me. He wanted to help me."

"Good for him, he's a nice person." Laura's needle paused, poised in midair. Her bushy, gray eyebrows arched. "Oh. Oh!"

"Exactly." Jennie plunged her needle into the cotton fabric with more force than necessary. "He said he was looking for *me* to help *me*."

"The man is nice, but he's lost his mind." Laura wrinkled her nose. "He's Mennischt."

Laura didn't have to elaborate. They both knew what that meant. He drove a car, used electricity, and his family traveled around the world planting new churches. He'd told her all about them at supper one night. The Mennonites came from the same roots, but their leader, Menno Simons, and others who disagreed about the severity of *Meidung*, had broken off from the Anabaptists to start their own church. Now there were all sorts of Mennonites with different rules and ways of living, just as there were Amish. The more modern ones were like Nathan. They wore more English-like clothes, met in church buildings, had Bible studies, and evangelized around the world. A person could hardly tell they once came from the same stock as the Amish. "I've never heard him talk about his faith, but he certainly blends in with our crowd. Everyone likes him."

Laura went back to her sewing, but her forehead remained creased with wrinkles. "Do you . . . like Nathan?"

"What kind of question is that? I'm mad at Gott, but I would never leave my faith—"

"I knew it." Laura stabbed her swollen index finger at Jennie, her needle dangling by its thread. "Finally, after all this time, you admit it. You're mad at Gott."

Let her think Jennie was mad at God for taking Atlee. Not the other thing. For giving her such a husband to start with. At least they weren't talking about Nathan anymore. "Aren't you?"

"After Eli died, all I wanted was for Gott to take me too. Freeman said it was his time, and I know that to be true." Laura paused, her eyes bright with sudden tears. Even after four years the memory of finding her husband dead in bed on Christmas Eve still caused her pain. A happy marriage did that to a person. "My days continue, but there were many nights when I lay down and I prayed I wouldn't get up in the morning. It's not up to me. Gott's plan is His plan. His will is His will. We have no business questioning it."

Laura swiped at her face with her sleeve. "I'm a silly old woman."

"Nee, you're not. You were blessed with a good *mann* for forty-five years. I'm so . . ." Jennie stopped. *I'm so jealous.* "Sorry for your loss. And on Christmas Eve. It's easy for others to say it's Gott's will. But to live it, that's another cup of tea."

Laura inclined her head as if acknowledging the truth of the words. "You only had fifteen years with Atlee. You must miss him something fierce."

A not-so-direct question. Jennie squirmed in her chair. The answer had been dammed behind a mountain of guilt and remorse for four years now.

"You never want to talk about it. Not even after all this time." Laura bent her head over her sewing as if she knew it would be easier for Jennie to talk if she didn't look at her. "I reckon there was more going on than meets the eye."

"Atlee wasn't an easy man to live with."

"I suspected as much."

"You did?"

"Child, he was a sourpuss at best. I can't imagine living with that attitude all the time." Laura leaned over the frame, her gaze fixed on her fine stitches. "Not to speak ill of the dead."

"I believe in 'spare the rod and spoil the child' as much as the next person."

"But he overdid it?" A fierce frown enveloped Laura's face. As one of the most sought after and experienced midwives in the area, she'd delivered all seven of Jennie's babies. She had a heart for children. "We are meant to discipline with love, not meanness. It's our way."

"It wasn't Atlee's way. Any little thing. Matthew dropped a serving bowl full of potatoes on the floor during supper and broke it. Atlee took him out to the woodshed." She took a shuddering breath at the memory of Matthew's bewildered face as Atlee dragged him by the arm out the back door. "He left welts on his backside."

"The boy didn't mean to do it, that's obvious."

"Atlee said accidents only happen when a person isn't paying attention. Matthew had to learn to pay attention. He wasted food. We couldn't afford to waste food or buy new dishes."

"All good points."

"The kinner were afraid of him. They were always tiptoeing around him. They never knew what might set him off. A rip in their clothes, a kapp not properly starched, a chore not done to his satisfaction." Jennie's stomach lurched just as it used to do when the thunderclouds gathered, dark and fierce, in Atlee's face. She put her hand to her mouth, willing her stomach to settle. She breathed and let it drop. "Too much noise at the supper table. The clicking of the fork on the plate when they cut the skin on the sliced tomatoes bothered him. I started peeling them before I served them. Chewing too loud bothered him. Cold food and food too hot or meat too tough set him off. Crumbs on the floor that didn't get swept up."

"And you?"

He often demanded from her what she didn't feel up to giving. Not to a man who filled her with such dread. Not to a man who saw nothing wrong with using his powerful arms and his brutal words to cow a child into submission. He said it was her duty. After the first time, she never denied him again. "I enjoyed the times when I was expecting. As I got farther along . . . less was . . . demanded."

He didn't touch her when she was carrying a baby. At first the months of peace had lulled her into thinking things were better. Until the baby came. She learned her lesson after Matthew and Celia.

"Certainly a double-edged sword, I should say." The kindness in Laura's face made Jennie want to cry. The older woman patted her hand. "A hard row to hoe and you never said a word all those years."

"I took the same vows you and the other fraas took." She let her hands drop to her lap. The quilt would have to wait until another day. "I didn't want to make it worse for the kinner. They didn't know better. They never knew anything different. I reckon they thought all daeds were like that."

"But they're not. Not all manns are like that either."

"I know that. I knew it then. But there was nothing I could do but pray that Gott would soften Atlee's heart."

He didn't. Instead, Atlee fell. His own team of horses trampled him. He'd been alone at the time. No one knew exactly what happened. No one knew she feared it an answer to prayer.

"Get inside. The laundry won't do itself."

The last words he would ever say to her. She shivered.

Cold air blasted her. The doctor left her alone with him in the tiny cubicle surrounded by curtains. The raspy sound, in and out, of the ventilator breathing for Atlee filled the air. Somewhere behind another curtain in the intensive care unit the disembodied voice of a man, hoarse and insistent, cried out, "Help me, help me."

Jennie needed help too. She put her hand to her mouth to keep from joining that poor soul in his lament. Instead she steadied herself on legs that didn't want to hold her. She forced herself to touch the place on Atlee's arm not covered with tubes and tape where an IV ran. Machines beeped, recording his heartbeat, his blood pressure, his respiration. His skin was cool to the touch and clammy. Black-and-blue bruises covered his face. Coupled with the swelling of his head, they made it almost impossible to recognize him as her mann. "Atlee? Can you hear me? Breathe. Just breathe. They say you can't breathe on your own. The ventilator is breathing for you. They can't take it out unless you breathe on your own. Can you do that?"

Nothing. Gott help her, nothing.

The doctor said Atlee wouldn't wake up. Ever.

She had to make the decision. What next. What would Atlee want?

Not this. Gott, not this. Please Gott, I didn't mean this.

"But he didn't, so now you're wondering if you'd be better off with someone who's not of our faith."

Laura's words, delivered in that tart tone she so often employed when observing something that didn't sit quite right with her, plunged Jennie back into the world she lived in now. A widow with seven children and a pile of medical bills that she labored to pay off even after five years. Several church districts had assisted with general donations. Cards filled with donations had arrived after pleas for assistance in *The Budget*. But monumental medical bills never seemed to dwindle. *"Set up a payment plan,"* the hospital financial counselor had said with a kind smile and eyes that seemed to say, *I've seen this before. I'll see it again. And again. And again.* She didn't know Plain folks. Their bills were always paid.

"It's not that." Jennie stumbled back to the present with its cold, empty bed and endlessly silent nights. "I'm not better off with anyone. Ever. Alone is better."

"You don't know what Gott's plan is. You can't."

"So bow in submission and take the chance." The chance it would happen again. How could she know? Atlee before marriage had been a different man from the one who died fifteen years later. How could she ever trust her own judgment? "I'm doing fine on my own."

Squinting, Laura slipped the needle into the blue square. "What about Leo?"

That ship set sail a long time ago. But Laura didn't know that. Black curly hair like Atlee's. Now streaked with gray. At least his eyes were a different color. What went on behind those amber eyes? "You've been talking to Bess and Aidan, haven't you?" She studied the material in front of her, not really seeing it. Seeing instead Leo's anguished expression at his father's funeral. "I know Aidan wants his cousin to find a fraa and Bess thinks I need a mann. Just because we're both in need, doesn't mean we go together."

"He's like another brother to Aidan. They just want him to be happy." Laura sighed. "But you have a right to be a little scared when it comes to men."

"I'm not scared." The thought rankled her. She would not let Atlee steal her courage, from the grave. Leo had the same look about him, with his dark hair, fierce eyes, and broad shoulders, but he talked to kinner the same way he talked to his horse—soft, sweet, kind. "And there's surely no reason to be scared of Leo. He's a gentle man. It's just that he's not shown an interest."

Not since their rumspringa. Now she was thirty-seven and he was a year older. Too old for romance.

"He's a quiet man." Laura tied off a thread and cut it with a definitive snip. "Sometimes they're the ones with the most to say, if you're willing to be patient and listen."

"I can't afford to make the wrong choice and have the kinner suffer again. I'm better off to raise them myself."

"That's up to Gott. The kinner need a daed. Freeman would tell you that. Cyrus too." Laura shook her head. "It's not easy. I'm old so they don't think much of it, one way or the other. But you're young, young enough to try again. Pray about it. Accept that you have been refined by the experience. You've walked through the fire and survived."

She didn't feel young or like praying much. "I prayed for Atlee and look what that got me."

"In this world there will be light and momentary troubles."

"Momentary?" Jennie's voice squeaked with disbelief. She breathed and softened it. "Fifteen years is momentary?"

"To Gott, it's a tiny blip. He has all of eternity on His hands."

Mary Katherine tromped into the room, a tray in her hands and her cadre of shadows skipping behind her. They'd been joined by Celia and Cynthia. All four had chocolate smeared on their faces. Rufus brought up the end. He had what looked suspiciously like crumbs on his graying snout. Mary Katherine's smiling gaze skipped from Jennie to Laura and back. "What'd I miss?"

"It's time to turn in, girls." Jennie stood. "I'm more tired than I thought, I guess."

Laura stuck her needle in a half-finished square. "A decent night's sleep will do us all good."

"But I brought tea." Mary Katherine stuck the tray on the table. "And we still need to talk about the store."

"I can't work at the store." Jennie waved her hands at the children, who were already engrossed in their play again. "They need me at home. Home is where a mudder should be."

"You'll get no argument from me there." Conflict warred in Mary Katherine's normally serene face. "I understand it's not easy."

No doubt she did, even though her youngest daughter was almost eighteen and likely courting some special boy by now. Still, Mary Katherine carried the biggest burden in making the store solvent. Her savings, her elbow grease, her time. She had jumped into this business to give folks like Jennie another way to earn money. "I will work hard this week and bring you new goods to sell as soon as they're ready. We should have strawberry jam shortly."

"It's just that Lazarus Dudley is back from his Florida vacation."

Lazarus Dudley, the Jamesport businessman who owned the antique store next to Amish Treasures, always wintered in Pinecraft, Florida.

"Did he come into the store?"

"Not yet. But I know he will. Dylan, who manages Antiques and Beyond, told me yesterday, he's getting settled in and then he's coming after us." She rubbed her hands together. "He says Seamus O'Rourke should've given him first option. He says Seamus knew he wanted the space next to his shop and should never have leased it to us it without talking to him first. He's convinced there was some big conspiracy between us and Seamus."

Seamus O'Rourke, the butcher who decided to close shop and toddle out west in a used RV with a lady from St. Louis, likely would beg to differ.

"I told Dylan we have a signed lease. There's nothing dirty or underhanded about it." Mary Katherine picked up a glass of tea and sipped it as if to hide her expression. "We need to have lots of traffic, lots of customers, to offset our initial expenses and to show we're making a success of it. Dylan says the town doesn't need another Amish tourist shop."

"Yet Lazarus wants to expand his antique store—as if we don't have a lot of those already. From the crowds we had in town last summer, I'd say the more the merrier." Laura's chair creaked as she stood, her knees cracking at the same time. "What does all that have to do with working shifts at the store?"

"Annabelle has morning sickness something fierce. Joanna's *schweschder* is going back to Indiana to take care of their mother so she can't watch Joanna's kinner. We don't have enough workers. We need to keep the store open a full complement of regular hours."

"If you want me to work a few shifts, I'd be happy to do it." Laura picked up her canvas bag and hugged it to her ample bosom. "I used to work at my parents' vegetable stand on the road many years ago."

The woman had passed seventy with no slowing down in sight. She'd delivered nearly every Plain child in a ten-mile radius in the last forty years. Shame ran through Jennie. "Standing all day will give you pain in your knees and your back."

"Feeling useful is good medicine for what ails a person." Laura winked at her. "It's been a long day and nothing has to be decided tonight. It's getting dark and I don't like to be on the road too late. Early to bed, early to rise."

None of them cared about wealthy, but wisdom seemed to elude Jennie at every turn.

EIGHT

DID PARENTS FEEL THIS BAD WHEN THEIR CHIL-
dren were in pain? Leo suspected they did. He forced himself to shake
loose his fists. He shifted his feet, inhaling the comforting scent of
hay and manure that wafted through the barn on a dank breeze and
brought with it the first day of May. Red whinnied, his head whipping up and down as he tried to pull away from Todd's touch.

The vet muttered soothing, sweet nothings as he ran an experienced hand down the horse's legs. He shook his head and looked back
at Leo, his smooth-shaven face somber. "Come here. Feel this."

Todd was like that. Every visit was a teaching opportunity. Leo
eased closer to Red. The horse was as skittish as a cat beset by a pack
of wolves. Leo touched the horse's leg. "Right here, that's the digital
pulse. It's pounding."

"I felt it yesterday." Leo slid his hand down the groove between
Red's tendons and ligaments. The pounding had accelerated in the
twenty-four hours since he'd used the phone in the shack up by the
road to call Todd. It was one of the rare occasions when Leo had been
glad for the shack on his property. Unfortunately, Todd had been

caught up in delivering a breech foal out at an English man's farm near Trenton the day before.

"You shouldn't be able to feel that. A horse's pulse should be rather hard to find. When it pounds like that, it indicates inflammation and pain."

"It's obvious he's in pain." Leo patted Red's back and then ran his hand through the horse's tangled mane. Red's head dipped and his neck stretched as he turned as if to get closer to Leo. "Is it laminitis?"

Red sank to his belly with a whinny that could only be his version of a groan of pain.

"Yep. He's doing anything he can to get off his hooves. That's some severe pain. Poor baby." Todd pulled a white handkerchief from the back pocket of faded, baggy blue jeans. He wiped sweat from his face and neck. "Easy, buddy, easy. We're going to help you out. I promise."

"How fast can you get him relief?"

"We'll start with bute. It's an anti-inflammatory." Todd tucked the handkerchief away and turned to a huge black backpack that served as his medical bag. He produced a syringe filled with a pasty-looking substance. "When you described his symptoms, I figured that's what it was so I came prepared. It tastes terrible, but he'll be glad he swallows it after a bit."

Todd went on to give Leo a series of instructions that included pouring cool water on Red's feet two or three times a day, putting him on a low-carb, low-protein diet, adding plenty of hay to his stall to give him a softer place to stand, and getting his hooves trimmed before special boots could be put on them. "It's up to you how much you do, but the more you do, the more relief he'll get. It'll cost you money, but a good blacksmith who knows what he's doing should do the trimming."

"I'll get Zeke over here right away." Blacksmith Zeke Hostetler and Leo had grown up together as best friends before Zeke decided to leave his Plain faith behind to marry an English girl. "He has experience with this."

"You can always owe me for my services." His dark-brown eyes intent, Todd delivered the medicine to Red, who did his best to avoid treatment. Todd was a skinny guy with no girth, but he had a way with the massive animals that made him one of the best vets around. He also had an uncanny way with people. He could've been a people doctor. "I'm betting Zeke is the same way."

Leo studied the barn rafters for a second. He hated owing people money, almost as much as he hated talking to them. "I'll pay you as soon as I can."

"How about this? Samantha has a hankering for one of your rocking chairs. The double rocker. Make me one of those and I'll owe you."

Barter for services was a time-honored tradition in these parts. "Oak or walnut?"

"Which is best for putting twins to sleep?"

"Twins?" Todd and Samantha were expecting, Leo knew that, although Todd had said little, knowing how circumspect his Plain friends were about discussing such things. "You're doubly blessed then."

"Yep. It's an amazing thing to see those two beating hearts in a sonogram." Todd ran both hands through thinning blond hair. He likely would be bald before those twins were in high school. "Two girls."

English medicine was amazing, but it took the joyous surprise out of the miracle of birth in Leo's way of thinking. "Two daughters. A blessing indeed."

Todd's grin stretched so wide it must hurt his cheeks. "You're telling me, buddy. I'm over the moon. So is Samantha. So what do you think? Make me the rocking chair. She and I can rock our babies at the same time."

"Consider it a baby gift." A twinge that started in the vicinity of Leo's heart spread across his chest. He had no need for a rocking chair. No fraa. No babies to rock. No lullabies to hum. "You'll need a lot of things for two babies."

"No way. We'll be even on my services, but I'll still owe you. I know what those chairs run. And you need the money." Todd stopped. His face turned radish red. "I mean, man, I'm sorry. I open my mouth, insert foot, all the time. I'm just saying, I want to pay you for it. It's too big a gift, too valuable."

"And I know what your services run." The lack of money truly didn't bother Leo much, or he would've overcome his loathing of mixing with folks. That other feeling, so like a writhing snake of envy, bothered him more. He'd avoided thinking about his lack of a fraa for so long, the sharp twinge of pain took him by surprise. He still had feelings. He didn't want feelings. They only led to the pain of loss. Of unseeing eyes and lolling heads. "I want to do this for you and Samantha. They're your first."

After three years of marriage, they'd been concerned. He could see it in Todd's eyes when he talked about their plans to add bedrooms to their little bungalow house—when they needed them. It had taken them longer to need them than they had expected. Then the joy when the news came that there would indeed be a baby. Now two babies.

Leo had expected at some point to have a wife. Only he hadn't. Because having a wife meant talking to the girls. Going to the singings. Taking a girl for a ride. He had done it one time—with Jennie

Troyer. It had been so awkward and he'd been so bad at it he hadn't tried again. It meant taking a chance and he simply hadn't been able to do it.

"You need to charge me because you're gonna have to get yourself another horse. Red, here, won't be able to work for quite a while, if ever."

"I know he won't, but I'll find more work. It's not for you to worry about. A gift is a gift."

A man having twins needed to save his money for diapers and car seats and more diapers and high chairs and cribs. And more diapers. Double the trouble and double the money.

What a good problem to have.

"Horses are good company. But so are women." Todd busied himself packing his doctor bag. "If you catch my drift."

Leo did. They'd been friends a long time. Todd had never stuck his nose in Leo's business so much in one day. "I'm fine."

"There's nothing like it, man. Women are something special. I used to heat up a burrito in the microwave for supper. I'd drink beer and watch baseball on TV. I thought I'd died and gone to heaven. Then I met Samantha." He threw his hands in the air, head back, eyes rolled, in a dramatic, comic rendition of his condition. "Talk about heaven. There's no comparison, whatsoever."

"It's not for everyone."

"Yes, it is, my friend. It is. I promise you." He slapped Leo on the back so hard, he stumbled forward a step. "Try it, you'll like it."

"I'll stick to horses and furniture."

"You are stubborn as a mule. So, I'm gonna go. I'll be back tomorrow to give him another dose. In the meantime, low-carb, low-protein diet." Todd grasped his bag and slung it over his shoulder. "You can bandage his feet with poultices made from bran and Epsom salts, but we don't really know if that helps."

"Can't hurt."

"Neither can getting on with your life. A guy has to man up and do it, sooner or later."

Tough words from a man who knew what Leo had been through. Their paths had crossed when one of Leo's dogs had been sick. Todd was the new vet in town, taking over from Doc Carter, who had held the spot for a good thirty-five years. Todd stayed all night, sitting cross-legged on the floor in the front room, keeping Leo company until Tinker passed. An unlikely friendship forged in loss and a mutual love of animals. "We'll see."

"Just think. A son. Or a daughter."

The possibilities seemed like stars that twinkled in the night sky, then disappeared behind a blanket of clouds.

He might end up with something akin to what Todd had. A wife. Twins on the way.

Leo might not sell his work in town because of the money, but could he do it for the company of a good woman? For the possibility of children? Of family?

The thoughts twisted themselves into a knot in his chest.

Todd was almost to his black Chevy Traverse before Leo caught him. "Hey, wait."

"Whatcha need?"

"Give me a ride into town?" He eventually would have to borrow one of Aidan's horses until he could figure out something else. Not being a farmer, he didn't have extras the way his cousin did. "I need to get a couple of things."

Talk to Mary Katherine Ropp. There was something about the

woman that made the words come a little easier. And he'd heard her working on Jennie more than once. Jennie of the sweet, heart-shaped face and soft, strangely sad voice.

"How will you get back?"

"I'll hitch a ride."

Someone from the district would be in town at the grocery store, the hardware store, or one of the Plain shops. They always were.

Not having his own ride would keep him from losing his nerve and turning around.

NINE

FIFTEEN MINUTES LATER LEO THANKED TODD FOR the ride, hitched up his pants, took a deep breath, and strode toward Amish Treasures. He thought of it as Mary Katherine's shop because she was the driving force behind it. Really, it belonged to a bunch of them. All working together for a single cause. Holding on to their farms. Holding on to their way of life. It was nestled next to a huge antique shop in a long, two-story red-brick building probably built sometime in the late eighteen-hundreds. The building had some wear and tear on it, in other words. A bell tinkled when he opened the glass door with its hand-painted sign.

Inside, things were looking good—better. The store was a work in progress.

Mary Katherine, Jennie, and the others had worked for weeks removing the meat display cases from the store, ripping out old linoleum, restaining the original wood floors underneath, and painting the walls a pale robin's-egg blue. Unused light fixtures still hung overhead, but the store was filled instead with light from half a dozen windows that ran top to bottom along the front. Bright and airy. The sweet scent of lavender and roses mingled, a far cry from the earthy smell of raw steaks and sausage.

Mary Katherine stood next to a far wall where a series of king- and queen-size quilts were displayed on long dowels that stuck out from the wall. She was talking to an English woman who patted at her damp face with a tissue in one hand and held a chubby toddler balanced on her hip with the other.

"I don't know how you stand it in here without AC. Why don't you turn on those ceiling fans at least?" The woman grimaced as she pointed at the fans overhead, her tone like that of a whiny teenager. "It's a sauna in here."

"The breeze is nice." Mary Katherine gestured toward the open windows. "We're selling cold lemonade, if you're interested."

Leave it to Mary Katherine to capitalize on the English folks not being used to the heat. Most of the English stores were too cold in the summer—at least for Leo. Even if Mary Katherine wanted to turn on the fans—the *Ordnung* gave them some leeway on the use of electricity, computers, and such for business purposes—she didn't dare. The electrical wiring was old, according to an English friend who'd helped with the renovations. It was a wonder faulty wiring hadn't caused the place to burn down around Mr. O'Rourke with all his freezers, meat display cases, AC, fans, and lights.

"I'd rather have a pop." The tourist shook her head. Dangling earrings shaped like leaves danced. She wore a sleeveless blouse and short-short shorts, revealing an assortment of tattoos, mostly flowers of various colors. "That's an awful lot of money for a quilt."

"It's handmade, every stitch. Sometime when we are having a quilting frolic, we'll have an open house so folks like you can see what goes into making such a piece as this." Mary Katherine's tone remained respectful. No doubt she heard this refrain frequently. Tourists loved the quilts, but they also wanted a bargain. Quilts were not manufactured comforters like the ones found in bed bags at discount stores. No doubt they would complain about his furniture too. "It's well worth the price when you think of all the work. And it will last forever. You'll be able to hand it down to your daughter someday."

The curly-headed toddler on the woman's hip chose that moment to clap her hands and giggle as if tickled by Mary Katherine's observation.

"She's fourteen months old. Someday is a long way off." The woman plopped the child on the burnished wood floor. The little girl immediately sat as if her sagging diaper was too heavy for her. "I'd hoped to get two, one for my bedroom and one for the guest bedroom."

"We have several others in a variety of patterns." Mary Katherine waved her hand toward the display. "Feel free to look around and think on it. Getting just the right one—or two—is a big decision. They'll be in your house for a very long time."

Would he have to do this kind of sales job? Leo's gut tightened at the thought. His throat went dry. Sweat dampened his armpits. He couldn't. Mary Katherine smiled at him and waved. She held up one finger as if to say *I'll be right with you.*

He edged toward the door. She shook the finger at him. "Wait, Leo. I'll be right with you."

He halted. Maybe if he stood still he'd blend into the background like a deer hiding in plain sight from hunters. Directly in front of him stood a shelf filled with books. Shelley Shepard Gray. Beth Wiseman. Amy Clipston. English authors who wrote stories about Plain people. The tourists would like those. On the shelf right next to them was Mary Katherine's compilation of short stories. The Plain folks liked to read those, and the elders approved of publishing stories if it gave folks something to read that was wholesome and God-centered.

He wasn't much of a reader, but folks said Mary Katherine had a special way with words. Which explained why she served as the district's *Budget* scribe. Her pieces were colorful and full of interesting anecdotes from Jamesport. Those he managed to read. Since he didn't get out much, he often learned things in the newspaper he didn't already know about his neighbors. Something Mary Katherine would call a sad commentary.

She talked like that.

"All my friends have quilts in their guest bedrooms to show off when they have company." The whine had returned to the woman's voice. Leo glanced back. The baby stood on plump legs and headed for a shelf filled with wooden trains, wagons, and pull-toys made by Angus Plank. The woman caught the straps of the toddler's sundress and tugged her back. "No you don't. Stay."

Like the child was an unruly puppy.

With her free hand, she dug around in an oversize leather bag and came up with a cell phone clad in a pink sparkly cover. "I have to talk to my best friend. See how much she paid. I'll get back to you."

Leo studied the small framed paintings of flowers and birds over the counter. Lorraine Hostetler had made those. He didn't want to see the woman rub her sweaty hand over the quilt's pristine squares while she alternately gabbed into the phone and scolded the child, who'd discovered the faceless dolls. Quilts were just blankets, after all. Something intended to keep a person warm in the winter. Not for bragging rights. Mary Katherine trotted in his direction. "I'm so glad you came." She clapped her hands as if applauding his decision. "I hope that means what I think it means."

He folded his arms across his middle, afraid if he left them loose they would accidently collide with jars of jam or honey or a rack of hand-embroidered tablecloths or pieced rag rugs. The store held a treasure trove of goods that represented the hard work of many of his friends, even family members. His cousin Timothy's wife, Josie, made the sweet-smelling candles on the shelf above them. "I don't understand why they make such a fuss over blankets."

Mary Katherine shrugged and straightened a pile of Iris Beachy's crib quilts, which were just the right size for a cradle. "The Amish are a mystery to the rest of the world. They don't understand our ways. It's almost as if they want a little piece of us to help them find their way back to a simpler life closer to Gott. They like that we live close to the earth. They see our way as peaceful when theirs is full of strife and noise and far from Gott."

"Guess they don't notice the hard work it takes to live this way." He tapped down the grumpiness in the words. The English folks' money allowed his friends and family to supplement their income. He shouldn't criticize while holding out his hand for some himself. "And my furniture will give them that feeling too?"

"You'll do it? You'll sell your furniture here?" Her smile lit up her face. He felt like a scholar who'd won favor with his teacher. Something he never actually did when he was in school. "How soon will you have something to display? It would be lovely if you could work on a piece here in the store on Saturdays when we'll get the most walk-in business."

His stomach roiled. The demo. Explaining to people what he did and how he did it. "Do I have to?"

"You sound like the kinner when I used to tell them to clean the chicken coop. It's not that bad. See that area over there?" She pointed to a long, narrow empty space that ran the length of the front of the store. "That's the demo area. On Saturdays when the foot traffic is highest and on craft days, we'll have our craftsmen set up there. You'll be with other folks doing the same thing. You won't be the only one. I'll do something out front with free cookies and coupons so folks will come on in. They love seeing craftsmen at work."

"Like me?" He found that hard to imagine. They simply wanted to watch him work. "Why?"

"Because it's interesting to them to see how you sand a piece of wood smooth and stain it. You could make small pieces like step stools or miniature rocking chairs for little kinner. They'll like that." She gestured with both hands, her face lit up with enthusiasm that made her look much younger. "We'll have some of the women doing needlepoint and samples of jellies and jams with homemade biscuits and recipe cards, and Laura and Jennie can give quilting lessons if we can get Jennie on board. Poor thing is almost as shy as you are—"

"Jennie?"

The name came out of his mouth before he could stop it. Shy. He never thought of himself as shy. Simply independent. Maybe Jennie saw herself the same way. Did her mouth go dry and her armpits dampen at the thought of showing English shoppers how to quilt? Did women's armpits sweat like his? What he knew about women would fit on the head of a nail.

Mary Katherine's hands stopped moving. The smile stretched even farther. "Jah, you have a problem with Jennie being here, or does it seem like a good idea to you?"

"Nee, I just—"

The door swung open and the topic of conversation trotted

through, a large box in her arms, four children in her wake like bows on a kite's tail. Jennie slammed to a halt when she saw him. Her son Mark careened into her. The box slipped from her hands and crashed to the floor.

"I didn't know you were here."

Those were the first words out of her mouth. Of course, she didn't know he was here. What made her think he would think she did? And why drop the box? "I'm leaving."

"Nee, don't leave. I was just dropping off these goods for sale." She knelt, looking as if she had a toothache. "Mark, Elizabeth, help me."

Strawberry jam oozed from a broken jar onto a dresser scarf filled with tiny, fancy embroidery stitches. The look of anguish on Jennie's face was unmistakable. She jerked her sewed goods away from the jars. The stain spread.

"It's okay, Mudder." Elizabeth sounded much older than her years. "Celia and Cynthia will sew more."

"And we'll pick more strawberries so you can make more jam." Mark squatted next to his mother and patted her back with a small, dirty hand in what must be the spitting image of something he'd seen grown-ups do. "It's okay, we'll make more in a jiffy."

They were so loving and so concerned for their mother. It said something about the kind of mother she was. A beloved one.

Pretty and a good mother. A good wife, no doubt. She'd been a good scholar. Good at reading. Not like him. Numbers were easier for him than words. Graduation couldn't come fast enough. Then he didn't see her anymore. His father died. He stopped going places. Never got the hang of singings. Then he heard she was marrying Atlee Troyer.

He had no one to blame but himself. He squatted. "Let me help."

"Nee, it's fine."

"I promise not to eat any more jelly on my biscuits." Elizabeth knelt next to Mark. "Francis won't either, right, Francis?"

Without a word, Francis scooted around to Leo's side. He squatted as if mimicking Leo's action. His dirty hand rested on Leo's thigh. His hand was so small and tender. Something about it made a lump swell in Leo's throat. He cleared it. "With all the rain we had this spring, the fruit has been plentiful."

More jelly could be made. The children wouldn't have to give it up, would they? "I'm good at picking berries if you need any help."

Francis leaned closer and burrowed his head in Leo's arm. His cheek was warm and sticky.

"Don't worry yourself. I'm sure you have plenty of work to do." Jennie looked alarmed. "Francis, stop it. You'll get Leo dirty. You're a mess."

"He's fine." Leo extricated himself from the boy and patted his small back. "Does he like to fish?"

"He loves to fish." Mark piped up. "We all do."

"Sometime we'll fish."

Why had he offered this? Something about Francis's chubby face and the way the boys looked at him as if he were a strange, foreign species they rarely saw and longed to examine more closely. They were starved for attention from a man. What would it cost him to give it to them? A little bit of time and he had an excuse to fish, something he loved to do.

"You promise?" Mark whooped. "I can't wait to go home and tell Micah."

"We clean now." Elizabeth, a practical little girl it seemed, frowned, a picture-perfect image of her mudder. "We help Mudder clean."

They were all so intent on making her feel better. Why did a broken jar of jelly and a stained dresser scarf make her feel so bad?

"Jah, jah, we clean. There's still five jars of jelly." Mark imbued the words with great enthusiasm. "And the set of dish towels with the days of the week on them and two more dresser scarves. They'll fetch a nice price. We'll be able to buy material and groceries as soon as they sell."

So that was it. Money. They needed the money. Why didn't Atlee's family help or hers? Maybe she was like him, not wanting to ask, wanting to make it on her own. He understood that.

Four little figures in descending order bent next to Jennie who sniffed and wiped at her face. Her eyes were red, but her lips curled up in a determined smile. "I am so sorry to make a mess right in your doorway." She kept her gaze on Mary Katherine, as if he wasn't there. "You have a washrag? I'll get it cleaned up."

"No problem, no problem." Mary Katherine sped behind a counter that held a huge old-fashioned calculator and an antique cash register. She produced a roll of paper towels and a spray bottle of cleanser. "Accidents happen. That's why they're called accidents."

She handed over the goods to Jennie. The paper towels dropped to the floor and rolled. Mark retrieved it and handed it back to his mother. The children tried so hard to help. They were good children. Not like Atlee Troyer. Leo could never understand what Jennie saw in him, but then, he shouldn't criticize her choices. He'd never stepped forward, never offered himself as a choice. In all likelihood Jennie had been better off with Atlee.

"I was just explaining to Leo about the demonstrations we'll do in the store." Mary Katherine seemed oblivious to Jennie's discomfort. And Leo's. "You two will be big draws for the tourists."

"Nee, nee." Jennie popped up from the floor. Jelly stained her apron. She handed Mary Katherine a wad of dirty paper towels. "I can't."

She gestured at the box. "It's obvious I can't."

Mary Katherine dropped the dirty paper towels into a nearby wastebasket. She hugged her friend. "You can, you really can."

She needed the money just as Leo did. "If I can do it, you can do it."

The smile Mary Katherine bestowed on him felt like a special gift. Jennie, on the other hand, turned and fled toward the door.

He'd made it worse somehow. She not only didn't want to do the demo, she didn't want to do it with him.

"I guess that was the wrong thing to say."

Mary Katherine shook her head, a delighted look on her face. "Nee, it was the right thing to say. The absolutely perfect thing to say."

Jennie didn't get far, however. Her escape was blocked by a parade of English folks entering the store led by a man Leo could have gone a month of Sundays without seeing. One Lazarus Dudley, antique dealer and self-proclaimed wheeler-dealer.

From the expression on his face, he'd come to do some wheeling and some dealing.

TEN

Jennie inched toward Amish Treasures' door. She'd made a mess of everything. She didn't belong here. She didn't belong anywhere near Leo, either. At best, he felt sorry for her. At worst, he thought she was a clumsy cow. Like Atlee had. Lazarus's contingent of four men, a local contractor named Bill Weatherford, an electrician whose name she didn't recall, and two others she didn't recognize, blocked her escape path.

She gathered up her scraps of dignity and sought to make her way out, her children behind her in a tight hand-holding row. "Excuse me."

They dodged the man in a suit made of a shiny material. It looked like it belonged to a much larger owner. He had a skinny notebook in one hand, pen in the other. He barely glanced up from his scribbles. The man behind him, on the other hand, loomed large, his navy polo shirt with its golf course emblem on the pocket stretched tight above a well-fed belly that hung over his khaki pants. His shoes made clacking noises on the wood floor. He wore cleats of some kind. Why, she couldn't fathom. Despite a distinct look of discomfort on his face, he summoned a smile in her direction. "Sorry, I'm so sorry. Do you need something to wipe off with?"

He pulled a wrinkled mess of a handkerchief from his pocket and held it out.

"It wasn't your fault, but thank you."

"Wait, Jennie." Mary Katherine's voice was much higher than normal. It held a note of trepidation, something Jennie had never heard there before. "If you don't mind."

Her friend needed her. Taking a deep breath, she stopped. "Cynthia, take your bruders and schweschder outside. Sit on the bench. Don't move until I come out."

"But—"

"No buts."

Cynthia did as she was told. Francis's delighted grin told Jennie she didn't have much time before her daughter would be chasing her youngest son down the street. Still, Mary Katherine needed her. She straightened her shoulders, pivoted, and slogged back through the men to her friend. "What is it?"

"I don't think Lazarus is here to buy a quilt. This involves all of us."

"You are an intelligent woman, Ms. Roper." The obvious surprise in Lazarus's tone turned a compliment inside out. So did the faint disdain on his thin face with its oversize nose and thin lips. His head was bald except for a fringe above his neck that flipped up in the same curl as his thick gray mustache. He wore a black suit, white dress shirt, black bow tie, black-and-white dress shoes, and leaned on a matching black-lacquered cane. He pointed the cane at the other men. "This is my team. You know Bill. He renovates space."

Renovates space?

They had fixed up the store. It needed no renovations. At least the parts that showed. The back room and storage area hadn't been touched, except to squeeze in all the stuff that didn't fit or was no longer needed up front. For now. To get the store open as quickly as possible. Jennie had done her share of ripping out the old linoleum and refurbishing the wood floor under it. And painting the walls until her shoulders ached and she could barely lift her arms. She had blood, sweat, and tears represented in this "space." All of them did.

"This space has already been renovated." Leo spoke up, his tone noncommittal, but his stance, legs apart, hands on hips, was firm. "It is suited to its purpose."

"As I told Ms. Roper—"

"It's Mary Katherine Ropp."

"As I told Mary Katherine, this was to be my space. Seamus promised it to me."

"Promised it?" Leo's eyebrows lifted and settled. "In writing?"

"We were closing in on an agreement." Lazarus brushed the words away with his tone and his hands. "He promised me he would wait to close until I returned from my vacation. My wife insists we take one every winter. She hates winter. She loves the beach. But I digress." He pulled a folded sheaf of paper from the inside pocket of his suit jacket. "My attorney had even drawn up the paperwork."

He held it out to Mary Katherine.

Her hand came up. Leo shook his head. Her hand dropped.

"If it isn't a signed document it has no legal standing."

"I understand that, but I'm relying on your people's reputation for goodwill and for getting along, thinking you'll want to do the right thing here."

"Give up the lease to you?"

"Yes, out of the goodness of your hearts." His voice had taken on a pleading note. "You see, I need this space."

He didn't say it, but his words implied it. *More than you do.*

"There's a difference between need and want." Jennie ventured into the fray. Maybe a woman should keep quiet in these circumstances, but she was Mary Katherine's friend. If anybody knew the difference between need and want, the mother of seven children did. "You already have the lion's share of the space in this building."

"I need all of the space." He pointed to the silky suit man. "Kenneth knows about opening coffee shops. Not like the mass-market franchise shops. A real coffee bar with a barista and espresso, cappuccino, and so forth. People who love old things, they love coffee."

He waved the cane around in the general direction of the quilt racks. "I'm envisioning round tables, nice, lacy golden-yellow tablecloths. Adirondack chairs. A few love seats. Bookshelves with old books for sale. Wi-Fi. They can do their research on my antiques while they sip."

"We don't have to do this right now." Kenneth snapped his pen's lid on and off in a steady, nervous racket. "There's plenty of time once the ownership issues have been resolved."

"I need cost estimates for my investors." Lazarus tapped his two-tone black-and-white shoe on the floor. "Bill, what do you think?"

Bill tugged a measuring tape from his pocket and held it up. "If y'all don't mind, I can get the measurements real quick and get out of your way."

"We're open. We have customers." Mary Katherine's tone was polite but cool. She looked far cooler than Jennie felt. "It might be best if you came back if and when Lazarus owns the place."

Seemingly oblivious to the consensus of the group around him, Lazarus turned to the electrician. Kyle. Kyle Barlow. That was his name. "What about you, Kyle? How much work do you think it needs?"

Kyle, a beanpole man in a spotless white T-shirt and green

work pants, shrugged. "The wiring has to be as outdated as what you have in the antique shop." He had a lazy accent that said he wasn't originally from these parts. "Those big coffee makers pull a lot of juice."

"But you can do it?"

"With time and money, everything is possible." He tipped his Kansas City Chiefs ball cap at Mary Katherine. "And with permission. I don't touch wiring without permission. Too much liability."

"It'll be resolved shortly." Lazarus grimaced and gave a half bow toward Mary Katherine. "I had right of first refusal. I turned my back for a second and that old goat bailed out and skipped town. My attorney will be in touch with him. And eventually, with you."

He turned and limped out, leaning on his cane, his entourage behind him. "We'll be back."

Jennie didn't like him much and she didn't like that feeling. They were expected to like folks. Even if they made it difficult.

That didn't mean they had to turn their shop over to them. She headed for the door.

"Where are you going?" Mary Katherine called.

Jennie shoved the door open and looked back. "To get busy making more jam to sell. And more dresser scarves and tablecloths. We need to stock up. People can go to Kramer's or the Stop N Go for coffee."

Mary Katherine grinned. "Perfect. And I can put you down to work a shift?"

"Jah, you can. But let me work on inventory first."

With a whoop Mary Katherine darted forward and held up her hand in a high five. Jennie reciprocated and did the fist bump she'd seen the children doing. It was silly, but it felt good.

Mary Katherine turned to Leo. He ducked his head and stared at his boots. Mary Katherine patted his shoulder. "We'll get you next time."

Next time.

Realizing just what she'd agreed to do, Jennie fled.

ELEVEN

FOOD STAPLES OR MATERIAL? THE QUESTION GAVE
Jennie a headache. She bent over the treadle sewing machine, her
feet pumping as her hands guided the material under the needle. Or
maybe it was the time she had spent sewing after making cookies all
morning, to sell at the store, that caused the ache. They all had to pitch
in and earn the money to pay the bills and still earn a profit. They
could not give in to Lazarus. That wasn't an option. Stewing about
the store kept her mind off the scene she'd made the previous week.
Not thinking about that look on Leo's face. A mixture of puzzlement
and pity. Pity for what? Because she was the clumsiest woman on
earth? Because she spent all that time embroidering dresser scarves
and canning jam only to drop the whole kit and caboodle on the floor?

Still, the look on Leo's face when Francis put his hand on his leg
had touched Jennie. A strange mixture of tender sadness and lost
hope. A look that made her heart constrict in painful recognition. His
heart hurt the way hers did for dreams lost or broken.

Just because he had an interest in children didn't mean he had an
interest in her. He was simply being kind.

Nee, she could never be sure.

He felt sorry for her. That was all.

"If I can do it, you can do it."

Had he really said that? Had he meant it?

The image of the two of them working side by side in the store, her showing women daisy stitches and French knots, him sanding wood and staining it, filled her mind to the brim. Both were such peaceful pastimes. Creating something pretty and yet useful. She found peace when she sewed. It took her to another place, a quiet, restful place. Likely, Leo found that place when he created a piece of furniture that would last for decades or longer. It would become part of a family and a storehouse of memories for the owner.

A nice image, but it wouldn't be like that. She would drop something. Stain something. Stutter and jab herself with a needle. Atlee said she was a clumsy cow. The clumsiest woman he knew. He said she had given birth to equally clumsy children.

She had no time for feeling sorry for herself. First she would sew clothes for the kinner. Then she would pick up the embroidery again. She had enough pale-blue poly/cotton to make another dress for Elizabeth. Enough black tri-blend denim for one more pair of pants. She liked this material because it didn't require ironing and the tri-blend didn't fade the way regular denim did. Mark needed them worse than Micah, but they both had sprouted up so much in the last month, their pants had become high waters. She chewed her lip. The cookie jar in the kitchen contained enough cash to buy flour, sugar, coffee, and a few other staples she needed or more material. Not both. Enough to do, but not enough money to do.

Which took her right back to the store. Bills outweighed the money in her pocketbook every day. She had to do whatever was necessary to take care of her children, but they also needed her at home.

They needed a mother who was present in their lives, not going into work in town three or four days a week. Women with husbands did not have this dilemma. Plain wives and mothers didn't work away from home. It was frowned upon. Widows were different.

In every way.

The screen door opened and Cynthia barreled in. Her hands occupied by a large wicker basket of clothes fresh off the line, she let the door slam behind her. "Can we get a trampoline?" She settled the basket on the floor with a thud next to the table and picked up the first pair of pants. "Sarah and Rachel have one in their backyard. It would be fun for all of us, something we can do together when the chores are done."

Sarah and Rachel's father, Isaac Plank, could afford the extras, it seemed. Not that a trampoline was an exorbitant thing to want. Jennie had already looked through the ads in *The Budget* and the asking price even for used trampolines didn't fit in their meager budget. "I'll ask Matthew to put the tire swing back up." It fell when the children decided to try a family ride—six of them at once. Only Matthew refused to participate, saying he was too old for such silliness. The sight of them sprawled all over the ground, hooting, hollering, and tickling each other, had made even Mister Sourpuss smile. "You can push Elizabeth and Francis. Celia can push you. You like the swing, don't you?"

Her sweet face somber, Cynthia nodded and plopped another pair of pants in the pile. "It's okay. Is it because there's no money?" This daughter, at ten, was the wise owl in the bunch, with her black-rimmed glasses sliding down her nose. She was also the one who looked the most like Jennie. Sandy-blonde hair, pale-blue eyes, a solid frame made for childbearing. She even had the same slightly crooked lower front teeth and a dusting of freckles that reminded Jennie of her childhood spent picking peaches, blueberries, and apples at her parents' farm. "Matthew can take me and Celia to the store tomorrow to give Mary Katherine your Log Cabin quilt and some more of the embroidered pillowcases. They'll sell fast. The tourists are starting to flood in by the busload what with the nice weather."

"That's a good idea. We'll have a table at the next market days too. You and Celia can run it." The children didn't need to concern themselves with money. Most everything they needed could be grown on the farm. Almost everything. Jennie flipped up the lever to release the material and picked up the scissors to snip the thread. "Did you get the eggs from the chicken coop?"

"Jah and Celia milked the cow. We can have egg taco casserole for supper and drink the milk."

"Sounds good. Grab a jar of peaches from the basement and I'll make a pie for tomorrow. I have biscuits in the oven for tonight."

They would never starve as long as they could grow their own food. The canned goods in the basement occupied an entire wall of shelves. Flour and baking soda were relatively cheap. Cynthia's response was lost in the sound of a familiar, cranky engine revving outside the open windows. Jennie stood and peeked out.

Nathan.

The waves in Jennie's stomach heaved and lurched, back and forth.

She hadn't seen him since the day on the side of the road with Leo's lame horse. He had looked so concerned, so afraid he'd caused her harm. That look could lull a woman into thinking a man could be kind, even gentle.

No. She'd been fooled before.

He'd also looked perturbed when she drove off with Leo. Nathan didn't like it, her giving Leo a ride. He didn't have any business liking or not liking what Jennie did with Leo—or anyone, for that matter.

Why did he care? Was that the doo-doo he'd mentioned that day before tromping off to talk with Freeman and stare at her from a distance?

"Is that Nathan? Yippee, it's Nathan." Cynthia cast aside one of Elizabeth's dresses and raced to the door. "I wonder what books he brought today." Shoulders hunched, she halted at the door and looked back. "I know. We can't buy books, but he can stay for supper, can't he?"

Jennie forced a smile. Of all her children Cynthia loved to read the most. She'd plowed through the entire Little House series during the long, cold winter months. A copy of *Sarah, Plain and Tall* lay on the table, a bookmark stuck at the halfway point. She read even when the great outdoors called to the other children. "Maybe next time."

"It's okay. That's the nice thing about the library. We can get all the books we want for free." Grinning, Cynthia jerked the door open. "And Nathan doesn't mind. He says he wants us to read because reading opens our minds up to the world and new thoughts and ideas. He just comes here for the pie and the company. That's what he says."

Not necessarily what a Plain parent wanted—the new thoughts and ideas of a fallen world. But Nathan wasn't Plain. The van and his choice of occupation told that story. A *clomp, clomp* told Jennie when he started up the steps, then strode across the porch. A second later, his *rat-a-tat-tat* knock announced his arrival at the door. "Hey, Cynthia, how are you, girl?" He peered through the dark netting of the screen, his face a shadowy gray on the other side. "Long time no see."

"What do you have today?" Cynthia held the door open wide.

"Mudder says we can't afford to buy books right now, but you can stay for supper. Can you stay? I'll get the Life on the Farm out, or would you rather play Scum?"

Embarrassment coursed through Jennie like a terrible fever. Cynthia didn't need to be so free with information about their financial situation. Her expression blithe, Cynthia let the screen door slam, then turned and skipped to the kitchen and the basement door before Nathan could answer.

Jennie teetered heel to toe, trying to get her balance. "Sorry, she's so rambunctious. You don't have to feel obligated to play games or stay for supper. I'm happy to look at the books. Do you have anything on sale today?"

"And don't you feel obligated to look or to buy."

"I don't."

His face reddened until it was the color of the shirt he wore today with his khaki pants and dusty red sneakers. His Cardinals cap had been replaced with a John Deere one. Surely a gift from one of his customers. The man had never been on a tractor in his life. He busied himself with the backpack full of his wares, children's books of all kinds, all suitable for Plain children. He made sure of that. Nice, good-quality books that would hold up under many readings and the chunky hands of children who hadn't learned yet to treat books with that special care they should always receive. "I know books can be seen as a luxury when you're trying to put food on the table."

"Is that the sales pitch you usually use?" The snippiness in her tone shamed Jennie. She fought to soften it. It wasn't Nathan's fault she was embarrassed. "Books are a good thing for kinner. It's just that they spend more time outside playing and doing chores than inside reading in the summer."

True, but not why she couldn't buy.

"You don't want them to lose the reading ability they gained during the school year over the summer, but I know what you're saying. I generally have fewer sales in the summer for that very reason." He laid out a series of books she hadn't seen before. A family crossing the country in a covered wagon in early America. "But that's okay. That's why I'm . . ." He stopped, a guilty look on his face.

"Is something wrong?"

He shook his head. "I like playing games with the kids."

She picked up one of the books, then laid it down. "You must have other families to visit."

"I like your cooking better."

The heat that roared across her face told her its color surely matched his. "Not tonight, you won't. It's egg taco casserole." A recipe she'd made up when she had no meat. "But the biscuits will be hot."

The smell of something burning hit her nose. "Oh no. The biscuits!"

She ran to the kitchen. Celia bent over the oven and pulled out the pan. She sniffed and turned. "I smelled them out back." She wrinkled her nose. "They're only a little singed. If we eat them with butter and strawberry preserves, we won't even notice."

Celia was Jennie's optimistic child, the one who could find the silver lining in the darkest of clouds. Jennie patted her back. "I'm so glad you caught them in time. Can you help Cynthia get a jar of strawberry preserves from the basement? And a jar of hot sauce for the casserole. Green beans too. She can't carry it all, with the peaches."

Hot sauce made the eggs seem less plain.

Celia planted a kiss on Jennie's cheek. She was also the most affectionate of the children. She looked like her father, but had none of his volatility. She was a beautiful girl with dark hair, fair skin, and enormous blue eyes. Her slim figure would make her popular at the singings in a few years. Not something to which Jennie looked forward. "The blueberries are blooming. Everything is early this year. And the purple martins are building their nests already. I saw eggs in one of them."

"*Wunderbarr.*" Jennie turned to glance back, following her daughter's gaze. "Nathan has come by."

Nathan nodded a greeting. "Why don't I fix that step out front before someone trips over the loose board?"

Jennie couldn't put him to work when she wasn't even planning to buy his wares. It wasn't right. "Matthew will do that when he gets back from working at Peter's."

"He'll be worn to a frazzle after cutting hay all day in the sun." Nathan offered her a smile that turned his rather plain face into one Jennie might see when she closed her eyes at night. "I'll have it done in a jiffy."

"But—"

"No buts. I'm earning my supper. Consider it a fair trade."

If she were serving pork chops or brisket, maybe. But eggs for supper? She watched him go, a grin on his face that said he didn't plan to take no for an answer.

Much pounding and talking ensued, the chatter from Cynthia, Elizabeth, and Mark floating through open windows while Jennie threw together the casserole ingredients and popped it into the oven. She opened the jar of green beans to stretch the meal. The children wouldn't complain about the plain fare. Neither would her company. Their company. He wasn't there to see her. He liked the children.

Jennie knew Francis watched every move Nathan made, not

because he spoke but because Cynthia kept telling him to move back. It became apparent some screens were also being fixed as well as a chair that had collapsed under the weight of three children who decided to sit in it together one evening in a fit of giggles. All this work gave her time to fix supper. It wasn't much, but it would do.

The meal was a lively affair with the children—all except Matthew of course—interrupting each other to talk to their guest. Nathan attempted to draw out her oldest son with questions about his day. Matthew grudgingly unbent enough to describe the horse that broke loose from the tedder and sent them scurrying after him midday. Nathan listened and nodded and asked questions in all the right places. Despite Nathan's encouragement, Matthew lapsed back into silence.

Nathan watched him with a puzzled look on his face, then smiled at Jennie. "This was good grub." He pushed back his chair and patted his belly. "You do know how to gussy up eggs. And that salsa wakes up a fella's tongue."

"It's just casserole." She scraped the last of it onto Micah's plate. He was a growing boy who had worked hard alongside Matthew and Peter's boys from sunrise to supper. "No need to fuss."

"You could learn to take a compliment." Nathan attempted to hide a burp behind one big hand covered by fine orangey-red hair. The sound made Elizabeth giggle. Which of course made Francis giggle too. Mark followed with a loud belch. Nathan chuckled. "That's compliments to the chef, I always say. I like your cooking. I like a lot of things about you."

He stopped, his ears as red as his face. "What I mean to say is I like a lot of things you cook."

The children tittered. Matthew arose and stomped from the room.

"Celia, Cynthia, get started in the kitchen." Jennie rose. Her hand smacked against her water glass, tipping it over. Water soaked the tablecloth and ran onto the floor. "I'm so clumsy."

Celia sopped up the table with her apron. "You're worse than Elizabeth, Mudder."

Getting scolded by her oldest daughter in front of Nathan didn't help in the least. "I can clean up after myself. You get the dishes. Micah, Mark, go help your bruder with the chores before it gets dark."

"I guess I should be going too." Nathan picked up his hat. "Y'all will want to turn in soon."

"Nee, we still have to play Life on the Farm." Cynthia balanced a stack of dirty plates in one hand and the casserole dish in the other. "Right, Mudder, we can play a game? It's early yet."

"I want to play Life on the Farm." Elizabeth chimed in as she grabbed the empty biscuit basket and trundled toward the kitchen. "Don't make him go, Mudder."

"*Don't make him go.*" Like she was being inhospitable. "I have sewing to do, but if you want to stay, stay."

The emotions that flitted across his face were indecipherable. He scooted back his chair. "Bring it on, Elizabeth. Life on the Farm it is." His tone made it a challenge. "Your mudder doesn't want to play games, but I do."

She liked to play games, but not the kind Nathan had in mind. Jennie grabbed the empty casserole dish from Cynthia and strode into the kitchen. Matthew stood at the kitchen screen door, his hands on his hips, staring outside.

"Go do your chores so you can come in and play Life on the Farm. They're getting it out now."

"I have other things to do besides play stupid little kinner games."

"You used to like to play games."

"I'm too old for games." Matthew's tone grew uglier, his voice louder. He sounded like Atlee. "Besides, someone has to do the work around here."

"You know better than to speak to your elders that way."

He swiveled and stared at her. "What'll you do about it?"

"I shouldn't have to do anything. You know better. I've raised you better."

"Like *Groossdaadi* raised Daed?"

"You're not like your daed."

"Try me and see." He surged through the door and slammed it so hard the pots on the counter rattled.

Exactly like his father.

Dufus. Nathan was a big dufus. He had the opportunity to tell Jennie and he hadn't. This was his last visit as a salesman. His two weeks' notice would be up and he could start his new vocation as a farmhand. If someone would hire him.

A mighty big *if.*

There were many ifs in his life these days. Walk by faith, not by sight. That would be his father's advice. His father made it look easy, but it wasn't. Not at all.

Nathan took the box covered with black-and-white cows and the big red letters that read *Life on the Farm* from Elizabeth. She settled Indigo onto the table, climbed up on the bench next to Nathan, and tugged the lid from the box. "I want the red pawn." He need only look at Elizabeth to know what her mother had looked like as a child, with her fair skin and blue eyes. "Red is my favorite color. Celia says it's too bright for Plain girls. I like bright. That's why Rufus wears a red bandana."

She pointed her plump finger at the dog, who curled up in a ball next to her chair. Elizabeth never lacked for company.

"I like red too, but lighter colors are nice." He knew what Celia was trying to teach her little sister. Plain boys and girls didn't want to stand out. They wanted to keep themselves apart from the world. He'd heard that speech from Freeman when he dropped by the bishop's house to tell him he'd given his two weeks' notice. Freeman didn't mince words. The possibility that Nathan would be able to give up all the trappings of the world and stick to it seemed small to the bishop. But that didn't mean Nathan couldn't take the lessons with Freeman and contemplate a future different from the one he saw in front of himself at this moment. "Rufus could wear a black bandana and he'd still look handsome."

Elizabeth frowned. "Black is your favorite color?"

"Blue is my favorite color," Nathan hastened to add. "Like the color of your mother's eyes. And your eyes too."

The slightest pause in the *thump, thump* of the treadle told him Jennie was listening. He hid a smile. The woman needed to learn to take a compliment. She needed to relax. She wasn't clumsy, either. Just a little nervous. He'd like to think it was because of him. She might have a tiny sliver of feeling for him that made her hands tremble. A start toward something more, with time.

Celia counted out the ten thousand dollars and handed them to Nathan, along with the white pawn. "I feel like I might win tonight. I feel lucky."

"We don't believe in luck." Mark shook the die. "I go first. Me first."

"I feel like retiring so I want to win. Just watch. I'll get my sixty cattle in no time." Nathan glanced at the back of Jennie's head. She bent over the sewing machine as if her eyes were going in the dusky evening light. "In fact, I've given my two weeks' notice. No more selling books for me."

"No more books!" Celia and Cynthia spoke in unison. They sounded disappointed. He understood that. He loved books. That's why he chose selling them as his job. If he had to sell something, he wanted it to be something he believed in.

The *thump, thump* stopped. Jennie's head came up, but she didn't turn around.

He waited.

Turn around, turn around, look at me. Please look at me.

The *thump, thump* began again.

He'd taken the easy way out. Telling her by telling the children. Instead of to her face. *Lord, forgive me for being such a coward. I've never done this before.*

He sometimes wondered why he hadn't found the right woman after all these years. Never even came close. A date here and there, but it always fizzled before becoming something real and warm and tangible. Books were easier. Losing himself in the pages was easier. Until now. Now it had to be this woman whose face he saw when he closed his eyes at night. This woman who could never be his unless she wanted a different life or he chose her life.

Freeman had made it clear there was little likelihood of either.

"What will you do?" Celia broached the question he'd hoped to hear from her mother. "How will you make a living?"

"Will we ever see you again?" Cynthia tugged on his shirtsleeve. "Where will you live?"

He rolled the die and moved his pawn, landing on the space Cow Auction. He bought ten cattle at five hundred a piece. Half his cash, but a herd was an investment. The first person to get sixty head of cattle won. He had a head start. *Stop beating around the bush.* "I'm starting a new career as a farmhand. At least that's the plan if someone will hire me." He counted his money, once, twice. Better hope he landed on the Collect Milk Check next. "I'm looking around for a little duplex or a house to rent. I have some money set aside for a rainy day."

The *thump, thump* continued.

The heat of the propane lamp made him sweat. He longed for a cool drink of water. "I'm thirsty. I'll bring out the pitcher."

"You're company. Let me get it." Jennie pushed away from the sewing machine. Definitely listening to every word. "I might as well make the popcorn. You know you'll want some before the game is over."

It didn't matter how much they ate for supper. They always had popcorn soaked in butter and sprinkled with salt during the game. Which led to more water.

He waited until she disappeared into the kitchen, then coughed. "I better get that water. I have a frog in my throat."

"A frog is croaking in your throat?" Elizabeth giggled. "I want a frog in my throat."

As if she didn't have enough pets. The girl had named all the chickens, in order according to the alphabet: Abby, Bertha, Cassie, Daisy, Emma, Fiona, Georgia, and so on. She claimed to know which one was which. The horses—Lulu, Buck, Samson, and Carmel—also received daily visits complete with carrots when they could be spared for use as treats for the animals.

"You can have my frog." He patted her kapp. "I'll be right back. I promise."

Maybe sooner if Jennie kicked him out of the kitchen. He found her standing at the counter, the water pitcher in one hand, staring out the window.

"Can I help?"

She jumped and shrieked. Water slopped onto her dress and apron, spreading in a dark swirl. Why did she jump every time he came upon her from behind?

"It's only me. I needed that drink of water. My throat is parched. It's hot for May, isn't it? I mean if it's this hot now, what will it be like in July or August?"

Why did he run on at the mouth every time he was around her? Talking about the weather? Seriously.

She didn't answer. Instead, she busied herself pouring water into a plastic tumbler. Her hand shook. Droplets of water splattered on the counter. She grabbed a towel and sopped them up in such a hurry a person might think water stained.

"Why are you so nervous around me?" He took the pitcher from her and set it on the counter. "I'm a friendly guy."

"It's getting late." She turned and faced him. "Time for the kinner to turn in."

"We just started playing." He folded his arms over his chest to keep from reaching out to her. "You were making popcorn."

"Popcorn is salty. It only makes you thirstier."

She said this as if it were a new piece of information that explained everything. Why did she look so troubled? Why did she shrink back if he dared to come too close? Why did she duck her head when she spoke to him? She reminded him of a puppy who'd been kicked by a previous owner and could never trust a human again.

She had been married to an Amish man. They were the gentlest folks around. Nonviolent. Conscientious objectors. It seemed unlikely Atlee would have raised a hand to her, but then no one truly knew what went on behind closed doors, especially among people as private as the Amish. "Is it because I said I'm staying in Jamesport for good?"

"It's none of my business where you stay."

"We're friends, aren't we?" If it couldn't be more, he wanted at least that much from her. An admission that they had more than a passing, polite interest in each other. "I promise being friends with me isn't a bad thing."

"I know that." She handed him the glass of water. His fingers brushed hers. They were callused. She drew back her hand as if he was the snake she so feared that day at the school picnic. "It's getting late."

"Maybe I should go. I'll slip out the back and you explain to the kinner that I wasn't feeling well."

He really wasn't. The look of fear on her face turned his stomach.

"I can't lie to them. I'll tell them I asked you to go." She drew an audible breath, then let it out, a painful sigh. "I'm sorry. They need to turn in. Dawn comes early."

"You really haven't done anything to be sorry for." Somebody had. Somebody had turned her into a woman fearful of a man's touch. Who would've done that? "I hope you figure out that I mean you no harm. I promise."

"It's not you."

She said the words, but her face said differently. It was him. And all the rest of the men in the world.

"I'm staying in Jamesport because I like the people here." He gulped down the water, hoping it would take with it the lump that suddenly lodged in his throat. "All of them, including you. It's a good place to put down roots. I've never had roots in my life—not since I was a kid anyway."

"That's hard for me to imagine." Her expression softened, Nathan caught a glimpse of what she must have looked like as a young girl, softer, even prettier, even sweeter. "I've never lived anywhere but here. Not in this house, but within miles of it."

"My family is flung to the four corners of the hemisphere now." Nathan held the glass out to her. She took it, her care in not touching him again obvious. He smiled. She smiled back. "My parents are in El Salvador planting a church."

"Planting a church like corn or beans? It's odd how different Mennischt have become from our kind." She set the glass on the counter and moved to the stove where she placed a thick cast-iron pot on the burner, measured out and added two tablespoons of oil, then adjusted the flame. Her back was to him, but he could see how her body hummed with tension in the set of her shoulders.

Still, she had changed her mind about the popcorn. That was a good sign. "Driving cars. Flying in airplanes. Evangelizing. But we mostly believe the same things, don't we?"

She turned and picked up a huge jar filled with popcorn kernels. "Do we?" She looked up at him, the wrinkle in her forehead and the quizzical look in her eyes accentuating the question as if she really wanted to know. "Do you believe in Meidung, then?"

He would never have to test his beliefs on the subject of shunning. His family was a family of believers. So much so they dedicated themselves to evangelizing others. Something else Jennie wouldn't understand. No wonder Freeman found it so hard to believe Nathan might be able to immerse himself in this life. "I'm not sure shaming people you love into toeing the line is the best way to bring them closer to Christ."

Who was he to judge? He was a poor sinner who felt an endless well of jealousy every time he thought of all the energy and love his parents expended to get others to believe. He hadn't seen them in almost three years.

"It's not shame. It's tough love and it keeps the rest of us from falling into the same patterns." The sizzle of oil punctuated her statement. She poured in a cup of kernels and set a lid on the pot. "It's our hope they'll realize what they're missing and return to the fold."

"Why are you making popcorn?"

Her gaze traveled from him to the pot and back. Her hand fluttered to her chest. She shook her head. "I don't know. You made me forget what I was doing."

"Maybe you really wanted me to stay."

The pause lingered longer than he hoped it would. *Pop-pop-pop* filled the air, slowly at first, then faster, along with the heavenly scent of popcorn that reminded him of watching movies and game nights with his own family.

"Nee. Jah. I mean, no, it's that I can't think straight sometimes. I have so much to do and I worry. I know worry is a sin, but I can't help it. I can't keep myself grounded in today. I keep thinking about tomorrow and what it will bring and if I'll be able to do what I need to do for them." She nodded toward the door. "I have to do the work of a daed and a mudder. I'm not always sure I'm up to that. Mostly, I'm sure I'm not. I don't know why I'm telling you all this."

"Because that's what a person does with a friend. Confides in him. I understand—"

The back door swung open and Darren barged through it. "Howdy . . ." His gaze swung from Nathan to Jennie and back. "What are you doing here?"

TWELVE

THE LOOK ON HER BROTHER-IN-LAW'S FACE SAID
it all. Jennie took a step back, out of a habit that never died even when
her husband did. Darren, although a few years younger, could've been
Atlee's twin. The same towering height, burly shoulders, wild hair,
and blue eyes that pierced through the skin to the marrow of her bones.
The same way of talking as if everyone should stop and listen. Right
now he looked as if she'd confirmed his worst suspicions. Standing
alone in her kitchen with a Mennonite man within arm's reach.

"I stopped by to show Jennie and the kids the latest books."
Nathan's tone was even, but the lines around his mouth deepened.
He must've been in his late thirties or early forties. Why had he never
married? Or had he and she just assumed he hadn't? He could be a
widower too or divorced. He never talked about it. "The kids wanted
me to play Life on the Farm with them. But now I'm headed out."

Headed out because Jennie asked him about shunning instead of
congratulating him on his decision to retire from life on the road and
settle down a hop, skip, and a jump from her.

Darren said nothing in the long pause that followed.

The smell of scorched popcorn tickled her nose. "Oh no." She whirled and lifted the pot from the stove. The handle singed her fingers. "Ouch. Ouch."

"A pot holder might be in order." More judgment from Darren. "I stopped by to see if Matthew and Micah can help cut hay tomorrow. We're behind and it's supposed to storm. I want to get it in before it rains."

"They worked with Peter today, getting his in."

Another long, awkward pause. Darren had to know her brother paid the boys for their work. Darren always offered to pay the boys and the money was needed, but she also knew he had his own bills to pay and mouths to feed. Atlee's brothers farmed his fields, which helped because she couldn't do it on her own. No one had much extra these days, but Atlee's family had been plenty helpful in the early days. She didn't want to keep asking them for help. It didn't seem right.

"I'll feed them and send them home with some meat." Darren shoved his hat back, revealing a suntan line across his forehead. "We butchered a cow yesterday and a hog today. We have more beef and sausage than we know what to do with."

Meat would be good. As good as cash. Better. She didn't know what it would feel like to have more than she knew what to do with. "We would appreciate that. The kinner like sausage, and we haven't had any in a while."

Darren nodded.

Yet another awkward pause.

"I better get going." Nathan adjusted his baseball cap. "Tomorrow I have to hit the road to Seymour and that direction."

"I heard you were thinking of hiring yourself out as a farmhand." Darren's voice held thinly veiled doubt. "Got any experience?"

"Not hands-on, but I'm a quick learner."

"Hmm."

"Let me dump the popcorn out in your trash can. It'll get the smell out of your house." Nathan grabbed a dish towel, picked up the pot, and moved toward the door. "I'll leave the pan and the towel on the back step. Tell the kinner I said I'll see them next time."

"Come up to my place once you get done with the books." Darren made it a statement, not a question. "We need another set of hands and a strong back. I can't pay much, but you might learn something."

Jennie gripped the counter's edge. Did her brother-in-law just offer Nathan a job? His expression was downright kind. She'd never seen that look on her husband's face. Darren had offered help over the years, even when it was obvious his own cupboards were getting low. How could two brothers be so different?

Nathan's face broke into that sunny grin that made the skin crinkle around those periwinkle eyes. "Much obliged."

"No reason to come down here to Jennie's on your own." Darren's words acquired a harder edge. "Her brothers and me and the rest of the family take care of the fields here."

"I reckon a person can always find a reason to visit with friends." His grin still in place, Nathan's tone was good-natured, but firm. "I try to help out with a few things around here when I can. Fix the steps. Clean the gutters. Work on the washing machine. Things friends do for a friend who doesn't have a husband to do it for her."

Everything about his tone suggested family might consider doing the same. Neither man backed down from the staring contest. He shouldn't poke at Darren like that. Jennie would pay the consequences. He'd be gone and she'd be left to explain to her brother-in-law.

"Matthew and Micah should be doing that. All they have to do is ask and we'll help." Darren was equally firm. "We're family."

Not an iota of capitulation in his face, Nathan tipped his hat to her and headed for the door, smelly popcorn pot in hand, stride jaunty.

He looked as if Darren had offered him his own farm.

Silence prevailed until the door closed behind him. Jennie scooped up the dishrag and scrubbed at an already-clean counter.

"I reckon, my bruder being dead and all, it's none of my business." Darren cleared his throat, a deep *harrumph* full of discomfort. "But you are still family so I'll say it anyway. I reckon the elders would have something to say about that kind of visit from a so-called friend. A Mennisch man."

"He came to sell books." Jennie scrubbed harder. "Like he does with everyone."

"He stayed for supper. Long past supper."

"The kinner invited him. They like having company." Atlee's family almost never visited anymore. Or invited her and the children for a visit. The family thread had grown thin and stretched over the years. It was her fault as much as theirs. "They like his stories. It's harmless."

"Tell Micah and Matthew to be at the barn at sunrise."

She turned to face him. "Do you want to poke your head in and say hello?" He was their uncle. If they hadn't spent a lot of time with him over the years, he couldn't be blamed. She wanted to put as much yardage between herself and the memories as possible. She hadn't been thinking of the children. "They're all in the front room."

"Can't. I still have animals to feed. Dawn comes early." He stifled a yawn behind his big hand. "If you need work done around here, have Matthew do it. Don't let him get away with being lazy."

"He's not lazy."

"Gut. Don't be a stranger." Darren trudged out the back door, letting the screen slam. Unable to stop herself, Jennie watched from the window as he strode to his buggy. The back of his head, the slope of his shoulders could be Atlee. But it wasn't. This man offered a job to another man seeking a fresh start. He treated her like family, even though she'd been the one to distance herself from him and the others. Nothing was black and white in this life. She could hear her dad saying those words. People can't be pigeonholed. They have some good and some bad in them.

Which brought her back to Atlee.

The Atlee she knew had kissed her on her parents' front porch that first time with such white-hot emotion that it burned a trail through her body from her heart all the way to toes that curled up inside her sneakers.

That was the Atlee she married. He was the one who picked her up and kissed her hard that evening down by the pond when he asked her to marry him. He whirled her around and around until she was too dizzy to stand after she said yes.

That Atlee.

Stop. Stop.

Atlee reached up, grabbed her arm, and jerked her from the buggy. Unable to catch herself, she fell to her knees. He released her. She cradled her arm against her chest, sure the bone had been ripped from its socket at the shoulder. "What is it? What's wrong?" She tried to stand. He shoved her back down and stood over her, hand lifted as if to strike her. No one had ever hit her, not ever. Her daed didn't need to hit. His quiet word was all she needed for correction. "Why are you acting like this?"

He hadn't said a word all the way home from her parents' house. Not a word. No answer when she asked if he liked her mother's lasagna. She thought to fix it for him if he did. In six months of marriage, she was still learning what he liked or didn't like.

"Don't ever do that again."

"Do what? What did I do?"

"You interrupted me in front of your daed. You disrespected me in front of your parents."

"I didn't. I was just making conversation."

"At my expense. A fraa doesn't do that. A fraa fixes the food, puts it on the table, and cleans up afterward. A fraa doesn't interfere in a conversation between men."

They'd been discussing repairs that needed to be made to the house. Changes that needed to be made. Atlee wasn't much for that sort of thing. He was a farmer. She'd told how the water spouted in his face when he tried to turn it off and work on the pipes in the bathroom. They'd laughed.

"I'm sorry. I didn't mean to disrespect you. I was just making conversation."

"You sleep on the floor tonight."

"What?"

"In the barn."

"Atlee—"

"You have to learn. You're like a stupid child who doesn't know any better. I'll have to teach you."

"I'm not a child. I'm a grown woman."

His hand flew out, catching her by surprise. The back side caught her in the mouth. Pain exploded. The taste of salty blood seeped from the inside of her lip and gathered in the back of her throat.

She gasped and threw her arm up to protect herself.

"Go on, get. Put the horse and buggy away. Get out of my sight. I can't bear to look at you."

He turned and stomped away.

That was the first time.

The first of many lessons she had to learn from the man who'd said he loved her and wanted to spend the rest of his life with her.

"It smells like burnt popcorn all the way in the front room." Cynthia skipped into the room and skidded to a stop. "Where's Nathan? Mark has been playing his turn. Why does it smell like burnt popcorn? Did you burn it again?"

Jennie propped herself up against the counter with one hand and held her stomach with the other. Nausea at the memory, as fresh as if it happened the day before, flooded her. "Enough questions, *Dochder*."

"But Nathan—"

"I sent him off. It's late and *Onkel* Darren came by. He wants Matthew and Micah to work for him tomorrow. Nathan didn't want to keep us up too late."

Cynthia shook her head. "Without popcorn? He never leaves before the popcorn."

"Tonight he did. Anyway, I burned it." Jennie held out the pitcher. "Take some water to your bruders and schweschders. I'll make some more popcorn, and we'll finish the game before we go to bed. I'll take his place."

"He plays better than you do."

"I'm sure he does."

She made the popcorn and carried the bowl into the front room. A stack of books on the table caught her gaze. She set the bowl down next to Mark, who was too busy arguing with Elizabeth over whether she had moved her pawn three spaces or four to notice.

The books were a series of historicals for children set in pioneer America. Smooth-covered hardbacks. Expensive books. He'd scrawled a note. "An early Christmas present. One for each. Nathan."

Seven books. She touched the covers, one by one. One for each child even though Matthew would sooner eat cockroaches than read a book now that he was done with school. Celia and Cynthia would love them. Elizabeth would grow into them. Francis would sit still a few minutes at a time for a story. Even Mark liked a good story if someone read it to him. It was too much. Nathan shouldn't have done it.

She picked up the last book. Underneath it lay another one. With another sticky note. *For you, Jennie. To give you comfort in the dark hours before dawn. Your friend, Nathan.*

As if he saw through her to the place where everything hurt. The sleeplessness that came in the middle of the night when her mind wouldn't stop going around and around, remembering, worrying, thinking, trying to pray, straining into the silence to hear God's answer. That smothering feeling of being deaf and mute, unable to have the most important conversation imaginable with a God who seemed to have disappeared into the darkness.

The book was a devotional Bible study on the topic of grief and loss. A popular one she'd seen in the bookstores in town. She ducked her head and sighed. Nathan might somehow have an inkling of her inner turmoil, but he still, after all this time, didn't understand her people's faith. They didn't do Bible studies. They believed God's

Word was God's Word, not open to a gaggle of interpretations by well-meaning laypeople. They didn't try to interpret the meaning by picking out individual threads from a beautifully, wonderfully woven blanket of God-breathed Scripture.

She hugged it to her chest for a brief second, then laid it on the table out of reach. No book was worth censure. To her surprise, she believed what her faith taught her. God's Word needed no interpretation. It simply was.

Her gaze dropped to the book. Still, she wandered in the wilderness a good part of the time. *Nee. Don't go there. Return the book. Explain. He'll understand.*

He'd left his book bag on the chair.

She could send the boys into town to return it and the Bible study.

Or he would come for it when he realized what he'd done.

Which would be better?

She picked up a book, held it close, and breathed its scent of paper and ink. The scent of a traveling book salesman.

Better for whom?

THIRTEEN

LEO DUMPED HIS SADDLEBAGS FULL OF SMALL PIECES of wood and tools on a workbench outside the stall in Aidan's barn. He'd used the drive in his English friend's pickup to his cousin's farm to work on his carved animals. No time to waste these days. Finishing a dresser in the week since his visit to the store had kept him occupied. With a desk also half done, he needed to start thinking about how he would move them to the store.

He cleared his throat. Aidan looked up and grinned from ear to ear as if he were the new father of a dozen or so pinkish-white piglets that squealed, wiggled, and tumbled over each other trying to feed. He squatted in the straw and muck of the afterbirth, muttering in soothing tones to the enormous white sow as if she understood every word.

The humidity-laden mid-May breeze that wafted lackadaisically through the open barn doors held the stench of hay and manure, a curiously homey odor. Sweat drenched Aidan's shirt from front to back. It trickled down Leo's temples and tickled his cheeks. The sporadic rain that fell on the drive had done nothing to cool the air. A good, hard rain would be a relief.

So would asking the favor and getting it over with. He needed to borrow a horse. If he intended to work at the store, he needed transportation. He settled his straw hat more firmly on his head. "Does she ever answer you?"

That wasn't the question.

Chuckling, Aidan smoothed the sparse white hair between momma pig's erect ears. "Sure she does."

He grunted and hauled himself to his feet. He was a tall man with sandy-brown hair peeking from under his straw hat and gray eyes that never missed a thing. He might be a lot younger than Leo, but he had a wisdom that came from hard knocks much like the ones Leo had experienced. "But I reckon you didn't come here to talk bacon and pork chops. What's up, Cousin?"

"I like bacon." Leo took a long breath. Even if Aidan, Timothy, and the other Graber men were like brothers, he hated asking favors. Aidan would give Leo the shirt off his back if he thought it would help. The thought settled Leo's ornery stomach. "I need a favor."

"Anything. You know that. I heard about your horse. A bad piece of news, for sure." Aidan stalked across the stall, the soles of his dirty boots making a sucking sound in the sow's mess. "How's he doing? Can you salvage him?"

"It's laminitis."

Aidan gave him a look of sympathy. "You're welcome to Star. I've got the Percherons."

Leo nodded in thanks. "It may be a while before I get him back to you."

"Take all the time you need." Aidan slipped through the stall door and shut it behind him. He looked tired but in good spirits. His hog operation was doing as well as the chicken-raising operation that had been in peril from bird flu not so long ago. "Gut thing Jennie came along when she did after the picnic. That's a long walk home."

Nothing remained a secret in this Gmay.

"Could have done without the Mennischt." The words sounded surlier than Leo intended. Nathan stopped to help. Because of Jennie, but still. He wrestled with his tone. "Nathan almost ran us down."

"Nathan has gut intentions."

Why would Aidan defend the man? Leo studied his hands. He had dirt under his nails from weeding his small plot of vegetables in the cool of dawn. A scar along his thumb and another across his index finger reflected the early days of learning his trade. He had no reason to dislike Nathan. He was not the source of Leo's problems. If Jennie had an interest in him, that was something for Freeman to manage. Leo had lost any claim on Jennie the day he'd decided not to ask her to ride home with him again.

Water long gone under a distant bridge.

"What are you looking so glum about?" Aidan strode to a huge bucket where he thrust his hands and arms into the water and then lifted handfuls that streamed over his face and neck. "Seems like this is about more than needing a horse."

Aidan saw too much. He always had. They'd grown up hunting, fishing, and farming together. When Leo's father passed, his uncle Dale took over the role. When Uncle Dale passed, they knit themselves together in a tight gang that made their grief more bearable for all of them. Now, with his sisters married and moved to Wyoming with husbands in search of cheaper land and more wide-open spaces, Leo counted the Graber brothers as the only family he had in Jamesport. "How did you do it?"

"Do what?" Aidan dried his face with his sleeve. He sniffed and sneezed, a sound so loud his German shepherd, Ram, looked up and woofed. "No worries, *hund.* Just a little water in the nose."

"Move on. You keep moving on."

"You make it sound like it was easy for me. It wasn't. It isn't." He jerked his head toward the door. "Glass of tea? Bess gave me some cinnamon rolls to bring home last night."

"Jah."

Leo slung his saddlebags over his shoulder, and they fell in step easily as they always did, traipsing several dozen yards through newly cut grass to Aidan's two-story white frame house with its crisp, fresh coat of paint and long wraparound porch. Someone—surely not Aidan—had planted sunflowers along the banister. They angled toward the sky as if seeking their namesake. Aidan dodged a streaking tabby kitten chased by a gray one. The breeze died. The heavy air weighed on Leo's shoulders. "Ugly weather."

"The weather is the weather." Aidan refused to be diverted from his train of thought. "Sooner or later, you have to make peace. Gott knows what He's doing."

"Will Gott strike me dead if I say I'm not so sure?"

"Nee, but Freeman might take issue with it."

"I want to believe." He should've borrowed the horse and kept his mouth shut. Fat drops of rain smacked his hat and shoulders. He lifted his face to them, hoping for coolness. None came. "It's not like a man can turn it on and off like a spigot."

"It takes work." Aidan eased onto the porch step and tugged off his dirty boots. "Sometimes I just said the words even if my heart wasn't in it. I kept saying them until I started to believe them. Your daed, my daed, they lived gut lives. They were gut men. I believe Gott saw that. They rest in peace. We're still alive. Gott has plans for us."

Leo let his gaze wander over the buildings where Aidan raised chickens. Bird flu had decimated his cousin's flock the previous year. He'd been forced to start over from scratch. Yet he managed to cling to his faith and have the guts to court a woman who'd been married to his best friend. His strength and faith served as an example that Leo couldn't ignore.

"Do you think that plan includes a fraa?" The moment he asked the question, Leo wanted to snatch it back. He tromped up the steps and tugged open the door, glad Aidan couldn't see his face.

"Nothing to be ashamed of, wanting a fraa." Aidan's voice followed him in. "I'm working on it myself."

Leo escaped through a sparsely furnished front room to the kitchen where he helped himself to two clean glasses in the midst of Aidan's leftovers from breakfast. A dirty coffee cup, a plate sticky with egg yolks and bacon grease, and a half-eaten, burnt piece of toast littered the counter. A salt shaker lay on its side on the pine table. Two chairs set askew. The man might be a good farmer, but he wasn't much of a housekeeper. "Like that's a big secret."

Aidan snorted and grabbed a pitcher of tea from his propane-driven refrigerator. He proceeded to fill their glasses, slopping some over the edge of the second glass in his haste. "Nothing's a secret around here. You should ask Jennie to take a ride with you."

"Is that you talking or Bess?"

"Bess thinks it's a good idea."

Bess wanted her widow friends to be happy. That was understandable, but what made her think he would make Jennie happy? Something twisted in his midsection. A woman like Jennie, who'd suffered the loss of a husband already, should get a second chance at happiness.

Not that God promised happiness in this life. That was apparent.

"You've never shown an interest in any other girl in your whole life. When Jennie married Atlee, you hunkered down and stopped trying. There's a reason for that. She must be the one. Just like Bess is the one for me. I tried to make it work with someone else, but I couldn't. You haven't. Jennie is the only one for you."

"But not for her. She chose Atlee."

"I reckon he didn't take no for an answer. I didn't know him all that well, but that's my impression."

"The girls liked him." Leo drew a square in the condensation on his glass. Then turned it into a circle. "I never could figure out why. But he asked Jennie and she said jah."

"He's been gone a long time. She's been alone a long time. Besides, it's a buggy ride. That's all." Aidan flopped into a chair and gulped his tea. He set the glass on the table and wiped his mouth with his sleeve. "You're worrying about what's ahead instead of living today. We have no promise of tomorrow. No need of tomorrow. Gott gives us today. That's it. If I've learned anything, it's that. Trust and obey."

Trust and obey. How could he trust? The image of his father's face flitted across his mind.

"You're thinking about your daed." Aidan leaned forward, his face animated. "It wasn't your fault."

"What?"

"You think it was your fault. It's written across your face every time someone mentions him." Aidan pressed his hands together in front of him in a gesture that was almost prayer-like. "I'm not old enough to remember much about him. But I know how Henry and Timothy liked him. I've heard so many stories about him. Everyone says you're just like him. Henry says he liked the same things you did. Hunting, tromping around in the snow, with his kinner. I reckon he died doing something he loved with someone he loved."

Breathless, Aidan stopped so abruptly he appeared to have run out of words or spoken his limit for the day. His face had turned red under his tan. He didn't like talking about this stuff either, but he cared enough to do it.

Leo could accept that, even if he didn't like it himself. The most unmanly of sobs burbled deep inside him. For that reason, he chose to let the memories and the pain lie buried below a ton of rock and the debris of his life. He shook his head, unable to speak, fearful of opening his mouth.

"Let him go. Let him rest in peace." Aidan threw his hands up as if despairing of making his point. "Trust Gott. Don't waste another moment."

The fervor in his voice enveloped Leo. He swallowed against the boulder in his throat. It didn't help. He sucked down half a glass of tea. At twenty-three, Aidan had watched his best friend, Caleb, die in his arms after a truck hit his buggy the previous year. He truly understood Leo's reluctance, his dilemma, like few could.

He inhaled once, twice, wrangling the emotion into the corral. "For a whippersnapper, you're a wise old man."

"I don't know about that, but I do know I'm no coward."

"Are you saying I am?" The words stung like a whip. The warm, brotherly feelings fizzled. "With everything I've endured?"

"You've endured? Life is rough for many. It's no excuse."

He might as well have said, "Get over it."

"She's taken with Nathan."

"She's not a fool."

"He's taken with her."

"That's a bird of a different color. He's a nice man, but Freeman will take care of him. Stop making excuses."

Leo used to like Aidan's penchant for being plain spoken. Not today. "It's not an excuse, it's—"

"Fear."

Back to calling him a coward. "I'm not afraid." He stood. "I'll saddle Star."

"*Bawk, bawk, bawk.*"

"You're a chicken farmer. You know they sound nothing like that."

Still, the *bawk, bawk, bawk* followed him through the house and out the front door.

Gott, I am afraid. Of hurting her. And me. Help me.

He stopped in the middle of the dirt road that led to the barn. A prayer. The first he'd offered on his own in a long time. Eons, it seemed. Would God still hear him? He'd lived his life a walking shell of a Plain man. Never feeling his faith. Going through the motions. Attending services. Kneeling in prayer. Singing the long, slow songs. His mouth moving, his brain disengaged.

Gott, please.

The wind picked up, hurling dust into his face. What kind of answer was that? The tree branches whipped. An empty milk can flew over and rolled. Leo picked up his pace. He'd be riding home in the rain, but he didn't really mind. A summer rain felt good. It washed away old dirt and sin.

He reintroduced himself to Star, who had a pretty face and a docile personality to go with it. She whinnied and tossed her long neck. "I know. I know. It's not your favorite thing, hauling folks around in the rain, but I've got work to do at home."

He saddled Star with practiced hands that moved quicker and

quicker as he thought about what Aidan had said. Time was a gift from God that should never be wasted.

If he intended to court Jennie, he needed to get busy and earn a keep—enough for her and seven kinner.

Instead of getting heavier, the load on his shoulder eased until it dissipated as if melted away by the rain that pelted his back as he guided Star toward the road and home.

FOURTEEN

THE INSTRUCTIONS HAD BEEN CLEAR. HITCH THE horses to the mower. Nathan glared at the massive, butterscotch-colored Belgians. Neither looked perturbed by his hesitance. In fact, they looked bored. How hard could it be? Flies buzzed. The horses stamped and took turns shaking their heads. Nathan shook his head too. He'd received his wish to spend the day working with Darren and the boys on Jennie's farm. She'd been digging potatoes when he rode up on the horse loaned to him by her brother-in-law. He wasn't offended by the look of surprise on her face. Two weeks had passed since he started his new job. He'd had two long sessions with Freeman. Having a working knowledge of the articles of faith gave him a head start. He knew all about obedience and humbleness and faithfulness. It was finding his way off the electrical grid that Freeman seemed to have concerns about.

Nathan would get there. Sooner rather than later.

Today, he would eat lunch with Jennie at her table in her house. All he had to do was survive until then. And not muck it up by not doing his fair share from simple ignorance.

"Start with the collar," Matthew whispered as he walked past. "Make sure the padding is on their shoulders."

Surprise blew through Nathan at Matthew's willingness to help. Jennie's oldest was a silent, morose teenager. Not one for talking.

The collar didn't want to fit over the horse's head.

"Put on the wide part over his head first." Matthew walked by again, some unidentifiable piece of equipment gripped in his arms. "Then turn it around. They have fat heads. Then the bridle. Then the harness."

"Thank you."

"The sooner you finish, the sooner we eat." The boy shifted his burden. He had broad shoulders and thick muscles for a kid. "We'll take the hitch cart and the tedder to the other side and fluff the hay that's already been cut so it'll dry faster. We should be able to bale it tomorrow."

Eating meant seeing Jennie. Sitting across the table from her. Maybe Nathan would have the opportunity to find out why she'd sent the boys to return the books he left for her and the kids. Why return a gift given with no strings attached?

Nathan attacked the job with more enthusiasm. Trial and error did the trick. Finally, the horses were hitched to the mower. The wheels turned the blades, moving back and forth. If he kept the team in a straight line and stayed awake, they might actually get the milo cut. It was a long, hot, tedious job shared with mosquitoes and flies. Would tedding be easier? So far, nothing had been easy. Not the first time he saddled the horse and it refused to move. Or the time he smacked himself in the face with pliers mending a fence. Or slipped and fell face-first in the manure pile. At least that got a laugh from Darren. A big belly laugh with no meanness in it.

The sun continued its trajectory across the sky. Birds chattered. He breathed hot, moist air. *This is good, God. It's good.*

Too bad Jennie couldn't walk by and see him working.

Now that was a stupid thought.

He smacked a mosquito on his neck, then brushed away a horse-fly the size of his thumb. His eyelids felt heavier with each passing hour. What would happen if he fell asleep at the wheel, so to speak? The horses probably knew how to do this job in their sleep.

His throat ached. His dry lower lip split. His stomach rumbled.

"Time to eat." Matthew's shout startled him from his revelry. "Come and get it before it's all gone."

Nathan didn't need to be told twice. He double-timed it to the house, careful to let the others go in first.

The heavenly scents of fried ham and homemade bread floated through the house. Matthew, Micah, and Mark jostled for position in front of Nathan, washing their hands and splashing each other with water. He was content to wait and watch—surreptitiously, of course—as Jennie bustled back and forth to the table in the front room. Ham, boiled potatoes soaked in butter, rolls, pickled beets, and green beans. Her cheeks were pink. Her apron was spotless, the dirt from a morning in the garden picking broccoli, cucumbers, radishes, and summer squash gone. The woman put on a spread and looked good doing it. She made three passes back and forth to the table, chattering with her daughters who helped and never looking at him, not once.

Maybe now he could ask her about the books. He cleared his throat.

His hat in one hand, Darren stomped through the back door and halted behind Nathan.

Maybe not the best time to compliment her looks. "Good day's work."

Darren's nose wrinkled as he wiped at his forehead with a semi-clean sleeve. "Barely a half day. We're just getting started."

"I just mean—"

"I know what you mean. How's the backside? Are you still walking funny?"

"Fine, fine." Heat billowed over Nathan. He'd never said a word about the aches and pains caused by the unfamiliar form of transportation known as horseback riding. "I'm getting accustomed to the changes."

"Sitting on a hot water bottle might help."

The boys hooted and hollered.

"You all hush now." Jennie shook her finger at her sons. "Move along, let Nathan get washed up. Sit down before the food gets cold."

"Ain't going to get cold in this weather." Darren sniffed in distain. "More like it'll boil."

"Where are your boys?" Jennie's tone was polite, but her expression seemed anxious. "You're not getting behind at your place, are you?"

"Nee, my boys cut our hay yesterday. They're bailing today." Darren splashed water on his face and began to lather his hands with soap. "Nothing for you to worry about."

Unspoken words hung in the air, something between Jennie and her brother-in-law that Nathan couldn't fathom. "Food smells great."

"Get washed up and have a seat then."

No smile accompanied her words.

He cleaned up and grabbed the seat between Francis and Mark, who immediately threw Elizabeth a triumphant grin. "I get to sit by Nathan."

"Quiet." Darren plopped into a chair at the other end of the long table.

Heads bowed. A few seconds later Darren said "amen" and the bowls began to pass. The platter of ham felt light in Nathan's hand. He studied the slices. Enough for one each, if he counted right. He let the plate pass.

"Don't you like ham?" Jennie's anxious tone had returned.

"Boiled potatoes are my favorite." He heaped several on his plate and ladled a few for Francis. "Green beans too. Pickled beets are a treat."

"Atlee liked fresh potatoes boiled too." Darren speared two big slices of ham without looking up. "Butter, salt, and pepper. A man could make a meal of them."

Jennie ducked her head. She pushed beets around on her plate with her fork.

The silence built.

"I like pie," Elizabeth piped up. "Apple or cherry. Or pecan."

"Me too." Grateful for small children, Nathan smiled at her. "But my favorite is strawberry."

"Mudder made strawberry yesterday," Cynthia volunteered. "Two of them."

"I imagine your mudder makes good pie." Nathan forked a potato and chewed, careful to avoid Darren's gaze. "Her cooking is excellent."

"More eating and less talking will get us back in the field quicker." Darren gulped his water and set the glass down with a smack. "The hay won't cut itself."

Would that it could. Nathan sneaked a peek at Jennie. Her head came up. She smiled and gave the tiniest shrug.

He hadn't imagined it, had he? Heatstroke could do strange things to a man's mind. He smiled back. Her smile grew.

On the strength of that smile, he could work in the field all day long.

And then some.

FIFTEEN

Everyone in the world wanted to go to the annual Purple Martin Open House at James and Olive Troyer's House the last week in May. Everyone except Jennie. She tucked unruly strands of hair under her kapp and stared at the road ahead. If she could slow the buggy down somehow, she would, but Bess seemed intent on getting to the Troyer house as quickly as possible. No doubt because Aidan, an avid birder, would be there. Their marriage still had not been announced, but Jennie knew in her bones it would be any day. They would burst from their happiness if they couldn't share it soon.

The *clip-clop* of the horse's hooves on the sun-hardened earth, the squeak of the buggy wheels, and the chatter of the children in the back filled the air. It should be a lovely ride. It was a lovely ride.

"Okay, tell me what's bothering you." Bess glanced back at a squeal from her son Joshua. Someone was tickling the toddler. "You've been a gloomy Gus ever since I picked you up. Spill the beans."

"A gloomy Gus? Have you been talking to Mary Kay?"

"Don't avoid the subject. Tell *Aenti* Bess all about it. You're not happy to be here. Why? It's fun. The kinner love it. They learn something about nature. People visit. What's not to like?"

"I just have so much to do at home. I need to make jam from the strawberries we didn't sell at the produce auction yesterday. I've got peas, spinach, and brussels sprouts to pick. I still haven't planted my flower beds. If I'm going to work at the store, I need to get my ducks in a row at home—"

"All that will still be there this afternoon. Tell me what's really bothering you."

"I don't know." The response escaped willy-nilly before Jennie could corral it. "Never mind me. I'm just out of sorts this morning. I didn't sleep well."

"It's me and Aidan, isn't it? I've found new love after only a year and you've been alone four years." Sadness laced with guilt filled Bess's sweet face. She was so young still, barely twenty-one. "I'm sorry. I know how lonely feels."

"It's not that. I'm happy for you. I'm happy for Aidan. It couldn't make me happier. I just don't understand."

"Understand what?"

"How it's possible? Aren't you terrified?"

Of course not. Bess was one of the bravest people Jennie knew. Unlike herself.

"I am." Bess shrugged. Her smile belied her words. "But if I've learned anything from what I've been through, it's that with Gott, anything is possible. Isn't it?"

"It is." Jennie forced herself to say the words with more conviction than she felt. "It's just hard to see it sometimes."

"I admit I haven't always thought that. After Caleb died, I was lost. You know that. You saw it." Bess rolled her shoulders and craned her neck from side to side. "But I'm going to marry again. Soon. We were going to wait until the fall, but now we both know we don't want to wait that long. And don't be spreading that around. It's supposed to be a secret still. A year ago I wouldn't have dreamed such a thing possible." She sighed, her expression a bittersweet mixture of the pain and happiness that was her life. "It took a lot for me to learn to trust Gott, trust His plan. I learned from Laura and Mary Kay and you."

"Me?"

"Jah, you. You trudge on, no matter how hard it is. You never give up."

"A person has no choice."

"I suppose not, but watching the three of you helped me to trust that there is a future for me in this place. In this community, I can have a family. It might look different from other families, but it will be a family."

Jennie tried to see what Bess saw in her future. It looked beautiful. And so tantalizingly close. Did Laura and Mary Katherine feel the same way? Did they see a new family in their futures? Neither of them had sallied forth with a new love, but they were older, much older than Bess. Single men their ages were not plentiful in Jamesport. They had lived and loved in long, fruitful marriages. Bess's first love had lasted only a fraction of a moment. "How were you able to risk it again?"

"I learned that the momentary troubles we have in this world are just that—momentary. Gott doesn't cause them, but He does walk us through them. I don't know how many days I have on this earth, but He does. I don't know how many Aidan has either."

The same words Laura had used. Momentary troubles. Jennie

clamped her mouth shut. Her friends were right, but it didn't make it any easier. God didn't intend for faith to be easy.

Bess pulled onto the dirt road that led to the Troyer homestead. A sea of buggies, vans, and cars lined its dirt shoulders. If past years were any indication, at least two hundred people, some from as far away as Iowa, Nebraska, and Pennsylvania, would stop by to see the purple martins that made their homes temporarily in houses built and maintained by the Troyers. Bess parked behind a battered blue pickup truck. "Whoa, whoa. We'll have to walk part of the way."

"I don't mind."

The longer it took, the better.

"Joshua needs a daed." Bess's face lit up with a smile. "Aidan will make a good daed."

He would. Jennie had no doubt of that. Bess and Aidan would have more children, God willing. Their lives would become more and more entwined. They would risk everything for each other.

Bess turned and hopped down from the buggy. "So would Leo."

How had they gone from anything's possible with God to Leo? Leo with his callused hands and his carved animals and his penchant for being at the right place at the right time. Leo who once took her on a buggy ride but never came back. She climbed down, keeping her back to her friend. "I can't imagine myself with a mann again."

"I couldn't either, a year ago, but here I am unable to wait a few more months to marry the man I *lieb.*" Bess's delight at the thought flowed through the words. "And you'll have all that time at the store to talk to Leo."

"He doesn't talk."

"Until you spend time with him. Aidan can get him to talk."

"Aidan's family."

"Aidan knows how Leo feels. He lost his daed early. Their daeds were brothers. They were close. Leo's like another older brother."

"I can understand that."

"So why don't you extend that grace to your in-laws?"

The words were uttered softly, but their points still pierced skin. "It's different."

"It's not. Olive and James are gut people. We used to get together with them on Sunday afternoons when I was little. Olive and my mudder were friends." Bess smiled at the memories. "She made gut zucchini bread. James went hunting with Daed. They lost a son. That's some hard times. You've been so wrapped up in your own misery, have you never thought of theirs?"

Her point, however delivered, stung. She couldn't tell Bess how hard it was not to blame James and Olive for Atlee's horrible behavior. "I am selfish, I know. For so long I was barely hanging on by my own fingertips. I couldn't take on someone else's feelings."

"I know how that feels." Bess did know. She'd lost her first love in a terrible accident. "There's no time limit on healing. For you or for them."

Such wisdom from such a young woman. James and Olive had tried to reach out to her a few times, but Jennie had chosen to go it on her own. They were the parents of a man who had hurt her. How could she trust them? But Bess was right. She was expected to forgive.

"You're right. It's time to get on with it." Feeling like a persnickety old woman, Jennie followed the children, who ran on ahead, Joshua on Celia's hip, Francis trotting behind, toward the backyard. A small crowd had gathered around the long pole that held one of several white bird-apartment houses spread across an open expanse of mowed grass. "I've kept them at arm's length for so long I'm not sure if I'm welcome anymore."

"You're all ready to move on—together. I can feel it in my bones." Bess picked up her pace, no doubt anxious to see Aidan. "What groossdaadi and *groossmammi* wouldn't want to spend time with their grandbabies? You're family."

"We'll see."

"We did a nest check yesterday and found we have 127 active nests with eggs or young with a total of 486 eggs laid so far, and 122 of those have hatched." James's voice was a deep bass. It carried over the excited chatter of nearly a dozen children who gathered in a tight knot around him. "That's a little better than last year's count."

That voice. Atlee's voice. Jennie shivered. Her in-laws stood side by side, smiling, happy to share their birding love with any and all who came. Olive was as short and round as James was tall and thin. His hair was black laced with silver and his eyes blue like his son's. Olive had fair skin and hair that had gone completely gray years earlier. Her eyes were a warm hazel. Nothing of Atlee in her. Nothing at all.

Bess looked back. "Are you all right? Are you coming down with something?"

"Nee." Jennie would not let the past rule her day. Atlee was gone. Her in-laws had done nothing to hurt her. "The kinner will enjoy it, as you said."

"There's Aidan. Oh, look, Timothy and Leo are with him."

Goose bumps prickled Jennie's arms. Leo bent over and picked up Timothy's youngest, Nyla. She wrapped her arms around her cousin's neck and squealed in delight over something he said.

"Leo, Leo!" Elizabeth broke away from the others and ran toward him, Francis on her heels. "How's Red?"

Leo turned. His gaze bounced from Elizabeth to beyond, seeking. For a second some emotion flitted across his face. Something like happiness. Then it was gone. Jennie couldn't be sure it had ever been there.

Bess's hand touched Jennie's sleeve. "He's looking for you," she whispered, her tone delighted. "Go say hello."

"Nee." She wasn't a teenage girl on her rumspringa. "Don't be silly."

"Don't be an old lady."

Leo patted first Elizabeth's head and then Francis's, but his diffident smile reached out to Jennie. He said nothing, as usual.

Jennie joined him in the dearth of conversation and tried to concentrate on the subject at hand. Bess slipped closer to Aidan. The kinner crowded around James. The sun heated Jennie's cheeks. Or was it the way Leo's gaze kept slipping sideways toward her and then back at James? Each time colliding with hers. *Stop it.*

"Hot day."

Was he talking to her? "Jah."

"Good day for this, though."

"It is." This was more painful than childbirth. "How is the horse?"

"Gut. Better."

"Gut."

Conversation with Leo had never been easy, but this was enough to make a woman choose to be alone for life.

Nyla tickled Leo's cheeks. He laughed and tickled the girl back. She giggled, an infectious sound that made Jennie smile. "Knock-knock, Cousin, knock-knock."

"Who's there, Nyla, who's there?"

"Cow says."

"Cow says who."

"Nee silly, a cow says moo!"

Leo's belly laugh made her smile as much as Nyla's high-pitched trill. Elizabeth and Francis joined in. It was all the more delightful because it undoubtedly was a rare occurrence to be treasured by the people around him. He grinned at her over the girl's shoulder, his awkward stance softened for a second. He might be her age, but he didn't look it. Time had been kind to him. All muscle and brown skin and only a little gray in his dark hair. She smiled back.

The moment stretched.

He ducked his head. "Been to the store?"

"Nee. I've been sewing, though. I have lots of pieces to sell and a few to finish. Mary Kay says Lazarus hasn't been back, but Kyle, the electrician, came in. She let him look around."

"No point in antagonizing them."

"Nee."

Nyla tickled his ears. He pretended to dump her from his shoulders and she shrieked with laughter. Jennie couldn't help but laugh too.

"Let's get started." Sounding irked, James raised his voice to be heard over the ruckus. He used a winch to lower one of the birdhouses.

The collective oohs and aahs that followed said the closest spectators were seeing hatchlings. Elizabeth and Francis squeezed in front of Mark, Cynthia, and Celia, who stood beside a half-dozen English children Jennie recognized from town.

"What are their names?" Elizabeth's voice piped up over the others. "Do they have names? Can I hold one? Can I name them? I named my kitty Indigo."

It had been a struggle to convince Elizabeth to leave Indigo at home. Only the assurance that her kitten would be tempted to eat the birds convinced her.

"Nee, little one. Touching them will interfere with them growing up proper." James's bass softened. "You want them to grow up big and strong, don't you?"

"All my pets grow up big and strong—"

"Hush, 'Lizbeth. Birds aren't pets. They fly away. What do they eat?" Mark put one hand over his little sister's mouth. She squawked and he removed it but kept his other hand on her shoulder. "Can we feed them?"

"They eat insects like flies, June bugs, grasshoppers, cicadas, and bees." James pointed his huge finger at the sky. "When you see them doing that aerial dance, diving and such, that means they're hunting for food."

"How come they only live here part of the time?" His expression intent, Mark edged closer to his groossdaadi. Of the boys, he looked the most like Jennie. He had a smattering of freckles across his upturned nose and fair skin red from the sun. "Don't they like their house?"

"They like it a lot." Olive spoke up. "That's why they come back to it every year on their trip from South America. We make sure it's nice and clean, and we put some pine needles in the little rooms. See how deep they are? That's to keep the starlings and the sparrows out. We're good landlords."

Indeed, they were. The purple martins chattered from their homes placed out in the open, just the right distance from trees to give them a chance to see enemies like owls coming in to attack and steal their babies. They were beautiful birds—the male birds especially with their glossy purple-blue plumage and blackish wings and tails. The momma birds might not be as fancy, but they looked nice too.

"Why does that bird have a yellow band on its leg?" An English man, whose Nebraska Cornhuskers T-shirt identified him as a tourist, held up his hand as if in school. "It looks like he's wearing a bracelet."

The children tittered, but James shushed them. "I'm glad you asked that question." He launched into an explanation of banding, permits, colors, and numbers that had little Elizabeth frowning and nodding.

Olive trotted away from the group, headed toward the two-story white house she'd shared with her husband since before Atlee's birth. Her gaze landed on Jennie. She swerved in her direction. "You came! I'm glad you came."

"Really?" Jennie stammered. "I mean, the kinner like learning about the birds."

Bess smiled at Olive and turned toward the birdhouses. *Traitor.*

"I was about to get a glass of lemonade. All this talking has made my throat dry." Olive's hand went to the hollow of her throat, then dropped. She nodded toward the house. "Join me?"

"No need to go to any trouble." Jennie stubbed her shoe on a rock and stumbled. Heat burned her cheeks. Always a clumsy cow around Atlee's family. "I should stay with the kinner."

"They're fine." Olive's smile was tentative. It almost begged. "Their groossdaadi won't let anything happen to them."

The emphasis fell on the word on *groossdaadi.*

"I know that."

Olive held open the door. "Come inside."

Not quite a command. More of an appeal. Jennie gathered her courage around her like invisible armor and went.

They tromped into the kitchen, neat as a pin as usual where Olive poured the lemonade, and settled at the scarred pine table with their glasses. The room still held the homey scent of bacon and fried eggs. Olive took a long drink of lemonade and smacked her lips in appreciation. "You must think it's strange that James and me would be bird lovers."

"He always has been, as long as I can remember. You too."

But not Atlee. He had no interest in the purple martins. Only birds that could be hunted for supper.

"Birds are like people." Chewing on her lower lip, Olive paused.

Jennie had no idea how to respond so she waited too.

"Only a few days ago the starlings ruined the flicker nest. And the day before that a wren got into a bluebirds' nest that had four eggs and filled it up with twigs. They just barge right in. They have no sense of decency when it comes to taking what they want."

"I see." Jennie didn't really see at all.

"The wrens sing so sweetly, but they have a dark side, I reckon."

"Like people."

Olive picked up a dish towel and wiped at the table. The lines on her face made her look older than she was. "Exactly. There's bad apples in every bunch."

What exactly were they talking about? "They still take you by surprise, though."

"We miss having the kinner around." Pink rose in Olive's plump cheeks. "And you too, for sure."

"There's so much to do." That Olive and James missed their grandchildren didn't surprise Jennie. That Olive would admit to missing her did. "With the house and the fields and the garden."

"I know how that is. 'Course I always had my mann to carry his fair share of the load. He has a lot to take care of here, but the boys help out. They can help you too." Olive traced the circle left by her glass on the table. "They're not like Atlee."

Olive knew what her son was. Her shame and embarrassment mingled on her face.

"I know. At least I think I know." The question that had plagued Jennie for years spun around and around in her head. "How could he be so different? Did something happen to him?"

The back door opened. Atlee's youngest brother, Raymond, stuck his head through the doorway. "We have another load just arrived. That man from Pennsylvania is here, RV and all. The one who wrote he was coming."

"I'll be right there."

Raymond let the door slam.

"Olive, was it something I did?"

"Nothing you did." Olive stuck the glass on the counter and wiped her hands on her apron. She stared out the window over the sink, her back to Jennie. "Nothing I did."

"But you thought it was."

Just as Jennie believed she had done something. Something that made her husband angry and frustrated and contemptuous.

Olive swiveled and learned against the counter. "I'm his mudder. I raised him. Me and James. We tried to teach him the difference between right and wrong. We tried to teach him the meaning of faith and family. We showed him how to work hard."

"What happened to him?"

The lines around her mouth and eyes deepened. She shook her head. "A person shouldn't speak ill of the dead. Especially family. Especially a son."

"I need to know."

"What's past is past. Move on. But James and me, we'd like to see more of the kinner. Of you."

How could a person move on without knowing why something happened? Why a husband acted the way he did? The stern set of Olive's face said Jennie would find no answers today. "It never felt that way. When Atlee died—"

"It seemed that we didn't want you around?" She shook her head, her eyes bright with unshed tears. "Nothing could be further from the truth. It was hard for us to get over losing a suh, that's all."

"Looking at his kinner remind you of him."

"The good parts of him." Olive headed toward the back door. "Bring that tray of cookies, will you? We like to hand them out to folks."

The good parts. They knew about the bad parts. They knew what he was like. Surely they knew why. "Olive, please."

"Try to give it up to Gott." Sadness flitted across the other woman's face. "Dwelling in the past changes nothing. You need to look forward."

"How can I when the possibility is always there that I'll make another mistake?"

"That mistake gave you seven kinner." Olive held open the door again. "I reckon Gott knew what He was doing."

SIXTEEN

Wave upon wave of nausea pounded Jennie. Her stomach heaved. She leaned over the dish tub, trying to breathe through it. She had work to do. She was supposed to fill in for Annabelle at the store today, her first shift as a worker, a day when she could barely stand upright. She retched, the bitter bile of a nearly empty stomach burning her throat and tongue. She gasped and swiped at her forehead. Her skin burned. Her throat ached with every swallow.

She closed her eyes. Purple dots danced against the dark side of her eyelids. *Breathe. Breathe.* She laid her head on her arm. Just for a second. Only a second. Then she would load the buggy and go. She would tell Mary Katherine the children were sick. She couldn't stay. Her first shift, and already she was unreliable. Atlee would've said "I told you so."

Atlee would never have let her go in the first place. Her job was at home, being his wife and mother to his children.

The dank June air oppressed her. No breeze stirred the curtains. The rain that fell earlier had only served to make the humidity worse. She didn't usually mind the summer heat, but today every muscle in her body ached. Her dress weighed a thousand pounds on her back.

Celia barreled through the kitchen door. "Mudder! Mark threw up in his bed." Her kapp was askew and she reeked of vomit. "It smelled so bad, Elizabeth threw up on the floor right next to his bed."

"What was Elizabeth doing in the boys' bedroom?" Having seven children meant sickness tended to spread like poison ivy's itch. She'd been through this with every childhood disease imaginable. Colds, ear infections, flu, slapped cheek disease, impetigo, pinkeye. If it was out there, her children caught it and passed it around like a shared lollipop. "She should be in her bed."

"She wet the bed. I think she felt too sick to get up. Poor Cynthia was lying next to her at the time." Celia wavered and slapped her hand on the door handle. She looked peaked herself. She would be the last child standing. Matthew and Micah had gone to help Darren cut hay earlier in the day, but both boys had lacked their usual gusto for pancakes, eggs, and toast for breakfast, a sign they'd likely be home soon. Matthew's face had been green when he trudged from the house to hitch up the horse to the wagon. That and the threat of rain that hung in the air, titillating, promising another round any minute. What they had cut yesterday wouldn't be able to dry either. "I was changing her sheets so she went looking for a place to lie down. Poor thing is burning up."

Elizabeth hadn't wet the bed in years. Jennie grasped the edge of the counter and fought another wave of nausea. Outside the kitchen window the sky had turned an ominous green like an enormous bruise. A ragged bolt of lightning zigzagged across the expanse. Thunder complained in response. A fainthearted breeze lifted the leaves on the oak that shaded the back porch. Then died a sullen death.

The weather matched her mood. "Put some water in the tub. Stick Elizabeth in there. It will cool her off and clean her up at the same time."

"Are you all right? You look puke green."

"I'm fine." Jennie wiped at her nose and stuck the hankie in her sleeve. Her arms felt too heavy to lift, but she positioned the stockpot filled with noodles in chicken broth—the closest she could come to chicken unless she slaughtered one of the egg layers—on the propane stove and turned the knob. "I'll warm the soup. We'll see if at least one of them can keep it down. We have saltine crackers too. They might help."

"We need to start a load of sheets and towels too." Celia's voice rose, high and weak. "I'm running out of clean sheets. I still need to strip the boys' beds."

To crawl between clean sheets and lay her head on a cool pillow sounded like heaven to Jennie. "I'll get the laundry started while you take the soup up to the kinner. Just bring everything down when you can."

Celia nodded, but she swayed.

"Are you feeling poorly too? Because if you are, you need to lie down."

The girl shook her head. She put her hand to her mouth. Her other hand went to her belly. She leaned over and vomited on the kitchen floor. "I'm so sorry." She gasped, both hands on her stomach. "I just made more work for us."

"That's okay. It's not your fault." The stench made Jennie's stomach rock. She swallowed against a lump the size of a watermelon lodged in the back of her throat. The coffee she'd consumed burned a hole in her stomach. "I'll clean it up. Go on upstairs and lie down."

"There's no place to lie down. Everything is dirty." Celia grabbed the tub of dish water and eased it to the floor. Water sloshed over the sides. She tumbled onto her knees next to it. Water soaked her dress and apron. "I can clean up after myself."

"Sick girls get a pass in the cleaning department." Jennie forced a weak smile. "I'll get the mop. You go."

"Nee, you can't do this all yourself."

Celia had a stubborn streak ten miles long. Surely something she inherited from Atlee. Still, Jennie appreciated her daughter's desire to tough it out. She had backbone. Atlee's flaws had been big, but he hadn't been all bad. Jennie would never have married him otherwise. The thought brought a strange measure of relief to her. Atlee worked hard. So did his children. He provided for his family. He had a mean streak, but he also could be generous. With others. Not so much with her. She hadn't been a total fool to marry him. Anyone could've been taken in by his better qualities.

Jennie wanted to sink to the floor next to Celia and stay there until the sick feeling in her gut subsided. "I'm the mudder, you are sick. Go."

Celia ducked her head, arms around her stomach. "I don't know if I can make it up the stairs."

"Then tuck yourself on the couch and rest for a while first."

"Francis is on the couch." She shook her head. Her kapp slid farther to one side. "He's curled up with his teddy bear in his arms, sleeping. He has his thumb in his mouth."

Francis hadn't sucked his thumb or carried around his old teddy bear in months. "I'll check on him as soon as I get the soup ready."

"I'll do it. I'll scooch him over and we'll both rest. He doesn't take up much space. Don't worry about him."

The back door swung open with a bang. Jennie jumped. Celia shrieked. In marched Laura, followed by Bess. They looked like two angels of mercy—if angels wore long dresses, aprons, kapps, and carried large black umbrellas.

"What are you doing here?" Jennie fought the urge to weep. Reinforcements. "Did we have a frolic planned that I forgot about?"

"Nee. Matthew told Darren you had sickness here. Darren told his fraa who told Iris who told Bess. Who told me." Laura popped the umbrella shut and propped it against the wall next to the wood-burning stove. Her glasses were beaded with rain. "And here we are. The wind nearly blew us off the road. We parked the buggy in the barn. We couldn't leave poor Lilac out in that mess."

The Plain grapevine curled its way from one buggy to the next, one gas-powered hay bailer to the one yonder, from one caring, loving mouth to the next. It wasn't the first time her friends had come to her aid. Given the age of her children and their penchant for sharing illnesses, it likely wouldn't be the last time. "You shouldn't have come out in weather like this. What were you thinking?"

"I may be old, but I still don't melt. It's only water." Laura took Celia's arm and helped her to her feet. "Go on, little one, go lie down. You're greener than a granny apple." She turned to Jennie. "You too."

"Nee. The soup is heating. Laundry has to be done. Sheets and towels. Elizabeth wet the bed. She hasn't done that in years." Jennie drew a breath, dizzy from the effort to carry on conversation. "Mark threw up in his bed. I need to get into town to work. It's my first day."

"The weather is really bad out there. Mary Kay will close."

"And you're in no condition to go anywhere. She'll understand."

Bess stirred the soup and turned down the heat. She trotted across the kitchen and gave Jennie a quick hug. She was like that, no thought for germs or her own well-being. "I'll get the laundry ready. You just sit there and rest."

"I'm so glad you didn't bring Joshua."

"He's had his own little cold, but his reflux is much better." Bess went to the cabinet, pulled out a box of saltines, and opened it. "Hazel was happy to keep an eye on him. She says the more the merrier. Of course, she's due any day, so I hate to impose too much."

Bess's sister-in-law from her first marriage was a sweet friend who'd lost a baby not so long ago. This one would be particularly welcome.

Jennie considered laying her head on the table and closing her eyes. Bess set a bowl of steaming soup in front of her and laid a saucer filled with saltine crackers next to it. "Try to eat. The broth and saltines will settle your stomach."

Jennie doubted that, but she complied. The soup was hot and the aroma alone had medicinal value far beyond anything found in a pharmacy. "Sit and talk to me. Take my mind off my sick kinner for two minutes. How's Aidan? When will they publish your plans to wed?"

Bess leaned forward, a twinkle in her lake-in-the-spring-sun blue eyes. Her voice dropped to a whisper. "Soon, very soon."

"You keep saying that." Jennie forced a bite of cracker. It hurt to swallow. She washed it down with a spoonful of broth, hot and soothing. "How is it with you and Aidan?"

How do you manage to trust again?

"It's still wonderful. It gets better with every day." Bess patted Jennie's hand. "I heard through the grapevine that Leo has finished three pieces for the store and brought them in. He hasn't actually done a demo, but he's working on it."

"Mary Kay told me." Jennie tugged her hand away.

"He's making progress, that's what Mary Kay told me." Laura strode through the kitchen, a pile of dirty sheets and towels in her arms so tall her face couldn't be seen behind it. How she managed to navigate down the stairs and through the house was a minor miracle. "She says he asked when you were starting."

"She shouldn't be spreading gossip. I'm sure he was thinking there is no need for us to work at the same time."

Mary Katherine had a mouth the size of a serving platter. A crack of thunder shook the house. It rolled and grumbled right over them as if God had heard and scolded her for being a negative Nelly. "It's getting worse out there. Is it raining? I hope Darren had the good sense to get the boys inside."

"Darren will exercise good judgment when it comes to weather and your boys. Don't try to change the subject." Bess shook her finger at Jennie. "Aidan says Leo is finally ready to burst from his turtle shell. Because of you."

"Mary Kay saw what she wanted to see."

"There's not someone else, is there?" Laura traipsed back through the kitchen. She grabbed a cracker from the plate as she passed by. "Everyone has been fed and everyone is sleeping."

She squeezed into the chair next to Bess and turned a stern gaze on Jennie. "The grapevine is vibrating with the news that Nathan Walker was over here playing games a while back and gabbing in the kitchen, big as you please. And then he cut your hay and ate at your table."

Heat toasted her cheeks. Darren also had a large mouth. Who

had he told? His wife, Bertha. Who shared it with the other sisters-in-law. Her mother-in-law. A grapevine that would never wither and die. "He's good with the kinner. They love playing games with him. He's working for Darren now. It's not like he was working in the fields on his own." She wouldn't mention the Bible study book or the gifts he'd left for the kinner, extravagant gifts by their standards. Gifts Micah and Matthew had returned to him the next day. "He's a kind, friendly soul and a hard worker. I think he gets lonesome, that's all."

"That's the way it starts." Laura's disapproval gave weight to the words. "Be careful. A lonesome woman and a lonesome man alone with each other. One thing leads to another."

"Not for me, it doesn't." Jennie pushed the bowl away. She couldn't stand the sight of food right now. It had been nice to see Nathan enjoy the food she cooked and furthermore, say so. It wasn't necessary but still nice. "I'm not a fool. I've learned my lesson."

"You just said he's a kind, generous soul." Bess helped herself to a cracker. "He wouldn't do anything to hurt you or the kinner."

"That's the problem." Laura splayed her knotted fingers across the pine table's rough wood. "Best intentions. We know where those lead. Nathan is looking for something, seeking something that's missing in his life. He thinks he'll find it here in Jamesport. And well he might. But he won't find it here in this house."

Laura sounded certain of that fact. As well she should. Jennie didn't disagree. She simply longed for the presence of another soul in her life, someone with whom she could talk and share her day. Someone who cared not only about her, but the children too. "I'm a widow. I look like I have given birth many times. I usually have oatmeal in my hair and gravy stains on my apron. My fingernails are ragged. I smell of bleach and I'm the clumsiest woman this side of the Mississippi."

"You are not." Laura's tone grew even sterner. "We may not be ones for complimenting or even noting appearance, but I can tell you that you are pleasing to the eye and you're no clumsier than the next woman who is busy raising kinner on her own. When you say things like that, it tells me you've been listening to the devil whisper in your ear instead of Gott who brings you all blessings, who made you fearfully and wonderfully. You were made in His image. Scripture says so."

Thoroughly chastised, Jennie found no words to respond to her friend's astute observations. She couldn't tell Laura that those words were whispered in her ear—and shouted at decibels that hurt—by her dead husband.

"You're a pig."

Jennie jumped. She hadn't heard him come into the bedroom. She tightened her grip on her kapp and lifted it from her head. Her bun looked worse for wear but not deserving of such a name.

"You left the kitchen a mess."

"I swept. I mopped. I wiped the counters and put all the dishes and pots and pans away." She kept her voice low, conciliatory, as she ticked off the tasks on her fingers, all the while racking her brain to think of what she might have forgotten that would displease him. "I got everything ready for tomorrow so I can get your breakfast on the table quick as a wink."

He didn't like to be kept waiting when he had a full day's

work ahead of him. She could understand that. He wasn't being unreasonable. She simply had to move more quickly in the morning. And that didn't mean spilling a small pitcher of maple syrup on his pant leg the way she had this morning.

"There are cookie crumbs all over the table."

She closed her eyes. The kinner had sneaked in for a quick snack before bed, no doubt. "I'll go wipe it down."

"Nee." He grabbed her arm as she attempted to slip by him. His grip tightened like a manacle, imprisoning her. "After."

He cast a glance toward the bed they'd shared for so many years.

She sucked in a breath and switched directions, her feet smacking against the bare wood floor. It was cold. Every part of her felt cold.

"You smell like throw-up." Distaste soured his words. "Is that spit-up on your nightgown?"

"I fed Francis before I put him to bed." Her voice quivered despite her best effort to keep it level. "He had a little tummy ache. Or he ate too much."

"A pig like his mudder." Atlee's gaze ripped over her, head to toe, then back, the corners of his mouth turned down. "Take it off."

"Atlee."

"Take it off. You can get a clean one later. I don't want you in my bed smelling like a mewling bopli."

She did as she was told. Just as she always did. The way a good wife should.

"Wives, submit yourselves to your own husbands as you

do to the Lord. For the husband is the head of the wife as Christ is the head of the church, his body, of which he is the Savior. Now as the church submits to Christ, so also wives should submit to their husbands in everything."

She shivered. Atlee had whispered those words in her ear one night in the darkness of their bedroom. That he could quote Scripture didn't surprise her. He read his Bible at night by the fireplace, his face placid and peaceful in a way that lulled her. Until he closed the book and jerked his head toward the stairs.

The gentle buzz of conversation around her drew Jennie back in a warm, comforting embrace. She inhaled a quivering breath. A pig. Who would want a pig like her? She would never have to know that kind of shame and embarrassment again. Ever. No man would ever treat her in such a fashion. Better to be alone. Or as alone as a woman with seven children could be.

She had her job, a God-given job of raising them. She needed nothing more.

A sharp, urgent rap at the back door interrupted Laura in mid-sentence grilling Bess about post-wedding plans. Where would they live? Who would they visit first?

Mary Katherine tugged the door open.

Sopping wet, rain dripping from his blue KC Royals baseball cap visor, Nathan barged into the kitchen. Micah and Matthew tromped in behind him.

"What are you doing here?" Besides dripping on her pieced rug and tracking mud on her wood floor. "In this weather?"

"A half-dozen funnel clouds have been sighted in the area. One of Darren's neighbors drove over to tell us the sirens are going off in town. He said to take cover." Nathan lifted his cap and wiped rain from his eyes. "One touched down on the ground only a few miles from here."

Instead of taking cover, he'd come here with the boys. "Why didn't you all get in Darren's basement?"

"Darren told me to make sure the boys got back all right and that you all took cover."

"The boys knew the way—"

"That's what I said." His face the spitting image of Atlee's when he had no patience left, Matthew brushed past Nathan. "But we got here faster in his van."

Thunder clapped so loud the house shook. The wind howled. Something banged outside the kitchen window.

Faster was good.

SEVENTEEN

THE FLU, FUNNEL CLOUDS, AND NATHAN AT HER back door. For a single second, Jennie tried to comprehend which presented the biggest danger.

Funnel cloud.

She lurched to her feet. The kitchen faded in and out around her. She grabbed the kitchen table to keep from sinking to the floor. "The kinner."

"I need to get to Joshua." Bess rushed toward the door. "He'll be scared."

"Hazel has him." Laura stepped into her path. "There's no time to go anywhere but downstairs."

Everyone moved at once. Laura's tight grip on her arm steadied Jennie. In a blurred rush that left her reeling, they converged on the front room. Matthew and Micah grabbed kerosene lamps. Nathan hurtled up the stairs ahead of Bess. Laura scooped up Francis and shook Celia's shoulder. "Get up, sweetie, a tornado is headed this direction. Time to rest in the basement."

Celia shrugged off the woman's wrinkled hand and muttered in her sleep, "Go 'way."

"Celia, honey, you have to wake up." Jennie tugged her oldest daughter upright. Thunder boomed. Rain pelted the windows. "You can nap downstairs. You have to get up off the couch. Now."

Celia's eyes jerked open. "Tornado?" She hauled herself from the sofa, swayed, and grabbed the back of the rocking chair. "Elizabeth? Cynthia? What about the boys?"

"We have them."

Nathan raced down the stairs, Elizabeth in his arms. Bess followed hand in hand with Cynthia and Mark. Rufus trotted down behind them, two steps at a time.

"Mudder, Mudder!" Elizabeth held out one plump arm. The other one hugged Indigo to her chest. "I want my mudder."

"Your mudder doesn't feel good either so you'll have to settle for me." Laura took the handoff from Nathan. "You can sit with her in the basement."

Elizabeth didn't protest. She took Laura's hand and sighed. Indigo, on the other hand, began to yowl. "I don't like the basement. Neither does my kitty."

"Me neither." Laura petted the unhappy kitten. "But it's a good place to tell stories, and it's an excuse to take a nap in the middle of the day."

"We need blankets to make pallets for them." Jennie kept supplies in the basement for times such as this, but she'd never envisioned a need for five beds. "They should lie down."

Six. If she didn't lay her head down soon, she would fall down.

"I'm on it." Nathan volunteered. "Just tell me where—"

Rufus barked at an ear-splitting decibel. The front door burst open. Clothes soaked, Leo whipped through it, his mutt Beau behind him, and slammed the door. Rain spattered his face and leaves stuck to his wet shirt. Leather saddlebags slung over one shoulder dripped rain. His straw hat was missing, leaving a mass of tangled black curls exposed. "Tornado coming," he shouted over the dogs, who barked at each other. "Basement. Go. Go!"

No time to talk. No time to ask what Leo was doing at her house. No time for blankets. The kinner scurried to the basement. Nathan led the way down the steep wooden stairs. Leo shut the door behind them. The dogs' claws made a *squitter-squitter* sound on the wood.

Bess held up the lamp so no one stumbled in the dark. The smell of kerosene, earth, and dust filled Jennie's nostrils, reminding her of her parents' basement when she was small. They'd spent many nights in the basement. She hadn't minded with her father and mother close. Now she did. Now that she was shut below ground with two men, one a Mennonite who'd made his interest in her obvious, and the other a Plain man folks claimed had more than a passing interest in her.

Hogwash.

Her stomach clinched. She breathed. The children came first. These two couldn't be allowed to get in the way. "I stacked old rugs in the corner and a pile of lawn chairs. There should be enough rugs for the children to curl up on and chairs for the adults to sit in."

The other women arranged the rugs side by side making a large pallet, then added the chairs in a semicircle around it. The dogs circled and sniffed each other, then planted themselves side by side on the cement floor. The two lanterns cast odd, flickering shadows across the walls, illuminating an enormous spider web that wavered in a slight draft that emanated from the house's foundation.

"Take a seat. Or lie down, however you want." Jennie nodded to Celia. She knew the girl wouldn't want to lie down in front of these folks, no matter how bad she felt. Jennie felt the same way. "You can sit with Elizabeth and Francis."

"I don't want to." Elizabeth clung to Jennie's skirt. "I want you, Mudder."

"You're a big girl."

Francis's arms flailed. He twisted in Bess's arms, reaching for Jennie.

"Easy." Leo took the boy in one smooth motion. He raised his voice to be heard over the wind and chatter of nervous, excited children. "I have something to show to you."

"First we should pray." That suggestion came from Nathan, which somehow surprised Jennie. "I mean, don't you think?"

Heads bowed.

The wind shrieked through the cracks in the foundation. Rain pinged against a small, solitary window where the basement wall met the house's foundation. Thunder rumbled.

Jennie wrapped her arms around her heaving middle and tried to gather her thoughts. Her parents, her brothers, their wives, their children, they were family, but the entire Plain community was family. All of Jamesport too. Neighbors, people with whom she'd grown up.

Gott, please. Keep them safe. Mudder, Daed, bruders, all of them.

"Amen."

Leo sank into the first chair and sat Francis on his lap. He nodded toward the next chair. Jennie tottered toward it. She weaved, left, right, then managed to plop into the chair. Her legs wouldn't hold her. Her skin as white as her small apron, Elizabeth climbed into her lap.

Leo tugged the saddlebags from his shoulder and eased them to the cement floor. "I've been working on something."

"What?" Elizabeth lost some of her listlessness. "Is it a surprise?"

"I reckon it is." Leo produced a package wrapped in brown butcher paper. His arms in front of Francis who watched with an intent face, Leo unwrapped the paper. A series of small animals carved from wood appeared. A turtle. A rabbit. A cow. A sheep.

"Me?" Francis touched the turtle with pudgy fingers. "Mine?"

More words than Francis had spoken in the last week. Jennie smiled. Leo's eyebrows lifted. He tilted his head as if to ask her an unspoken question. "Jah, if it's okay with your mudder."

"It's okay."

"Did you make them?" Mark joined in the conversation from his spot curled up on the rug.

"I did." Leo tugged a two-blade folded carving knife from the bag. "This is what I use to carve with. Do you want me to carve you something?"

His gaze locked on hers. He wanted to carve something for her. The man worked with wood building furniture all day and then carved figurines in his spare time. He truly loved his work. Creating, not tearing down.

"A kitty. Carve me a kitty." Elizabeth held up Indigo. "Like mine. This is Indigo."

Indigo yawned, her thin tongue delicate and pink, her tiny incisors pointed and sharp. She had no interest in making a new acquaintance, it seemed.

"Pleased to meet you, Indigo." Leo snapped the blades open and produced a chunk of wood from the bag's seemingly bottomless pit. "A kitten it is."

Not Jennie. Elizabeth. He wanted to carve something for Elizabeth, of course.

"I brought books." Nathan pulled half a dozen storybooks from his black backpack. His face turned red. "They can read while we wait for the storm to pass."

He always had books, even now, when he no longer sold them. Books were special to him and she had rejected his gift. Shame washed over Jennie. "It was nice of you—"

"We usually tell stories," Cynthia interrupted. "Can you tell us a story?"

Nathan's forehead wrinkled. "I'm sure I can think of something."

"I'm sure you can." Jennie wanted to offer him an apology for returning his gift. "You read so much, you must be full of stories."

He ducked his head. "Let me think about it."

"What about Onkel Peter and Aenti Kate and their kinner?" Celia didn't seem interested in animals or stories, but she was older and understood what the storm could mean. "Do you think they're okay?"

"And what about Lulu and Buck and Jake and Carmel?" Elizabeth sniffed. She clutched her kitten to her chest. Indigo meowed in protest. "What about Tammy? And Abby and Bertha and—"

"Peter will take care of Katie and the kinner. The animals are smart enough to take care of themselves." Jennie hugged Elizabeth tight. "We have to trust Gott."

Guilt assailed her. She spoke the words so easily to her daughter when she herself couldn't take her own advice.

Leo frowned. "Abby and Bertha?"

"Elizabeth has given names to every animal on the farm." And some not on the farm. Birds flying by were apt to get names. "Abby and Bertha are two of our chickens. Lulu, Buck, Carmel, and Jake are the horses."

"I like your names." Leo smiled at the little girl. "My dog's name is Beau and my horse is Red. You met him."

"He's sick like me. Does he feel better?"

Leo shook his head. "Little by little, he's getting better. Doc Todd gave him medicine. Do you need medicine?"

Elizabeth's face scrunched up in disgust. "Nee, medicine is yucky."

"I agree."

"I named my van Bunny." Nathan announced. He tucked a book into his backpack. "I think I have a story I can tell. It's about a boy whose parents leave him with an uncle so they can go on an adventure. He runs away to find them because he wants an adventure too. Boy, does he get one."

"Story, story." Cynthia tucked her hands under her cheek like a pillow and stretched out on the pallet. "Everyone listen to Nathan's story."

Elizabeth slipped from Jennie's grasp and curled up next to Celia for the story. A second later, Francis followed. It had better be a good one. Her children were used to Laura's stories. The bookseller turned storyteller glanced at her as if seeking approval. She nodded. He'd risked life and limb to bring her sons home. He deserved their attention. She smiled. Nathan's face lit up in a grin.

Leo stood and paced the narrow space that ran along the shelves filled with canned goods—green beans, tomatoes, pickles, corn, plums, peaches, beets, jams, jellies, a supply that would get them through a winter even if it didn't end for years.

Jennie glanced at her kinner. Francis sprawled on the pallet, half asleep. Elizabeth burrowed on Celia's lap. Cynthia, her arms wrapped around her middle, her face still a green hue, listened to the story. Mark had both hands behind his head, using them as a pillow while

Micah sat cross-legged next to him. Matthew sat in the corner, his dirty hands over his face, likely sleeping. That left Bess and Laura whispering at the other end of the horseshoe. Laura had her arm around the other woman's shoulder likely assuring her about her little boy's safety.

Inhaling the scent of kerosene and dust, Jennie eased from her chair and slipped into Leo's path. Her breathing quickened. She feared the answer to her question, yet something pushed her to ask. She had to know. Her heart did an odd *ker-plunk*. "How did you end up at my house today?" She kept her voice down. "Of all places."

"What's he doing here?" His voice low and brusque, Leo jerked his head in Nathan's general vicinity. "I thought he quit book selling."

"He was working at Darren's. He made sure the boys got home all right." Trying to ignore another wave of nausea, Jennie rearranged the jars of tomatoes and green beans. "How did you get here?"

Leo tapped a jar of bread and butter pickles as if counting the cucumbers used to make them. "I delivered a table and chairs to Louis Whitehair." He stopped as if that explained everything.

"And then what?"

"Louis had the radio on in the kitchen. He said they were broadcasting tornado warnings."

"So you came here?"

"After Deputy Delay stopped by." A pulse worked in Leo's jaw. He cleared his throat, the effort it took for him to say the words reflected on his handsome, clean-shaven face. "He said tornadoes had been sighted in six places in the county. Sirens were going off in town."

"And Deputy Delay drove around warning folks instead of seeking shelter?"

Leo shrugged. "They see it as their job to warn as many folks as possible."

Six tornadoes. So many loved ones who might be in harm's way.

Jennie stole a glance at Bess. She sat, fingers twisted in her lap, head cocked as if listening to the storm outside and not to Laura's well-meaning chatter. Bess, too, fought to cast her cares on God. "I hope Aidan is in a safe place."

"Timothy and all the others as well. They've got the brains Gott gave them. They'll be hunkered down in the basement, same as us."

"Gott will protect them?"

A bevy of warring emotions danced across his face. "Do you believe that?"

She peeked at her companions. They seemed enthralled by Nathan's story of a little boy on a big adventure, traveling alone on a bus across the country. The sound of the wind whistling provided background music with an occasional rumble of thunder. The kerosene lanterns flickered. "It's what we're called to believe. Don't you?"

"I'm trying."

She swallowed a lump in the back of her burning throat. "Me too."

"That's all a person can do."

Was it enough?

"I had to come." Leo's gaze flicked to the basement floor and then back up at her. "I wanted to make sure you were all right. I needed to—"

"It's passed."

Jennie turned. Bess stood midway up the stairs, finger pointed at the door. With her declaration, she had stopped Leo from making his. Jennie shivered. From the fever. Not from the thought of what Leo might have said, what the future might hold if he said it.

For the best. Or was it?

"The wind stopped blowing." Her voice tight with worry, Bess edged up the stairs. "Let's head upstairs. I need to get to Joshua."

Leo brushed past Jennie. "Come on, Beau, time to go."

The dog unfurled from his spot next to Rufus, who had the audacity to whine.

Jennie squatted and patted Francis. His eyes opened. "Throat hurt."

"Mine too."

Anxiety and dread mingled with nausea in the pit of Jennie's stomach. She followed Leo up the stairs, the others straggling behind, single file. The house still stood. *Danki, Gott, danki.* Two windows in the front were shattered. The curtains dangled haphazardly from the rods. Rainwater spattered the wood floor and the rug in front of the rocking chairs. One had tipped on its side. Papers from the desk, sopping wet and wrinkled, were scattered across the room. Jennie grabbed Francis and hoisted him to her hip to keep him from walking into the glass strewn across the floor. Silently they pushed through to the front porch.

The barn hadn't fared as well. The walls still stood, but the roof had disappeared, leaving a huge gaping hole. The animals had scattered.

Jennie's stomach heaved.

"No problem." Leo tugged his hat from the brambles of wind-blown rosebushes that curled themselves around the porch banister. "Windows and roofs can be replaced. Everyone is safe."

As far as they knew. How had the other families and farms fared? Bess squeezed Jennie's shoulder. "I hope everyone is all right."

Laura slid her arms around Bess and Jennie. Her head bowed. She was praying. Jennie tried to do the same. Words wouldn't come. *Gott, Gott.* It was the best she could do.

She cast her gaze across the landscape. A wheelbarrow hanging in the oak tree. The purple martin birdhouse smashed against the porch. Their buggy upside down, wheels missing, sat in the middle of the corral. The chicken coop perched atop the shed. The hay baler twisted into a nearly unrecognizable hunk of metal and rubber. The manure spreader had suffered the same fate. The corn binder a mess. Hail had decimated the vegetable garden.

She sat down on the step with a thump.

Leo squatted next to her. "Everyone here is safe."

"They are. Thanks be to Gott. But what about the others?"

"I'll go find them. Make sure they're okay."

"I'll go." Bess edged past them. "I need to find . . . the others."

"Aidan's probably in his cellar."

"Joshua first." She wiped at her face with shaking fingers. "And then I need to make sure."

"I'll take you in the van." Nathan turned, then turned left, then right. His mouth dropped open. His hand came up, finger pointing, then dropped. "Where did it go? I parked it right there by the porch."

The van was gone.

Laura turned to Bess. "Run out by the barn and see if our buggy is still there. If one of the horses shows up, take it. Just make sure everyone is okay."

The women hugged and Bess trotted toward the barn with its forlorn walls shorn of their roof.

His face pinched with worry, Nathan leaned against the porch railing. His fingers rubbed his smooth chin. "I could always buy a buggy. And a horse. Cheaper than a car, I suppose. The buggy shop in town is advertising a special 20 percent off. I saw the sign when I drove by the other day."

It would be a good deal, but the amount—any amount—was beyond Jennie's means. "Don't you have insurance?"

He nodded. "With a big deductible. I don't know if it'll be enough to get another car, and I'm not making diddly-squat as a farmhand. That makes it hard to get a car loan."

"Or just buy the horse." Leo stepped from the porch onto the grass. His boots sank into mud, making a sucking sound. "You know how to ride one, don't you?"

A faint note of sarcasm wafted in the rain-drenched air.

"I ride them all the time now."

"Best look around first to see if you see the van." Leo didn't look impressed. "You never know. Maybe it settled down easy someplace."

"That would be a grand thing." Nathan gestured toward Jennie. "I'll look at the buggy too. If it can't be fixed, maybe you can get one made in town."

Carl Trautman handcrafted the buggies from wood. Most of the manufactured ones were made with fiberglass nowadays, and the wood was more expensive. A manufactured buggy went for at least forty-five hundred dollars or more. Jennie couldn't image how much a wooden one brought. It might as well be a million dollars. Horse-drawn farm equipment had become so scarce the men often went to sales in Indiana to pick up new pieces. A corn binder went for as much as six thousand dollars earlier in the summer. "It's a thought."

"We'll all help with the barn roof. Between the lot of us, we'll figure something out." Leo raised his face to the sky. "I better get moving. The clouds out there look like they might not be done yet."

The thought that there might be more storms coming propelled

Jennie to her feet. "Some of those slats of wood on the ground out there might work to cover the windows."

Leo held out his hand to Elizabeth and opened his fingers. A tiny kitten posed to pounce lay in the palm of his hand. She swiped it. "My kitty."

"Your kitty."

"My kitty." She leaned over and vomited on his boots.

"Ach, Elizabeth." Jennie started forward. "Let's get you inside. Leo, there is a bucket of water in the kitchen if you want to wash off the boots."

Leo didn't flinch. "No problem." He patted Elizabeth's red cheek, picked her up, and handed her to Jennie. "I'll check on the livestock. We'll be back to see what we can salvage later. We can replace the roof in a few hours' time. Stay away from the barn. The walls could collapse on you."

Jennie took the child and balanced her on one hip. Elizabeth laid her head on her shoulder. Her body was warm and her breath smelled. She gripped the kitten in her small fist. Jennie rubbed her back. "You think the horses are still there?"

"I let them go before I came in. They'll come back when they feel it's okay."

He would make sure the animals returned safely. It was his nature.

"I'll get into town soon as I can and rent a car." Nathan hadn't budged. "Remember, you have friends and if you need help—"

"The community helps its own." Laura clomped down the steps, wiping her hands on her apron. "You men go do what you need to do. I'll help Jennie get the kinner back to bed and then start cleaning up here. I reckon Darren or one of the others will be by later to help with the damage."

Jennie's legs shook with the effort to hold Elizabeth's weight and her own. "What about the *dawdy haus* and your *kinner*?"

"I'm here." Laura's tone brooked no argument. "I'll help you and then head home to see what I can do there."

When it rains it pours wasn't simply an expression.

EIGHTEEN

BUNNY WAS GONE, CAPUT, FINITO. NATHAN TURNED the key in the rental SUV's ignition and glanced in the side mirror before he pulled out from his motel parking lot headed out of town to Freeman's house. He would miss her, but a car could be replaced. Only minor injuries had been reported from the rash of tornadoes. Not a single life lost. An adjuster would have to visit Bunny at her eternal resting spot—Otto's Junkyard Paradise—before an insurance settlement would be forthcoming.

The SUV guzzled gas, but it was all they had left only two days after the tornadoes. It would get him to Darren's farm until he finished his studies with Freeman. If the bishop allowed him to join the Gmay, he would invest in a horse and buggy. That would mean renting a place to live where he could keep a horse. Not a by-the-month motel room. He would soon be an old hand at saddling horses, riding them, and hitching horses to buggies and wagons. His skin was brown and his hands were starting to callus.

Plus, he didn't walk funny anymore.

He blew out air and flipped the signal as he turned onto the road leading to Freeman's house. Each visit with Freeman was like a visit to a specialist who couldn't figure out what ailed his patient and really didn't want to see him again. The bishop's skepticism was understandable. Someone not born into the faith probably couldn't fathom the necessity to sacrifice everything that connects him to the grid. But for Nathan it would be different. Being Mennonite meant he had a better understanding of the lifestyle. He wouldn't truly see it as a sacrifice. He would see it as an opportunity. Not just because of Jennie, although he would be truthful about her place in his picture of the future. He wasn't on the run from a calling, he was searching for another way to answer it. Instead of shouting from the rooftops, he wanted a gentler, more measured approach. A watch-and-learn approach.

He had to get past Freeman to get there.

He pulled up to the house and got out of the car. Freeman stood in the doorway of the one-story, ranch-style house with brick siding, his hat pulled down over his forehead. His jowls shook in a large yawn. "Come in, come in. I thought you might not show up."

"Insurance stuff always takes forever."

"Horse and buggy might be easier right now, what with everyone who has damaged cars trying to rent something."

"I considered it, but insurance doesn't cover a horse and buggy. Besides—"

"Besides, you're still sitting on the fence when it comes to your future." Freeman settled into a rocking chair next to a huge potted asparagus fern on the porch. "Take a load off. There's more of a breeze out here. We need to be quick about it. Thanks be to Gott, no one was hurt in the storms, but there's work to be done all over the country-side. We're raising the roof on Jennie's barn this morning. It's one of those things that can't wait too long, what with livestock and all."

Helping with the roof meant a chance to see Jennie. Nathan didn't have the money to buy her another buggy, but slinging a hammer he could do. He plopped into a lawn chair that had a drop in the seat so deep he feared his behind would drag on the porch. "We could skip this for today, reschedule, get to Jennie's."

"We're not skipping anything if all you can think of is getting to Jennie's."

Smart man. Nathan let his gaze meander over Freeman's yard toward a corral with its lone mare and young foal nibbling at grass by the fence. The bishop had been blessed. A few downed limbs had been the extent of storm damage at his place. "That's not what I meant."

Freeman didn't look convinced.

"Where do you want to start?"

"Let's talk about evangelism."

Freeman's voice held no judgment, but he'd driven straight to the heart of the matter.

To the heart of Nathan's predicament. Freeman had no way of knowing that, of course. "My parents are missionaries. They spend their lives helping folks in poorer countries with their physical and spiritual needs."

"Not you."

"I'm more of a set-an-example kind of guy." God might think otherwise. A smarter man might give it up and admit an omnipotent God was never wrong. Not Nathan. *Work with me here, God. Come on, work with me.* "A point in my favor, if you ask me."

"Yet you sound bitter."

"I try not to be." He schooled his voice. To say the words aloud would sound so childish and selfish. "Faith is important. Family is important. Balancing the two is important."

"We value faith first, then family, and then community."

"If you're always traveling, it makes it difficult to make family and community priorities."

"So that's it?"

His face burned. "That's the long and short of it."

"When did you last see your family?"

"My parents have been in El Salvador for about three years or so."

"It's hard for me to believe you don't know exactly how long it's been."

A person knew how long a wound had festered. "Three years and three months, give or take a few days. But that's just this time. They started leaving me with my aunt and uncle when I was in grade school for six months or a year at a time." His room at his uncle's had been decorated with a basketball theme. The images of basketball players on posters, framed and hung on the walls, flashed in his mind's eye. "They always came back, but they missed a lot of birthdays and basketball games."

Freeman clasped his fingers over his rotund belly and let his thumbs twiddle. "They bring people to Christ, to salvation, in their way of thinking. I reckon they figure that's more important than a basketball game."

"The most important vocation people can have." He searched for words under the boulders of his own resentment. "I don't begrudge them their mission or their passion. I simply believe as a parent I would try to find a better balance. Not bring children into the world only to abandon them."

"Abandon is a strong word."

"It's a strong sentiment."

"Have you ever told them how you feel?"

"I don't want them to feel guilty. Worse, I don't want to look in to their faces and realize they don't." Nathan swallowed the hard knot in his throat. Bitterness tasted of metal. "I keep thinking I'll grow up and get over it and recognize that nothing can be more important."

"How old are you?"

"Thirty-eight."

"Never been married?"

"No."

"Never had children?"

"No."

Freeman's harrumph held unmistakable disapproval. "And you chose a job that had you traveling around the country, never staying in one place, never putting down roots."

"I don't think it was intentional." He paused and schooled his voice. "And now I'm working in one place. With Darren Troyer. Farming."

Freeman snorted. "Not all that well, from what I hear."

Nathan had lost a load of hay on a sharp corner. And he still had trouble controlling a team of horses. But he had picked up the rhythm of horseback riding. "I'm learning. Quickly too."

Freeman picked up the stack of papers from the table and thumbed through them. He stopped at a page on which boldface type jumped out at Nathan. It read *XII. Of the State of Matrimony.* He cleared his throat. "Did you read what this article says?"

"I did. I was baptized in the church. I believe in the New Testament." Nathan slapped at mosquitoes that chose that moment to dive-bomb him. The latest version of the plagues. "I can marry in the Lord."

Freeman dropped the papers on the table. "You were not baptized in this church so you cannot marry in ours."

"One thing at a time."

"You deny your desire to join our faith springs from your interest in Jennie Troyer?"

Darren had been talking about more than his farmhand's penchant for mishaps with the equipment. Nathan had nothing to hide. "It's one aspect of several. I want to belong." A mosquito bit him. He smacked it and drew blood. "I want to find a way to be closer to my God."

"You cannot do that without first resolving your problems with your family."

Freeman was wrong. Nathan could find his way without them. "They have no bearing on my feelings for God."

"You resent Him for taking them from you for His work."

"Not true." He stopped. Being combative with Freeman would not serve his purpose. Only the truth would. "I resent them for not finding a way to do both. I don't resent a perfect and holy God. He doesn't make mistakes."

Which made it hard to argue a point with Him. Which didn't keep Nathan from trying.

Freeman removed his glasses and wiped them on his faded blue cotton shirt. "Why didn't they take you with them when they first decided to go on mission trips? Kinner go."

Something else Nathan didn't want to think about, let alone share. "I was sickly."

"Lots of kinner are."

"I had leukemia. They wanted me to have the best of care." The basketballs had been cruel. His aunt and uncle didn't see that. A theme for a sport he didn't have the strength to play. "They wanted me to stay in the states because of the doctors. They didn't want me exposed to germs when I was at risk for infection. They had good reasons."

"It's hard to imagine a mother leaving a sick child."

"You don't know my mother. She loves her children, but she loves God more. She wrote letters. She came for visits, when she could. When I was in the hospital having my tonsils out, she stayed for a month. But when the call came, she went. As she should. Scripture is clear. Jesus told the disciples to leave their families behind."

"Yet you sound bitter."

"I'm an imperfect man." Who had no business telling others about faith. Surely God could see that. "I figure sooner or later I'll grow up."

"I need to get to Jennie's." Freeman plopped the glasses on his long nose, stood, and stretched. "Come back next week and be ready to talk about the Holy Supper and the washing of feet."

Feeling as if he'd passed some sort of test, Nathan stood. "I appreciate your time. Don't worry about me doing something stupid. I know my place—for now."

"Worry is a sin. I'm doing my job. I drew the lot, but I don't know any more than the next man. It's all in Gott's hands." Freeman waggled his finger at Nathan. "And don't be in a hurry to change your life. You might find yourself in these discussions. You might find out who you really are."

"I know who I am."

"We shall see."

They would indeed. Nathan slapped his hat on his head and tromped down the steps. A dusty blue van plodded toward them. "Expecting company?"

"Nee, but that doesn't mean much when you're the bishop."

The van stopped, gears grinding.

The passenger door opened. A tall, lean man with auburn hair stepped out looking eerily similar to the one Nathan saw every morning in the mirror when he shaved.

"Nate! I tracked you down. Finally."

Only family called him Nate.

His brother grinned at him. "Aren't you gonna introduce me?" His grin broadened. "Are you wearing suspenders?"

Ignoring Freeman's inquiring gaze, Nathan strode into his brother's hug. "Shut up."

NINETEEN

PUTTING A NEW ROOF ON A BARN REQUIRED MORE elbow grease than carpentry skills. Leo stretched and craned his neck from side to side, careful to balance on the beam ten feet off the ground. He surveyed the scene. Rain-cooled air was a thing of the past. Heavy clouds hung close, but the sun broke through crevices, creating a stifling humidity. At least the storms had not returned. About thirty men wearing tool belts swarmed Jennie's barn. At this rate, the new roof would be in place in a few hours.

The frame was set, planks in place, and the *pop-pop* of dozens of hammers on nails against the tin sheets sang a syncopated song. Aidan and Timothy shimmed up the ladder with more tin sheets. Below, the women appeared in a steady stream, setting up the noon meal on picnic tables brought in from other homes.

Jennie stood near the barn, away from the others, talking to her oldest, Matthew. He gestured, his mouth wide, his shoulders stiff and set with anger. She took a step back, one hand on Francis's shoulder as if holding the little boy there. Probably trying to keep him out from underfoot. Matthew, who towered over her, took a step forward, both hands in the air now.

Leo waited until his brothers passed, then scooted along the beam until he could haul himself onto the ladder and climb down. He only had to take a few steps to hear their raised voices. That meant others heard as well. The look on Freeman's face didn't bode well. Nor that of her brother-in-law Darren.

"Nothing happened." Matthew's voice held distain one didn't usually hear when a Plain boy spoke to his parent. "I don't know why you're making such a fuss about it."

"You're too young to be sneaking out at night." Jennie let go of Francis, but instead of escaping, he burrowed into her skirt. "Your rumspringa doesn't begin for another two years."

"Why are we talking about this now?" Matthew jabbed his finger toward the barn. "I should be up there working."

"Because you'll sneak away again and I won't get a chance." Her voice rose. "Where are you going so late at night? What are you doing?"

Leo edged closer. "We could use some help getting the sheets of tin onto the frame." He jerked his head toward the barn. "Younger bodies, stronger muscles."

Matthew rolled his eyes. "Can I go?"

"Now you ask?" Her forehead wrinkled. She frowned, her face red in the heat. "Make yourself useful, but this conversation is not over."

Matthew took off like a dog after a rabbit.

"Sorry." Jennie dabbed at her damp face with her apron. "I shouldn't have confronted him here for the whole world to see and hear."

"Not the whole world." He studied the spot of mustard on her dress and waited for Cyrus to trudge by with his load of tin. "He's leaving the house at night?"

"I don't sleep through the night much so I get up and wander around—check on the kinner now and again." Her face went a deeper scarlet. Her hand went to her mouth. "I mean—"

"I don't sleep much either." Leo shrugged. She need not be embarrassed on his account. She hadn't revealed something about women he didn't know. They slept too, in beds in bedrooms. "Bad dreams."

Dreams of the dead and dying.

She nodded. "I found his bed empty."

"The older kinner, the ones on their rumspringa, they go to the tavern in town to play pool and watch TV some nights." Somehow Matthew had gotten it in his head that he could start his running around early. A rare problem in these parts. "One of them probably gave him a ride."

If Leo figured out which one, he'd give him a talking to.

"I'm not ready for rumspringa yet. I thought I still had time." She smoothed Francis's curly hair and glanced around as if to see who might be watching them talk. "He's not old enough to go into a tavern."

"It's a tavern and grill." The tourists frequented it because it was one of the few places open after dark in Jamesport. They surely got a kick out of seeing the girls wearing their dresses and aprons—but no kapps—in there. He'd gone in once for a late burger and found himself embarrassed when he ran into kappless girls he'd known since they were toddlers. "If he buys a BLT, they don't care."

"Where does he get money to buy a sandwich?" She took a whack at a mosquito that buzzed away unhurt. "Why would he start doing this now? He's so restless."

Because he had no father to keep him in line and he knew it. His size kept Jennie from taking him to the woodshed. Leo had experienced the same feelings of free falling, no one to catch him. Aidan and the others in his extended family had tried. "He's spreading his wings." Leo studied the boy, now halfway up a ladder, dragging a tin sheet behind him. Barely contained anger boiled below the surface. What Matthew had to be angry about, Leo couldn't fathom. His mother was a sweet, kind, hard-working woman. "I could give him work to do and keep him busy."

"Why don't you go play with the other little ones." Jennie gave Francis a nudge. He grinned up at Leo and didn't budge. "You don't have time."

"I know what time I have." He tickled the boy's cheek. Francis giggled and hid his face. "I could use a helper, if it doesn't cause Darren or Peter a problem."

"They have their boys, plus Micah and Mark." She hesitated. "But I need him on the farm. I don't like to always ask for their help."

"He can do both." Work him hard and long. "Between the two of us, we'll wear him out."

"Gut plan." She studied the ground for a second, her fair skin turned a deeper red. "You talk to him. If he knows it was your idea, he's more likely to be accepting. He suddenly doesn't do as he's told. I've never had that problem with the others."

"Something's chewing him up inside."

"He's growing up too fast."

A bang followed by jeers and cheers made them both jump and swivel toward the barn. Someone, Isaac maybe, had dropped a sheet from atop the frame to the ground. Everyone stopped to rib him. Jennie laughed. Leo joined her. He nodded at Francis. "And this one. Is he growing up too fast too? Does he need a job?"

She smiled for the first time and shook her head. "The opposite. My bopli refuses to turn into a little boy. He won't even talk."

Aidan walked by. He grinned at Leo and winked. Leo glared at him. "A boy after my own heart."

"You don't like talking much, do you?"

He put his hand to his forehead and peered at the sky. "Doesn't accomplish much."

"It lets people know what's on your mind."

Did she want to know what was on his mind? He'd come close to saying something in the basement, during the tornado. The thought of her endangered by the storm had propelled him through wind, rain, thunder, and lightning to her house. The moment had come to say something, to declare his feelings, but the storm had ended first. And he had been relieved. To say the words aloud was to give them power to hurt. Him and her. Sharing his heart with another meant accepting life's fleeting nature.

Could he do that?

Jennie had improved with age, and she was a sweet, pretty girl in school. Getting too close to her made his hands shake and his heart do a strange two-step that made it hard to breathe. Getting closer might make it stop all together.

"I better get cracking. You'll have your new roof in a couple of hours."

"I should get back to the kitchen." She glanced at the picnic tables. "The food is ready. Wouldn't you like a sandwich?"

A sandwich would stick in this throat. He shook his head. "The others first."

"I'll save you one." She inched a step toward him. He caught her scent. She smelled like cinnamon, like cookie. Like a woman should smell. Sweet, yet spicy. "Ham or bologna?"

"Ham."

"Peanut butter or oatmeal-raisin cookies." The way she said it felt as if she were making a list she'd pore over later and memorize. He studied her face. She had a tan now. Her cheeks were red. She smiled. Everything about her said she could be trusted. "Or snickerdoodles."

He swallowed and forced a breath. "One of each?"

"You're as bad as Francis. One of each then."

Feeling warmer than the summer heat warranted, he started toward the barn.

"Doo-doo."

What? The voice was high and small, too small for Jennie. He looked back. "Did you call me doo-doo?" Francis gave him a sly grin and held out a grubby fist. He smiled at the boy. "Are you giving me something?"

Francis's head bobbed. Leo held out his hand, palm up. Francis deposited the wooden pig on it. The one Leo had carved for him. "Nee, I made that for you."

Francis shook his head.

"Your pig will miss you."

Francis giggled. "You."

The boy didn't talk much, but he made himself understood. "Okay, my turn for now."

Francis nodded. Leo smiled and turned.

"Leo, wait."

Once again, he looked back. Jennie ducked her head. "He talked to you. He never talks to anyone except his bruders and schweschders. Not even me."

Leo shrugged. "He sees someone like him, I reckon."

"Someone he can trust."

"I reckon."

"Do you remember that buggy ride, the only one you and I ever took?"

It had been quiet and awkward. The silence dragged on and on. He searched his mind from one corner to the other and couldn't come up with a single topic of conversation. She looked so pained. Like she had a toothache. "I do."

"Why didn't we take another ride?"

At first, he hadn't asked again because he'd been afraid she would turn him down. The first ride had seemed so short and miserable. Then his life turned into a dark void. The light went out. Voices ceased to speak. Nothing seemed to matter much. "Daed died."

"I was so sorry. I wanted to tell you that, but I never had the chance." She eased closer. Her hand came up, then dropped to her side. "I always thought eventually you would come back, but you didn't."

"I'm sorry."

"Me too."

He couldn't break away from her gaze. Her eyes were dark with emotions he recognized. Loneliness. Sadness. Longing. Did she think he could assuage her feelings? He couldn't even find his way through the morass of his own feelings. Her arms tightened around Francis. He thought she would say more, but she didn't.

He opened his mouth to speak, then closed it. Her middle brothers, Silas and Luke, trudged by, their looks curious. All her brothers were spitting images of her dad. Blond hair, blue eyes, thick through the chest. Jennie looked like her mother. This wasn't the place. Jennie ducked her head. Her cheeks turned scarlet.

"I have to get back to work."

"Me too." She turned to the closest picnic table. Francis took off at a run and threw himself at Leo's legs.

He nearly tumbled back but caught himself in time. "You are a stinker." He grabbed the boy up in his arms and whirled him around in a circle, his little body flying, two times, then set him back on the ground, careful to make sure his feet connected with earth. "See how you walk now."

Francis chortled, took two wavering steps, and plopped down on his behind, crowing with laughter. "Again."

The boy could talk if he chose to do so. "Later."

"Later."

Leo had found a kindred spirit and he was four years old.

What did that say about Leo?

TWENTY

NATHAN GRITTED HIS TEETH, LEANED BACK IN his chair, and waited while the waitress in her pink flowered dress set two tall plastic glasses of iced tea on the Formica-topped table. Here he sat with Blake at the Kramer Family Restaurant, instead of putting a roof on Jennie's barn. He wanted to show that he cared and wanted to help. Leo was probably there right now taking care of business. Showing off his big biceps while he single-handedly replaced her roof.

The aroma of chicken frying and brownies baking mingled in the warm air, making his mouth water despite his desire to be somewhere else. A desire to not be sitting across from a brother he hadn't seen in three years, who'd shown up without warning and who had made small talk on the ride over instead of answering questions about what he was doing in Jamesport.

"Are you going to look at the menu or what?"

Startled from his peevish reverie, Nathan glared at Blake and took the menu from the waitress. "Give us a minute, would you, please?"

She smiled and backed away. Avoiding his brother's gaze, he sipped his tea. It was fresh brewed and tangy from a juicy slice of lemon. Still, it did little to quench his dry throat. His brother looked so at ease, so happy to see him, so oblivious to the emotions that his sudden appearance evoked.

Not even Blake, with all his happy-go-lucky nonchalance, could be that dense. Nathan dove in. "What are you doing here?"

"The waitress is cute as all get-out."

"She's not Mennonite." The simple truth was that they made more in tips from tourists if they dressed the part. "She goes to the Methodist church down the road."

Disappointment suffused Blake's face. Except for a few sun lines around his eyes and the sprinkle of silver in his auburn hair, he hadn't aged much. He was a year older than Nathan, but looked younger. He had Nathan's wide smile, blue eyes, and perfectly aligned nose. As kids they'd been mistaken for twins. "She's not the only one who isn't what he appears to be."

"What is that supposed to mean?"

"You haven't tried to be a part of our family in a long time."

"That's difficult to do when you're halfway across the country." He softened his tone. He had no desire to argue with a brother he hardly knew. Blake had gone with his parents on the mission trips because he had a knack with people. He had a photographic memory and could spout Scripture, book and verse, at the drop of a hat. People loved that in a young, barefoot boy with a gap-toothed grin and freckles. "Or halfway across the world as the case may be."

"That chip on your shoulder must get mighty heavy." His nose wrinkled, Blake perused the plastic-covered menu. He tapped the page. "Fried chicken, mashed potatoes, gravy, and corn. Comfort food."

"There's no chip."

"Seriously?"

"Why are you here?"

The waitress reappeared. Blake gave his order and looked at Nathan, eyebrows raised. "It's on me."

"I can pay my own way."

"Seriously, get over yourself and order already."

"I'll have the wiener schnitzel."

"Save room for the walnut brownies." Blake smacked his lips like a small boy. "Or would you rather have cherry pie? With soft-serve vanilla ice cream."

"We'll see."

The waitress scribbled on her little pad, took the menus, and returned Blake's smile. His widened. "What time do you get off?"

"Not for a long time." A furious blush scurried across her round cheeks and hid in the blonde hair not covered by her kapp. "My boyfriend is picking me up."

"Figures." Blake watched her walk away, her long skirt rustling. "I strike out again."

That his brother had never married—just like Nathan—had to mean something. Their brother Aaron married someone he met on a mission trip in Africa. Lottie and Maura married brethren who worked in the same home for the elderly in Pennsylvania. Keeping it all in the family. Only Nathan and Blake remained single with the forties approaching like a train car careening off the rails.

"You were going to tell me why you're here."

Blake lined up the metal paper napkin dispenser, sugar, catsup, mustard, and salt and pepper shakers in two neat rows of three. "I came to fetch you."

"Fetch me?"

"Mom and Dad are coming home. To Pennsylvania."

"That's not home."

"Home to me and Aaron and Lottie and Maura. You're the only renegade."

The only one who refused to fall in line with the family business of saving souls. "I have a life here."

"Book salesman." His tone held no censure. Blake—all his brothers and sisters—had been brought up to revere books. "You can likely do that anywhere."

"I quit. I'm working as a farmhand."

"That's what the suspenders are all about?" Blake's eyebrows rose and fell. Disbelief crept into his voice. "Looking the part?"

"No."

"What do you know about farming?"

"I'm learning."

Blake leaned forward and propped his elbows on the table, his gaze bordering on urgent. "Mom and Dad aren't getting any younger."

Life was like that. If a person was blessed, fifties led to sixties and so on. "Neither am I. I've decided to settle down. Here."

"Come home and see them." Blake's voice took on a pleading tone that surprised Nathan. Since when did his brother care that much? "At the very least."

"They never came to see me."

Blake slapped his napkin on the table. "You're still carrying around that grievance like a monkey on your back?"

"It's not a grievance. It's a fact."

"Dad has pancreatic cancer."

The world slowed. A bottomless, black void opened in front of

Nathan and engulfed the room. The aroma of brownies disappeared, replaced with the smell of dirt shoveled in the rain. Unexpected tears forced him to swallow and swipe at his face with a napkin. He wanted the menu back so he could hide behind it. He cleared his throat. "He's coming back for treatment?"

"Yep. They have to do a laparotomy—exploratory surgery—first to figure out how bad it is. Then they'll decide on a course of treatment. You know Dad. All sunshine and lollipops. God's will be done."

"You don't believe that?"

Blake switched the catsup and mustard to new spots. He stacked the pepper on top of the napkin dispenser. Nathan reached over and stilled his brother's hand. "Don't you believe that?"

Blake grabbed Nathan's hand and held on to for a second, then let go. His Adam's apple bobbed. "I think he's seventy years old. I think he's lived a good life. I think I'm more afraid than he is. I can't imagine this world without him in it."

"Seventy is the new sixty."

"Pancreatic cancer is usually advanced by the time it's diagnosed. The stats are ugly." Blake raked his hand through his hair, making it stand on end. "And you know Dad. He never bothers to go to the doctor until he absolutely has to do it."

Nathan didn't really know his dad. "Don't borrow trouble before it gets here."

"Will you come home—to Pennsylvania?"

"Has he asked for me?"

"He won't and you know it."

"What about Mom?"

The waitress settled his plate in front of him. The schnitzel—breaded veal cutlet deep fried in butter—came with mashed potatoes, corn, and a roll. He swallowed against sudden bile in the back of his throat. His stomach roiled. "Thank you."

She nodded and slid Blake's plate onto the table. "Anything else I can get you?"

A new pancreas for his dad. A cure for cancer. A miracle. "No thanks."

She trotted to the next table and smiled at an elderly couple intent on arguing the merits of the buffet versus ordering off the menu.

"Did Mom ask for me?"

Blake picked at the mashed potatoes and gravy. "I haven't actually talked to either one of them. Mom called Aaron."

She would. Aaron was the oldest brother. The one on whom she depended. Who had traveled the world with her. "When do they arrive?"

"Middle of July."

"They're waiting a month and a half to start treatment?"

"You know Dad. He's a stubborn old coot." Blake's voice broke. He gulped tea and set the glass down so hard liquid splashed over the side and ran down his hand. He dabbed at it with his napkin. His eyes reddened. "He says he has to stay for the revivals they have scheduled, finish a Bible study. Finish his work."

"It's a sign of overwhelming pride when a man thinks he's the only one who can do God's work."

"It's a sign of his commitment to God's work."

Their father had answered God's call at a later age than most. He'd uprooted his family and gone where he was needed. Nathan had no wife and children. Yet he found himself too selfish to follow his own father's example. "He always put that work ahead of everything— family, country, now his health."

"Jesus said, 'If anyone comes to me and does not hate father and mother, wife and children, brothers and sisters—yes, even their own life—such a person cannot be my disciple,' Luke 14:26." Blake picked up the chicken leg, then laid it back on his plate. "'Anyone who loves their father or mother more than me is not worthy of me; anyone who loves their son or daughter more than me is not worthy of me,' Matthew 10:37."

The exact Scripture Nathan had referenced with Freeman earlier. Great minds think alike? Only Nathan never had the verses when he needed them. "He's done his part."

"He won't rest as long as there is one more soul to save."

A worthy mission, but one that would never be finished. "I imagine him standing before the Lord and hearing, 'Well done, good and faithful servant.'"

Blake wiped his mouth with his napkin and threw it on his plate, covering food he'd barely touched. "Me too. I just don't want it to be anytime soon."

Nathan continued to eat, although he tasted nothing, even after a liberal squeeze of the lemon juice over his schnitzel. The food lodged in his throat and he had to wash it down with tea. His father had been the ultimate fisher of men. It wasn't fair. He would suffer a painful death with this disease.

Life wasn't fair.

"'In this world you will have trouble. But take heart! I have overcome the world,' John 16:33."

Blake always had a way of reading people.

"You're right. It's a fallen world." Nathan laid aside his napkin. "Is he in pain?"

"If he is, Mom's not saying."

"She's a good soldier."

"She is and she wants all her children together for this next season of their lives."

"She left me when I had leukemia." The image of her tucking him into his bed with the basketball sheets and comforter, her nose and eyes red, floated across his mind's eye. She wore a green turtleneck sweater, corduroy pants, and red socks with different-colored toes. She'd snuggled up against him, her curly red head propped on the pillow, and told him the plan. Her voice never wavered, but her lips trembled. She told him not to worry, that Jesus would be with him always. She kissed his hair and hugged him until he couldn't breathe. "I was just a kid."

"It wasn't an easy thing for a mother to do. She did what she thought was best. As a mother, as a wife, and as a Christian."

"I try hard to see it that way." He glanced around, seeking the waitress. He'd drained his tea glass and yet he needed more to swallow the lump in his throat. "Aunt Millie and Uncle Rex were good to me. They raised me like their own."

The mustard and catsup moved to the front of the line. Blake had returned to rearranging condiments. "They also are good Christians. You need to forgive and forget."

Nathan knew that. The monkey on his back had a stranglehold around his neck and he had no one to blame but himself. He stared at his plate. "I will."

"Good. You'll come back with me?"

Go now and give up his chance to be part of this community? He would lose his chance to belong and to be a part of Jennie's life. The story he'd been writing when Blake showed up at Freeman's door. "There's a woman."

Blake let out a whoop that made the elderly man look up, tea glass suspended in air, and held out his hand for a fist-bump. Nathan ignored it and his brother let it drop. "Get out of here."

"Don't sound so surprised."

"You've never stayed in one place long enough to put down those kinds of roots." Blake leaned back and crossed his arms, a smile stretched across his face. "Who is she? Tell me everything. Are you engaged? Is there a date?"

Nathan couldn't. Not until he had the right to talk aloud about Jennie. "I don't see a ring on your finger."

"There was a girl once. She passed before I could get the ring on her finger."

"I'm sorry."

Blake shrugged. "It was a long time ago, but I've never found anyone quite like her. Someone who makes me want to be her one-and-only."

"I know someone like that."

"Ask her to come with you."

The image of Jennie Troyer, seven children in tow, transplanting herself to Pennsylvania, caught Nathan's imagination for a second. He could read to Elizabeth and Francis before bed. He could give them piggyback rides. They could ice skate in the winter and play baseball in summer. He could get a job that brought him home to Jennie every night. The image shattered like an icicle crashing to the ground. What would they do on Sunday morning? "That's not possible."

"With Jesus Christ, anything is possible."

"She's Amish."

"Ah. Explains the suspenders. You finally decide to go for the gusto and you choose someone who's out of reach?" Blake gave him a thumbs-up. "That's my little brother."

"She's not totally out of reach. That's what I was doing at Freeman's. He's the bishop."

"You're converting?"

"I'm thinking about it." Thinking hard. "It's not such a huge leap for a Beachy Amish Mennonite."

"And you could stop feeling guilty about being the odd man out in the family."

"I don't feel guilty." A lie. He did feel guilty. He couldn't bring himself to tell his own brother of his nightly battles with an insistent God. If he said the words aloud, he would be forced to admit he had no choice but to follow God's command just as his father and mother had. "I'm conflicted."

The understatement of the year.

"And resentful."

"I don't feel resentful." Nathan paused, searching for a word that encompassed his lingering dissatisfaction over his strange childhood. "I feel disappointed."

"Disappointed in God or in Dad and Mom?"

"Yes." There, he'd admitted it. "My disappointment is only outweighed by God's disappointment in me for not asking Him to take this journey with me."

"Have you prayed about it?"

"Until I'm blue in the face."

"Maybe you need to talk to Dad. Tell him how you feel."

"Now that he has a life-threatening disease?"

"Now that you might not get another chance."

TWENTY-ONE

JENNIE SAT UPRIGHT IN THE BED. SHE GASPED FOR air. Sweat burned her eyes. It soaked her nightgown. She threw off tangled, damp sheets. A nightmare. A nightmare relived again. A memory from long ago, yet every detail had been painted in stark contrast against a background of disbelief. Atlee's anger had not been directed at her only. Matthew had suffered too. He carried scars no one could see so they couldn't possibly understand why he acted the way he did.

She did understand. Somehow she needed to tell him that. She needed him to understand he could come to her with his pain.

She wrapped her arms around her thin pillow and inhaled its scent of outdoors. It comforted her. The dream revolved around a simple, innocent conversation after church. Leo had broken his long-standing silence to congratulate her on Francis's birth. A short conversation as all were with Leo.

His supreme effort to make small talk with her that day had meant a lot. She hadn't thought of what it might look like to Atlee. It had been a simple conversation after church. Leo had been kind, his voice soft, a little gruff, the effort apparent in the way he ducked his head and his jaw worked.

Atlee took it the wrong way. She paid the price. Matthew saw it and tried to stop his father, earning a trip to the woodshed.

Suddenly cold, she shivered and pulled the sheets back over her body.

Their time spent in the basement during the tornadoes had reminded her of that day. As did the conversation during the roof frolic. Seeing him at church. At the store these past few weeks. His attentive stare that made her think he was waiting for something. For her to do something or say something. Which probably brought on the nightmare. The thought rankled. He was a kind man and he did so well with the kinner.

As did Nathan with his sweet storytelling and playing games and leaving books for her. His looks over the supper table after a day working in the fields.

Two kind, gentle men were paying attention to her. Both seemed intent on protecting her. A second chance. Did she deserve a second chance? Did she dare try again? How could she be sure it wouldn't happen again? The same old doubts tormented her. Nathan was Mennonite. Not so different from the Amish, but not the same. She couldn't do that to the children, could she? Not with their eternal salvation at stake. She'd only begun the journey with them. Matthew's rumspringa would begin in less than two years. Then it would be time for him to seek a wife and decide about baptism. The children had to come first. Leo had his own problems, his own void to fill. She couldn't take care of another person. She had enough on her plate.

Jennie struggled from the bed and lit the kerosene lamp. Still shaking, she padded on bare feet from the room and down the hall.

She had to make sure Matthew was all right. He had intervened on her behalf, to save her, and he had paid the price. No wonder he felt such fury now. He didn't know how to deal with his feelings. He had his father as an example of how a husband treated a wife.

She peered into the bedroom shared by her boys. Francis was curled into a ball, his hands under his cheeks. Micah sprawled, one arm thrown over Mark, who lay on his belly, snoring.

The narrow bunk bed that belonged to Matthew held only rumpled sheets and a pillow tossed at the foot.

The sound of a door squeaking broke the silence. She whirled and sped down the hall to the banister. Matthew stood at the front door below.

"Where are you going?"

He jumped and turned, but his hand remained on the knob. "Out."

"Nee. It's late."

"Why are you up?"

"I couldn't sleep."

"Me neither. That's why I'm going out."

"Stay."

"Nee."

"You're my suh. I'm your mudder." She hated the shrill pitch of her own voice. Trying to soften it, she climbed down the stairs and went to him. "Go upstairs and get some sleep. We have church tomorrow."

"Nee."

He sounded like a small child whose first word was no.

"Do as you're told."

His hand dropped from the knob and fisted. He shook his head, his face contorted in a familiar sneer. She took a step back, her dream raging around her. He took a step forward, his boots loud on the wood floor. "What will you do? Drag me off to the woodshed for a whipping?" He stepped yet closer. "Would you leave me in the basement all night in the dark?"

"Nee. I wouldn't do that."

"No, that was Daed's job." The bitterness in his voice made bile rise in her throat. "I can take care of myself. I'll be back in time for morning chores."

"You didn't deserve the punishments you received."

"Spare the rod and spoil the child."

"With love. Punishment should fit the crime. It should be offered in love."

"Are you saying Daed didn't love me?"

"Nee, nee." She scrambled for words that wouldn't come. She couldn't explain Atlee's behavior. It made no sense then and it made none now. "I'm only saying that I hope you can forgive him for being unjust and know that you don't have to follow in his footsteps."

"Have you forgiven him?"

Nee. She'd tried. Gott knew how hard she'd tried. "I'm working on it."

"I hear how people talk."

"What people talking? About what?"

"Why don't you marry again?" His voice cracked, the voice of a boy trying to grow into a man. "It's expected."

"With time, but it's not something for you to worry about."

"I'm not worried." He jerked the door open. The smell of night air wafted through it, sweet and light. "I'm not worried about anything."

His tone said the opposite.

"Church is tomorrow."

"I'll be there. Don't worry. I'll not shame you."

"Why are you doing this?"

He shook his head. "I don't know."

"Stay home."

He slammed the door behind him.

TWENTY-TWO

LACK OF SLEEP DIDN'T LEND ITSELF TO STAYING awake during a three-hour church service. Bleary-eyed, Jennie breathed a sigh of relief as the last words of Freeman's benediction rang out. She stood and shooed Francis toward the barn doors. The four-year-old had done well with his plastic horse and her handkerchief–especially considering she'd forgotten to pack his snack. Thank goodness Mary Katherine always carried extra crackers in her bag. Elizabeth needed a diversion as well. The humid heat in Freeman's barn hadn't helped. Jennie wanted to lay her head on the bench and close eyelids that drooped more with each passing minute through two sermons, half a dozen hymns, and two kneeling prayers. She would never do that. Just the thought made her already warm cheeks burn.

Lying awake, staring at the ceiling, afraid to sleep, afraid of the dreams that would come meant she needed to drink an entire pot of coffee before church on Sunday morning. Thinking about Matthew, where he might be, what he might be doing. Images of the twisted metal of the plow, the buggy upside down in the corral, the barn without a roof. The store and her need to work there. The empty cookie jar that held no funds for materials or groceries. A thick morass of worries that whirled around and around in her mind until she wanted to weep.

But she didn't. She had more backbone than that.

"You look a little peaked this morning." Mary Katherine patted her shoulder from behind. She had nudged Jennie twice during the second sermon. "Still feeling poorly?"

Jennie glanced around. Church was not a place to pour her heart out. "Nee. I had trouble sleeping last night. Too much on my mind." The heat wasn't the problem, but it didn't help. "I don't think I got a wink of sleep."

"The harder you try, the harder it is. I get up and make a list of my worries and set it aside." Mary Katherine moved into the steady exodus from the barn. "But I'm so worn out from working in the store, it wouldn't matter. I'd sleep well either way."

Hint, hint.

Mary Katherine's farm and the store had been spared damage from the tornadoes. Jennie didn't try to understand why one would be spared and another destroyed. Freeman said God didn't make bad things happen. They happened because of a fallen world that dated back to Adam and Eve. God wanted them to turn to Him in times of distress. Jennie tried, she really did, but often a cold, dark void filled the space where comfort should've been. She shook it off. *Think of others.*

"How are things going at the store? Any more visits from Lazarus and his crew?" She squinted against the bright sunlight as they passed through the barn doors. "Has his lawyer shown up?"

"No, but Lazarus walks by several times a day, and once I saw that business partner of his measuring the front window. They're having trouble tracking down Seamus. They can't do a thing until they do."

"I'm sorry I haven't been there to help. The tornado wrecked my plans—and my barn."

"Don't worry. Take care of things at home. We'll manage until you can bring in more of your sewing goods and your jam. I have some earnings for you when you do."

Without coming out and saying it, Mary Katherine had offered her a lifeline. Her friend was truly a friend. "As soon as I finish the laundry tomorrow, I'll come in."

"Let the girls do the laundry."

Again, that slight but kind pressure. "I'll get them started and come on in."

"Did you see Nathan sitting through the service? With a stranger who looks just like him?" Her face full of curiosity, Mary Katherine cast a glance over Jennie's shoulder. "He's headed this way. What do you think he wants?"

Jennie had seen him. Who could miss his red head? Seated next to a twin tower and only a few seats from Leo. Their gazes had locked more than once during the service. She'd found herself studying one man and then the other. Instead of following the sermon. It was a wonder God hadn't struck her dead for such inattentiveness.

Surely Nathan had seen the surprise in her eyes at his presence. Freeman must have sanctioned it. But the other man? Who was he? A relative, obviously.

"Good day, ladies." Nathan's big smile had an anxious air to it. "Those were some serious sermons. I'm glad Freeman gave me a copy in English so I could follow along. Quite a lot to chew on, don't you think?"

"The words come from Gott, according to Freeman." She waited for Nathan to introduce his friend. Or say something. The pause grew. "Will you be coming to all the services from now on?"

His face reddened. "I hope so. Freeman gave me permission, suggested it, actually." The other man gave him a nudge and cleared his throat. "This is my brother, Blake. He's . . . visiting."

Jennie took the hand the man offered. It swallowed hers whole. "Will you be staying a while?"

"Yes."

"No."

The men's dueling answers were simultaneous.

"Either way, welcome to Jamesport." She wanted to ask more questions. Why didn't Nathan want his brother to stay? "Did you get a new car?"

"That's what I wanted to tell you, to ask you." He shoved his ball cap—St. Louis Cardinals this time—back on his forehead. His auburn hair sprang out in all directions. "I heard there are plans to go to Indian Creek this afternoon for fishing and barbecue. I thought I might take you and the kids. You can have a ride in my rental. It's huge, so there's plenty of room. I'm just using it until I decide . . . what to do." He finished in a rush.

If he planned to convert, he would have to give it up altogether. Buy a horse, as Leo suggested. Not Jennie's business.

Leo, who reminded her of her school days and buggy rides. Her face felt warm just thinking of him. Better to focus on the here and now.

Francis skipped across the yard. One cheek bulged with food of some kind. The child couldn't sit still long enough to eat. She should be supervising. "The kinner would like that."

His cheeks reddened. "Would you like it?"

A drive to the beautiful state park would be fun. His company would be nice. She liked talking to him. She felt comfortable in his presence. He had a gentle soul and so far, he'd asked nothing of her. She felt none of the confusion that Leo's presence evoked in her. They had no old memories that cut skin like broken glass. Nathan talked. A lot. She would always know what was on his mind.

Laura's words of warning flashed through Jennie's mind. She couldn't get tangled up with a man who wasn't Plain. Still, it was a simple outing. One the children would enjoy.

"Hey, Aenti." Hannah, one of her more than forty nieces and nephews waved as she squeezed through the crowd, her three little brothers in tow. "See you at the lake."

"Jah, see you then."

Her brother, Luke, Hannah's father, would be there with his wife and the rest of the kinner. Freeman would be there. Darren and his wife and children would be there. Her other brothers and their wives. Her parents might even go if they felt up to it. The audience would consist of concerned family and friends.

They thought she should marry again. But not a Mennonite. Not Nathan. They all liked Nathan. They trusted him, considered him a friend, but not marriage material. Not yet, anyway.

She forced herself to smile at him. "How are your visits with Freeman going?"

"Slowly." He drew a line in the dirt with his sneaker. "We could talk about it. You could explain some things to me. Help me understand."

Help him learn to be Plain. She barely understood the articles of confession herself when she went to the baptism classes more than sixteen years earlier. She didn't have to understand, only believe. At least that's what her mother and father had said.

Indecision wracked her. He was waiting for her response. Blake looked from her to his brother and back. They both waited for a response. "Laura and Mary Kay are going. And their children and grandchildren. We'll ride with them and see you there."

He dug his hands into the pockets of his khaki pants, disappointment plain in his expression. "They have their own vans?"

"Mary Kay has someone she uses all the time. Laura has many great-grandchildren. They may need a van. You should ask them."

"Sure." He rallied. "I will. We'll see you then, I guess."

Nathan turned toward the road where his car was parked. His brother followed behind him like an overgrown puppy dog. Jennie fought the urge to stop them, to say yes, to ignore the naysayers. No. She was a grown woman. She knew better. Resolute, she whirled and headed for the house. Grinning, his cheek still bulging, Francis skipped toward her. He stumbled and pitched forward.

His hands went to his throat. A gagging sound filled the air. His mouth gaped open and closed. He coughed and gagged again. His face turned red, then purple.

"What is it? Francis?" She dashed across the yard. "What's the matter?"

He gasped, but no words came out. He stumbled to his knees, arms flapping.

"He's choking." Leo bounded up from a nearby picnic table. "He had a sucker."

She saw no stick. The boy had chewed the candy from it. She reached for him. Leo got there first.

He grabbed Francis from behind, arms around his chest, and lifted him off the ground. Once, twice, three times.

The ball of candy sailed through the air, smacked against Jennie's apron, and fell to the ground. Francis coughed, a hard, rasping sound.

"Got it." Leo set him on his feet. "No more candy for you, little one."

Sobbing, Francis whirled and buried his head in Leo's middle. Leo squatted and hugged him back. "You're gut, you're gut."

He nuzzled Francis's hair with his chin and whispered soft words until her son stopped crying. The look of longing that blossomed on his face touched Jennie's heart in a place she'd thought permanently inaccessible and marked with Do Not Enter signs. Stones in a wall so high she couldn't climb over began to crumble and fall away. She scrambled to reinforce them.

"He shouldn't eat candy." Leo looked up at her with those amber eyes. His usual Stay Out signs, looking so like her own, reappeared. "Suckers, anyway."

"No more suckers." She breathed, hoping the quiver in her voice would ease. "No more candy, ever."

"He's fine." He patted Francis's back, then straightened. He gave the boy a gentle shove. "Go play with the others. Look, they're jumping on the trampoline."

Grinning, his fright already forgotten, Francis took off without a word as usual. Jennie shook her head. This one would be the death of her. The others seemed easy in comparison. Except for Matthew. The oldest and the youngest.

Leo frowned. "Are you gut? You look a little peaked."

"Jah." Her heart still banged against her ribs. Whether from the shock of Francis choking or from the realization that she'd allowed Leo to get through her defenses for a split second. "My heart stopped there for a second."

"Mine too."

"You think fast."

"My daed taught me to be ready for what life brings." Sadness flitted across his face. "I should've learned better, I reckon."

"You've rescued Francis twice."

He shrugged and shifted from one foot to the other. He ducked his head. After a second he chuckled. And then guffawed.

"What? What is so funny?"

"I reckon you're thinking of starting a new trend."

"What?"

He pointed toward the ground. Jennie looked down. She didn't see anything unusual, just grass and dandelions ready for their seeds to be blown away on a breeze, along with a child's wishes. "What is so funny?"

"Do you always wear shoes from two different pairs, or is that a new thing you're trying out?"

She focused on her shoes. Both black Sunday shoes, but one had a thick rubber sole like a sneaker and the other a short heel. They both tied, but the laces were different. She wore shoes from two different pairs.

"It's not that funny."

Still she chuckled. The chuckle turned into an outright laugh. She laughed so hard she snorted. Laughter born of a sleepless night and worry that robbed her of her peace. It felt good.

Leo laughed with her. People paused in their conversations to look at them. She gasped, put her hand to her mouth, and swallowed another snort. "It's not that funny."

"Plain folks don't care about things like shoes matching." His grin made him look years younger, like the boy she'd known in school. A little mischievous, like there was a lot going on behind the smile. To her chagrin, warmth spread through her, head to toe. His knowing look didn't help. "But it does make a person wonder what you were doing this morning that you didn't notice."

"Rushing out of the house. I didn't want to miss the service."

"Me neither." He sounded surprised at the thought. "But my shoes match."

A Plain man's church shoes were virtually identical in every way.

"You don't have seven children to get ready and herd out the door."

Six. Matthew had stayed home.

Leo looked around, took a step closer. He took off his hat and twirled it in his fingers. "I was thinking of stopping by tonight."

"Tonight?" She glanced back. Nathan had taken a seat at a picnic table, his brother across from him. Both stared with unabashed interest. "To talk to Matthew?"

"To take you for a ride." His face turned a deep scarlet. He glanced up as if looking for inspiration in the tree branches overhead. "You asked me why I never came back. I reckon better late than never."

New to courting, she hadn't been able to find a topic of conversation. His silence had intimidated her. The long pauses had grown longer. The ride had been short. And now? Now would they find the rhythm they'd lacked all those years ago? She found a place in her heart that wanted to know even as she shied away from the thought.

Nee. How could she trust him? He was different than Atlee. He had a gentle touch. The hands of a carpenter who built things up, not tore them down.

Embarrassment coursed through her. She would not think of his hands touching her. No man's hands had done so in four years. His were callused. Not like Nathan's salesman hands. Leo's carpenter fingers were stubby. Silky black hairs blanketed the backside. Muscles burgeoned in his arms. His chest seemed to burst from his shirt. Muscles. Strength. Hugs that would leave a person breathless.

The familiar drink of anguish and fear burned her lips, her tongue, and her throat when she swallowed. She couldn't take such a chance. To find herself wrapped up in the physical response to a man who then turned on her in a heartbeat. A hand that stroked her skin could so quickly become a fist. She breathed and stood tall. "I already have plans."

If she weren't going to the lake, would she have said yes to Leo? Some part deep within her cried out to say yes. To trust enough to say yes. Atlee's raised fist loomed, its memory never far. Would it never fall to his side and stay there?

Leo's gaze skipped to Nathan. The tentative smile that reminded her of his younger years died. His shoulders hunched. "I see."

"We're going to Indian Creek Lake. Everyone is coming. You could join the group."

The doors, open for a scant few seconds, closed. The expression in his eyes died. "I have to check on Red."

Something important slipped beyond Jennie's grasp. She wanted it back. "Matthew will come see you on Monday."

"Fine." He slapped his hat on his head. "I best get home. Chores to do."

"Maybe another time." Why had she said that?

"If you're not busy." Sarcasm dusted the words. "Sometime."

"Thank you for helping Francis."

"No need to get fancy. It's what anyone would've done."

He had the knack of being there when Jennie needed him.

The painful thud of her heart told her she hadn't returned the favor.

TWENTY-THREE

HOT DOGS ALWAYS TASTED BETTER EATEN OUT-doors. Jennie balanced her paper plate and spooned pickle relish onto a hot dog already swimming in mustard and catsup. The pungent smell of condiments reminded her of childhood, backyard picnics, and camping trips to Stockton Lake. A breeze through the leaves on a towering oak tree made a melodic rushing sound that at once cooled her and soothed her. She relaxed for a second, letting thoughts of money, the store, Matthew's anger, and storm damage seep away. The children's laughter filled the air as they splashed each other in the ankle-deep water on Indian Creek Lake's shore. The sound and Mary Katherine's attempts to hop and jump in the water made Jennie smile as did the croak of the frogs and the hum of the cicadas. She loved summer sounds. They warmed her and melted fears and gloomy depression.

"Do you want some chips with that?" Nathan sidled closer, a bag of sour cream potato chips in one hand.

Jennie's moment of peaceful contemplation dissipated in a split second. She nodded. "Thank you."

Nathan glanced around as if gauging who might overhear their innocent conversation. Beads of sweat dotted his forehead. His damp hair stuck out from under his ball cap. He smiled and held out his offering as if it were precious. He looked younger in his T-shirt and jeans held up oddly enough by suspenders. He seemed to have taken a step in a certain direction, only to waver.

She found herself taking that same quick look around at the other picnic tables spread across the grounds. She took the bag from him and settled onto the bench at the closest picnic table. "Did you get some?"

"I prefer Doritos. Nacho flavored are my favorite."

The only person close enough to hear would be Laura, and she sat on an old blanket in the shade of a hickory tree, her hands in her lap, eyes closed. Her friend had stayed within arm's reach since arriving with a group of Mary Katherine's children and grandchildren in Nathan's SUV. Freeman had settled at a picnic table nearby, his expression benign. Her brothers and the kinner had immediately scattered to the lake shores, fishing poles in hand. Blake remained by the lake, his head bent over his fishing pole, his cap turned so the bill was in the back. Giving his brother time alone with her?

"Mind if I join you."

She inhaled and almost choked on her first bite of hot dog. She glanced around again. Freeman and Peter were talking, hands moving in animated agreement over who knew what. She couldn't hear, which meant they couldn't hear her. Would it be wrong to say yes? Would it be rude to say no? Nathan waited, his expression so like the one she saw on her children's faces when they wanted a second piece of pie. "Jah. Yes. I mean, go ahead."

He settled onto the bench across from her and set down a plate laden with a hot dog, barbecue chips, Doritos, and half a dozen Oreos. She suppressed a smile. He had a child's approach to food.

He took a bite. Catsup oozed and dripped on his hand. He chuckled. "I'm a mess."

"The messier it is, the better it tastes."

"True." He dabbed at the catsup, which dripped onto his shirt. He shrugged and took a long swig of his grape pop. He ate and drank with a gusto that she liked. "So, I'm glad we have a few minutes to talk alone."

Her heart revved. They were not alone. Darren and his wife sat at the picnic table at the next pavilion with three children who were still eating. Silas, Luke, and her other brothers cleaned fish they planned to grill on the spot and eat. Her sisters-in-law had spread blankets on the grass and put babies down for naps. Her parents, thankfully, had not made the trip. Still, her community surrounded them. Her community, not his.

It had seemed perfectly natural until he said that word alone. Everyone had been chatting all afternoon. About the wild turkeys and the raccoon they'd seen, the rabbits hippity-hopping across the grass, about books they liked and didn't like. The men had told tall tales of fishing, and Nathan and Blake had matched the others story for story. Laura and Mary Katherine had nattered on about their sons' love of fishing and hunting and all manly things.

"How long is your brother staying?" The question was the first flung from a whirlwind of thoughts she couldn't harness.

"That's definitely not what I want to talk about." He grimaced and broke a Dorito in two places with his thumb. He moved the pieces to far regions on the plate. "He hasn't said, but I don't expect him to be here long. He came to . . . tell me something. He's told me. He'll go soon."

She waited, not sure where Nathan was going.

"I think Freeman is beginning to see how well I would fit into this community." He studied his plate. "That's why he decided to have me come to church. So I could learn more. He wants me to spend more time with the people who would be my community. I need to understand how the faith is practiced on a regular basis."

"Converting is very hard. Most can't do it."

"Most aren't me *and* I'm Mennonite, not so different from you."

"I don't know a lot about what Mennonites believe aside from the Meidung issue. I only know that they live their lives differently." She picked her words with care, not wanting to hurt him or his enthusiasm for a worthy cause. Having him as part of their community might be a good thing. But it would force her to face issues she wasn't sure she wanted to face. Not yet. "You may be working on a farm, you may wear suspenders, but you're also driving a van and wearing jeans."

"I'm moving toward the goal, one step at a time." He wiped at his mouth but missed the spot of catsup on his chin. "I gave up book sales and settled down. I'm learning a new trade. That's a lot of progress in a month's time. I'm moving as fast as I can."

"It's not just how you live your faith. It's the faith itself. The reason behind the way you live."

"I know." He picked up the hot dog, then dropped it back on the plate. "I'm working on that part too. The fact is I would do anything for you."

His declaration came in a soft whisper, but his gaze didn't waver. Jennie swallowed against a knot of emotion, not sure whether fear or delight would win out. She would not get caught in this web. Not again. Especially not with a man who had so far to go in his quest. "I appreciate—"

"Mudder, Mudder!" Mark raced across the grass and stopped short of the table, dancing around on dirty, bare feet. His face was red with sunburn, exertion, and possibly embarrassment. "I split my pants."

"You what?"

He whirled around and showed her his backside. Indeed, he had a big split in the seam. "I'm getting too big for my britches. And there aren't any more in my room."

How was that possible? She and the girls had done all the laundry on laundry day. She couldn't keep up with the sewing. She needed more material, which meant more money. "We'll have to see if Micah's hand-me-downs fit you. In the meantime, it's just us. We don't care if you have a hole in your pants."

"Mudder!" His hands went to his behind. "The girls will see."

"Sit down. I'll make s'mores in a minute. Do you want to go home or do you want to eat s'mores?"

"S'mores." He backed away as if they hadn't already seen the damage. "They'll make me even fatter. All the seams will explode."

"You're not fat." Nathan tapped the box of graham crackers. "You're a growing boy. You'll burn off the calories in three minutes."

Mark dashed off again, chortling and shouting to the others about the s'mores.

"You didn't get a chance to answer me."

"I can't."

"Can't answer me or can't be with me?"

"We can't talk about this."

"Okay. For now. Until I totally earn the right." Nathan ducked his head as he swirled a chip in the catsup. "But I'm not giving up. Let's talk about the kids. I know it's hard to keep up with their needs. Is there some way I can help?"

He didn't know their ways. Leo did. Leo could help. She glanced at Nathan's hands. He had blisters and the beginnings of calluses. The beginnings of a working man's hands. But still gentle. "The girls and I will sew more pants. I'll be able to afford the material when I sell more items on consignment at the store."

Until Lazarus took it away from them and this source of income dried up.

"Have you been able to put the money together for the new buggy?"

Jennie had wanted one afternoon in which she didn't have to think of these things. These problems didn't disappear because a person chose to run and hide. "I'm working on it. Some donations are coming in from people who want to help everyone who had damage. It's the Plain way."

"I want to help you." He dropped his dog on the plate, looked around, then slid his hand across the table until his fingers touched the tips of hers. His were warm and damp. "Do you understand what I'm trying to say?"

Memories rushed at Jennie. She had no place to go, no way to escape.

Atlee's fingers bit into her shoulder. Tight, tight. They hurt. He leaned down until his bristly beard brushed against her check. His hot breath smelled of onions. "It's time to go."

She glanced at her mother, humming an old hymn as

she pulled a pan of chicken-and-rice casserole from the oven. "But we haven't had supper."

"Don't question me."

Mudder turned and smiled. "Supper's almost ready, Atlee. Would you like a glass of tea while we put it on the table?"

"We're going."

Her smile faded as she glanced from Atlee to Jennie and back. "I made lemon bars."

"Kinner who can't behave go to bed without supper."

"Surely they don't deserve—"

"Get up." He grabbed Jennie's hand and jerked her up from the table. "Neither do wives who don't obey."

Abject humiliation turned her muscles to water. She stumbled. His grip around her hand crushed tiny bones. She cried out. Her free hand covered her mouth. She swallowed the pain and strove to keep up with his stride.

"Jennie?"

She looked back. Her mother stood motionless, a pot holder forgotten in her hand. A terrible sadness mingled with pity on her wrinkled face. Shame billowed through Jennie. "It's fine, Mudder, I'm fine. I'll be here for the canning frolic."

It would never be fine, but Mudder didn't need to know the depths of her shame.

Jennie jerked her hand back and half stood. "Nee. Nee."

Nathan's hands retreated to his lap. His face turned a deep red. "Wait, what's the matter. You just went white as a sheet? What did I say?"

If only the earth would open and swallow her up. Her heart pounded inside her chest. She couldn't breathe. Atlee's face reappeared, full of revulsion. Revulsion for her. She slipped from the table. "We should go."

"No, no." Nathan's tone implored, but he kept his voice down. "Please don't run."

She gripped the edge of the table and forced a smile. *Don't make a scene.* She plumbed the depths for a soft voice, a calm expression. "I'm not running from anyone."

"I'm sorry. I'm sorry." He slipped from his seat and busied himself cleaning the mustard bottle with a napkin. "Are you only afraid of me or of all men? How did you get this way? What did your husband do to you?"

He could never know what a poor wife she'd been to deserve such treatment from a husband who could not be satisfied, no matter what she did. The children had gone to bed without supper that night and so had she. She never knew—and neither did they—what they'd done to deserve that punishment. "Nothing. Nothing."

"Sit down. I swear I'll leave the subject alone."

"Plain men don't swear." Her breathing slowed. The past receded. Atlee was dead and buried in the ground. Guilt pulsed through Jennie. Could God ever forgive her for being relieved? She could make supper with no fear that it wouldn't please. She could go to bed at night with no fear he would be there, shirt off, face expectant, when she entered the bedroom. Had God given her this sweet release? Could a fraa ask for such a thing? Legs weak, she eased back on the bench. "We shouldn't be having these conversations. They're for special friends."

"I want to be your special friend."

"That's not possible." The way he said it was so sweet, so loving, the ache where her broken heart resided eased a little. That a man like Nathan might see something in her after all these years, it was a healing balm. If only he were in a position to offer such a thing to a woman like her. "Even if it were, it would be wrong to try to become Plain in order to court me."

"I know that. There's a host of other reasons."

"Are any of them about faith?"

"Yes. I'm looking for a faith that fits me. My Mennonite life doesn't."

What did that mean? A faith that fit. Could he shed one that was like a coat too tight through the shoulders for another? Could anyone? There had to be more to it. "You need to do what you need to do, with no regard for feelings you may have for me."

The idea that he might have feelings for her seemed so farfetched as to be a silly tale, like the ones Elizabeth and Cynthia made up at night to entertain each other before bed.

"You could never have feelings for a man like me?"

"I'm not good fraa material."

His forehead furrowed. "You look good from where I sit."

He couldn't begin to know her shortcomings. Atlee had found them out quickly enough. "You don't know me."

"I want to get to know you. Give me time to do that."

"It won't change anything." She grasped for a way to end this conversation that went around and around and never arrived at its destination. "You started a new occupation. You have family visiting. You have your time with Freeman. Focus on those things. Leave me out of it. Please."

Nathan sniffed and pushed chips around on the plate. "My

brother's here because he wants me to go back East with him to see my family."

To his true family. Another reason Nathan had no business talking to her as if he planned a future in Jamesport. His words could not be trusted. "You should do that."

He fiddled with the loop on his pop can. "You're here."

Fear made her stomach rock. Hot dog and chips rebelled as if they would no longer stay in their proper place. She bit her tongue and tasted salty blood. "That is of no consideration for you. It can't be."

"What are you so afraid of?" He leaned forward, his fingers splayed as if longing to touch her again. She scooted back. His hands withdrew. His gaze sought hers. She couldn't hold it. He sighed. "What happened to you?"

"I'll make the s'mores. It's getting late." She stood again. "We'll have dessert and get back. We have chores to do."

He threw his half-eaten hot dog in the trash can. "And pants to make."

"Exactly."

He picked up the bag of marshmallows and handed it to her. "Someday I hope you trust me enough to tell me what happened to you."

"I might say the same of you."

"Touché." He shook his head, his eyes sad. "This wasn't the way I wanted this to go."

"You can't spring something like that on a Plain woman and expect her to be right there with you."

"You have no feelings for me at all?"

She closed her eyes for a second, trying to see a distant speck in the future where she might be able to have the courage to try again. A faint figure far, far away beckoned to her. She couldn't tell who it was and what he wanted. Leo's face earlier in the day as he comforted Francis filled her mind's eye. A good Plain man who wanted to take her for a buggy ride. A man with callused hands that worked hard, had strength, but then turned gentle. Suddenly, it seemed as if she had choices where before there had been none. Neither man could change her past. Could she somehow become a good wife pleasing to the husband either would be?

Jennie fumbled through the dark corridors of her mind looking for that simple, sweet feeling of love for another, fresh and new. She couldn't find it no matter how hard she tried. Atlee had turned the air around her black. It smelled of distrust and fear. "It's not that simple."

"It never is." Nathan stuck three fat marshmallows on a stick with sharp thrusts as if skewering them for bad behavior. "But I won't give up."

The idea that he would pursue her, the least desirable of women, almost made her laugh—almost. "You need to focus on your faith first. Work your way through what it means to be Plain and whether you truly can do it. You can't stick your toe in the water and expect someone to jump in with you."

"Smart and pretty."

Her cheeks burning, she turned to the fire pit. She blew the flames out on her marshmallows and slipped them on top of the graham cracker and chocolate bar lying on the paper plate waiting for the perfect middle. "I'm going to call the kinner."

"Don't run away."

She wasn't running. It would be undignified. She settled for a fast walk—as fast and as far away as possible.

✳

Women were a mystery. Nathan remembered to shut his mouth as he watched Jennie trudge from the pavilion. She looked as if she wanted to break into a run. Only innate dignity kept her from fleeing. The look of fear on her face burned through him. The fear on her face when his fingers brushed against hers had been immediate and all encompassing. What did she fear? What had happened to her? He couldn't begin to reach her if she wouldn't tell him. When would he have another chance to speak to her again? Opportunities were few and far apart when he worked for her brother-in-law. He couldn't simply show up at her house uninvited now that he had no books to sell. He slapped his marshmallow stick on the table and started after her.

"Let her go. You've bent her ear enough."

He stopped. He'd forgotten about Laura's presence. She'd looked so relaxed and peaceful napping in the shade of the old hickory tree with its sweeping boughs that dipped low to the ground. Not napping, apparently. She stood, the cracking of her knees loud in the sudden silence. She brushed leaves and twigs from her dress.

"You were listening to our conversation?" His outrage made the words come out in a semi-stutter. What passed between Jennie and him had been meant for no other ears. "It was private."

"I was napping. At first." She sniffed and shrugged. "Chalk it up to an old lady's prerogative. Besides, Jennie is my friend."

"And mine also."

"Plain women don't have single men as friends." She stretched and yawned. More popping and cracking of joints. "Why do you think Mary Kay and I are here, if not as chaperones? Not to mention her brothers. She is a good Plain woman who needs good friends who know what it's like to be a widow to help her navigate."

"How is a man to get to know a Plain woman then?"

"A man like you doesn't." Laura's tone was firm but kind. "You have to do things in the right order. Have patience. One step at a time. That is what a Plain man would do. Jennie gave you some good advice."

"You need to focus on your faith first. Work your way through what it means to be Plain and whether you truly can do it. You can't stick your toe in the water and expect someone to jump ahead of you."

"I heard her."

"Did you? She's been through a lot. Being a widow in a community built around husband and wife isn't easy. Finding a way to fit isn't easy. Don't make it harder for her." Laura meandered into the pavilion. She picked up the paper plate that held a s'more, a sudden smile appearing. "I love roasted marshmallows, don't you?"

The last thing Nathan wanted to do was make it harder for Jennie. He wanted to make it easier. The thought that he had done the opposite hurt like lashes from a whip on his bare skin. "She's been through a lot. What does that mean? What happened to her?"

Laura plopped onto the bench and lifted the s'more to her mouth. It remained suspended in air for a few seconds. "We all want to see her happy, to see her remarry. It's what the Gmay wants for her. None of us want to see her make a bad choice and be hurt."

The words again reverberated in the air. "Was there something with her first husband, something that no one is saying?"

"Jennie's story is Jennie's story to tell. Not mine." Laura took a big bite, the graham cracker breaking into pieces that fell onto the plate she held under it. Marshmallow oozed out and dripped on her fingers.

She licked them. A blissful smile made her look younger. She would have been a pretty woman. "My advice to you is the same as hers. Get your house in order before you start barging into someone else's."

He hadn't asked for Laura's advice. But she was Jennie's friend. She'd known her since childhood. "I have no intention of hurting her. Quite the opposite."

"If you make her care for you and then decide you can't or won't pursue joining our faith or the bishop determines you're not fit to join, you will do damage to someone who's had her share of pain in this life."

"What, what pain?"

"Don't concern yourself with the past, only with the future."

If only it were that simple. His own past turned up in the form of a brother he hadn't seen in years. His father's future, on the other hand, invaded his dreams at night. "I can't map the future without learning from the past."

Had he said those words? How could he be so interested in her past when he hadn't addressed his own? He thrust the thought aside and concentrated on trying to read Laura's face.

"It seems to me you have to learn from your own past first."

Was she a mind reader? He shook his head, baffled at her insight. Age or female intuition? "What do you know about my past?"

"Why does your brother want you to go home to see your family?"

"Eavesdropping is not a desirable habit."

"Being old means I can get away with a lot. I've earned the right. Did you know I delivered all seven of Jennie's kinner?" She rubbed together swollen hands, a look of discomfort on her wrinkled face. "They're like my grandkinner. Practically family. I have a right to weigh in on any man who might become important in their lives."

"I can understand that." He did understand. He wanted family relationships like that in his life. "I would never hurt them."

"Sometimes things don't work out the way we want them to. Sometimes our actions and desires cause hurt." She contemplated the pieces of chocolate and graham cracker on her plate. "No matter how sweet our intentions." She fixed him with a stare so sharp it seemed to slice through old memories and scar tissue. "Gott's plan is Gott's plan. We don't know what it is. You need to pray long and hard before you take another step that affects people around you. People like that sweet woman coming this way."

The sound of laughter floated on the air. Blake's laugh, a deep chuckle, mingled with higher and sweeter trills.

"Your brother fits right in." Laura didn't sound pleased about it. "He's not fishing for an Amish girl too, is he?"

"No. No, of course not." Nathan surveyed his brother from afar. He was chasing Cynthia and Celia with a handful of night crawlers, gooey, nasty, wiggly worms. "He may be older than me, but he's still a big kid."

The kids, including Blake, rushed into the pavilion, pushing and shoving. Jennie trailed behind with Mary Katherine. Without looking his way, she began to stuff hot dog buns and condiments in bags. Preparing to go.

"S'mores, s'mores, we want s'mores." Celia and Cynthia chanted. "Lots of s'mores."

"Me too, me too." Blake joined in. "Double-deckers, all around. I'll help."

Laura handed Nathan a chunk of chocolate. "Stick to s'mores. They're easy."

He glanced at Jennie. She didn't look his way.

Nothing was easy.

TWENTY-FOUR

A PERSON COULD ONLY HIDE OUT SO LONG IN A
barn. Leo adjusted the poultices of bran and Epsom salt around Red's
legs, patting each one to make sure it held firmly in place. He planned
to stay here as long as Red needed him. He wasn't hiding, just being
a good steward of his resources. Red neighed, but the sound had
ceased to be frantic in recent days. He shifted his feet and his long tail
swished away the flies that buzzed them both.

The barn's warm air was dank with humidity. Bits of hay and
dust swirled, backlit by sun that seeped between boards shrunk with
age and weather. Sweat soaked Leo's shirt and dampened his face, but
he felt at home, at ease. Red still needed him, pure and simple. No
expectations for more than food, water, and banishment of his pain.

"I'm glad you're feeling better." He patted the horse's rump. "One of
these days I'll be able to get you some company. Would you like that?"

Red's head bobbed. His long, velvety nose brushed against Leo's
chest. It was "thank you" in any language. Leo scratched the spot
between the horse's ears. "You're welcome."

He received a soft whinny in response. Like Leo, Red didn't talk
much, but when he did he made it count. Leo stuck his hand in a

canvas bag hanging from the stall railing and brought out half a dozen apple slices. "A treat because you deserve it." He held out two. Red nibbled at them with a surprisingly delicate touch. His lips tickled Leo's palm. He grinned and held out two more. "For good measure."

People would think him crazy, talking so much to a horse, but Red asked little in return and seemed thrilled beyond measure with what he received. Most animals were like that, unlike humans. Leo longed for a poultice that would stop the pain where his heart should be. The wound that never quite healed. The memory of the previous day's scene with Jennie after church reared. He lassoed it back into its corral with a desperation born of yet another sleepless night. He'd picked up the gauntlet thrown down by Aidan before the tornado. He'd gone out on the limb and Jennie had cut it off behind him.

The strange, yet familiar look of longing that had spread across her face even as she said no still baffled him. He breathed through a pain so persistent it was like an old friend on whom he could always depend. It didn't matter. He still wanted to help her. He still needed to help her. With Matthew. And with the buggy. Somehow he would find a way to pay for another buggy or find one she could borrow. Plain folks were good about that sort of thing, but most of them didn't have an extra buggy sitting around the homestead.

In the meantime work served as the only remedy. He would finish with Red and get to work. Red's head bobbed. He whinnied as if he'd read Leo's mind and agreed. Leo chuckled. "We're a fine pair, aren't we?"

Beau, who'd been stretched out on his back, paws in the air, sleeping, barked, a loud, vociferous sound, rolled over, and stood. They had company, it seemed.

Matthew Troyer stood half-in, half-out of the barn door. He had a contemptuous look on his thin, pimpled face that reminded Leo more of Atlee than Jennie. His head swiveled as he glanced around the barn. "Who are you talking to? To yourself?"

Beau continued to bark, his tail wagging in an ecstatic welcome. The dog loved visitors. He could not be counted on as a guard dog, however.

"Beau, be quiet. I'm talking to Red. Come on in." Leo picked up a brush that he'd laid on the stall gate and began to curry the horse's coat. He might not be able to swing the buggy yet, but Matthew had shown up and Leo was ready to help the boy solve his woes. "I'm surprised you came."

Matthew stooped and patted Beau. The dog's tail thumped on the floor in a rhythmic *thwack, thwack.* He followed when the boy leaned up against the stall, both arms propped on the ledge. He was tall for a fourteen-year-old, broad through the shoulders and sturdy from years of field work. He probably wasn't done growing, either. He was the spitting image of Atlee. Same black hair and big blue eyes made all the more brilliant by a deep tan. Same way of staring a person down. "Why do you say that?"

"It doesn't look to me like you do much of anything your mudder asks—or tells—you to do. Like showing up here days after we roofed the barn."

Matthew snorted in that disdainful way that reminded Leo of English kids he'd seen gathered outside the convenience store when he went into town. Like they knew what the whole world didn't. "Things she asks me to do don't always make much sense."

"She's your mudder. It doesn't have to make sense." He laid the brush down and wiped his hands on his pants. He tried to see some trace of Jennie in Matthew. A little in the nose maybe, the shape of his chin, the dimples. He had none of her sweet disposition. "Where did you learn to be so disrespectful—from your *Englisch* friends?"

"If I wanted to be pestered about how I act and what I do, I would've stayed home." Matthew's face contorted in a sneer. "Mudder was wrong again." He started toward the door.

Leo couldn't fail in his commitment to help Jennie with this, her oldest boy. She might never take that buggy ride with him, but he would do this for her. She had far, far to go with seven children. How she fared with the first would set the tone for all the rest. Much as he hated to talk, for her he would talk. And probe and keep at it, just as he kept at his efforts to help a horse in pain. He would do more for a boy who so obviously had pain. "Your daed and I were friends when we were kinner."

Matthew stopped. His shoulders hunched. He turned, the sneer gone. "He had friends?"

The wondering tone spoke volumes. Why would a boy think his father had no friends growing up? "We all played together, but he was one of us that went to Indian Creek Lake to fish and went hunting and swimming, all the stuff you do now."

Matthew kicked at the dirt with his boot, his effort to not care plain on his face. "Did you ever figure out what's wrong with your horse?"

He wasn't ready to ask the real questions yet. "Vet says it's laminitis." Leo explained the disease and motioned for Matthew to come into the stall. "Feel here. That's his pulse."

A look of concentration on his face, Matthew nodded. His fingers were long and thin. He let them run up Red's leg. The horse tossed his head as if wondering who this interloper was and why Leo let him into their domain. "Is it painful?"

"Jah, but Todd has given him medicine for it. It's much better.

Laminitis is something a farmer should know about. Are you planning to farm?"

Matthew shook his head. "I came over here today because carpentry is better than being stuck outside plowing a field in the hot sun all afternoon."

Pure honesty. Leo couldn't help but laugh. Honesty was a good start. "What do you know about carpentry?"

"You make things out of wood."

"Then we best get started." He gave Red a last pat and led Matthew to his work shed, a modest structure he'd built himself. Squat, square, serviceable. His favorite place to simply be. Quiet reigned most days except for Beau's snoring or the mingled chatter of birds and crickets outside the open windows. He had a view of Missouri fields planted in milo and corn that arched and waved in unison in a summer breeze. Not another soul within miles. Most days, he liked it that way.

"That's a lot of stuff." Matthew surveyed the shop, with its hodgepodge of tools and materials, his face intent. "A lot of tools."

Inhaling the familiar, calming scent of cut wood and sawdust, Leo tried to see it through Matthew's eyes. It was a lot of stuff, but everything had a job to do, everything in its place. A miter saw, a band saw, the gas generator he used to run the power tools, piles of wood, finished chairs, half-finished chairs, sculpted pieces of wood held tight in braces until ready for assembly, cans of varnish, tubes of glue, piles of sandpaper, worktables, cabinets, all the tools of the trade hanging from peg boards on the walls.

Matthew nudged a pile of walnut with his boot. "You start with a pile of wood and make something."

"Something useful *and* beautiful."

"We don't care if it's beautiful, do we?"

By *we* he meant the Gmay or Plain folks in general. The likes of Freeman Borntrager held utility in more esteem than beauty. Understandable, but a man could view the world in more than one way. "I give myself room to care." He wasn't sure why, but it meant something to him that his furniture was more than a place to sit or a drawer that held clothes. "Memories happen in the chairs. Meals are shared on the tables."

A fanciful notion but one that got him through three or four days of sanding seats, arms, back slats, headrests, and rockers.

Matthew ran a hand across the double rocking chair that sat on the worktable, assembled but still requiring days of sanding and then the finish. "How many have you made, do you think?"

"Single rockers, at least fifty or sixty." Leo moved to stand next to him, contemplating the days he'd spent cutting and sculpting the wood, creating the joinery, building the something from the nothing. "Doubles, only a few. Maybe a dozen."

"How long does it take to make one?"

"I can make a single in eight or nine days."

"It's a lot of work."

"It requires patience."

"You don't get bored?"

"I think. I think about the people who will sit in it and what they'll talk about and the boplin they'll rock." The words jostled inside his head. So many words. He'd never told another soul. Words he longed to say to Jennie, he said to her son. Because he had promised to help. "The stories they'll tell while they sit in it. Maybe a mudder and then the groossmammi in the afternoon, holding the bopli while the mudder fixes supper."

"You think about all that?"

"I'm not just building a chair, I'm building a part of someone's life." He picked up a piece of sandpaper. After hours of sanding, it seemed an extension of his fingers. "A rocking chair lasts for generations, if it's made right and sturdy. It's passed down and its stories go with it."

"Never thought about it."

Matthew likely hadn't thought about much of anything at his age. "Same way when you're out there working in the fields."

"What do you mean?"

"Farms grow crops that feed people's bellies." Leo ran his hand over one of the seats. He'd spent hours sanding it to a high sheen, bringing out the natural grain. "They'll sit at the supper table and eat corn on the cob or green beans or tomatoes or bread and talk about their days."

"It mostly feels like hot, sweaty work."

"Work feels good." Leo offered him a smile. "Work gives us purpose."

"How come you don't farm then?"

"Because I do this." He waved his hand at the shop. "I like working on my own."

The sneer was back. Like a reflex Matthew couldn't suppress. "Then maybe you don't want me around."

Leo handed him the sandpaper. "I'm no fool. If I can get someone else to do the sanding, I'll take it."

Matthew laughed, a rusty sound as if he wasn't used to it. "For how long?"

"Takes three or four days."

"Three or four days!"

"It'll be a thing of beauty by the time you finish." And he would learn the value of patience. Two birds with one stone. "It's a present for Todd Riker and his wife. They're expecting."

"You're doing all this work for a present." His expression baffled, Matthew took a swipe at the arm with the sandpaper. "You'll not make a penny from it?"

"They'll sit in this chair with twin babies." Leo took sandpaper to the other arm, demonstrating the smooth, even stroke. "Like this. What could be better?"

Matthew shrugged, but he began to sand with a softer touch.

Satisfied at this small start, Leo stood back and watched. The boy had shown up. He'd listened. Now he worked.

All was not lost with Matthew Troyer.

Jennie might have gone to the lake with Nathan Walker, but she had entrusted her son to Leo.

TWENTY-FIVE

JENNIE GATHERED HER BOX CLOSE TO HER CHEST and shoved with her shoulder through Amish Treasures' door. Her latest load should bring a good sum toward replacing her buggy and the other equipment destroyed by the tornado. She couldn't keep using Peter's. The tiny bell over the door tinkled its welcoming notes. The sun peeked in the windows, promising a hot mid-June day in the making. Inside, half a dozen shoppers were spread out, one looking at quilts, another holding a Plain doll in one hand, and another perusing the paperback books.

Mary Katherine looked up from the cash register, smiled, and waved, before going back to her customer, who appeared to have purchased one of Iris Beachy's crib quilts and several candles. The aroma of lilac floated in the air, mixed with a hodgepodge of other scents emanating from handmade sachets, potpourris, and dozens of candles. Nothing anxious or fearful about this place. In fact, it seemed light and sweet and full of happy thoughts.

Jennie slid the box onto the long counter that ran from the cash register to the door that led to a storage room. Mary Katherine bid her customer good-bye and hustled over to Jennie, her skirt rustling with purpose. "You made it." She peered into the box, her smile widening. "That scarf is a beautiful piece of work. The tablecloths too. These will fly off the shelves."

Jennie clasped her hands in front of her, willing them to stop shaking. "The barn is fixed. Everyone is healthy. I had time to make several pieces. Do you have me on the schedule to work today?"

"I didn't, but I do now." Mary Katherine clapped so hard a customer looked up from a set of wooden blocks. "Rachel has a sick child so she's not here today. I could use another set of hands."

"Celia is keeping an eye on the kinner. The boys are helping Peter combine oats, and the girls are digging up the first of the potatoes for the produce auction. I can stay."

Mary Katherine wiped her hands on her apron and moved toward the cash register. "You know how to use this thing?"

Jennie shook her head. "Never had cause to learn."

"A woman who runs a household like yours alone can learn anything." Mary Katherine proceeded to give her instructions and a demonstration. She was right. It seemed simple enough. "Next customer is yours. I'll get a card table and some chairs for the demo area. Did you bring your sewing supplies?"

Jennie wanted to hightail it out the door. Instead, she nodded. "But I don't have to start—"

"They'll love it. I'm telling you, they're nice folks for the most part. You have nothing to fear but fear itself."

That seemed unlikely. Jennie's palms were sweaty, and if the damp feel of her dress was any indication, so were her armpits. Her throat, on the other hand, was dry.

Mary Katherine disappeared into the back room, leaving Jennie with a lady who had a long white braid wrapped around her head, a woman in a pink sundress that looked like something a little girl would wear, and a mother pushing a double stroller containing a girl and a boy who were engaged in a push-pull tussle over a doll dressed in a cowgirl outfit.

Breathe. Breathe.

"How much is this?"

The woman who wore the pink sundress held up a faceless doll.

"The price should be on it." The words came out in a stutter. Jennie cleared her throat. "On the tag pinned to the back."

"If it had a tag, I wouldn't be asking." The customer flopped the doll back and forth in the air. "*Nada.* Nothing."

Nada? Jennie trotted from behind the counter and took the doll. The customer was correct. She picked up an exact replica. "Here it is. Twelve dollars."

"Good heavens. For a homemade doll with no face? That's crazy." Frowning, the woman deposited the doll back on the shelf. She huffed and moved on to a collection of carved wooden animals. Leo's work. Leo who had looked so disappointed at church on Sunday. The customer studied an owl, then placed it back in the basket. "They're toys, after all."

"Handmade toys. Handcrafted." Leo took time from his furniture business to make these carved animals. They were beautiful. A person wouldn't find anything as well done anywhere. Jennie swallowed the rest of her retort. If she'd learned anything from listening to Mary Katherine, it was that a person earned more sales with honey than vinegar. "A lot of work goes into each piece. The craftsman picks out the wood. He carves out the animal, he sands and smooths the wood, and then he stains it and varnishes it. It's careful work and each piece is unique. It's not like buying a toy at a discount department store."

"I'm looking for something different for my nephew. He has enough DVDs and toys that make noise." The woman picked up the horse. It was a stallion with one foreleg stretched above the other in a fierce pose. She cocked her head. "He might like this. He likes horses. My sister can't afford a real one."

"Nine dollars."

"I'll take it."

Relief billowed through Jennie. Her first sale. "Anything else?"

"That's it. Everything else is too rich for my taste."

"If you'll come over to the counter, I'll ring you up."

She turned to see Leo coming through the door.

She'd conquered her fear of talking to customers. Now she would have to conquer her other fear.

Leo.

Eating a big breakfast had been a bad idea. Leo shifted his box under his left arm and gritted his teeth against the heaving mess where his stomach should be. He'd hoped he would be there before Jennie. Matthew said she was planning to work today. Leo wanted to talk to Mary Katherine first. To tell her he wanted his share of the proceeds to go to buying a buggy for Jennie. He could sell enough furniture to English folks to recoup the cost if Mary Katherine would loan him the money up front. It didn't matter that she had chosen the lake and Nathan over him. Leo still had to help her.

Jennie was here. Now. Another opportunity from God? His chance to have what he'd been missing all these years? For now, he would tell Jennie about Matthew, who was back at the shop sanding at this very moment. She looked good. The pink in her cheeks no doubt was caused by nerves, but it added to her appeal. He wasn't a teenager, still he couldn't help his response to her. They had something to offer each other. Hope, comfort, the end to loneliness, but so much more. Mind, heart, and body. Heat barreled through him at that last thought. He stomped across the store toward her.

"You're here." She fumbled with a bag for a customer's purchase—one of Leo's carved animals. "Mary Kay didn't mention you were coming in. She'll be happy to see you."

And you? Thankful he hadn't voiced the question aloud, he settled his box on the counter. "I'll get tables and chairs from the storage area so we can set up."

"Mary Kay is back there. She said she would bring them out."

"I'll help her. It's a mess in the storage room. She'll have trouble getting them out of there."

Helping Mary Katherine would keep him from dealing with customers for a little longer. No matter how many days he worked in the store, he still didn't feel at home talking to people.

Jennie counted out change to the customer and closed the cash register drawer with a bang. "I think she's counting on us to do demos today."

He'd already done demos a few times and it helped pass the time. Working calmed him, even with people watching his every move. "It sounds like you plan to spend some time here."

"I told Mary Kay I would." She handed the bag to the customer and thanked her for her business. "If you help her with the tables, I'll deal with these customers."

"Right." He paused. He couldn't wait any longer to tell her. "Guess who showed up at my place."

Her face broke into a smile. "Matthew?"

"Jah."

"That is gut news."

"I put him right to work."

"Did he say much?"

"Nee. But neither do I."

She lifted a box from the floor, set it on the counter, and rummaged through it, producing a half-finished dresser scarf and a handful of brightly colored skeins of thread. "Did he seem like he had an interest in carpentry?"

Before he could respond, the door opened and the bell tinkled. Neil Reilly, the postal carrier, ambled into the store, a grin on his ruddy face. "Hey folks, got a registered letter here!" He held up the slim, white envelope. "Mary Kay needs to sign for it."

He didn't want his conversation with Jennie to end, but Leo had no choice. He strode to the back room and called Mary Katherine to join them. A few minutes later, she used a letter opener to slit the envelope and read the letter it held. Leo carried out folding tables and chairs in the meantime and Jennie began pricing her items.

"Well."

The single syllable told him little, but Mary Katherine's expression spoke volumes. Disappointment. Concern. And anger. An emotion he had never seen on the woman's face in all the time he'd known her. "Bad news, then?"

She whipped the paper back and forth, using it to fan her face. "Not for Lazarus Dudley."

Jennie gave up on her task and crowded to her friend. "What does Lazarus want now?"

"Apparently, he finally tracked down Seamus. Seamus is

exercising the thirty-day clause in our contract." She snapped the letter with her fingers. "The one that says either party can decide to end the lease with thirty days' notice."

"Why would you agree to that with what was needed to turn this from a butcher store into a tourist shop?" Leo didn't consider himself a businessman. He was a carpenter. One who barely made a living. Who was he to question? "It just seems shortsighted is all."

"He insisted and we didn't know if we would be successful. We didn't want to lock into a year lease and then find we couldn't stay afloat." Mary Katherine sighed. "We lacked faith. We were shortsighted. All of the above."

"Why would Seamus do this?" Jennie put an arm around her friend. "He wanted out of the business. Is retirement not working out for him?"

"Nee, it's working out well, it seems. He's selling the whole building to Lazarus. Instead of leasing the space. He's getting out of the rental business."

Jennie plopped into a chair. Mary Katherine did the same.

"How long do we have?" Leo picked up a piece of wood from his table and let his fingers rub the rough edges. Jennie needed this. He wanted to replace that buggy for her. He needed this. "Is there anything we can do to stop it?"

"I'll talk to Freeman about consulting a lawyer." Mary Katherine fanned herself with the letter. "He and the others will want to decide the best course of action. They may feel it's best to let the store go rather than getting into legal wrangling with Englischers."

"Could we match Lazarus's offer for the building?" Jennie's expression as she asked the question said she already knew the answer. "I know. We can barely afford the lease payments. If only we had more time to build up the business."

"When one door closes, another opens." Mary Katherine dropped the letter. "In the meantime, we still have customers."

She bustled over to the quilt section and asked an elderly shopper carrying a huge bag if she'd like to stow it behind the counter while she shopped.

Jennie stood and went to the window, her back to them. Leo followed. "Look at it this way, at least we won't have to make change and answer questions about our clothes."

She nodded, but her eyes were wet. She sniffed. "We can't just give up."

"Mary Kay's right. We have to talk to Freeman and the others."

Knowing Freeman's aversion to wrangling with outsiders, Leo could guess the outcome of that conversation.

A customer barged through the door with a bang. "Quilts? You have quilts?"

Not for long. Soon they would be replaced with a barista and her choice of cappuccino or espresso.

TWENTY-SIX

BEST-LAID PLANS. LEO CHEWED ON THE PROBLEM
as he drove into Jamesport with Matthew to deliver Todd's rocking
chair. He wanted to get the chair done and delivered so he could get to
the store. They only had a few weeks left before it reverted to Seamus
and Lazarus got his hands on it. In the meantime Leo would come up
with another plan to buy Jennie's buggy.

Matthew had been mostly silent on the trip, as he was at the shop.
Silent, but not sullen. It worked for Leo. He needed the time to plan.
His apprentice worked hard and didn't complain. Whatever burr he
had under his saddle had been absent in the days since he'd started
coming to Leo's shop. The opportunity to find out what that burr was
had not presented itself, which was fine with Leo too. Talking about
feelings wasn't high on his list, either.

The delivery was a surprise. It might have been easier for Todd to
pick up the chair in his SUV, but a gift should be delivered. Todd went
home every day for lunch. If Leo had timed it right, both Todd and
Samantha—whom Todd called Sam—would be there. Without a word
Matthew hopped from the wagon and helped Leo lift the double rocker,

wrapped in some old blankets to protect it, from the back. He lifted the chair with an ease that made Leo feel old.

He studied Todd's house. The chair suited it, with its white wood frame, green shutters, and graceful wraparound porch. Baskets of potted begonias hung all along the front, splashes of pink, purple, and red against the white. Sunflowers spread in haphazard abundance in flowerbeds that hugged the foundation, like a welcoming committee that leaned toward its visitors.

"They'll like it."

Matthew's words surprised Leo. Had he read something in his boss's face? "I hope they do."

"What's not to like?"

The boy was observant. He saw Leo's hesitation and his desire for affirmation that he did good work. He had more depth than Leo would've credited him with. They settled the chair on the porch and Leo knocked.

A few seconds later, the door swung open and Samantha gazed up at him. Her round face lit up with a smile. "You're here." She threw her waist-length blonde hair behind her shoulder and held out her arms as if to give him a hug. He had no idea what to do. She hugged him anyway. "It's good to see you. You've made yourself scarce lately."

She let go and offered Matthew the same all-encompassing, *I-love-the-world* smile. "And who is this?"

Leo made the introductions. "We brought the chair."

She squealed and clapped. "I knew it. When Todd told me, I didn't think I could wait to see it. I'm so excited. It's going to be perfect for the nursery. You have to see it."

She threw back the door and held it with one hand, arm stretched, to give them room to pass by her in the narrow alcove that led to the living room. Her belly protruded in a too-tight white T-shirt and blue knit shorts that revealed long, slim legs. It was the fashion, it seemed, for English ladies to wear tight clothes when they were expecting. Not like it used to be when they mostly wore tentlike dresses that made a man wonder if they were fat or expecting.

They hustled the chair into the living room. She followed and then padded around them in flip-flops that smacked against the hardwood floor. "This way, this way. Todd, they're here. The chair's here."

What would it be like to be married to someone so naively innocent at twenty-five or twenty-six years old? She was a kindergarten teacher, and Leo could imagine her sitting on the floor, legs crisscrossed, looking at picture books with the same sense of wonder and awe as her students.

Todd clomped into the room, a napkin in one hand and a glass of iced tea in the other. "Do you need help?" He wiped his chin. "You caught me in midbite."

"We've got it."

"Sam's been chomping at the bit to see it. She wanted to come out to your shop, but I refused to let her spoil the surprise of seeing it for the first time." He set the glass and napkin on the coffee table. "Come on. Might as well settle it in the spot she's been saving for it."

They wrestled the chair down another hallway and through a narrow doorway. It just fit. Todd and Samantha had decorated the room in a soft shade of evergreen with trim that featured lions, tigers, elephants, and giraffes along the top of the walls. Curtains in a darker evergreen covered two tall windows. A pair of white bassinets sat side by side. Beyond them stood one crib, already complete with matching bedding in the jungle theme. A changing table and long dresser crowded the other wall.

"When are the babies coming?"

"In about six weeks." Todd chuckled. Samantha pretended to pummel his arm. "Sam's a little anxious as you can see."

"We're having girls. Two girls. We've seen them twice in sonograms." She picked up a frame from the dresser and flashed it at them. It held a gray photo of what looked like blobs to Leo. "See. Aren't they gorgeous? That's Jessica and Janine. Or Ashley and Annie. Or—"

"Suffice it to say, we haven't come to a meeting of the minds on names yet." Todd put his arm around his wife and squeezed, his smile as wide as hers. He tugged the frame from her hands and settled it back on the dresser. "We have plenty of time, God willing. They still need to bake a little more."

"Yah, we don't want them coming out before they're fully baked."

Baked? Formed? "Is that a likelihood?"

"With twins, it happens more than we would like." The look of sheer, unadorned, naked love on Todd's face as he hugged his wife to him embarrassed—and shamed—Leo. Had he ever loved someone that much? Todd touched one of the bassinets with his free hand. "Sam is to stay home and take it easy from now on. Not quite bed rest, but no heavy lifting, no running around, no nothing."

Samantha giggled. "And Todd is making sure I follow all the rules. He's cooking and washing dishes and he even ironed his own church pants the other day."

She planted a big, smacking kiss on her husband's cheek. Todd ducked his head. His big ears, like saucers, turned red. "Hey, Leo and Matthew don't want to see any PDA."

"This isn't the public, it's our nursery for our babies." She said it with such glee. They'd been married three years and they still acted like newlyweds. "Okay, enough stalling. Unveil it."

Glad to be done with the subject of kissing, Leo obliged. He slipped the tattered quilt from his creation. Samantha gasped. Her hand went to her mouth and then took Todd's. The vet shook his head. He touched the back, then the arm. "It's beautiful. Really beautiful. You've outdone yourself."

Leo didn't know about that. It was a piece of furniture after all. But somehow, this piece spoke to him as only a few others did. He'd spent extra time shaping and sculpting the seats for comfort and the arms and back slats. The finish shone in the sun that filtered through the curtains. The walnut grain was warm and homey. He'd spent four days sanding the entire chair, sanding until his arms, shoulders, and back ached. He had thought of nothing else as he worked, only making the wood curve and connect and become something that would be handed down from one generation to the next. It would be there at night when a baby had colic or whooping cough. It would be there through night terrors and the grumpy terrible twos. It would be there for the twins and God willing, the babies who came after them.

"I'm glad it pleases you."

"I have to sit in it." Samantha let go of Todd's hand. She slipped into the first seat. "Come on, Todd, try it out."

Todd eased in next to her. Samantha's eyes filled with tears. Todd's hand went to her burgeoning belly. They leaned close to each other, their expressions filled with such a hope and such a vision that Leo had to look away. His friends shared a private moment in which he had only a passing hand. He and Matthew built the chair, but Todd and Samantha made it part of their home, part of their life, and part of their unborn babies' lives. He wouldn't know how to go about such a thing. He made furniture, not family.

Todd sniffed and wiped at his nose with his shirtsleeve. "Thanks, man, thanks."

"It's just a rocking chair." Matthew spoke for the first time. His expression perplexed, he shifted from one foot to the other. He crossed his arms as if he didn't quite know what to do with them. "He's made about fifty of them."

"Not for us, he hasn't." Samantha snuggled closer to Todd. They began to rock, their feet pushing off the floor in unison. "We've waited a long time for this. I started to wonder." She gulped and hid her face in her husband's shoulder.

"No more wondering." Todd smiled. "We've seen our girls. They're real and soon they'll be here."

"Why only one crib?" Leo liked the furniture they'd chosen. It was manufactured, not handcrafted, but a solid walnut all the same. It matched the rocking chair, if that were important to them. "For twins."

"At first they'll be so small they can sleep together." Todd's hand rested on Samantha's belly again. Leo let his gaze wander to the windows, covered with curtains that surely Samantha had made, with their giraffes, lions, and tigers parading across the material. A husband and wife were never closer than when creating another human life. Todd's happiness grew in proportion to his wife's. "They're used to being close to each other. They'll comfort each other."

"We have the second crib—my parents bought them both," Samantha added. "We'll put it up when they're bigger. Both of them turn into toddler beds so we're set."

"All we need are the babies."

"Fifty-six days." She grinned at Todd. "But who's counting?"

"We should go." Leo squeezed past Matthew, headed for the door. "Todd needs to get back to work. We have orders to complete too."

"No, no, let me feed you first." Samantha hoisted herself from the chair, one hand on her hip. Todd propelled her from behind. "Meatloaf sandwiches."

"We have to get back." Leo begrudged Todd none of his happiness. He wished them only the best. Somehow, though, he couldn't be in the same room with it. Not now. He gritted his teeth against a feeling of unbearable loneliness that left his heart cavernous in its emptiness. "I have an order for a dresser that has to be done by next week."

"I'll pack the sandwiches, and you can take them with you." Samantha plodded past him. "No arguments. Matthew is too skinny, and your pants look like they might fall down any minute."

She sounded like his mother.

Before she died. He breathed. Matthew had hunger written all over his face in big block letters. "Meatloaf sounds good."

So did life in a white frame house with green shutters and a nursery filled with a double rocking chair, lions, tigers, elephants, giraffes, and the love between a husband and wife.

Leo was hungry too, but not for meatloaf.

Todd followed them to the door. He pulled a checkbook from his hip pocket. "Let me pay you for this. It's beautiful and it's obvious how much work you put into it."

"It's a gift."

Todd smacked the checkbook against his leg. "You're something else. But I was telling my sister about it and she wants one and so does my brother-in-law's wife. You need to get cracking because I know half a dozen people who are waiting in line for high quality stuff like this." He chucked Matthew on the shoulder. "It's a good thing you've got help. You're gonna need it."

Samantha loaded Matthew down with a brown paper sack full

of sandwiches, chips, and cookies. Leo shoved his hat down on his head and strode to the buggy. Physical nourishment was good, but he needed something else, something far more filling. He would do what he needed to do to help Jennie. And at the same time, he would learn to help himself.

TWENTY-SEVEN

THE HOUSE SMELLED OF ROASTED CHICKEN, CHOCO-late cake, and childhood memories. Jennie shut the front door behind her and took a deep breath, inhaling the scent of happy days gone by. They'd opted to have her mother's seventieth birthday dinner in the big house where Peter now lived with his wife, Kate, and five children. The dawdy haus was too small for all the children and grandchildren. Jennie paused, letting her ears adjust to the noise made by dozens of children chattering and running through the house. They were not only cousins, but friends who played together every chance they could. Jennie loved the sound.

She loved the sight of her mother seated in a recliner, her skinny frame dwarfed by its navy-blue padding. Daed sat ramrod straight in the hickory chair across from her, his gnarled fingers wrapped around his cane. His silver beard reached almost to his thin waist. Mudder had laid a lap quilt over her knees as if she were cold on this broiling-hot July day. Daed peered at her as if waiting for the answer to a question asked minutes earlier.

They looked smaller and more fragile than they had even on Sunday. How was that possible? An errant memory scampered through her mind. Mudder at the stove, stirring a pot of beans, steam rising in the cold December air. Daed sat at the table, reading spectacles on top of his head, a perplexed look on his grizzled face. He asked Mudder where his glasses were. She pretended not to know. Then she skipped by, snatched them from his head, and perched the thick, black frames on her own nose. How they'd laughed.

Jennie had believed all parents laughed like that. All parents played practical jokes on each other. All parents kissed by the fireplace after dark when they thought the children were asleep. She loved their give and take. She thought all couples had that. Until Atlee. She wanted it. Now, after all these years, she still wanted it.

Her throat tight, she placed the brown paper-wrapped box that held a new shawl she'd knitted and a lavender-scented candle Celia had made on the table next to a stack of presents left by her sisters-in-law. "We're here. How are you two?"

"Peachy, Dochder." Mudder's face lit up with a smile, but her unseeing gaze landed somewhere near Elizabeth, who scooted across the room with a crow of delight and threw herself into her grandmother's lap. Mudder patted the girl's back, her smile broadening. "This would be Francis, right?"

"Nee, nee, it's me, Groossmammi. It's Elizabeth." The girl shook her finger at Mudder and climbed onto her lap. "Don't you know me?"

"Of course, I do." Mudder giggled, sounding just like Elizabeth. "I'm only teasing. You smell like little girl, not little boy. What did you bring me for my birthday? A kitten? A puppy? No, I know, two chickens and a partridge in a pear tree."

"Nee, Celia says I can't put animals in boxes and wrap them. I don't know why. I would poke holes in the box. I'm smart." Elizabeth giggled so hard her kapp flopped back over her shoulders. Francis tried to climb onto Mudder's lap, but his big sister cordoned off the open space with her chubby arm, obviously not wanting to share. "Besides, it's a surprise. You open after supper. With cake."

"Anyhow, it's not too exciting." Micah leaned against his grandfather's chair, his tone disdainful. "Mudder made it and it's too hot to wear it."

"Micah! Presents are surprises." Celia chased over him, pretending to try to cover his mouth with her hand. "Besides, mine smells good and Groossmammi will like it."

"The worse my eyes get, the better my honker smells." Mudder tickled Elizabeth, who writhed and shrieked. She gathered up Francis and pulled him onto her lap despite Elizabeth's best efforts to keep him out. She hugged both of them with an abandon that made Jennie feel stingy with her own displays of affection. Mudder leaned back and chortled. "I love smelly things. And cake."

"A little sliver for you, Mudder." Jennie hated to be the spoilsport on her mother's birthday. "Did you take your insulin?"

"I did. I'm set. And I'll have a chunk of birthday cake if I want." Mudder flapped both hands as if sweeping away any objections. The doctors diagnosed the diabetes when Jennie was sixteen. Mudder did a good job of controlling it. Yet it had taken her sight and given her pain in her feet and hands. She wasn't one to complain, though. "I might even have ice cream this once."

"Nee, no ice cream."

Daed dealt with the episodes when she had too much insulin. Or not enough. He would have the final word.

"Go on, girls, go help Kate put supper on the table. The sooner we eat, the sooner your groossmammi can open the presents and the sooner we eat cake." Jennie shooed them from the room. Knowing

Peter, there would be homemade ice cream as well. She could use the sugar. She sank onto a fabric-covered stool next to her mother's chair. It felt good to sit down. It felt good to inhale her mother's scent of vanilla and soap. "Boys, make yourselves useful. See if Peter needs any help finishing chores before we eat."

Elizabeth, who would insist on being in the center of the preparations, skipped after Celia and Cynthia. Francis, to Jennie's surprise, slid from her mother's lap and trotted after his brothers, leaving her with a few unusual moments alone with her parents. She should help in the kitchen. Her legs protested. So did her arms. She wanted to simply sit and enjoy this moment. She couldn't remember the last time she was alone with Mudder and Daed. With six older brothers, it was a tiny miracle.

"The little one still doesn't talk?" Daed broke the silence. "He's four now, going on five, isn't he?"

"He can talk. He just doesn't want to." The image of Leo and Francis huddled together, Leo comforting the little boy, leaped into the forefront of her mind. "It's too much effort to get a word in edgewise."

"He'll talk when he's ready."

"It won't be around the big bunch here today." Mudder chuckled. "Do you think all sixty of us will fit around the table?"

"Peter brought in the picnic tables." Daed's voice held approval at his son's resourcefulness. "The kinner can sit outside. The rest of us will scoot together. It's a good thing we like each other."

They did. Most of the time. Jennie liked her big brothers. But they were brothers. Growing up, she'd longed for a sister to whom she could unburden her heart, seek advice, and share secrets. Boys weren't good for that. They were good for teasing their little sister, for tickling her until she nearly wet her pants laughing. They were good for hiding her dolls and putting salt in her tea. They were good for carrying her over their shoulders like a ten-pound sack of potatoes.

Then they'd grown up, married, and got on with their lives. They'd offered their help over the years in practical ways—fixing a fence, rebuilding the chicken coop, sharing their harvest of sweet potatoes or rhubarb when they could. They were a practical lot, who like most men, would rather die than tell her how they felt. Instead, they showed it when they could. But they weren't friends, and neither were their wives. Now that she was older Jennie had Mary Katherine, Laura, and Bess. She was blessed. "I should help Kate with supper."

"Your sisters-in-law are in there. The kitchen is full to the rafters. Stay. Talk to us." His expression somber, Daed let his cane rest against his leg while he rubbed his knotted fingers together. "You've not had an easy row to hoe. We know that."

The words were more than he had expressed to her on this subject in all the years since she married Atlee. Something told her more would come. They'd heard something. Someone had said something. Mudder took Jennie's hand. Her skin felt like crepe paper, thin and wrinkled. "We should have said more, did more, before."

"It wasn't our place to interfere." Daed shook his head. His beard bobbed. "The business between a mann and his fraa is private."

"It was fine. Everything was fine." She smoothed her hand over Mother's. Her bones were tiny, like a newborn kitten's. "I did the best I could and so did you."

"Where's Matthew?" Daed's tone reminded her of when he had to punish one of the boys. He didn't relish the idea, but he did what he felt a father should do. "I didn't see him in that mess of kinner that rolled through the door."

"He didn't come."

"Where is he?"

How could Jennie explain the inexplicable? She no longer had control over her oldest son. Another who went against the grain just as his father had. Plain men were quiet, peaceful, fair. They could be stern but not mean. Plain boys Matthew's age did what they were told. They saved their running around for rumspringa. But not her son. She'd failed in her marriage, and now with Matthew. She lifted her chin, despite the urge to hide her shame. "He left the house without telling me."

Freeman would say apples with bad spots grew on every tree. Then he would say they had to be made into pie or thrown out.

"You don't know where he is?" Surprise married with dismay in her father's voice. "How does that happen?"

Jennie's rumspringa had been tame. But six older brothers surely meant a time or two—or more—when her parents had wondered where they were and what mischief they were getting into, even before rumspringa began. "It's not as if I can drag him to the wood-shed for disobeying. He's a good four inches taller and fifteen pounds heavier than me."

Excuses. It sounded like excuses offered in a whiny voice.

"Freeman stopped by." Daed's voice deepened the way it always did when a topic pained him. "He had some concerns."

Someone had carried tales about Matthew to the bishop. Surely not Leo. He had his own issues with the Gmay. "About Matthew?"

"About him and about you."

Not only Matthew. "Why didn't he talk to me?"

"You're our dochder, our only dochder. And you have no mann." Daed cleared his throat. His face turned red. He plucked at his beard.

"He felt it would be more suitable, I reckon. It wasn't a conversation he would have with a woman, it seems."

"Which is the problem." Mudder sighed. "It's not your fault, but you must take great care."

Jennie had been on her own for over four years. In her community none of that would matter. She understood that. She'd tried to be careful, to follow all the rules. She'd done her best. "I haven't done anything wrong."

"They're watching." Daed's eyes narrowed behind his thick black-rimmed glasses. "You're old enough and wise enough to know that."

"Freeman is watching?"

"Everyone is watching. Your bruders. Peter came to your father the other day, so did Luke." Mudder's tone was softer. "You know how it is. They mean well. They want what is best for you and for Matthew."

"What am I supposed to have done?"

Daed wiped at his face with a white handkerchief as big as his head. "A conversation was had at the lake, it seems."

The talk with Nathan. She had been careful, but not careful enough. That was the problem. People watched and made assumptions. "I tried to discourage him. Peter and the others couldn't hear the conversation so they don't know that. He made assumptions."

"I would never be ashamed of you, child. You can't imagine how blessed I felt the day you were born. I loved my boys, but a mudder likes to have a dochder too."

"You liked having someone to help with the cooking, cleaning, and gardening." Jennie made her voice playful to hide the tears that welled at her mother's words. "Having six boys was a lot of work, for sure."

"Now you're all grown up, but I still pray for you daily in this widowed state of yours." Mudder's voice trembled. "It can't be easy and I've been blessed to not know. My mann is still here."

"Fraa, don't get all weepy on us." Daed's harrumph was half-hearted. He wiped his face again. "The point is this man, Nathan, is a good fellow. Everyone says so. But he's Mennischt. Take care that you don't stumble in his direction."

"I haven't stumbled in any direction."

If Daed's face turned any redder, his voice any gruffer, he'd faint. "We want happiness for you, don't we, fraa?"

"We do." Mudder's voice broke.

Daed raised his head. His gaze met Jennie's. She saw there the depth of his concern. As much as this conversation pained him, he was willing to have it for her sake. It made her heart hurt. Her parents wanted for her what they had. She couldn't aspire to fifty years of wedded happiness. That had not been her lot. But to ask for a few years—just a few—surely, that wasn't too much. A second chance for however many years God allotted. She saw a wisp of something with Nathan, a chance at something. She stood on a precipice, Nathan below. He had his arms lifted halfway. The promise in his eyes said he would catch her if she chose to jump.

But first he had to jump off his own precipice. He had to choose her way of life. She would never leave it. Never. Did she feel something for Nathan when he looked at her with those blue eyes that held a hint of lilac? The feelings that swirled hinted at something. At the possibility. Not the torrent of emotion that had engulfed her when Atlee hugged her to his broad chest and kissed her so hard her legs gave way beneath her. She couldn't trust those powerful emotions. They had served as camouflage that allowed pain and shame into her life. They had caused her to make mistakes. Someone like Nathan with the gentle foray into simpler, softer emotion that he represented. He would be a safe choice.

She didn't want breathless love that carried her away in its undertow. She couldn't afford that mistake again. "How did you know Mudder was the one?"

They both laughed, a sound that took her right back to the supper table, every night. He delighted in making Mudder laugh with silly jokes. She made him laugh with stories of what the babies had done in his absence. They bickered some, but they laughed more.

"I thought your daed was silly."

"I thought your mudder was snooty."

Daed stared at Mudder as if back at a singing. She could no longer see him at even the short distance between the recliner and the chair, but her expression revealed that she too meandered down that path where he had been a strapping twenty-year-old with an open-seater and a penchant for driving too fast on backcountry roads. Neither seemed to breathe or move for several seconds.

Jennie looked from one to the other, then back. Feelings smoldered there. After fifty years? At seventy and seventy-one? She shook her head, trying to shed the thought. Her parents had been in love like she loved Atlee once. And still were. "What happened?"

Mudder answered first. "He told me a joke one night after a singing."

"And it was funny?"

"Nee. But he tried so hard that it made me giggle." Mudder smiled. "After fifty years he still makes me laugh. If you have that in a marriage, you're halfway there."

"I was funny," Daed protested. "I told you she was snooty."

They both laughed as if they were the only ones in the room.

Jennie tried to remember if Atlee made her laugh. Surely at the beginning. No memory popped up. Not a single one. She sometimes smiled when he sang as he worked. He sounded like an unhappy dog that had his paw stuck in a barbed-wire fence.

"Supper's ready!" Kate called from the kitchen. "Call the menfolk."

Daed rose. He wielded his cane with the ease of a man who'd come to terms with his infirmities. He stopped by the chair and held out his hand. Mudder laid her lap quilt over the chair arm, took his hand, and he tugged her to her feet. They paused as if steadying themselves for a long trek. With care, her hand went to his forearm and he started forward, leading her.

"Come along, child. It's time to eat." Mudder held out her free hand. "I'll help you up."

Jennie took her hand. The blind leading the blind.

TWENTY-EIGHT

THUNDER. HAMMERING. POUNDING. NEE. JENNIE swam up through a lake of heavy, dark dreams of a baby crying and a man's deep, angry voice. Pounding. Someone pounded. A voice shouted. She sat up, pillow wrapped in her arms like a buoy. The door. Someone was at the door downstairs. Shivering despite the dank July night air, she listened to her own heart pound and breathed. Only darkness seeped through the window across the room. Nighttime. No good came of a nighttime visit. She slipped from the bed on weak legs. More pounding.

A man's voice. She couldn't make out the words, but the tone demanded immediate attention.

"Stop, stop." Silly to think the visitor could hear her. Whoever it was would wake the children. Not a problem with the older ones, but Francis had a penchant for waking and staying awake, playing with his wooden animals until light. She fought with her dress, first her head stuck, then her elbow. She wound her hair into a ragged knot and stuck it in her kapp as she raced down the stairs on bare feet. "Coming. I'm coming."

At the door she stopped and drew a long breath. Bracing herself, she opened the door. A Daviess County sheriff's deputy stood on the porch, Matthew next to him. She closed her eyes and opened them. The image did not disappear. It wasn't a dream. "Why didn't you come on in?"

"He wouldn't let me." Matthew's hangdog look matched his tone. "He said people have been shot for less than entering a farmer's house in the middle of the night."

"You're Matthew's mother?" The deputy had a deep voice that matched his solemn air.

She nodded, her throat tight with dread.

"We need to talk." The man removed his hat and introduced himself as Deputy Seth McKenzie as he entered the living room. He smelled of spicy men's cologne. He was a beanpole with a deep sunburn, crow's feet around his blue eyes, thinning white-blond hair, and a beak nose that reminded her of a rooster. "I'm sorry for intruding in the middle of the night, but we have a situation that needs to be addressed."

Matthew was now a situation that needed to be addressed in the English world. The Gmay would not be happy. Freeman would not be happy. No one would be happy. Jennie nodded toward the chairs by the empty fireplace. "Have a seat then."

He was so tall his knees seemed to touch his chin in a chair too small for him. "Is your husband here?"

"My husband passed."

A look of concern mixed with outright pity flittered across the deputy's face before he shuttered it behind a neutral gaze. "Fine, then we'll get down to business. Dispatch got a call from Delbert Wilkins about a bunch of kids overrunning one of his pastures." Deputy McKenzie tugged a tiny notebook from his front pocket, flipped it open, and stared at squiggles that might pass for cursive writing in some corner of the world. "He heard a motor backfire and loud music playing at eleven o'clock at night. He got his shotgun, saddled up a horse, and went to take a look. Called dispatch when he saw a kegger happening right under his nose. Smart man, he didn't let them know he'd seen them. 'Course they all scattered when they saw us coming. Your guy didn't move fast enough. I grabbed him."

Jennie stared at her son. He studied his boots as if he'd never seen them before. His broad shoulders hunched. His mouth, so like his father's, turned down in a half sneer, half frown. A scarlet blush spread across his face under his tan. She waited, hoping he would offer some explanation that would help her make sense of this strange behavior.

Nothing.

"Suh, what do you have to say for yourself? Were you out there drinking?"

His head sank some more.

"Most of the kids out there know to drop the cup and run like crazy." The deputy turned his stern glance to Matthew. "Yours just stood there like a moron, a red cup full of beer in his hand."

"I'm not a moron." Matthew's head snapped up. His scowl deepened. "And I wasn't drinking. I just had the cup in my hand."

"I put him through a field-sobriety test and he passed." Deputy McKenzie's voice was stern. "I'm inclined to believe him. Which is why he's here and not in jail with half a dozen of his buddies."

"They're not my—"

"Matthew, hush. The deputy is giving you a break." If he went to jail for drinking, he might never recover in the eyes of the Gmay. He would be forgiven for his mistake, but folks would remember.

Freeman would always be watching, even more than he did now. "Why were you there?"

"I was just having fun, you know, talking, listening to music." His gaze sideswiped the deputy, freewheeled past Jennie, and landed on the empty rocking chair beyond her. "There was no harm in it."

"You were on private property." Deputy McKenzie shook his head. "You were with a bunch of minors who were drinking. You were in possession of alcohol."

The scarlet blush spread down Matthew's neck in ugly blotches. "I like them. I like . . . the girls."

"You're fourteen years old–"

"Almost fifteen."

"Too young for girls. For alcohol. To be running around with Englischers. That's for your rumspringa. You're way ahead of yourself."

Silence reigned for a few seconds. Jennie didn't know where to begin. She didn't understand. Plain boys didn't do this. Not Mary Katherine's children. Not Laura's children or grandchildren. Not her own brothers growing up. They waited until they were sixteen and the time was right to explore life outside the rigid rules of the Gmay. Parents expected it. They accepted it, because they believed God would guide their children back to their families and to faith.

Freeman would say no community was without its trouble-makers. Her oldest son had meandered–no raced–off the path. Where had she gone wrong? What had she done? Or not done?

Gott, save him. Please save him.

For the first time in four years, supplication came easy. Her own trials forgotten, she cried out in silence. *Gott, forgive my absence. Forgive my stiff neck. Save him. Show me what to do to help him.*

"Say it." Matthew shot from his chair, hands clenched in fists, his voice raised. "Say it, go on, you know you want to."

"Say what?" She worked to keep her voice soft, gentle, a mother's voice. "What ails you?"

"I'm like him, aren't I? You look at me and you think I'm like him."

"Sit down." Deputy McKenzie stood. He towered over Matthew, who was by no means short. He had six inches and fifty pounds on the boy. "Show some respect to your mother, or I will cart you right down to the jail and throw you in with your buddies."

Matthew subsided.

"I don't know what you mean." Jennie struggled for words to assuage a hurt that so obviously existed but was beyond her feeble means of comprehension. She tried never to show her concern over the way Matthew sometimes acted like his father. "I think you're a confused boy who needs to talk to a man about some things. I'm sorry your daed's not here to help you with these things that I'm not capable of understanding."

"No, you're not." He spat out the words. "You're glad he's gone. So am I."

She couldn't, shouldn't lie. "It wasn't easy with your daed. I'm sorry."

"You did what a fraa does." He said the words grudgingly. He was old enough to know his words were true. She couldn't intervene, as much as she'd wanted to protect him. Even if Atlee hadn't been bigger, stronger, and angrier. Always angrier. "That's why you were glad when he was gone."

How could a boy so young see so much? Did all her kinner see and know? "I wanted . . . peace, but not like that. Not that way."

"Obviously there are family matters that need to be worked out here." Deputy McKenzie sank back into the chair. He slapped his notebook closed. "Here's the deal. Delbert said he wouldn't press trespassing charges if it didn't happen again."

"We weren't doing nothing wrong."

Matthew knew it was wrong. He felt guilty and ashamed. In his heart, he knew it was wrong. Everything about the set of his shoulders and the fisting of his hands said so.

Deputy McKenzie stood and turned to Jennie. "I'm counting on you, ma'am, to talk some sense into this boy and to keep an eye on him. He's getting a second chance here. He won't get another one."

"I understand." She swallowed a bitter lump of anxiety and rose to follow him to the door. "I'll deal with it."

His hand on the knob, Deputy McKenzie looked back at Matthew, who sat, elbows on his knees, head down, staring at the floor. "Your son has some anger-management issues, ma'am. It's better to address them now rather than later when they get out of hand."

She thought she had with Leo and the carpentry apprenticeship. "I'm trying. We're trying."

"The fact that you recognize the problem is half the battle. I know you folks keep to yourself, but you might consider taking him to a specialist. Someone he can talk to."

"Mostly, we talk among ourselves and that works for us."

"Sorry for your troubles, ma'am." He tipped his hat, his mournful smile reflecting his sincerity. "If there's anything I can do to help, you know where to find me."

The smile also said he knew she would never take him up on the offer. Plain folks solved their own problems—especially when it came to their children. She watched him drive away, took a long breath of night air, and went back inside. Matthew was halfway up the stairs. She called out to him. He looked back and kept climbing.

"I have to talk to Freeman about this. You know I do."

He stopped, his shoulders hunched. "I don't care."

"You do care. You don't like acting this way. You're a good boy with a good heart."

He whirled and sat on the steps.

"How do you know? Most of the time I act like a snot."

"You do." She had to concede the truth. "But you work hard for your onkels. You do your chores. You pick up Francis when he falls down. You found Indigo for Elizabeth when the kitten was lost. You wouldn't do those things if you were a mean boy."

"I feel mean."

"Maybe it's because you don't understand some of things you saw, the things that were done to you." She went to the bottom of the stairs and put her hand on the banister. "I don't understand either and I'm a lot older than you are."

"A while back me and Leo took a rocking chair to the vet's house." He stuck his elbows on his knees and rested his chin on his hands. He chewed on his lower lip for a second, his brow furrowed. He looked so like his father. "It was a present because she's expecting."

"Jah?" He was telling her something important to him. Jennie tried to understand the significance. "Leo is generous."

"They looked really happy about it."

"That's gut."

He raised his head. He fiddled with his hair. "They are happy."

"Most married couples are. They have bumps in the road and they bicker, but mostly they are happy."

"Not you and Daed."

"Nee." She couldn't lie to him. He was old enough to remember. What he remembered hurt him. He had invisible scars just as she did. Those scars made him act up. He couldn't be faulted for that. Nor could he be allowed to stray down this path. "I'm sorry you had to see the things you saw. I'm sorry he treated you the way he did. You can be better than him. You can do better."

"You couldn't stop him."

"Nee."

"I should've done something."

"You couldn't." The image of his small face, streaked with tears, hiding behind his bed all those years ago, flashed in front of her. "You were too small. You were only ten years old."

"Too weak."

"Nee. You were only a boy and he was your daed."

He stared down at her, his face full of pain that flowed from him into her. "Why didn't you leave him?"

"It's not our way." The words sounded weak in her own ears. A mother should protect her children from this kind of hurt. She should have done more. "I took vows."

"Do you think you'll do it again?"

"It's hard for me to imagine, hard for me to trust, but I want to."

"It doesn't bother you when Nathan comes around, sniffing at your heels, or Leo?"

The sarcasm made Jennie count to ten, slowly. "It's scary, to be truthful."

"How can you trust anyone?"

"I'm trying to trust Gott."

"I'm never getting married." He whirled and ran up the rest of the stairs, pounding out his frustration and his anger in the thud of his boots against the wood. "Never."

"You'll get over it in time," she called after him, more hopeful than certain.

Like she had?

TWENTY-NINE

CELIA'S BELLOW WAFTED THROUGH THE OPEN WIN-
dows. Jennie ignored it as she tied her bonnet strings. She'd sent
her oldest daughter to bring the buggy they'd borrowed from Peter
around to the house so they could load up the kinner and head to the
school fund-raiser auction. She wasn't in a hurry and there was no
need to yell. She straightened the bonnet and picked up her canvas
bag from the kitchen table. They couldn't afford to buy anything at
the fund-raiser, but it was the social event of the summer. People,
especially women, went to visit with friends, to see who bought what,
and to eat homemade ice cream and funnel cakes. The kinner loved
to attend.

The thought lifted her spirits despite the gloom that descended
every time she thought of the scene with Deputy McKenzie and
Matthew the previous night. Matthew's angry, belligerent face. The
deputy's urgent warning: *"I don't want to come out to tell you he's in jail
or worse."*

Matthew would not go to the auction. He would stay here and do
chores. They had agreed to that. He would not leave. He had given
her his word.

Could his word be trusted?

She had to talk to Leo. So far, his apprenticeship had not borne the fruit for which she had hoped. Matthew sought something she couldn't help him find. Her own experience with love had caused her eldest son to have a troubled spirit in need of healing as much as her own. Regret ached in her throat. Tears burned eyes red from lack of sleep. *Gott, help me.*

Maybe Leo could help her talk to Freeman. He had experience with this. She didn't. Freeman would be just. *Gott, please let him understand.*

She paused, surprised at her own prayers. She had lost her way after Atlee's death. Perhaps the fog over the road ahead had begun to clear.

Gott?

"Mudder, Mudder!" Her face flushed, Celia skidded to a stop in the doorway, Elizabeth and Francis behind her like little shadows. "Didn't you hear me yelling? Come on, come look, come look!"

"Lookie, lookie," Elizabeth added in a singsong voice. "Come, come."

Francis grinned and said nothing.

"There's no need to yell." Weary to the marrow in her bones, Jennie trudged toward the door. "I'm not in a big hurry. The auction will go on until dark."

And they wouldn't be buying anything so there was no rush to wade through the crowd to get close enough to bid or be jostled by the would-be buyers. It would be a slow, simple day of fun. She was determined to enjoy it. No matter what. Tomorrow, she would talk to Leo about Matthew and then she would go to the store and work until it closed. Freeman and the other men were discussing the fate of the store. So far, no answer had been forthcoming. She needed to make money while she could.

She would solve her money problems and she would be the mother Matthew needed.

"Melvin is here. He's brought—you have to see. Come on."

Celia dashed out again, Elizabeth and Francis trotting after her. Her curiosity piqued, Jennie hurried through the living room. Melvin had been in Jennie's class in school. He was a nice man, hard worker, married with half a dozen children about the same age as hers. They hadn't exchanged more than ten words in ten years. Now he was here and he had something to show her.

She pushed the front door open and stepped onto the porch. Celia danced around like chopped spuds thrown into a skillet full of grease. The two little ones tried to mimic her excitement, but Francis ended up taking a tumble onto the wooden floor. He sat on his behind and clapped while Celia tugged on Jennie's arm. "Look at it, Mudder. It's beautiful, isn't it?"

A run-of-the-mill buggy sat parked in the spot where buggies usually parked. So Melvin had driven over. What was so special about this one? Melvin, huffing and puffing as if he'd jogged the last few miles, seemed to be unhitching the horse that pulled the buggy.

"Guder mariye." She stepped onto the porch. "Is something wrong?"

"Not a thing." Melvin straightened. He stood as wide as he did tall. Every year added a few pounds to his squat frame. His round, sun-toughed face wrinkled in a smile above his brown beard. "I'm just delivering your buggy."

"My buggy?" Jennie wavered on the first step. "I don't understand."

"Our buggy, our buggy!" Celia danced a little jig. "I'll get the others." She raced toward the barn.

"Your friends pooled their funds and bought this buggy for you." Melvin patted the bay's rump. "I'm dropping it off as a favor to them."

"They bought me a buggy?" The words didn't add up. Buggies were far too expensive to be given as gifts. Jennie had resigned herself to the borrowed buggy for as long as Peter could spare it. "That's not possible. No one asked me about it."

"That's what makes it a gift." He mopped at his chubby, dimpled cheeks with his sleeve. "I have to get going. My fraa wants to look at the beds they're selling at the auction. Ours broke down."

Could it be his husky frame? That was beside the point. Jennie circled the buggy. It had a well-worn look to it, but it was sturdy. The reflectors were in place, the battery-operated brake lights seemed fine. Rearview mirrors stuck out from both sides. The seats were amply padded. It was a thing of useful beauty. "Who did this? Who bought this for us?"

Melvin's nose wrinkled. He donned a mischievous grin that made him look twelve instead of closing in on forty. "That's for me to know and you not to find out."

"Nee. I can't accept it."

"Don't be a naysayer. A gift's a gift." He busied himself pulling a saddle from the buggy and placing it on his horse. "The givers prefer to remain anonymous." He drew the last word out in four long syllables as if he'd never said it before. Likely, he hadn't.

"I need to be able to thank someone and then pay him back."

"No sense it getting fancy about it. You needed a buggy. Now you have one." He doffed his straw hat at her and hoisted himself into the saddle with ease for a man of his girth.

"Melvin, wait!"

"I'll never tell." He turned the horse around and then looked back with feigned seriousness belied by a distinct twinkle in his blue eyes. "Nothing you can do to make me spill the beans."

"Danki."

"I'm just the delivery man." He waved as he started off toward the road. "Use it well."

The children tumbled from the barn, laughing, talking, running toward her and the house and their new buggy. Sometimes a person had to accept unexpected, undeserved gifts for the sake of others. She contemplated the buggy. She would find out who gave it to her. She would find a way to pay them back. But first she needed to thank whoever it had been for a gesture that began to sew up the wound where her heart had once been.

THIRTY

THE LINE BETWEEN ONE PERSON'S JUNK AND another's treasure was never thinner than at these school auctions and fund-raisers. Still in a blissful state over the unexpected gift of the buggy, Jennie wandered through aisles of buggy parts, old dishes, farm implements, and furniture, bemused by the stuff people thought would sell. The July heat beat down on her. She lifted her face to the sun, glad it shone on her day of blessing. She paused to peer into a box of flowerpots and garden tools. Nee. She needed to save her money to pay back the generous friends who had bought her family that buggy. Somehow. Generosity would be repaid with a pleasing attitude of gratitude. The children ran on ahead, Elizabeth in Celia's keeping and Francis in Cynthia's. They loved to look, even if they couldn't afford to buy. Jennie had enough change to get everyone an ice cream if the price hadn't gone up since last year.

Everyone but Matthew. She shoved away the thought. Matthew was too old to be placated with ice cream. His malaise went deeper, so deep she couldn't fathom how she would cure it. The sight of Freeman's fraa, Dorothy Borntrager, and her closest friend, Josephine

Beachy, wife of Deacon Cyrus Beachy, made Jennie do an about-face and head the other directions. The thought that they might have heard of the deputy's visit to her home during the night sent long chilly fingers up her spine despite the sun's heat. She ducked her head and trudged toward the long line of wringer washing machines. She could use a new one, but that too would wait.

"The pink one looks like it would suit you."

Leo. Just the person she needed to talk to about Matthew. Her heart began to pound as she turned to look up at him. His grin said he knew how silly the notion was. One pink washer in the midst of all those run-of-the-mill white washers. It would never do. The neighbors would frown at her choice to stand out in the Plain world. She swallowed her anxiety and managed a smile in return. "Just looking."

"Me too." He held a bowl of ice cream in one hand and two white plastic spoons in the other. "It's really hot today." His tone was tentative, his expression uncertain. "Share with me?"

He offered her a spoon. She hesitated as she looked at his face. Such a tender expression. Such sweetness. His eyes were the color of warm chocolate. His lips were full. Not like Atlee's that thinned in anger until they became a line drawn in the sand with fury that said "Don't step over me."

"I don't have a cold or anything. No germs, I promise."

She took his offering. Their fingers brushed. A jolt of longing, a heat that had nothing to do with the sun, surged through her. She longed for the touch of his strong hand. His warm embrace. Something in his gaze said he offered both with no reservation. Her heart sought such an offering, but her head held on to fear. A soft touch could turn to stone in a mere second. She thrust aside her heart's desire.

"You can have the whole thing if you'd rather not share with me."

The disappointment in his words registered. Emotions warred in his face, then disappeared behind a careful neutral stare. But not before she saw a loneliness she recognized from her own constant and overwhelming supply.

"Nee, we'll share." She offered a smile. His returned. He held out the bowl. She dipped her spoon in the ice cream. "Soft serve."

"I like it that way. It doesn't give me brain freeze." He stuck a heaping spoonful in his mouth, closed his eyes in mock adoration, and swallowed. "Meredith and Bess made it. They're selling out as fast as they can finish a batch."

"It's very gut." She took another small bite, savoring the creamy texture. "I planned to buy some for my kinner."

"I already did."

"You shouldn't have done that."

"I wanted to." Emotion laced the words. His gaze met hers and, for once, didn't back away. She found she couldn't, either. Her heart began to pound. He opened his mouth, then closed it. Finally, his gaze strayed over her shoulder to the buggies parked on the other side of the road. He sighed. "I like them. Especially Francis."

"Francis likes you."

His head bobbed in acknowledgment, but his gaze remained fixed on the buggies.

"So do I." Where had that come from? Now her heart raced. Heat burned across her face. "I mean—"

"I like you too." Red spread under his tan. His gaze dropped to her face. "Always have."

She couldn't breathe. This was dangerous, dangerous territory, not where she had intended to travel at all. "I can't—"

"It's only ice cream." His amber eyes told a different story. "Don't worry. It's sweet and it's good, like you."

She opened her mouth but found no words came out. Her throat hurt. Tears formed but could not be allowed to fall. They could not. They could not. She would not cry. Instead she nodded. He smiled and nodded at the bowl.

She took another bite, then another, glad for the cold creaminess that cooled a heat she couldn't explain.

They took turns bite for bite without speaking. The auction sounds flowed around them, three different callers bleating out numbers in a singsong. People talked, horses whinnied, and children screeched as they played hide-and-seek among the buggies. Life ran on around them.

Leo scooped the last of the ice cream onto his spoon and held it out to her. "You should have the last bite."

"I had the first."

"I want you to have it." His spoon wavered. "Among other things."

Her mind ran in a thousand directions, trying to imagine those other things. She'd come to an auction because that was what a person did. Now this man declared himself with a bowl of ice cream and a gaze that saw through her.

She heaved a breath and allowed him to feed her that last bite. "I should find the kinner. They'll get into trouble if left on their own too long."

"Wait. They're gut kinner. They'll be fine." He tossed the bowl and spoons into a rusted trash barrel. "I wanted to give you something."

He ducked his head. He looked for a fleeting second like the boy she'd known in school, who never wanted to be the one to read aloud or answer the teacher's question. The best softball player and the worst speller. She'd always liked that boy. "You already gave me ice cream."

"You looked disappointed that day in the basement. When I gave the animals to Elizabeth and Francis, you looked like you wanted one too. I felt bad." He shifted from one foot to the other. "I never want to disappoint you again."

He knew she'd been disappointed long ago. "Nee, don't be silly. I'm all grown up."

"Not too old for this, I hope." His face red, neck to ears, he thrust a balled-up paper napkin at her.

A lump in her throat, she unfolded the napkin. A small, wooden horse lay in her palm. Its back arched, front hooves high, as it reared. The wood, something dark and rich in grain, had been polished to a high sheen. Leo loved horses. He loved animals. That he'd chosen to share that love with her was not lost on Jennie. "It's beautiful."

"It reminds me of you."

"Me? Why me?"

"You want to loosen the reins of something in your past."

After a moment she remembered to close her mouth. She sought a response but found none. He touched the horse. "You're beautiful too."

Plain men and women didn't aspire to such a thing. But the words touched something broken inside her. The carpenter took the pieces and, with great care, put them together again in something new and different. Something complete. To Leo, she wasn't a clumsy cow or a pig.

Her throat ached with the supreme effort not to cry.

"Danki." She breathed, in and out, in and out.

Ice cream. A carved animal. The rocking chair for Todd and

Samantha Riker. *Leo has a generous nature.* She'd said those words last night to Matthew. "I received another gift today. A buggy."

Did his expression shift? She couldn't tell. He cleared his throat. "That is gut news."

"A buggy is a very big gift, too big for a person to accept." She studied his face. The corners of his mouth turned up. "I need to find out who gave it to me so I can pay them back."

"If it's a gift, I reckon they're not looking for payment."

He definitely looked uncomfortable. She crossed her arms. "Regardless, I need to pay for it."

"You can't afford to pay for it, that's why they gave you the gift."

"How do you know why they gave me the buggy?"

"I'm just speculating." He studied his dusty boots. "I know you were thinking you'd earn the money at the store to buy another one, and now the store will probably close."

He knew her burden and wanted to help. She could see it in his face, no matter what his words said. A person should accept such a gift with grace. "For now, I'll say danki then."

He couldn't deny it without lying. The struggle played out across his rugged face. "Is Matthew here?"

So he changed the subject. "Nee." Heat burned her face hotter than the July sun. He'd given her the opening she needed. "He stayed back to do chores. I want to talk to you about him."

"I know." Leo took her arm, forcing her to halt with him at the end of the long row of washers. The desire to lean into him grew. The desire to feel his fingers against her skin. His grip wasn't gentle. Nor her reaction. Not like the sweetness that overtook her when she thought of Nathan. She should tug away, but her heart, warming after a long, dark cold, held her there, close to him. "Word gets around."

"You heard already? How?"

"Delbert Wilkins was at the coffeehouse this morning complaining to his buddy Louis Barton over pancakes and fried eggs. Isaac Plank was there with his fraa."

To tell Hazel was to tell everyone she knew who in turn would pass the word. A fund-raiser like this auction allowed the grapevine to twist and turn and grow in one fell swoop. "Freeman and Cyrus know?"

"I reckon."

"He said he wasn't drinking. He went to listen to music and talk to girls."

"Drinking or not, he had no business being out there at his age."

"He talked about your friend Todd and his wife, Samantha. He said you took them a chair. I'm not sure what that has to do with him sneaking out of the house to go to a kegger, but in his mind, they're connected."

His expression somber, Leo studied the crowd around the auctioneer's stand in the distance. He sighed. "It is connected. I saw what he saw at Todd's house."

"What? What did you see?"

His face suffused with red. He shuffled his feet. "Lieb."

"He's a boy."

"Too young to understand what he feels, but not too young to feel it."

"It has to do with his daed . . . and me." To have this conversation with Leo surprised—and embarrassed—her. But he seemed determined to have it. And to help her understand her son. His words would help her to show Matthew the grace he needed. "He's old enough to remember how things were."

"Whatever happened with you and Atlee, you can still teach Matthew how things are supposed to be."

If only he was right. "I'm glad you think so, but you have no idea what this is about."

"Tell me then."

She looked over his shoulder, across the road, to the lot where all the buggies were parked. Too far to run. "It's a long story."

"I'm a patient man."

The words sounded like a promise. She struggled against unfettered emotion. "Matthew needs time to heal."

"From what?"

"This isn't the time or the place."

"I've been down this road of looking for a way to put a bandage on a hurt that won't heal. Others will not be as patient."

His tone warned her. She followed his gaze. Freeman and the deacon approached from across the fairgrounds. Even at a distance she could see their expressions were somber, their tread heavy. Leo swerved, putting more space between them. "Quick, before they get here, tell me you'll take a ride with me. Later. One night this week. We'll talk. About Matthew. About everything. About us."

With the sweet taste of his ice cream still on her lips and the weight of the Gmay bearing down on her, she didn't have time to think about it. To worry it like a ragged thumbnail. To see the many destinations where such a decision would take her. To fear the known and the unknown. "Jah."

"Gut." A gusty sigh followed that single syllable. He smiled, which seemed a gift in itself. "It'll be fine."

She wasn't sure what he meant. The ride or the conversation she was about to have with Freeman and Cyrus.

✳

It didn't matter if the president of the United States himself approached now. Leo wanted to sing. Jennie would take a ride with him. Bringing her a bowl of ice cream had taken every bit of courage he had. Getting her the buggy had been easier. Because Melvin Plank had been willing to deliver it. Walking up to her with a bowl of ice cream and starting a conversation—it had almost been too much. She was like a skittish horse to be handled with gentle care and patience.

There were ways other than words to show a person you cared for them. The barn roof. Matthew's apprenticeship. Francis and the snake. Francis and the candy sucker. The buggy. Between the orders for his furniture at the store and from Todd's friends and family, and Mary Katherine's help, he was able to swing a deal with Melvin to take his old back-up buggy off his hands. Leo had his work cut out for him, but he liked the work and liked her. At a certain point a man had to speak up. Say the words. Words were the hardest part for him. He would find them, starting with this conversation with Freeman and Cyrus. He turned, planted his feet, and faced the two men.

They approached looking like twins with their paunches, their silver beards, and their thick-rimmed glasses. They had the same ponderous tread, the same way of swinging their arms as if clearing the way. The same solemn expressions. Men on a mission. No others stood in the area around the washing machines, but it wouldn't have mattered. Their gazes said they'd found their targets in Jennie and Leo.

Freeman nodded at Leo, acknowledging him before Jennie. Cyrus did the same. Leo returned the nod and crossed his arms over his chest. He had had many conversations with the bishop and the deacon. He would hold his own and then some. He always did. "Gut turn out."

"Indeed." Freeman brushed the comment away with the flick of his tone. He turned to Jennie. "I've been told of a visit to your house by a sheriff's deputy. Last night."

"Jah." Her cheeks stained red, which only made her prettier. Her voice quivered. "I'm sorry to say."

Freeman shoved his spectacles up his long nose. Cyrus did the same. "You should've come to Cyrus immediately. This is a matter that affects the entire Gmay. Law enforcement coming to your home. It's as if he came to all our homes. It reflects on all of us."

"I know. I–"

"She spoke to me about it." Leo kept his tone conciliatory, as much as he wanted to jump to Jennie's defense. She did her best. And Matthew was not a bad boy, only confused, angry, and sad. As Leo had been for so many years. "Matthew is my apprentice."

Freeman's eyebrows disappeared behind the brim of his straw hat. He exchanged glances with Cyrus who tugged at his hat and frowned. "Your own behavior has not always been what it should be. Are you sure you are the proper one to take responsibility for Matthew?"

Leo had his own history of meetings with the deacon. Stretches of time in which he didn't attend church. Or failed to materialize for Gmay meetings. He couldn't, in good conscience, go when all he felt was anger–at the loss of his father, at the death of his mother, at events that others said were God's will. God's plan. He understood Matthew's anger and pain. Leo's had only just begun to subside. Healing took time and the right people. Aidan and Timothy had been his. Matthew had no older brothers. "I can help him. He needs help before his behavior goes farther and he cannot be helped."

"Discipline is what he needs." Freeman didn't raise his voice, but the words were icy. "Teach him now or lose him later."

"You have no children of your own. No suh." Cyrus sniffed as if smelling something rotten. "You know nothing of how to reach them."

"My daed died when I was the same age as Matthew is now. I understand what you cannot."

"I do understand." Freeman's voice softened. "But you know as well as I do that Gott knew the days his life would number before he was born. Just as He knows ours. We're only passing through this life."

"I do know." Leo lowered his own voice. "Kinner are not always as able to understand something so sudden."

"It's been explained to you and to him many times."

Leo stared at the crowd. Hundreds of people. All had their heartaches. All had experienced pain and loss. Each dealt with it in his own way. Once he'd wanted to be like them, to be accepting, to stop hurting, to trust. But he couldn't. He didn't know why. Gott made him thus, hadn't He? "Sometimes the spirit is wounded and takes longer to heal."

"Has your spirit healed then?"

Leo glanced at Jennie. She stared at him, emotion churning in her face. She knew how he felt. She felt it too. She had loved and lost. She understood. "Today it's better." He cleared his throat. "Let Matthew stay with me for a while, at my house. Give me a chance to smooth his path."

"You would do that?" Jennie plucked at her apron. "I can't ask you to do that."

"You didn't ask. I offered."

"Can you not handle your own suh?" Cyrus frowned at her. "What does that say about your other kinner? Will you handle them?"

"She'll handle them well." Leo smiled at her, hoping to convey the strength of his conviction. "Each one is different."

Jennie nodded. "I'll be vigilant."

"We'll help her." Leo would do everything in his power to aid her. "That's what we do, isn't it?"

Freeman squinted as if trying to see a cloudy future. "I'll want to speak with him."

"We'll bring him to you."

Freeman's eyebrows rose and fell. "I'll see the three of you on Monday then." He did an abrupt about-face. Cyrus lumbered after him, puffing in his effort to keep up.

"I can't believe you did that." Jennie's voice held wonder and relief. "I have to go home and tell him."

"I'll see you there later."

She smiled up at him. "Are you sure about this?"

"I like Matthew." He waited a beat. "And I already told you how I feel about you."

Her smile disappeared. She ducked her head. "I don't know—"

"You don't have to know anything right now." He took a breath. Everything rode on how he made her feel safe. He didn't know why or how, but Atlee had done something to her that caused the sweet, happy girl Leo knew growing up to disappear into a shell. He would do whatever it took to draw her out into the light once again. "Right now, we help Matthew."

By helping Matthew, he helped her. For now, that was enough.

Besides, she'd already agreed to the buggy ride.

THIRTY-ONE

A GOOD BOOK ALWAYS PROVIDED EXCELLENT COM-
pany. Nathan stuck his bookmark into Larry McMurtry's *Dead Man's
Walk* and laid it aside. He scooped up his change and the receipt,
dropped a generous tip on the table, and stood. The book went into
his backpack, along with his wallet. The waitress waved and wished
him a good night. It wasn't a bad night. Just not the one he imagined
when he decided to stay in Jamesport. A table for one for a late supper
at the Grill and Tavern. He was indeed independent. In a lonely sort
of way. *Stop feeling sorry for yourself.*

He shoved through the door and out onto the street. On a Saturday night in a small town like Jamesport, there wasn't much to do.
Folks barbecued or went fishing. They had fish fries with watermelon and homemade ice cream. He hadn't scored an invitation to a
family gathering. Working as a farmhand didn't have the same cir-
culation as a book salesman. People had forgotten about him already.

Stop feeling sorry for yourself.

The *pop-pop-pop* of firecrackers fractured the silence. He jumped
despite himself and dropped his keys in the street next to the rental.
They went on and on, put to the music of raucous laughter.

A knot of a dozen Plain teenagers, some of whom he'd seen playing pool in the tavern earlier, loitered in a semicircle in the parking lot across from the tavern. One of the boys lit another string of Black Cats and threw them on the asphalt. The sound ripped through the air.

Talk about nothing to do. The girls, their hair loose down their backs, clapped and tittered. The boys guffawed. Nathan recognized several of them. None looked his direction. They probably told themselves if they didn't see him, he couldn't see them. Not that it mattered. During running around, their parents made it a point not to know what their children did, trusting they would find their way back home and to their Plain ways in short order.

Mostly, they did. He picked up his keys and hoisted himself into the SUV, his mind wandering back to his teenage days and his forays into drag racing on the back roads of southwestern Kansas. A gangly, sickly kid with a terrible layup and few social skills, he'd been lonesome then too.

His cell phone chirped like a cricket.

He didn't want to look at the text message. The only person texting him these days was Blake. Over and over again. His brother needed to go home. He had been pestering him all day to do something fun, as he put it. He figured if Nathan wouldn't go with him to Pennsylvania, then he should consider this a vacation of sorts while he worked to convince him. Go camping at Stockton Lake. Drive to Branson for a show. Have a holiday, he said.

All by text while Nathan was talking to Freeman and putting in a shift at Darren's farm.

A man starting a new career as a farmhand could not afford a holiday.

A man who wanted to be Plain couldn't be answering texts all the time.

If he told Blake where he'd been, he'd have to admit to eating out for supper without inviting him. Choosing self-imposed loneliness over his brother's company. Whose fault was it Nathan was estranged from his family?

He shoved the thought away and dug the phone from his jeans pocket. Sure enough. Blake.

Where r u?

Nathan had to retype his response twice. His fat thumbs didn't help.

Headed back to my room.
Meet u there.
Tired. Turning in.
Need to talk. now. 911.

His brother's idea of 911 could very well turn out to be a craving for a Dairy Queen soft-serve ice cream cone dipped in chocolate that couldn't be assuaged in a little town like Jamesport. According to Blake a road trip was never out of the question. He was a thirty-nine-year-old teenager. Muttering under his breath, Nathan hurled the phone from his window and took off without looking back.

Feeling a hundred pounds lighter, he drove to the motel, parked, and climbed out. Blake stood, arms crossed over his chest, as if at attention outside Nathan's door. The parking lot lights cast shadows that hid his face. He stepped away from the door onto the sidewalk.

Wetness shone on his cheeks. His eyes were red. His trademark Walker grin was nowhere in sight.

"What is it?"

"Not out here." Blake's voice cracked. He jerked his head toward the door. "Let me in."

The miniscule room, crowded with a double bed, dresser, table, and chairs, mostly covered by stacks of books, had a musty smell of Nathan's last shower and shave with a hint of Old Spice. He planned to rent a house or a duplex, at the very least. He kept putting off looking. Excuses seemed to abound. The tornado. The rental. The change in jobs. What did that say about his desire to put down roots?

Sick of his own thoughts, Nathan dropped his keys on the dresser that held the TV and sat in an overstuffed chair wedged between it and the tiny table. "What's wrong?"

"It's Dad."

A dirge began to play somewhere in the vicinity of Nathan's heart. Drums began to beat, a mournful sound that pounded so loud in his brain, he couldn't think. His lips didn't want to form the question, didn't want to know what came next. He swallowed. *Man up. Get it over.* "What happened?"

"He died."

Blake hung his head and sobbed, the big, hacking sobs of a brokenhearted man who had no experience with crying. Like Nathan, he likely hadn't cried since childhood. Women cried. Children cried. Babies cried. When someone like Blake cried, the bottom of the world fell out. Nathan heaved a breath, then another. His throat ached from his lips to his stomach. His eyes burned. He lifted his hands to his face. It was wet. "He had cancer. They just found it. It didn't kill him that fast."

It couldn't be allowed. Nathan wasn't done being mad at his dad. He hadn't offered forgiveness yet.

"He's dead." Blake wiped tears and snot on the sleeve of his polo shirt. "Don't you get it, you idiot? He's gone. We'll never see him again. Ever."

His brother's hoarse anger propelled Nathan from the chair. He stumbled the few feet to where his brother sat on the edge of the unmade bed and folded him into a fierce hug. Blake's head dropped to his shoulder. His ragged breathing filled Nathan's ears. He gripped his composure with both hands. "I heard you. It's hard to get it through my thick head. He was indestructible." Indestructible. Bigger than life. Noah and Moses and Elijah rolled into one. "How can it be? What happened?"

"Mom called Aaron who called me so I didn't get much. Aaron was too broken up to talk." Blake cleared his throat and straightened, wiping at his face again. "He just said it looked like a heart attack. His heart got him first."

"His heart was bigger than two men's."

"He was twenty-five pounds overweight, and he worked all hours day and night like a thirty-year-old. He didn't sleep. He didn't exercise. He loved his red meat."

Nathan let his hands drop to his lap. He didn't know what to do with them. They should be doing something, going somewhere, fixing something. "How did Mom take it?"

"She said he's the blessed one. He got to go first. He went on ahead of the rest of us. He's with his King and Savior." The racking sobs returned. Blake put his hand to his mouth and took a shuddering breath. "She is faithful. I'm so ashamed."

"Ashamed?" Nathan man-patted his shoulder. "You loved your father. You were a good son."

"I can't find it in me to see it as Mom does. I'm selfish. I wanted a few more years with him here. I wanted him to be grandpa to my kids. My hypothetical kids. I waited too long. I took it for granted he would always be here."

"You're human. You're allowed that grief."

"I believe he made it. I believe he is standing before the throne receiving the 'good and faithful servant' speech." Blake's Adam's apple bobbed. "I should be happy for him."

"You're right, but you're his son."

"Why do I feel so rotten?" His voice rose. "I should be filled with joy for him."

"You loved your father."

"So did you."

Not in a way that showed. Nathan had run away. He'd kept him at arm's length. He'd punished him for having a life dedicated to his passionate belief. "I never told him that."

"He knew." Blake shrugged. "Fathers know."

"I wish I believed that."

They sat in silence for a few moments, listening to the hiss of the air conditioner unit. Nathan sniffed and looked around the room for a box of tissues. No woman's touch. Toilet paper would have to do. He went to the bathroom and returned, a piece for himself and another for Blake. Nose blowing filled the air. Blake sighed and produced a watery smile. "Sorry about that."

"Nothing to be sorry about."

Nathan was the one who had something to be sorry about. He

would never have the opportunity to resolve his issues face-to-face with his dad. Never stretched to eternity and beyond.

"Don't tell anyone I lost it."

"Your secret is safe with me."

"Thanks. We're blessed, I guess." Blake went to the window, his frame silhouetted by the neon sign that flashed in the parking lot. VACANCY. "Imagine what it would be like to be a nonbeliever who watches a loved one be put in a hole in the ground and thinks that's it. Worms and dust. Nothing more. Nada. Kaput."

Nathan gripped his hands together in his lap. His knuckles hurt. He forced himself to flex his fingers. He cracked his knuckles, one by one. Finally, the question found its way out. "Have you prayed?"

Blake turned. He looked as surprised as Nathan felt at the question. "All I could think was to find you, to tell you. Some big brother I am."

"You can be my big brother now." Nathan lowered his head and closed his eyes. "Pray for Mom. Pray for us. Pray for me."

The mattress sank when Blake returned to the bed. The springs creaked. Blake's arm came around Nathan's shoulder in a tight, warm half circle. His deep voice filled the cramped room, illuminating the darkness and making space for their grief under an endless, healing sky. The words surrounded Nathan. He wanted to grab them and cloak himself in them. He needed protection from the frigid cold that invaded his body when he imagined his father's still, lifeless body.

Tattered pieces weren't enough anymore. He longed for the whole blanket of his Father's love. He would give anything for it. Whatever was required. He needed it all.

THIRTY-TWO

JENNIE LET HER BREATH OUT. IT FELT AS IF SHE'D held it for the entire meeting with Freeman. Matthew's red face suggested he had done the same. Only Leo seemed unfazed by the bishop's ponderous speech. Matthew would return home and immediately pack his scant belongings and go with Leo to his house. There, he would work as a carpenter apprentice until Freeman found him fit to return home. He would eat supper with his family on Saturday and Sunday nights. He would attend services without fail. He would not leave Leo's house at night. If he did otherwise, he would find himself before the Gmay and the entire community would decide his fate.

He was only fourteen years old. Too young for rumspringa but old enough to know better. Jennie swallowed tears of shame and relief. The wobble in his walk toward the door told her he, too, felt relief to have survived Freeman's scathing treatise on proper behavior. No excuses allowed.

She followed Leo through the screen door and out onto the porch. Freeman didn't join them. Probably resting his vocal cords after such a lengthy discourse.

"Hey."

Jennie looked up at the single syllable. Nathan walked around his car and started up the steps. His red-rimmed eyes were clothed in dark circles. He had a five o'clock shadow on his chin and cheeks that she had never seen before. His clothes were rumpled as if he'd slept in them.

"What's wrong?" The question was involuntary. She had no right to know how Nathan was or wasn't. "You don't look well."

His gaze went to Leo, then lingered on Matthew, who brushed past him and headed to the buggy. "I'm fine. How are you?"

"We had to visit with Freeman." She didn't owe him an explanation, but he looked so heartsick she couldn't bear it. "Matthew's been having some problems."

"I heard. Delbert Wilkins's farm. Drinking beer and rabble-rousing." Nathan rubbed his eyes with both hands. "Sorry, I didn't mean to be so crude. I haven't slept in a while."

"What is it?" The strange urge to comfort him overwhelmed her. As a friend, as someone who recognized another soul in pain. "Can we help?"

We. As if she and Leo were a *we.* Or did she mean a community *we?* The Plain community helped friends in need.

Leo clomped down the steps until he stood face-to-face with Nathan. "Sit down on the porch before you fall down. You've suffered a loss, haven't you?"

He looked so concerned and sounded so kind. That kind of *we.* Leo, who had helped her with Matthew, would help Nathan. He was that kind of man. She took a quick breath and stood back. Nathan staggered up the steps and sank into the chair.

He gave a harsh sound, like a stifled sob. His chest heaved. "My father died."

"I'm so sorry."

Leo nodded toward the other rocker. Jennie took it. He leaned against the porch railing, his arms folded over his chest, his face full of caring. "I also am sorry. Do you want to tell us what happened?"

Nathan related his story in quick, breathless fits and starts. Afterward, he stared at his hands in his lap. "I feel so guilty."

"Guilty?" Leo straightened. "He died thousands of miles away."

"Exactly. Because I am a stubborn, stiff-necked jerk, I hadn't seen him in years." He sniffed and wiped at his nose. "Now I never will."

"It wouldn't have mattered."

Nathan looked up at Leo. "What do you mean?"

"No matter how much time you spent with him, it wouldn't have been enough." Leo's jaw worked. His eyes grew dark with emotion. The pain told Jennie he relived his loss at that moment and every day.

"Your father lived a good life. He used up every minute of his time on earth." Plain folks might not evangelize, but Jennie understood the good it could do. They brought folks closer to God. "His time was done and now he rests, a good and faithful servant."

"I begrudged him that." Nathan hung his head. "I was selfish. I wanted him for myself."

"All kinner feel that way." Leo's voice held urgency. "All of them. I did. I was so angry with Gott when my daed died. I wanted him for myself. I thought I had a better plan than Gott. Such bigheadedness."

"And now?" Had he healed enough to get on with his life? Could he be trusted? Could he teach Matthew these lessons? Or did Matthew have to learn them on his own? "Can you see now what Gott's plan was for you?"

"I can see He has one and He's waiting for me to get on board." Leo grimaced. "I reckon He's waiting on all of us to do that."

❋

Wise men came in all shapes and sizes. As did fools. Nathan tore his gaze from the look on Leo's face. The guy had it bad. He was a good, kind person who loved Jennie and couldn't hide it. He didn't want to hide it. Nathan understood that feeling. Until now, he'd thought himself to be first in line to express it. He stood as Jennie squeezed past him and started down the steps. She smelled like cookies. Snickerdoodles, all cinnamon and vanilla. His throat ached. His already-battered heart shrunk under the flurry of blows. She had brought Leo with her to talk to Freeman.

Like a stand-in head of household. A stand-in father. He was Plain. Nathan was not. He had history with her, that was obvious. Nathan did not.

"Leo, wait."

His eyebrows tented and Leo frowned. He swiveled and glanced at Jennie's departing figure. His expression seemed to say "I'm with her."

"Just for a second. Alone."

"I'll be there in a minute." Leo called after Jennie. She nodded and kept going.

Leo came back up the steps. He remained standing.

"What are your intentions with Jennie?"

"Pardon?"

"Are you dating her?"

Leo's mouth opened and closed. Clouds swept across his face. The pulse along his jawline pounded. "Why?"

One terse syllable.

"I've thrown my hat in the ring."

Leo's headshake was so vigorous his hat shifted, until it was in danger of falling to the ground. "I'm sorry about your father. Take care of yourself." Again, he started down the stairs.

Nathan stood. "She knows how I feel."

"She'll ignore it."

"I'm in love with her."

"You're Mennischt." No disdain marred the words. Leo offered it as a respectful statement of fact.

"I could make her happy."

"We were just talking about Gott's plan for you."

"I know."

Leo's words were nearly lost in the stamp of his boot against the wooden steps. "He's chuckling now, you can be sure of that."

What did that mean? Nathan watched them drive away, the words ringing in his ears.

"There you are. I thought maybe you got lost." Freeman pushed through the screen door. His tone held pique. "We're late getting started. Are you ready to discuss Articles Sixteen and Seventeen?"

Ecclesiastical Ban or Separation from the Church. Of Shunning the Separated. Where the Amish and the Mennonites first parted ways. How fitting.

He faced the bishop. "My father died yesterday."

"I'm sorry for your loss." Freeman's smile disappeared. He settled into the rocker and pointed to the other chair. "You'll be leaving us then to be with your family, your mother?"

"Not for a week or two. It'll take that long, maybe longer, to wade through the red tape, to bring him home from overseas."

"Then you have time to continue your studies." Freeman paused, his expression thoughtful. "If you plan to come back."

His father's death hadn't changed his plan. Had it? The look on Leo's face had changed nothing. Jennie had nothing to do with his plan. Okay, Jennie wasn't the only reason.

The plan hadn't changed.

Had it?

"As far as I know right now, I'll be coming back."

"Sit. We'll talk about it."

Nathan sat. He wiggled his behind, stretched his legs, and pointed his shoes. No words presented themselves.

"I ain't getting any younger." Freeman's voice was kind, despite the words. "Neither are you, suh."

The word *suh*—son—burned the soft skin of Nathan's heart. Son. His father would never say that word again. He stood. "I shouldn't have come. I'm messed up right now."

"Sit."

His back to Freeman, Nathan gripped the porch railing. "My brother is having a hard time with this."

"You both need to be with family."

"I hardly know my family."

"Which is why you want to adopt this one."

Nathan pivoted so he could see Freeman's face. The other man's smile held a question. Nathan didn't want to answer it. "No. Maybe. Is that so wrong?"

"Doing something for the wrong reason can torpedo a man." Freeman steepled his stubby fingers propped up on his ample belly. "Maybe a change of topic will help you clear your mind. Let's talk about the Confession of Faith articles. Did you read them?"

Nathan had, but he hardly remembered. It seemed years had passed in a scant week. "I understand the concept of tough love."

"Could you shun your brother or your sister if they chose not to follow the Ordnung?"

"I've shunned them for years."

"Out of anger, not love. When we shun a wayward lamb, it's to teach him a lesson that will help him return to the fold. You simply wanted to punish."

Nathan closed his eyes. They burned with unshed tears. His throat ached. His chest ached. Everything ached.

"Turns out, you only punished yourself."

Freeman's words were like a sledgehammer to the chest.

"Get right with your family before you make a decision about your future, your faith, and who you'll share both with."

The big man hoisted himself from the chair and went inside, shutting the screen door with great care as if Nathan slept and he didn't want to wake him.

Nathan didn't move. His body weighed a thousand pounds. His eyelids, a thousand more.

Get right with your family before you make a decision about your future, your faith, and who'll you'll share both with.

What Freeman really meant was get right with God. Nathan had to do that first, before all else.

God, how do I do that?

THIRTY-THREE

THE SNORES REACHED A CRESCENDO. NATHAN LAID the articles of confession aside, stood, and stretched. He didn't mind Blake's noisy improvisations. At least it meant Nathan had company. Blake had passed out on Nathan's bed for the second time in as many nights. He stayed close as if guarding Nathan. As if he feared losing another family member in a sudden, cruel, inexplicable second.

Nathan felt the same way. Despite his determination to persevere on this path—to demonstrate to Freeman he was wrong—Nathan had been staring at the pages for more than an hour. He remembered nothing of what he'd read. Was this God's plan for him? He had been so sure it was. Now, nothing seemed sure.

While Blake found solace in deep, mindless, sleep, Nathan found only a restless, toss-and-turn, endless parade of thoughts he couldn't turn off. Every time he closed his eyes he saw images of his father in his Sunday black suit, standing on the sidewalk in front of his uncle's house in Arlington. He clapped his hands and urged them into the car. His mother, clothed in a flowered dress and black sneakers, hugged him tight. She smelled of the sweet scent of Dove soap. She kissed his cheek and then again. He held tight until his aunt peeled his fingers away and wrapped her arms around him from behind. His mother waved from the car until he could no longer see her.

Nathan turned off the lamp and slipped out the door. He tugged it shut with a gentle click. He turned up the collar of his Windbreaker against a heavy mist that did little to cool the night air. Ten o'clock and it still felt like an afternoon air heavy with heat and humidity. He stuck his hands in his jean pockets, ducked his head against the dank wind, and walked. He had no idea where he was going, but he needed out of that room. He needed to escape his thoughts. The more he thought, the faster he walked. His thoughts didn't give up. They pursued him, playing cat and mouse with him.

Why had he spent all those years avoiding his father? Wouldn't a man step up and face the past? Why had he spent all those years traveling around selling books to people, never settling down, never having a family? Because he liked being alone? Because he didn't want a wife and children of his own? What was he so afraid of? Did embracing the Amish faith with its simple precepts and even simpler life represent a way to meet his obligation to Jesus? Or a way to avoid it?

Stop, God, stop. Please stop.

His steps carried him faster and faster, past the grocery store, the restaurant, and dark buildings that had been shuttered for the night. Business owners had turned out the lights, closed the doors, and headed home to the warm companionship of family.

He turned onto Grant Street, barely aware of his surroundings. His heart pounded in his chest. It hurt. Everything hurt. His shoulders, his clenched jaw. He halted and bent over, hands on his knees. His chest heaved. Was this what it felt like to have a heart attack? Had his father suffered this inability to draw a breath of air?

Breathe. Breathe. He sucked in air. *Now out. In. Out.*

He swallowed the bitter bile that rose in his throat.

In. Out.

The weakness seeped away, replaced by a strong desire to look up. He raised his head.

A church loomed over him. Yard security lights illuminated its red brick walls and windows trimmed in white wood. A small steeple rose in the front. The long, narrow stained-glass windows were dark. It wasn't a large or imposing building. Simply one that said "for where two or three gather in my name, there am I with them."

Seriously, God? Signs. Smack-me-on-the-head signs?

He sank onto the cement steps in front and laid his head in his arms. No thought came. Not a single, solitary one.

"Are you all right, son?"

The gravelly voice came out of the dark night. Nathan rocketed to his feet. A *whoosh* of adrenaline shot through him. "Where did you come from?"

"I live down the street." The elderly, whiskered man wore a Frank Sinatra hat tipped at a rakish angle, black pressed pants, and a black suit coat. His white shirt was buttoned to the top button, tight around the loose, wrinkled skin of his neck. He utilized an ornately carved wooden cane in one hand. The other hand came up in an "I come in peace" motion. Raindrops sparkled on wire-rimmed glasses that perched halfway down his bulbous nose. "Where did you come from?"

"The motel."

"I reckon those steps are more comfortable than the beds at the motel, but I don't think I'd sleep there." He tottered a step closer with a gait that said the effort caused him pain. "Is there something I can do for you?"

"I don't plan to sleep here."

"What do you plan to do? Sit here until the raindrops wash your sins away?"

What did this stranger know about his sins? "Just resting a minute."

"Isn't the seat of your pants getting damp?"

As a matter of fact, it was. All of him was wet. Outside with rain. Inside with tears for the dead and the lost opportunities. He wiped rain from his eyes. Only rain. Not those persistent, nagging tears. "I don't mind."

"Sure you do. Wouldn't you rather come inside?"

Nathan glanced back at the doors. Solid, wooden, white. Closed for business. "I didn't think—"

"It's true most churches aren't open for business twenty-four-seven, but the Son of God never sleeps." The man dangled a key chain crowded with a dozen keys of various sizes and origins from his stubby index finger. "Join me for a late-night behind-in-pew powwow with the Big Guy?"

"I don't know."

"Isn't that what you're here for?"

"I don't know."

"Sure you do."

"Are you the preacher at this church?"

"I'm Clyde, the caretaker." He trudged past Nathan and teetered up the steps where he took his time unlocking the door. It squeaked, then groaned in protest when he opened it. "God is the proprietor of this establishment. What's your name?"

"Nathan. Nathan Walker."

Clyde cocked his head. "Join me." Then he disappeared into the dark interior.

Nathan raised his face to the rain. Sit out here in the rain or go inside? God was more likely to strike him down with a bolt of lightning outside than inside His own building. With a tiredness that made him feel a hundred, Nathan hoisted himself from the steps and shuffled inside.

The narthex was small and dark. He couldn't make out much. Dim light spilled through an interior doorway. He followed it and found himself in the sanctuary. Clyde sat in the last pew, his hat in his lap, his shiny, bald head bent. After a second, he looked up and patted the pew. "Have a seat, have a seat. It's warm in here, we turn the AC down when no one's here—but it's dry. And peaceful. I sit here all the time. Just me and my Savior."

Nathan slid into the seat, keeping some distance between himself and this man he'd only just met, Savior or no Savior. "Thanks."

"Don't thank me. You found your way here all on your own." Clyde moved his cane to the other side of the pew, fussed with his jacket for a second, then fixed his stare on Nathan. "All righty then. Spill the beans."

"Pardon me?"

"What's on your mind? You don't know me from Adam. You might never see me again. You might decide to see me every Sunday morning, I don't know. But we won't know, will we, until you tell me what you're doing here."

"And you'll fix it. Fix me."

"Good gracious, no. I'm only a conduit. Sometimes it's easier to tell the flesh-and-blood person than it is to converse with the Father. Tell me, knowing He'll hear. Pretend we're sitting in our lawn chairs at the lake slapping at the mosquitoes, we've known each other for years, and you're filling me in on your week over a glass of lemonade."

"You don't want to know."

"I do or I wouldn't offer."

It worked. Nathan opened his mouth and the words fell out in neat, complete, orderly sentences. Everything. His childhood. The leukemia. Drive-by parenting. Years as a traveling salesman. The Amish. Jennie. His desire to join the Plain faith. Blake. His father's death. The incessant voice of God in his head telling him to get to work. Now.

Or maybe he was simply nuts. Nutty as a fruitcake.

Clyde didn't interrupt. He didn't ask questions. He simply nodded, his gaze fixed on Nathan's face with a fierce concentration that prodded Nathan to keep going. He talked until his throat was dry and his eyes burned and his back ached against the wooden pew.

Finally, he finished.

Silence.

"Well?"

Clyde heaved a sigh and picked up his cane. "Well, what?"

"What do you think? What should I do?"

"Heavens, I don't know."

"You don't know? Why did you have me tell you all this?"

"You weren't telling me, young man, you were telling your Father." He pointed up, a look that could only be described as mischievous on his wizened face. "I sometimes act as an interpreter, but mostly I let the Heavenly One do His thing."

He grunted and stood, his joints popping. "Stay as long as you like. I have a cot in the back. I think it's time for me to rest. Turn out the lights and pull the door shut behind you when you go."

"Seriously?"

"I couldn't be more serious, young man."

"What do I do now?"

"Now you listen and you take heed."

He squeezed past Nathan and made his way down the carpeted aisle, his cane making a *thud, thud* sound. "Nice meeting you, Nathan," he called back just as he disappeared through the door.

What now?

Nathan closed his eyes. Darkness enveloped him. The anger, hot and fierce, washed over him in giant waves. "Father?" He whispered the word at first, then louder. Yet louder. "Father. Father. Father."

The single word encompassed all his fury, pain, his entreaty, his need.

"Father, answer me. Answer me. What now?"

Silence.

He lifted his head and glared at the ceiling shrouded in darkness surely as deep as that which lie within him. "Speak up. Speak up! What do you want from me?"

Silence.

He sank onto the pew and lowered his head into his hands. The tears seeped through his fingers. "You could've fooled me," he whispered, his voice hoarse and unrecognizable in his own ears. "What now, Lord? What now?"

THIRTY-FOUR

Most people slept at night, didn't they? Jennie sighed, set her glass of water on the table, and slipped from the rocking chair. She padded on bare feet to the front window, wide open to allow entry of a halfhearted breeze. She could stare out at the moonlit night, inhaling the perfume of fresh-cut grass baked by the July heat. It was no wonder she couldn't sleep. She'd finally made the leap of faith and gone to work at the store. Now, it would be gone in a few weeks and with it the extra income. Leo was around, giving her gifts, taking on her son, and tearing down her walls. The image of Nathan on Freeman's porch, his face wracked with grief, crowded her. Her mind reviewed the images. Nathan at the lake. Leo at the auction. Both so appealing even to a woman as wary as she was.

When Leo dropped her and Matthew off, he'd said he would be back. So far, he hadn't shown. Did she want him to come? She kept telling herself no. Yet her entire body ached in the emptiness of her house. The image of Leo's hands—carpenter hands—touching her cheek, her arm, or fingers entwined with hers, enveloped her. He had strong arms with muscles honed by years of manual labor. The thought of those arms around her waist made her shiver.

Grown women shouldn't act like teenagers. Plain women didn't act like this. Did they? She had no experience beyond Atlee and look where that had taken her. She let the curtain drop and headed for the stairs. Wise people slept at night.

You can never trust your instincts.

What about Gott's instincts? O ye of little faith?

The sound of buggy wheels squeaking and horse hooves on the road penetrated the silence. She spun around and darted across the floor to lift the curtain once more. She couldn't see the driver at first. He hopped from the buggy and tied the reins to the hitching post. Broad shoulders, not too tall. A dark shadow against the moon and stars.

He started up the steps two at a time.

Jennie's heart banged in her chest. He had said he would come. Leo was here.

Before he could rap on the door, she tugged it open. "You came."

"You're awake."

"I couldn't sleep."

He ducked his head. "Sorry I'm so late."

"You weren't going to come."

"I was . . . Then I wasn't."

"Why?"

"Let's take a ride."

"I can't take a ride."

"The kinner are sleeping. You don't want to leave them alone." He shifted his feet, his hand on the door as if he feared she would shut it. "Still, we could take a walk down the road and back."

She studied his face, half hidden in the shadow of his hat. He'd come all this way. After all this time. For some reason, she couldn't bear to disappoint him. He'd had his share of hurt in his life. "Jah."

His face broke into a smile. The smile looked good on him. "Come on then."

"Let me get my shoes."

"Gut idea."

Jennie made quick work of it and then they strolled side by side along the dirt road, grasshoppers popping out of the grass that lined it as if they'd disturbed their sleep. Cicadas serenaded them. Bullfrogs added their two cents' worth. The silence between them was nothing like the one on that buggy ride so long ago. It felt comfortable. Light.

"I'm sorry about the store." Leo's voice dropped another notch, so gruff she could hardly hear him. "I know you were trying to make a new start of it there."

"You too, I reckon."

"I've realized something. Making a new start is up to me." He smiled. "I can have it anywhere."

"What are we talking about, exactly?"

"I'm sorry everyone put so much time and effort into making a butcher shop into Amish Treasures, and now it'll be something else." He stopped at the corral fence and propped his arms on the top rail. "And we'll lose this way of earning money that everyone worked so hard for, but I'm still a carpenter. You're still good at sewing and making jams and such. We can start over somewhere else. Simple as that."

"Is Gott trying to tell us something, then?"

"More likely Lazarus is trying to tell us something."

"Like what?"

"Like greedy human beings will go to great lengths to get their way no matter who it hurts."

"I suppose you're right."

"Maybe you and I are right to be so distrusting of people."

"I can't speak for you." Jennie settled in next to him. She watched the leaves of a massive oak tree dance in the moonlight. She tried to order her thoughts. They wouldn't have light conversation. It wasn't his way. "My experience is that most people are kind, but somehow it's the not-so-kind I remember."

"Human nature."

"I suppose. But it shows a lack of faith in people that shames me. Most are not like Lazarus."

Or Atlee.

"You have your reasons, I reckon."

He didn't know, but somehow he understood. His massive hand moved. His fingers wrapped around hers and squeezed. Heat flooded her from head to toe. Then his fingers were gone again. He gazed straight ahead. Fighting to catch her breath, she glanced sideways at his profile, trying to read that impassive face. She saw something. A want. A question. A hope.

Like he must see in her.

She blinked against the tears that burned her eyes. "It's no excuse. People are good, for the most part. None of us is perfect."

"I'm not, that's for certain." He turned to face her. "I should've tried harder."

"We were too young to know better."

"I missed all those years." His hand came up and he traced the line of her jaw with one finger. "I don't know what happened between you and Atlee, but I see hurt and distrust in your face. I'm sorry for whatever you went through. It makes me want to make it better for you."

She was caught by his touch, immobilized by the fear that he would stop. She wanted that touch. His touch. Not just any man's. Leo's. After years of being afraid, her want of him exceeded her fear. How could he have that effect on her? The thought released her. She caught his hand in hers, entwining her fingers in his just as she had imagined. His skin was warm, his fingers strong, his skin callused. He had a strong grip, but no anger or hurt lurked there.

He leaned down and caught her in a kiss that seared her to the bone. His lips warmed every inch of her body. She ceased to breathe. Her free hand slid up his chest and touched his neck. His pulse pounded. Everything cold and hard in her melted. She'd longed for this, missed this, needed this.

Nee. Don't be caught in the trap.

Don't be a fool. Not again.

The memory of a raised hand and a raised voice sucked the light from the moon. Darkness descended. This would only lead to hurt and heartache. Pain that had nothing to do with a physical blow. Letting go would lead to an agony of uncertainty day in and day out. She jerked away and stumbled back. "I can't." Her hand went to her lips. They trembled. "Don't."

"Why? You don't like it? Like me?" Anguish stained his words. He raised his hands as if in surrender. "I'm sorry if I did something—"

"It's not you." The words came in a rush. He didn't deserve to be hurt. "It has nothing to do with you."

"Then what? Did Atlee do something to you?"

"What makes you think he did something to me?"

"Some things Matthew said. The way you act around me, like you're scared."

She covered burning cheeks with her hands. She'd spent years not talking about this. Now she had to do it or lose this chance—lose Leo and everything he represented. The words stumbled over themselves, trying to escape. "Atlee wasn't a nice man."

Leo frowned. "He could be mean-spirited."

"It was more than that. Sometimes he hurt me. Mostly with ugly words, but sometimes with a raised hand. Sometimes his punishment of the kinner was too much. More than their transgressions deserved."

Staring up at the stars, marveling at the beauty of the night sky, she told him her story, her voice barely a whisper. The fear, the pain, the ugliness, the endless nights, the words that left scars.

He didn't interrupt, but his grip on the wood tightened until his knuckles were white. His expressions ran the gamut from shock to horror to fierce anger.

Finally, she stopped talking. Night sounds filled the sudden silence.

Leo straightened and wheeled around, as if looking for the object of his fury. "If I had known—"

Jennie caught his arm. Shaking his head, he eased around, shock mingled with sadness in his face. "There would've been nothing you could do. I married him. I spoke the vows."

"I promise you I would've set him straight about how a man treats a woman. It would've ended or I would've ended him."

For a Plain man to make such a statement spoke of the depth of his feelings. A shudder ran through Jennie's body. It was better for him that he hadn't known. The Gmay wouldn't allow one man to interfere in another's marriage. "I believe you."

"I'm sorry you suffered through that for all those years." He inched closer. His fingers moved on the wooden railing but didn't quite touch hers. His gaze sought hers, his expression begging for permission. "I would never hurt you."

"I want to believe you."

"I struggle to trust too."

She fought the urge to lean into him, to lay her forehead on his chest, and allow him to hold her up, if only for a few seconds. "To trust Gott?"

"Jah." His voice was a hoarse whisper. He pulled her forward. His arms wrapped around her in a tight hug that far exceeded her imagination.

She leaned into it. His chin rested on her head. He did indeed hold her. The fiery heat of a few moments earlier simmered just below the surface. She ached for another kiss. His lips brushed her cheek. "You have to trust Him first. We both do."

She wanted to trust, but fear trapped her on the other side of a deep void. "How?"

"I don't know." Leo's arms tightened. "But I think this is the first step."

"I want to trust Him. I want to leave all the ugliness behind."

"Refined by the fire."

"Healed."

Leo's hands slid down to her waist. They stayed that way, not moving, not speaking, for a long time.

"I have to ask you something."

His tone warned her. She inhaled his woodsy scent one last

time and tugged from his grip. Their gazes locked. She longed for a breeze to dispel a heat that had nothing to do with summer in Missouri. "The thing that kept you from coming tonight. What was it?"

"Nathan."

On the ride home, she'd asked Leo what Nathan wanted with him at Freeman's. He said nothing important, but his expression said differently. "What about him?"

"He said he was throwing his hat into the ring. For you. He wanted me to know."

"I'm not a prize to be won." The words came out sharper than she intended. "He has let it be known that he's interested. I told him I would never leave my faith or my community—not for anyone."

"Do you have feelings for him?"

She could simply say no and enjoy this moment. Keep it whole and hopeful for a memory box that didn't hold many like it. "I don't know."

"That's not an answer."

She gripped her hands in front of her until her fingers ached. Nathan was a gentle man who didn't rock her with feelings that left her vulnerable to new hurt, new pain. "I don't trust my feelings about anything. Not when it comes to men."

"That doesn't mean you don't care for him." The space between them grew. "Why did you come out here with me?"

"To find out."

"Find out what?"

"If I have feelings for you."

"Do you?"

"Do you think I let just anyone . . . get so close?"

"Do you think I do?" His voice brimmed with despair. "Maybe I shouldn't have. Maybe I shouldn't have come." He whirled and strode toward his buggy.

"Leo, wait."

He kept walking.

"When I was married, I learned that love isn't always kind. It isn't always patient. It isn't always gentle. A person doesn't heal from a deep wound like that with a few hugs and kisses."

"It wasn't love. A man who would do such a thing to a woman or a child isn't capable of real love." His voice deepened, strained with feeling. His face radiated with all the kindness, all the patience, all the gentleness she could ever hope for. "I can wait. Until you stop being afraid. But you have to decide. There's only room for two in love."

Then he was gone. And Jennie was alone again. She stood at the corral fence for a long time, waiting for the feel of his hands on her to fade. It didn't. It stayed with her as the clouds wafted across the sky, revealing the light of the moon and stars that shone more brightly than they had the night before. Could she trust the feelings—sensations—that ran through her white hot? Her response to Nathan was nothing like what Leo made her feel. Nathan was simple, sweet, gentle, a pond with only an occasional ripple. Leo was a riptide, full of fierce passion at one moment, and gentleness the next. Like her feelings for Atlee had been.

How could she trust that?

THIRTY-FIVE

FOOL ME ONCE, SHAME ON YOU. FOOL ME TWICE, SHAME on me. The old saying kept running through Leo's head. He pulled on the reins and stopped in front of the tavern. This would be Matthew's one chance. Jennie had entrusted Leo with her oldest son, and he didn't intend to let her down. He'd felt Matthew's absence the second he arrived home from his visit to Jennie's farm. After living alone for so long, he was acutely aware of a presence—or lack thereof—in his house. Only Beau's dog snores broke the silence. His mistake had been trusting the boy to stay put.

The ride into town had been more time for Leo to think and feel, neither of which he had a hankering to do. He could still feel Jennie's skin under his, her lips, and her warmth. After years of being alone, getting that close to her was almost unbearable. Better to never experience it than to have that one tiny glimpse of happiness, only to have it slip beyond his reach again.

The grapevine in the Gmay had rippled with stories, but he never knew for sure what went on between Atlee and Jennie. She had been hurt. She was scared. She was confused. Thanks to her dead husband. Her feelings were understandable.

Nathan was no help at all. If the man truly cared for her, he would bow out. He would leave. He would recognize their differences were insurmountable. If Leo had the opportunity, he would tell Nathan as much.

And then he would wait. As much as it pained him, he would wait for her to be ready.

In the meantime, he had to make good on his promise to straighten out Matthew. Jennie's son would either come back to the house with Leo or take his chances before Freeman, Cyrus, and Solomon. Leo shoved through the tavern's door and stopped for a second to let his eyes adjust to the low lights. A few tables situated near the bar were occupied by people he didn't recognize. Likely tourists who'd waited too long to eat supper and found themselves with two options—eat at the tavern or head out on the highway to Chillicothe. The smell of hamburgers and deep-fried onion rings hung in the air. The chatter of folks seated at the long bar mingled with the noise of a huge, flat-screen TV that hung on the wall over it.

Leo waved at Sam Tate, who nodded, slung a towel over his shoulder, and went back to tending the bar. The owner's bald spot shone in the overhead lamp. His sparse white hair had become even sparser since Leo's last visit. Matthew wasn't among the patrons at the bar. That didn't surprise him. The real draw was the pool tables in the back where the kids on their rumspringas congregated.

Gritting his teeth, he forged ahead. It had been years since his own rumspringa. This had been one of the few places they could go in such a small town. Sam tolerated it as long as they didn't try to sneak a beer or make a ruckus.

Sure enough. Matthew leaned against the wall, a cue stick in one hand, his gaze fixed on a TV from which blared music that sounded like birds shrieking. He looked up when Leo entered the room. His boot dropped from his spot on the wall. He straightened and leaned his pool stick against the table. His expression didn't change.

Leo exchanged greetings with the other kids. None looked happy to see him, but neither did they scatter. They knew he would say nothing. They also knew their parents were aware of their activities. Jamesport was a small town. And this was rumspringa territory.

Matthew had no business in this territory.

"Let's go."

Matthew picked up a pop glass, wet with condensation. He took a sip and settled it back on a round high-top table. "Nee, I don't want to go."

Leo leaned in close. He kept his voice low, despite the TV's incessant blare. "You want a big scene?"

"I want to be left alone."

"No, you don't. You're seeking something you can't find."

"What do you know about it?"

Leo gripped the boy's arm and cocked his head toward the door. "Outside. I can't hear myself think in here."

Matthew's entire body stiffened. A fierce red blush scurried across his face and enveloped his neck. His scowl reminded Leo of the one he'd seen on Atlee's face when the man came across Leo talking to Jennie at a singing. It hadn't intimidated him then. It certainly didn't intimidate him coming from a fourteen-year-old boy who didn't know his head from a hole in the ground.

"Hey." Elijah Weaver made as if to approach. "Why not have a pop–?"

Leo fixed him with a stare. "I reckon one of you gave Matthew a ride here. You know better." Tightening his grip, he focused on Matthew. "Now."

Matthew shook loose of Leo's grip and shuffled past his friends.

A chorus of "Bye, Matthew" floated from the girls seated in a circle of chairs arranged so they could watch the boys play pool. Matthew ducked his head and plowed forward.

Outside on the street, Leo sucked in air, glad to be out of the smoky, damp air and the noise.

Matthew whirled and faced him. "Why did you have to go and do that? Why can't you leave me alone?"

"There's too much riding on it."

"You afraid Mudder won't like you if you don't make good on your promise." Matthew sneered. "You won't get to take her for a ride, give her a smack on the lips?"

Leo forced his hands to remain loose at his sides. He counted silently to ten, then back to one. "It's something much bigger than that." Fury at such insolence burned through him. Counting to twenty wouldn't assuage it. *Gott, tell me what to do. How to reach him.*

The sound of a car engine rumbled down the street. Seconds ticked away. His hands fisted, Matthew planted his feet, legs wide apart. Everything about him spoke of challenge.

"It's about you. Your future."

"My future is fine." The boy's voice faltered. "It's not your worry, anyway."

"I don't want you to end up like me."

Alone. The words, spoken and unspoken, hung in the warm, humid air between them.

"I have no plan to be like you."

"You have no plan at all." Leo grasped for words. This wasn't his strength. God knew that. Why put him in this position of trying to reach a boy who reminded him of himself? "You need help, but this is the only way you know how to ask."

"I don't need your help."

"You need somebody's."

"How can you help?"

"I know what it's like to have my father die."

"I reckon your daed wasn't nothing like mine."

Leo eased onto the curb and pointed to the space next to him. Matthew ignored his gesture and went instead to Star. He stroked the animal's head, his back to Leo.

Atlee was nothing like Daed. That a man could abuse a woman and children made Leo's blood run hot and then cold. His heart hurt for Jennie and for Matthew. The man had surely faced his maker and paid for his sins. "You didn't deserve to be treated badly."

The silence lasted so long Leo figured Matthew wouldn't answer. Matthew picked up a few pebbles and tossed them one by one into the street. "What do you know about it?"

"Only what your mudder told me. It's wrong to treat anyone like that, but especially someone you're supposed to love and protect."

"I didn't do anything to stop him."

The crux of the matter. "You were a little boy."

"He hurt Mudder."

"But he'll never hurt her again. And you'll be a better man."

"That's what Mudder says." Scorn mingled with shame in Matthew's words. "I was glad he was gone."

"That doesn't make you bad. You're human."

Matthew leaned his forehead against the horse's neck. A sound like a sob seeped into the air.

"You're afraid you're like him."

"I do stuff." His voice cracked. "I say stuff."

"That doesn't make you like him." Leo brushed dirt from his hands and let them rest on his knees. "It makes you a boy who doesn't have a daed to guide him."

"I should be the one to take care of things at home."

"You will."

"Mudder doesn't understand."

"She's afraid for you. She wants what's best for you." Leo gathered words that were so hard to find, his head hurt from the effort. "Your mudder is afraid for your eternal future, not just the one around the corner."

"I want to find out if I'm like my daed. I need to know."

"If you don't want to be like him, you won't." Who was he to give advice about things like this? He'd waited and Jennie had ended up with Atlee. If his head had been screwed on right, he might be talking to his own son now. Leo wished Atlee stood in front of him for one minute so he could see what his actions had wrought in his son. "You're not like him. You will choose to be different. You will choose to be a godly, kind, good Plain man." He stood.

Matthew pivoted and stared up at him. "How could you know?"

"I'll help you. Your mudder can help too. You need only follow her lead. She is the kindest woman I know."

Why had God let her become yoked to Atlee? Because He could see something they couldn't. Something good that would come from it. In the seven children they would have together. Because Jennie could offer Atlee something he needed. If time had allowed, maybe she would have softened his heart and led him to the place where he needed to go.

It wasn't for Leo to say. Only to accept.

Like his father's death. And then his mother's.

Gott, thy will be done. For the first time those words rang true. He could accept them for himself. For his mother and father, who rested easy even when Leo did not.

He waited, letting the indecision play out in Matthew's features. He might have Atlee's blue eyes and curly black hair, but he had his mother's chin and her mouth. Gott willing, he had her heart.

Matthew shook his head and growled, a guttural sound of an animal in pain. "I'll try." Tears trickled down his face. He wiped at them with his sleeve. "That's all I can promise."

"It's all any of us can promise."

"Are you going to tell Freeman?"

"Not if you commit to not letting it happen again."

"I won't. I promise." Matthew brushed past Leo, headed for the buggy.

Leo grabbed his arm. "Not so fast."

"What now? I said I'd try."

"You're walking home."

"What?"

Leo pointed at the street. "You left my house in the middle of the night. I had to come looking for you. Consequences."

"It's miles to your place."

"I'll keep you company." Leo climbed into the buggy and picked up the reins. "Better get started. It's your turn to make breakfast in the morning. I have an order to fill by tomorrow afternoon."

"Do you want bacon?"

"There's no bacon. It'll have to be sausage."

The conversation echoed on the empty street as they made their way out of town. Leo had a feeling God shook His head. But He might be smiling as He did it.

THIRTY-SIX

THE PHONE'S RING FILLED THE DARK MOTEL ROOM.
Nathan tossed aside the lumpy pillow that smelled like cheap deter-
gent, rolled over, and grabbed the receiver. He hadn't been sleeping.
Apparently, he would never sleep again. Two days had passed since
his discussion—okay, argument—with God at the church. He was
more baffled about his future than ever. If he couldn't sleep, he might
as well talk to someone—anyone on the phone. It was probably a
wrong number, anyway. No one ever called his room. Anyone who
knew him called his cell. The one he didn't have anymore.

He peered at the red neon numbers on the clock radio next to
the bed. One a.m. Who sold stuff at one a.m. aside from the shopping
channels on cable? "Do you know what time it is?"

"Nate."

The voice on the line was sweet with a hint of Kansas in it.
"Mom?"

"Did I wake you?"

He sat up and swung his bare feet over the side of the bed. "Are
you all right? Where are you?" Stupid questions. She was alone in a
foreign country. Her husband had died. "What's going on?"

"I've been trying to call you on your cell, but you never answered." She whispered the words so softly, Nathan strained to hear. "Blake says you got rid of it. Something about turning old-order Amish. Is that right?"

He didn't want to talk about it with her in the middle of the night, far, far away. "It's been so long since we talked." Whose fault was that? No one's. His. He'd shrugged off the opportunities, nurturing his grudge against both his parents like a hothouse plant. "I'm sorry about that. I should've called."

"I don't blame you for holding a grudge."

"Dad did."

"You learned how to do it from him." She sighed. "He was a good Christian man who loved his children. He wanted you to come running to him like the prodigal son. He thought you would, eventually. He thought it would be a lesson you would pass on to your sons. He never thought . . ." Her voice broke. Her ragged breathing filled the space.

"I'm so sorry, Mom. I'm so sorry."

"For what? You didn't do anything."

For not doing anything. "I'm sorry he's dead. I'm sorry you're there, dealing with this all alone."

"Honey, I'm not alone." Her voice strengthened. "God is with me. And the folks in our community are with me. They loved your father. They love me. They're helping me."

Of course, they were. His parents were the epitome of community everywhere they went. They made family from strangers. Something he had never done. His relationships with his customers were light and air, short on substance. "Hello, how are you," and move on. "When will you be able to bring him home?"

"It takes time. And money." The pause was laden with thoughts

Nathan strained to hear. "Did you know when someone dies at home and the cause is unclear, there has to be an autopsy to confirm the cause of death?"

"Even in a foreign country like El Salvador?"

"Even here. The embassy in San Salvador is helping us. A funeral home has to handle everything once we . . . once he . . ." Her voice broke. A small, half-stifled sob, like a tiny hiccup, came and went. "Once they have him, they'll do what's necessary to help him get ready to come home."

She made it sound as if they were helping Dad get dressed for a special occasion. "How long?"

"It could be a few weeks. There's so much red tape—paperwork—involved in repatriation of remains. That's what they call it. Bringing your daddy home." A bigger sniffle followed. Then a sigh. "You even have to have an export permit from the Ministry of Health."

An export permit as if Dad were fruit or furniture. Swallowing the lump in his throat, Nathan stood, picked up the phone, and tugged on the cord so he could shuffle closer to the window. The lights in the parking lot glowed through the thin curtains. "What can I do to help?"

"You can forgive me."

"Forgive you? I never blamed you for anything."

"No, you blamed your dad when I convinced him to leave you with Millie and Rex. I left you with them so we could do God's work. You thought it was him, but it was me."

"You don't have to take the blame for him." Nathan sank into the single chair in the room and dug his bare toes into the soft carpet. He counted them silently, one by one. No way it was her. It was him. All Dad all the time. "I know he was the one who had the calling."

"Yes, he had a calling, but so did I. Think about the women in the

Bible who gave up so much because they believed. Hannah gave up Samuel in service to God. What do you think Isaac's mother, Sarah, was doing when Abraham took him up to the mountain to be sacrificed? He was her only son. I knew what I had to do and I knew it was best for both of us."

She ran down, finally. It was as if she'd been storing up her defense, her arguments, for years.

Nathan let the pause drag for a beat, then another, trying to swallow his anger. "How? How was it best?"

"I was afraid for your health. I didn't want to drag you around the country and overseas. Your dad didn't want to leave you. He said a family should stay together no matter what. He said you would toughen up. That it would be good for you. I insisted."

The band around Nathan's throat tightened, making it almost impossible to breathe, let alone speak. He closed his eyes, seeing the bedroom with the posters of basketball players on the walls. The smell of Aunt Millie's chili, the whining of her Pekingese dog Clover at the door. They did what they could. They were good people. His body rocked. *God. God. God.* The band eased.

"Nate? Are you still there?"

"I was a kid. I didn't understand." He transferred the receiver to his other ear. "How could you expect me to understand?"

"I tried to explain—"

"You didn't want to feel guilty."

"I wanted to have both worlds."

"You shouldn't have had kids."

"Don't be mean. Don't say things you'll regret."

"It's true. For years I blamed Dad, and all along you decided to leave me behind like an old discarded piece of furniture."

"No, I prayed and prayed for you and me and your dad. I prayed to discern what was best."

"Leaving me was best?"

"I felt it in my bones. We are the sum of our experiences. What happened to you shaped who you are, just as it did me."

"I had to go through all that for some reason that will be revealed to me some day?"

"Or sooner." Her sigh filled the phone line. "I don't have all the answers. I can only beg your forgiveness and ask you not to let bitterness stand in the way of fulfilling God's plan for you."

"Was it worth it?"

"It broke my heart. I missed you every single day. I still do. Sometimes we're called to do hard, hard things."

He breathed and swallowed, unable to speak for fear of sobbing.

"We could work together now. We could do God's work together." Her voice filled with a certainty he didn't feel. "It wouldn't make up for lost time, but it could be a new beginning. Think about that. He's waiting for you to step up."

How did she know? How could she know of the calling that came to him in the middle of the night or during breakfast or while reading a book? "I'm not made for it."

"You're a salesman. I think it's a similar skill set."

After a few seconds her words sank in. He laughed, a hoarse disbelieving sound in his own ears. "I have other plans."

"Do you know what God does when He hears our plans? He laughs. He loves us so, but He also knows what's best for us. I have to go now. We'll talk about it when we get your daddy there."

Leo had said the same thing. God found humor in His children's feeble attempts to mold their own lives.

"How do you know He's waiting for me?"

"Read Isaiah 6:8."

"Just tell me what it says."

Silence greeted his demand. She was already gone.

He stood. Then sat. Then stood again. There would be no sleeping now.

His Bible lay on the end table. He flipped through the pages to Isaiah 6:8. "Then I heard the voice of the Lord saying, 'Whom shall I send? And who will go for us?' And I said, 'Here am I. Send me!'"

One of the basic tenets of the Amish faith was obedience. The irony was not lost on Nathan.

He didn't have his mother and father's calling. Or their wanderlust. He had plans. He would show his faith the way his Amish friends did. By example. He would woo Jennie, marry her, and settle down as a Plain man who put faith, family, and community ahead of all else.

I have plans, God. Do you hear me?

The response resonated in the darkness. *Son, do you hear Me? You're meant to woo many for Me, not just the one for you.*

Son? His father or the Father?

His mother's words rang in his ears. *"God laughs at our plans."*

THIRTY-SEVEN

A BOUNTIFUL CROP OF SWEET CORN MEANT PLENTY for canning after the first load went to the produce auction. A blessing. Sweat dripped down Jennie's back and ran between her shoulder blades, tickling her as she sliced the kernels from the cob onto a thick cutting board at her kitchen counter. Considering Leo's visit a few nights earlier, a day off from the store was a blessing too. She needed time to gather her thoughts and understand why she'd let him think Nathan might have a chance with her. He didn't. Not anymore. Not with the feelings that swept over her when she got close to Leo.

Feelings stronger than any that had ever assailed her before. Even with Atlee. So why did she tell him she might have feelings for Nathan?

Fear. Pure and simple.

The scent of spicy pickles bubbling in a huge pot on the stove tickled her nose, mixing with the corn's sweet aroma. She scooped up the piles of kernels and dumped them into hot jars, leaving a one-inch space at the top. She'd done this a thousand times, yet today she had to stop and think about how to do it. The other women's chatter soothed her. Laura and Bess had arrived bright and early for the canning frolic. Others were on the way. Her friends had no idea that the red on her cheeks had nothing to do with the hot July air. Every time she thought of Leo's visit—or more specifically his kiss and his touch and his words—heat billowed through her. She couldn't tell them any more than she'd told them about Atlee all those years ago.

But she wanted to. The words ached to be out.

"What are you thinking about? The store?"

She started at Laura's question. The ear of corn slipped from her hand and fell to the floor. "Nothing. Jah, the store."

Laura snatched the corn up before Jennie could grab it. Their heads came precariously close to banging. She laughed and Laura joined her. "Aren't we a pair?"

"Freeman, Cyrus, and Solomon have met. They've decided."

Laura patted Jennie's shoulder. "It's for the best."

The elders had decided they didn't want a legal battle with Lazarus Dudley. They felt it was best to let the store go. For the community. It wasn't their way to fight battles in public. If Lazarus so badly needed the space, he should have it. They would start again elsewhere or make do.

Jennie was used to making do, but it still hurt. She'd just begun walking this path and now the gate had closed. "That doesn't mean I have to like it."

"Nee, you're only human." Laura chuckled. "We all are."

"What's so funny?"

Jennie glanced back. Olive stood in the doorway, her hands clasped in front of her, as if waiting for permission to enter. Jennie offered her mother-in-law a smile. "I'm glad you could come."

"Me too. Where shall I start?"

Laura handed Jennie the ear of corn. "I'll go see what's taking Bess so long to bring up that box of jars from the basement."

She trotted past Olive, who moved aside, her smile uncertain.

"There's lots to do." Jennie motioned toward the table. "You can husk corn if you want, or if you'd rather—"

"Husking is fine." Olive sank into a chair and picked up an ear of corn. "I saw the girls in the garden, picking tomatoes."

"We're lucky to have any, the way that tornado ripped through here."

"It wasn't you."

Jennie stopped slicing corn from the ear in her hand. She swallowed, laid the knife on the table, and sat across from Olive. "Then what was it?"

"The grapevine is working overtime. Something about you and Leo Graber." Her smile was tentative. She shrugged. "You have a right to know so you won't be afraid to move on or afraid of making the wrong choice. You could still have a mann. The kinner could have a daed."

Jennie sucked in air. To move on, to have a life to lay aside her fear and anxiety, she had to tear the bandage from the wound and let it heal in the light of day. "What happened to Atlee?"

"Nothing." Olive ripped the husk from the corn cob. Corn silk flew. "That's what makes it so hard to understand. We raised him exactly as we did our other boys. But he turned out different."

"Something must've happened to him to become so hard, so bitter, so—"

"Mean?" Olive dumped the husks in a paper sack on the floor. She seemed oblivious to the tears that ran down her wrinkled cheeks.

"I've gone over it a million times in my mind. I can't find anything that made him mad or hurt or angry. Believe me, I've searched my soul over and over again, longing to find a reason, if only to ease my own sense of guilt at having brought such a mean man into this world."

"He wasn't always mean." Jennie no longer pretended to work on the corn. Her hands sank into her lap. "He took me for buggy rides. We went to the singings. We took walks and talked. I never saw a glimpse of that ugliness before we married."

"Because he wanted something from you that he couldn't get any other way." Olive raised her head. Her gaze locked with Jennie's. Her nose began to run. She wiped at it with her sleeve. "He knew how to manipulate. He knew how to hide the darkness that lurked in his heart. I saw him with the other kinner. Cajoling them into doing things they knew they shouldn't and then laughing when they earned a trip to the woodshed."

"I thought he loved me."

"I don't think he was capable of loving." Olive's voice cracked. "A man who loves wouldn't intentionally hurt the person he loves."

"He loved the kinner. He saw disciplining them as a way of showing it."

"As something he made, he owned, maybe." Shame radiated in the way Olive hunched her shoulders. "It breaks my heart to speak of my own suh this way, but you have to know it was nothing you did. He was the bad apple in the barrel, not you. They are scarce—thanks be to Gott—in a Plain community. You can try again. It wasn't your fault."

No, it wasn't. The burden on Jennie's shoulders rolled away, but not the sadness. She would always carry it with her. She was sad for herself, but sadder for this mother who had raised a son so hard to love. She was sad for a man who had such ugliness inside him and not the strength to fight it or overcome it. Not even the desire to try.

"It wasn't your fault, either."

"I know." Olive rubbed the last remaining corn silk from the ear and laid it, its kernels, shiny and tender, on the table. "It's taken a lot of time to accept it. I'm sorry we didn't help you more. We want to help you now. You and the kinner. Any way we can."

"Danki for telling me." Jennie stood and gathered her mother-in-law in one quick squeeze. "I know it pained you something awful. You did the best you could for him."

Olive managed a tremulous smile as she looked up at Jennie. "Is it true about Leo?"

THIRTY-EIGHT

THE URGENT *BEEP-BEEP* OF A HORN WAFTED THROUGH the workshop's open door. Leo straightened. The sandpaper in his hand dropped to the floor, landing in a cushion of sawdust and wood scraps. He stooped and scooped it up again. With a soft growl deep in his throat, Beau uncurled from his spot in the shop's doorway and disappeared into the yard. Customers usually got out of their cars and came inside. It didn't seem very neighborly to honk and expect him to come running. Still, beggars couldn't be choosers.

What he had thought was a new beginning in the store, a new way to market his pieces, would soon dry up. He would have to figure this out on his own. Make his own way. Something he knew how to do. Mind over matter. "Sounds like we have company."

"Hallelujah." Matthew backed away from the dresser drawer he'd been sanding for the last two hours. "I'll go see who it is."

"You just keep working. I'll go." Leo had no intention of letting the boy off the hook. He'd rousted him from bed at dawn, watched him make sausage and eggs for breakfast, and set him to work as soon as the last dish had been washed. This had become their routine since the night he ran off to visit the tavern. "When you're done with that drawer, start on the bottom one."

Rubbing red-rimmed eyes, Matthew went back to work without replying. At least he'd learned not to argue. That was progress. Leo dusted his hands on his pants and strode out into the summer heat. The midday sun beat on his face. He put his hand to his forehead to shield his eyes. Beau stood, tail wagging furiously, in front Todd's black SUV.

The window rolled down and the vet stuck his head out. "Hey, I was out driving around and thought I'd come by to see how Red is doing."

"He's much better." Leo wiped sweat from his eyes with his sleeve. "Want to come in and say hi to him? He likes a visitor now and then."

"Sure, but first I have something to show you." Todd rolled down the back windows with the touch of a button, shoved open his door, and hopped out. "Take a look."

His grin stretching so wide it must've hurt his face, he opened the back door. Leo peeked inside.

Matching car seats faced the back of the SUV. They held tiny mounds of sleeping baby. Two bite-size humans dressed in pink Onesies and little pink knitted booties. Bits of fluffy blonde down kept them from being completely bald. One stretched, and her tiny fists batted air, then subsided.

"They're here." Leo didn't know what else to say. Babies baffled him. They might even scare him. They were so tiny and defenseless. So needy. They made his heart contract and then swell with the need to do something, anything, to make sure they were never hurt. Even when they weren't his own. "I mean they're born."

The English likely did a lot of back slapping and congratulating.

It wasn't the Plain way, certainly wasn't Leo's way, but the blissful look on his friend's face deserved a response. "You're blessed."

"I am. They came ten days ago. Three weeks early, but healthy as can be. Five pounds, more or less, apiece." Todd rubbed the stubble on his chin. Dark bags hung under his red eyes. "Now we're both sleep deprived, exhausted, and out of our minds with happiness." He pointed at the far car seat. "That's Kaitlin. This little wiggle worm is Katherine."

The wiggle worm chose that moment to open her eyes, open her mouth wide, and wail.

"No, no, you'll wake sissy." Panic in his eyes, Todd unstrapped the baby with nimble fingers and lifted her from the car seat. "I just got them to sleep."

"Why did you bring them here?"

"Actually I was just out driving them around." Todd's confession came with a rueful laugh. "I couldn't get them to sleep, and Samantha is so worn out from getting up every two hours at night to feed them, I wanted to give her a break. They fall asleep in the car. Both at the same time. It feels like a miracle. I remembered that you hadn't seen them yet so I came this way. Your rocking chair is getting a lot of use these days."

"It's your rocking chair."

Todd rocked the baby in his arms for a second, then held her out. "Want to hold her?"

"Nee." Both hands up, Leo stumbled back a step. "I'll break her."

"Don't drop her and you'll be fine." He sounded a little desperate. "Babies don't break that easy."

Leo couldn't remember the last time he'd held a baby that small and helpless, but Todd seemed to need his help. "You sure I won't scare her?"

"She'll love you."

Todd settled the baby in Leo's arms. She looked even tinier against his enormous biceps. "Hello, bopli."

She stared up at him, her expression startled. She might look a bit like Todd, but more like Samantha. She smelled like spit-up, baby soap, and wet diaper.

"Look at you. You're a natural." Todd backed up and sank onto his SUV's front seat. He sighed. "Feel free to walk around with her. Sometimes that puts her to sleep too."

Nee, Leo wouldn't go too far in case she changed her mind about him. She gurgled. "I think she has the hiccups."

"That happens."

Her skinny, wrinkled legs and arms flailed. More hiccups. She was sweet and lighter than a splinter of wood in his arms. She stared up at him. He stared back. With her birth and that of her sister, everything in Todd and Samantha's life had changed. They were parents. They were a family. Nothing would ever be the same again. Leo tried to imagine a smidgeon of how that must feel.

Like the best feeling in the world and the worst, most horrible fearful feeling all wrapped up together. He'd like to find out.

Katherine began to fuss. The fuss grew in volume to a wail. "Hush, hush, you're all right, hush." He tried rocking her the way Todd had. More fussing. "Shhh, shhhhh."

The wailing reached a crescendo. Kaitlin opened her eyes and joined her sister in a crying chorus.

"Welcome to my world." Todd trotted around to the other side of the car and extracted the baby from her seat. Her sobs subsided to a low roar.

"Well, look at you." Matthew stood in the doorway. He crossed his arms and leaned against the frame. "Boplin look fine on you."

Leo was tempted to send him back to his sanding. Instead, he smiled. "I think so. You want to hold her?"

"I have six younger bruders and schweschders. I've done my share."

"So how do you get them to stop crying?" Todd put twin number two on his shoulder and patted her back. He didn't seem to see any irony in asking a young boy the question. "What's the secret?"

Matthew shrugged. "There's no secret. My mudder always checked the diaper first, then fed the bopli, then burped him, then put him to bed."

"What if he—or she—still cries?"

"Sometimes they need a little rocking. Sometimes they just need to get over it."

Fourteen and an expert. Matthew knew more about babies than Todd and Leo put together. "You'll make a good daed someday."

Matthew's face reddened. He ducked his head. "I better get back to work."

"Sure you don't want to hold her?" Leo held out his crying baby. "Maybe you'll have better luck."

"I reckon you need the practice." The boy chuckled as he turned toward the shop. "Mudder's not too old for boplin, but you better hurry. She isn't getting any younger."

After a minute, Leo remembered to close his mouth. He shifted Katherine to his shoulder and began to pat. From the mouth of a boy who didn't know his head from a hole in the ground. Matthew knew better than Leo did what Leo wanted and needed. He knew what it would take for Leo to go after it. "I think she needs a diaper change."

Todd sighed. "So does this one. All the time. Like I said, welcome to my world."

It was a world Leo wanted. Plain men didn't change a lot of diapers, but Leo was willing to do what it took to have what Todd had. "You think they might like to say hey to Red too?"

Todd's look of comic despair blossomed to a smile. "They're my kids. They're gonna love animals, especially horses."

"Change the diapers and we'll go introduce them. Might as well get them started on the right foot." Leo handed the baby back to her father. Todd shifted baby number one and took number two like he was already a pro at juggling twins. "It couldn't hurt for me to pick up a tip or two on how to do it."

"Is there something you're not telling me?" Todd nestled Kaitlin in her car seat and went to work on Katherine's diaper in the front seat. "Spill the beans, buddy!"

Leo refused to say a word—not yet.

He needed get himself in order before he could expect someone else to rely on him. Trust him. Love him. If he could do it, so could Jennie. With time. He would give her the gift of time and pray that God sent a certain Mennonite man far, far away. Soon.

THIRTY-NINE

SOMETIMES GOD USED A FRYING PAN UPSIDE THE head to get a man's attention. Sometimes He used a butterfly fluttering in the distance. Leo stared at the invoice in his hand, aware of an unfamiliar feeling of optimism that made his muscles hum with anticipation of work to be done. The early morning sun beating down on his shoulders, he stood in the dirt and gravel drive that separated his shop from the house and watched the new customer's dusty red pickup truck drive away.

Todd had something to do with this, Leo could be sure of that. The vet might be up to his ears in dirty diapers, but he somehow found the time to send work Leo's way after his visit with the twins earlier in the week. A job for an English family from Trenton included a dining room set with a table, six chairs, and an elaborate hutch. The deposit alone was enough to buy a new serviceable horse. Sweet Red would enjoy the leisurely pace of early retirement. And the proceeds from the finished furniture set would allow Leo to pay off the buggy he and Mary Katherine had given Jennie.

He could do this. He could have his own business, run his own shop, and deal with the customers. One step at a time. For himself. And for Jennie.

I get it, Gott. Through bad and gut, You are here.

Leo straightened his hat and strode to the open shop door. He stuck his head inside. "Let's go."

Matthew looked up from the dresser drawer he'd been sanding for the last hour. A look of relief on his sweaty face, he dropped the sandpaper on the workbench. "Where're we going?"

"To see a man about a horse."

Forty-five minutes later they parked the buggy next to dozens more lined up in a field next to Jonas Miller's barn. It was the second day of a two-day consignment auction with the big items such as carriages, buggies, and more than seventy-five horses on the auction block, according to the sales bill he'd picked up at the hardware store the previous day. Trucks, cars, and horse trailers of all makes, models, and colors packed the field on the other side. Bidding would be competitive, as usual.

Matthew at his heels, Leo threaded his way through trailers loaded with tack and saddles. Long before they arrived at the corral, he could hear the auctioneer at work, his raspy voice vibrating with obvious glee as the bids for what he described as a beautiful chestnut American Saddlebred grew. Together they squeezed into a space between a farmer in gray overalls and a John Deere hat and a cluster of Plain men from Seymour. Raymond Stultz's son, Josiah, put the horse through his paces in the center of the corral with a steady hand and quick feet.

"He looks gut." The animation in Matthew's voice surprised Leo. Finally, something that excited the boy. "Gut proportion. Strong."

"Jah, he'll go high." Leo craned his head and scanned the crowd.

It would be unlike his cousins to miss an auction involving horses. Both Aidan and Timothy were good judges of horseflesh, and horse auctions served as social events for the men. "Too high for me."

Aidan stood at the far corner of the fence, but his brother Henry, not Timothy, stood next to him, an older, shorter version of the other two men. Aidan turned just as Leo spotted him and waved. He grinned and headed their direction.

"I wondered if you would be here." Aidan slapped Matthew on the back. "Are you helping my cousin find a decent horse?"

His face red, Matthew nodded. "Are you buying too?"

"Nee, but Henry is."

"We'll see." Henry shrugged. "One of my Percherons is getting too old to pull a plow, but the nags they're selling today don't look much better."

"Really?" Straining to see over a sea of straw hats with black bands, Leo pulled his own hat down to shade his eyes from the sun and tried to tame his natural-born affinity for almost all animals on four legs. "You didn't see anything you liked for pulling buggies?"

They discussed the pros and cons of half a dozen possibilities before Aidan suggested they head inside to the barn and get a closer look at the best of the lot before it was too late.

As they zigzagged around farmers mixed with cowboys in blue jeans and boots and then two-stepped to avoid large piles of steaming horse droppings at every turn, Leo studied Matthew. His color was high, his smile as wide as Leo had ever seen. "You really like horses, don't you?"

"Lot more than I like furniture. No offense."

"None taken." Leo winked at Aidan, who grinned back. "Ever consider getting into the horseshoeing business?"

Matthew halted. "Hey, that's an idea."

"You're blocking traffic." Leo gave him a gentle shove. They started walking again. "I'll talk to Zeke to see if he's in the market for a helper."

Zeke Hostetler had been one of the gang when Leo and Aidan were kids. Then he grew up, met an English girl, fell in love, and left the faith. Many of the Plain community used his blacksmithing services, even if his family wasn't allowed to visit with him. Finding Matthew a vocation that would suit his temperament and be to his liking would make Jennie happy. Which would make Leo happy.

Thinking of Zeke naturally made Leo think of the other members of their once tight-knit group, Aidan's youngest brother. "Have you heard from Paul lately?"

"Got a letter last week." Aidan sidestepped a plastic water bottle someone had thrown on the ground. He stooped, picked it up, and tossed it into a rusted trash can. "He says he's doing okay in Sugar Creek working with Onkel Luke. He also says you're welcome."

Leo chuckled. Paul was a quiet man, but he did have a sense of humor. "We could've worked together. The two of us could've had a shop."

"Paul is about as inclined to work with others as you are." Aidan slapped at a huge fly that buzzed his head. "And he talks about as much as you do. Who would take orders from the customers?"

Paul's carpenter skills were strong. Leo would've been happy to work with him. Instead, his cousin had struck out for Ohio the previous year for a fresh start. Aidan had a point about the talking, though.

"If he has a girl, he isn't admitting it." Aidan elbowed Leo. "Also like you."

"Oh, jah, Leo has a girl," Matthew crowed. "My mudder."

"Hush your mouth." Leo picked up his pace, leaving the other men a step behind so they couldn't see his face. They laughed. "None of you knows what he's talking about."

"I'm getting us some lemonade." Henry jerked his head toward the concession stand manned by three of Jonas's children. "Help me carry it, Matthew?"

The two took off on their mission, leaving Leo under Aidan's obvious scrutiny. He ducked into the line that coursed by the stalls in the enormous barn. The air was thick with dust, bits of hay, and humidity. The smell of manure mingled with the odor of animal and man sweat. Flies buzzed. Leo inhaled and relaxed. Aside from his shop, this was where he felt most in his element. "That's a nice Morgan."

Aidan stepped in front of Leo and slapped both hands on the railing of the stall that held the object of Leo's admiration. "Don't try to avoid the question."

"What question?"

"This's Licorice. Don't laugh. My granddaughter named him." The horse's owner, a man with leathered skin, deep crow's feet, and a tan sweat-stained cowboy hat, curried the horse's glossy coat. "He's a good horse, nice disposition. A willing worker. Fifteen hands, strong back."

The black Morgan held his head and his tail high as his breed usually did. His tail, like his mane, was thick and full. He dipped his head and whinnied softly.

"Nice to meet you, Licorice."

The horse huffed and sidestepped closer when Leo held out his hand. His breath was warm, his eyes dark and intelligent. Leo patted his broad face.

"You'll talk to the horse and not to me?"

Leo ignored Aidan's frustrated snort and focused on the owner, who introduced himself as Charlie Hanson, a farmer from Chillicothe. "How much you hoping he'll bring?"

"Hoping for two thousand." Hanson smoothed his wrinkled hand along the horse's back. "He's twelve years old. He's good with a buggy or a wagon. And he's saddle broken."

A decent price. "Care if I come in?" Leo pointed to the gate.

Hanson nodded.

Leo took his time examining the horse from his ears to all four hooves while Hanson kicked dirt off his scuffed cowboy boots against the stall railing. The horse was solid, like his owner.

"Morgans don't get a lot of leg or foot problems," Hanson offered. "It's a known a fact."

"Good to know." It was after Red's laminitis. "Why are you selling him?"

"Truthfully? Things are tight and I don't have a need for three horses." Hanson patted Licorice's nose as if to offer an apology for his words. "The grandkids put their names in a jar and Licorice came up on the short end of the stick."

Leo nodded his thanks to the man and they moved on to other stalls, looking at a pinto, an Appaloosa, and several Standardbreds after Henry and Matthew joined them with the ice-cold lemonade. None of the animals caught Leo's eye like that Licorice. By mutual consent they returned to the corral, but Leo knew Aidan wouldn't give up. His cousin leaned in close and raised his voice to be heard over the auctioneer. "There comes a point in his life when a man has to put up or shut up."

"I know that."

"Do you?"

"Why do you think I decided to buy a horse today?"

"Because you didn't want to keep Star too long?" Aidan scrunched up his face like a scholar trying to please his teacher by guessing the right answer. "Because Star is eating you out of house and home?"

"I got a big job today. One that will pay for a horse and help get me on the road toward opening my own shop."

"Your own shop?" Aidan's mouth dropped open. He seemed oblivious of the bidding war that had developed over a nice-looking dapple-gray mare. "On your property or in town?"

"My property." Leo glanced at Henry and Matthew. The older man had the boy mesmerized with his considerable knowledge of horses. "I'm hoping I'll have some others join with me."

Aidan edged closer and lowered his voice. "Like a certain widow."

"None of your business."

"It's her!" He let out a whoop, then hunched his shoulders when several men looked around, frowning. "Why now? What changed?"

Leo pointed at the corral. Hanson had entered with the Morgan. "I changed."

"You're . . . ready to let the past go and move on?"

"Jah. I'm ready." The question remained if—and when—Jennie would be ready. His willingness to turn over this new leaf might serve as a sign to her. He prayed it did, but Aidan didn't need to know all that. He elbowed his cousin. "Now shut up. I'm trying to buy a horse."

And he did.

FORTY

THE WEDDING WAS LIKE NO OTHER IN JENNIE'S memory. She'd attended many ceremonies, to be sure, but none for a young widow and mother about to embark on a second life with her first husband's best friend. People from all over the Midwest—Indiana, Iowa, Ohio—had arrived to celebrate with them. Bess's face shone with happiness as she slipped to the front of the barn with her younger sisters as her witnesses. Everything about the way she carried herself spoke of hope and delight and no looking back.

Was Bess thinking of Caleb? The father of her child? The man who'd been taken from her in a terrible truck-buggy accident on a cold winter day? Was Aidan thinking of Caleb, who'd been as close as a brother?

If someone so young and inexperienced could find her way to this second chance, surely Jennie could too. She could let go of fear and distrust. She could rely on God's plan for her.

To have a second chance seemed so hopeful. A woman expected only one such wedding, one such promise, one such beginning.

Atlee grabbed her hand and tugged her back into her seat at the wedding *eck*. Around them the conversation of happy friends and family members flowed as they ate cake and pie, oblivious to the frown on the new husband's face. "Don't."

No.
No.

She shook her head. Then she looked around. Everyone was focused on the beautiful, sacred ceremony in front of them. They hadn't noticed her lapse. She would not stumble down that painful memory lane ever again. Those memories would no longer hold sway over her. She didn't know if Atlee found peace in death or faced his due, but she had to forgive. Forgive, forget, and move on. She had to look forward. She still lived. She still had a heart that ached to be filled with love.

With every touch and every look, Leo told her he could fill her up with the love she craved.

She bowed her head. *Thy will be done, Gott. Thy will be done.*

"Do you promise if he should be afflicted with bodily weakness, sickness, or some similar circumstance that you will care for Aidan as is fitting a Christian wife?" Freeman's voice echoed from the barn's rafters.

Jennie opened her eyes and raised her head.

Bess smiled. "Jah." Her voice was strong. No hesitation.

God's grace was so bountiful. It covered them up. Jennie swallowed hot tears as she listened to the remaining vows. Each day required a leap of faith. Some bigger than others.

Aidan and Bess clasped their right hands together. Freeman's hand covered theirs. "So then I may say with Raguel, the God of

Abraham, the God of Isaac, and the God of Jacob be with you together and fulfill His blessing abundantly upon you, through Jesus Christ. Amen."

They were pronounced husband and wife. Freeman wiped away tears with a simple, unabashed swipe. As many times as he had performed this duty, he did not lose sight of its significance.

But he was only the conduit. God oversaw it and worked through him.

He had done so when Jennie married Atlee. Why she had to go through it, she couldn't say. But she was a different person for it. Honed by the fire. Refined. Ready for what came next.

She stood with the others, waiting for a chance to give Bess a hug before she left with the wedding party to travel to Timothy and Josie's house where the festivities were being held.

Waiting for Leo to see her face.

Waiting to start again.

Leo couldn't put his finger on what had changed. He had served as a witness at Timothy's wedding. It was an honor and a joy. But now, with Aidan's marriage to Bess, Leo wanted to do all sorts of unmanly things. Shed tears. Bear hug his cousin. Shout. Someone alien had taken over his body for a few minutes. Surely, he would right himself if he could just have a few moments alone.

He waded through the crowd, nodding at relatives he hadn't seen in years. People from Iowa, Michigan, Nebraska, who crowded the barn, squeezed together like sausages, smiling, nodding, chatting as they watched the wedding party depart for the noon meal at

Timothy's. They would follow and the feasting would begin. Aidan and Bess's new life would begin.

He swallowed against the tight lump in his throat. To see his cousin so happy eased the pain in Leo's heart. Aidan waited a long time for this. He was a good man who put his best friend's happiness first. He deserved this.

You deserve it too.

The words were whispered in his ear. The voice was kind and gruff, deep, like his father's.

He glanced left and right. The crowd flowed around him.

You were a child. You could've done nothing.

In this world you will have trouble. But take heart! I have overcome the world.

The words erased the pain in his heart. The deep wound knit itself together.

He blinked against tears that burned his eyes and heaved a breath. He surveyed the crowd. There. Jennie stood near the door, but she wasn't leaving. She didn't move. She waited. He caught her gaze and she lifted her hand in a swift, small wave.

He moved toward her, dodging small children and clusters of guests.

"They'll be happy, won't they?" She spoke first. "I'm so happy for them."

"God has blessed them."

"He's blessed all of us." She smiled. "You and me, even."

"We only have to learn from the lessons."

"I have."

"Me too." Was she saying what he thought she was saying? Her gaze didn't shift from his. "Are you sure? There's nobody else."

"Nobody."

He glanced around at the crowd flowing past them. This wasn't the time or the place to talk about their future, but her gaze promised that the time was coming and it was up to him to choose the place. There was someone's future they could discuss, however. "Did Matthew talk to you about the horse auction last week?"

"Nee, he hasn't said much, but he has been smiling a lot more lately. What happened at the horse auction?"

"It turns out your suh has a special place for horses in his heart."

"Indeed?" She looked puzzled. "And that makes him smile?"

"He's smiling because Zeke Hostetler has agreed to take him on as a blacksmith apprentice." Leo studied her face to see if she understood what this meant. Her smile broadened. He grinned back. "He has found an occupation that suits him better than carpentry."

"He'll be okay then."

"More than okay. He'll be happy." They could all find happiness, with time. "We'll talk more soon. I'll find you later."

She nodded. Her smile made him long to take her into his arms and kiss her hard, in front of God and everyone who attended this wedding. The kiss would have to wait.

But not long.

"Jennie, over here!"

Leo turned to see Laura threading her way through the crowd. "It will be our turn to serve by the time we get to the house." Her gaze meandered from Jennie to Leo and back. "Or did you have other plans?"

"I have to go." Jennie's smile widened as if she read his thoughts. "You need to get going since you're in the wedding party."

He'd forgotten his role was not over. "I have to go."

Neither of them moved.

Laura laughed and tugged on Jennie's arm. "Let's go, my dear, everything in its time."

The wisdom of age.

His and Jennie's time would come soon.

FORTY-ONE

THE BLACK PLUME OF SMOKE DRIFTED ACROSS A
cloudless, early morning August sky. Concern swept over Jennie.
Jamesport's downtown consisted of only a few blocks. A fire in one
building jeopardized every building. The menacing plume spiraled
as she waited for the light to change at the intersection. It took her
mind from endless speculation over whether Leo would be at the
store. His role in the wedding party and hers as server had kept them
from having their talk after the wedding on Thursday. Friday had
fled in helping the newlyweds clean up and taking care of visiting
guests who weren't departing until the weekend.

Now Saturday had arrived. Their last day to work at the store
before they needed to begin packing up and moving out so Lazarus
could claim it for his coffee shop. Mary Katherine was probably
already there, marking everything down in hopes of selling as much
as possible by the end of the day. Jennie's friend didn't seem perturbed
by the turn of events. Mary Katherine loved the store, but she was
much better at accepting change than Jennie.

Which brought her back to Leo. The emotions in his face had
been unmistakable. She had no doubt that he had read the same in

hers. A heat that could not be attributed to the August sun enveloped her every time she thought about him.

Which had been dozens of times as she tossed and turned in her bed all night long.

Lulu neighed and tossed her head. She sidestepped and tried to bolt. "Whoa, whoa, you're fine. Don't get in a hurry." The light changed and Jennie eased up on the reins. That made Lulu happy. The buggy jolted forward. "What's your problem this morning?"

She turned the corner and headed up the street toward Amish Treasures. The caustic smell of burning wood, insulation, plastic, and rubber hit her. Smoke billowed in the air.

Smoke billowed from Amish Treasures.

Lula tried to bolt again. "Whoa, Whoa!" Jennie tugged on the reins until the horse gave in. She parked next to two other buggies, leapt from the buggy, and tied the reins to the hitching post.

Ignoring Lulu's indignant whinnies, she picked up her skirt and ran. Smoke seeped through the cracks around the windows and doors of the antique shop to Amish Treasures' left. It deepened and spread with each passing second, seeping into their store, with flames sure to follow.

Leo stood on the sidewalk. She raced toward him. "What happened?"

"I don't know. I just pulled up."

Three buggies parked on the street. Hers, Leo's, and a third. Her heart banged in her chest. That and the thickening smoke made it hard to breathe. "Where's Mary Kay?"

"I haven't seen her." He darted to the Amish Treasures' door and pushed hard. Nothing. "It's locked. She's not in there."

"Then where is she?"

"Are you looking for your friend?" Lazarus's business partner—his name swirled away in the smoke—Mr. Silky Suit, stood a few yards away, wringing his hands, Kyle, the electrician next to him. "She went in with Lazarus. They were discussing the handoff of the store when they saw the flames. He ran in. She flew after him."

"And you're just standing here?" Leo started toward Antiques and Beyond. "How long ago was that?"

"A minute. Ninety seconds."

"And you're still standing here?"

"I called 911. Fire & Rescue should be on the way."

Jamesport's Fire & Rescue was a volunteer-run department. How quickly the firefighters arrived would depend on how far away the volunteers were when they received the call. It could be a few minutes or it could be fifteen or twenty.

"He wanted me to go in there and fix whatever it is," Kyle added. "I told him I'm an electrician, not a firefighter. He was mad. And he's crazy."

"Is it an electrical fire?"

"I can't tell without getting in there and looking at it." Kyle sounded apologetic. "And it's too late for that."

Leo grabbed the antique store's door and threw it open.

Jennie grabbed his arm. "Leo, nee."

"Wait here."

"Nee."

"Tell the firemen I went after them." He disappeared into the smoke.

One second, two seconds, three.

Flames licked at the windows, lighting the interior. Black smoke poured out the door.

Jennie couldn't stand here. She couldn't lose that second chance.

She couldn't lose him. She couldn't lose her best friend, the woman who'd been there for her day after day for all these years.

Her heart pounding so hard her chest might explode, Jennie barreled through the door after her second chance.

"Hey, you can't go in there."

She ignored Kyle's and Silky Suit's shouts and plunged into the smoke. "Leo? Leo! Mary Kay?"

Blackness. Her eyes stung. Her mouth tasted bitter, burnt rubber. Her lungs burned. One hand over her mouth, the other flailing in front of her, she inched forward. She could see nothing.

She stumbled over a piece of furniture, fell to her knees, and knocked her arm against a wall.

"Ouch, ouch!" She righted herself. "Leo! Mary Kay!"

No response.

She'd never been in this store before. She didn't know the layout.

Tears strung her eyes from the acrid smoke that smelled of burning wires and old wood. She closed them for a second. The darkness wasn't much different. She opened them.

Shapes loomed. A china closet of some kind. Chairs. A display cabinet. Flames licked at the wood. She coughed. Her lungs burned. "Leo, please."

Gott, please. Help me. Help them. Don't take them. Please. I don't deserve a second chance, but I want it. I'm ready for it. I'm trusting You.

She couldn't breathe.

Stay close to the ground. Smoke rises.

She'd learned that long, long ago. At a May Day community fair when the volunteer firefighters had brought out their pumper and tanker trucks and raised funds for new equipment. The kids climbed around on the trucks. The air had been crisp and clean and fresh.

She longed for that air.

She crouched on her hands and knees. "Leo! Mary Kay!"

"Jennie."

Leo's voice was hoarse, barely a whisper. "Here. She won't wake up."

Jennie scrambled toward his voice. Menacing flames danced along the walls. Leo knelt over a body in the far corner, next to an open door.

"Are you all right?"

"It's Mary Kay." Leo coughed, a gut-wrenching, hacking sound. "She's breathing, but she's passed out. I can't find Lazarus. We have to get her out."

"Take her. I'll find Lazarus." She crawled around him and kept going. It was so black she could see nothing.

She bumped into a wall.

"Nee, don't go in there. That's where it started. The storage room."

The heat intensified. It scorched her cheeks. Fear enveloped her. *Gott, I can't see. Help me.*

Her hand landed on something warm and soft. And limp.

"Lazarus? Lazarus!" She patted harder. An arm. Then his face. "I found him. I have him."

Leo's outline loomed in the black smoke. "I'll drag him. You get Mary Katherine. She's lighter."

Jennie tried to rise.

His arm gripped hers. "Stay close to the floor. Less smoke."

On her belly she inched back to Mary Katherine. She rose to her knees, tucked her arms under her friend's armpits, and began to drag her out. Time stood still. The flames leaped higher and closer. A wall collapsed. She shrieked and ducked as embers flared and floated around her.

"Keep going. It's spreading fast," Leo yelled. He sounded close but she couldn't see him. "Move!"

She coughed, bent double under Mary Katherine's weight, but she kept going. She had to keep moving. For their future. "Come on, Mary Kay, come on."

For Leo's. Even for Lazarus's.

And her children. They'd lost their father. They couldn't lose her too. She pushed forward.

The door appeared. A gush of fresh air flowed over her.

Air—sweet, fresh air.

A firefighter in his slick yellow jacket burst through the door. "You got them?"

Jennie recognized him as Lou Stover, an employee from the hardware store. "We got them," she yelled. "Help us."

Lou tugged Mary Katherine's weight from Jennie. Craig Lohman, a plumber who had his own shop, squeezed in next to him and helped Leo with Lazarus. "Anybody else?"

"No, the store wasn't open yet."

"Get out."

They pushed through the door and out into the lovely, beautiful, fresh air. Jennie inhaled big, gulping breaths. Leo sank to his knees, his fingers rubbing at his soot-blackened face. "What were you thinking?" He gasped and coughed. "I told you to wait."

"I had to rescue you. You think you have to rescue everyone." Adrenaline ebbed, then flowed again at the thought of losing him. "Sometimes you have to be rescued."

Jamesport's Fire & Rescue pumper and tanker trucks filled the street. Sirens screamed as a Daviess County ambulance sped toward them and halted behind the trucks. Firefighters dodged around them, unwinding hoses. Shouted orders reverberated. Water sprayed. Leo loomed over her, sweat—or smoke-induced tears—creating rivulets down his dirty cheeks. "I didn't need help."

"Jah, you did, and I wasn't going to stand here and watch my life go up in smoke."

Firefighters helped the EMTs ease Mary Katherine and Lazarus onto waiting gurneys. Lazarus's entourage clustered around him. The man stirred and groaned. "My shop, my antiques."

"You're alive." The EMT—her name escaped Jennie—slapped an oxygen mask on him, stopping further outbursts. "You're lucky. Running into a burning building isn't smart."

"What about Mary Kay? Is she all right?" Jennie brushed past Leo and laid her hand on her friend's arm. The woman's face was red, her lips cracked and blistered. Her kapp was missing. Jennie smoothed her dirty apron over her skirt. She looked so old and vulnerable. "Mary Kay, wake up, please wake up."

The EMT—Diana, Diana something—applied an oxygen mask to her face. Mary Katherine's eyelids fluttered. Her fingers moved, then her hands. She tugged at the mask until she had it down around her chin. She coughed so hard she began to wretch. "The store is burning up." She gasped. "It's burning."

"Don't talk. Just rest."

"I tried to stop it."

Around them firefighters pulled hoses and yelled instructions. A cooling mist floated in the air around them. Puddles formed around their feet. Sweet, cool water. "It's okay. We'll survive."

Mary Katherine wiped at her mouth with shaking fingers. "I'm glad you finally figured that out. You are a survivor."

"I meant—"

"I know what you meant." Mary Katherine coughed again and tried to sit up. "I don't need to go to the clinic."

"Lie back, right now. You're going."

"You're not the boss of me."

"I am right now."

She sank onto the gurney. "I'll rest for a minute while you go apologize to Leo."

"Why do I need to apologize?"

"From the look on his face, you did something."

"Did not."

"Go."

"Fine."

Mary Katherine closed her eyes again.

Diana settled the oxygen mask back over Mary Katherine's mouth. She turned to Leo and Jennie. "And you two? Let me get a look at the stupid hero and heroine."

"I'm fine." Leo took a step back. Angry red burnt spots marred one cheek. His hat suffered from a big hole on top. Fire had singed the hair on both arms. "Look at her first."

"I'm fine." Jennie crossed her arms. Her lungs and nostrils ached. Burnt holes from floating sparks and embers peppered her dress and apron. A patch on her palm looked and felt like it did when she grabbed a pan without a pot holder. "Just worry about them."

"It's primarily smoke inhalation." Diana took Jennie's hand and examined it closely. She made a *tut-tut* sound and let it drop. "We'll take them over to the clinic in Trenton so the doctors can examine them both. You should go as well. Get this looked at."

"I can doctor it at home. I've doctored seven kids with worse."

Leo turned his back and stomped away. He coughed, his hands on his hips, his shoulders bent.

"You need to have her look at your face." Jennie strode after him. "You're not fine."

He whirled. "You didn't listen to me. You didn't stay safe."

"You can't keep people safe. You have to take chances and trust in Gott." She stopped, listening to her own words. "Trust Gott. And I'll do the same. I know what I want now. Do you?"

His blackened hands gripped her waist. She could think of nothing else, only him, and what it would be like to lose this second chance, to have to fill each day that might come without the hope of the life Leo offered her.

She leaned in. He met her more than halfway. His lips tasted salty. The heat had nothing to do with the fire that raged behind them. She inhaled the scent of him, saving the memory for when he was beyond her grasp.

The sound of clapping and a few ragged cheers reminded her where they were. She didn't care. She wanted this to last forever. Leo stepped back. His gaze startled, and he shook his head. "Sorry. To be continued."

"That's not quite what I meant by apologize," Mary Katherine called, her voice hoarse. "Courting is private."

"Sorry." Leo looked the way she felt. Stunned. "We'll talk later."

Talk and touch and kiss the way people who loved and cared for each other did. With no price to pay and no hurt or pain to bear in return. It seemed almost too good to be true.

Trust. You have to trust.

Gott, help me trust.

"Jah, we will."

He leaned close, his lips near her ears. "I promise I will never hurt you."

He was so close it was all she could do not to raise her lips to his again. "I'm scared."

His smile was ragged. "Me too."

FORTY-TWO

"CAN I TALK TO YOU FOR A MINUTE?"

Jennie looked up from wiping her sooty hands on her apron to see Nathan standing at the door to the store. He wore jeans and a red Kansas City Chiefs football jersey. The suspenders were gone, replaced by a brown leather belt with a big silver buckle. Red-and-black Nikes replaced his work boots. He looked tired.

She glanced at Mary Katherine, who shrugged and went back to sorting through wet, stinking black rubble with garden-glove-clad hands. Jennie smiled at him. "Sure. Come on in, but be careful where you step."

"You're making progress."

She nodded. The others would arrive soon to help. Everyone— Laura, Bess, Aidan, Peter, even James and Olive would come. Mary Katherine had been a rock throughout the aftermath of the fire. She said God had other plans for them. They need only wait to see what those plans would be. The store would be Lazarus's once he got back on his feet. It would be a while. He'd suffered a heart attack on the way to the clinic. The ambulance had diverted to the hospital in Chillicothe.

Fire & Rescue did what they could, calling in fire departments from five surrounding towns. They managed to contain the fire to this one building, a minor miracle considering the closeness and the age of the buildings in Jamesport's downtown.

In the meantime Jennie and the others were doing what they could to clean up before they had to turn the place over to Lazarus. What could be salvaged would be removed. Everything else thrown out. It would be up to him to renovate and rewire. The fire, caused by old, faulty wiring, had destroyed almost everything in his antique store as well as Amish Treasures.

Life would go on, of that Jennie had no doubt.

"I came to tell you I'm leaving today." Nathan's Adam's apple bobbed. His periwinkle eyes were troubled. "I wanted to tell you in person and see you again."

She didn't need an explanation, but he was a friend going on a trip and stopping by to tell her was sweet. "Your dad is coming home?"

"Yeah, my mom gets into Wichita tonight with his body." He shifted from one foot to the other. "I'm going down to get her. I wanted to talk to you about something first."

She leaned over and picked up a faceless doll covered with soot and sopping wet. "Go ahead."

"Could I have your undivided attention?" He took the doll from her and tossed it in the growing discard pile. His hand, callused from a summer of backbreaking work, turned black. He didn't seem to notice. "I want you to know I meant everything I said to you at the lake. I thought I would have more time, but I don't. I need you to know I care for you now. I love you. I know I could make you happy."

"Nathan—"

"Let me finish, please." He took off his cap and folded it in two in

352

his sooty hand. "I have a calling. I've been avoiding it, trying to out-run it, trying to hide from it, but I realize now I can't. I can't join the Amish faith. God's calling me. I have to go. I want you to go with me."

He was so sweet and so earnest and so full of love. Hurting such a kind heart made Jennie's own heart ache. To make his declaration in front of Mary Katherine must've been doubly hard. To spare him more embarrassment, she would risk being seen with him again. Soon he would be gone and the flapping tongues would have nothing to gossip about.

She threaded her way past him and pushed through the doors, looking back to make sure Nathan followed. Together, they sat on a wooden bench in front of the burnt, sodden remains of the store. "I'm so sorry, but you know that can never happen. I won't leave my faith or my children."

"You have family here to care for them. My mother did it." His breathless tone told Jennie his mother's choice had come with great cost—to her and to her son. "I didn't want to see it for a long time, but now I realize women have this calling too. They give up even more than men, sometimes. I'm working on letting all that go, not letting it get in the way. I need to answer the calling. If you go with me, you can trust me. I would never hurt you."

"Plain women, or men, for that matter, don't get this calling you talk about." She took a breath. There was another reason she couldn't go with him. She had the hope—the promise maybe—of another love, but it wasn't with Nathan. "Regardless of that, we're not meant to be together."

The wounds had begun to knit, bit by bit. The scars grew smoother with each passing day. She had only to think of Leo. God had blessed her with this second chance. She didn't understand why she had to go through the trials in her past, but she was stronger for them. She sought words that wouldn't hurt Nathan any more than necessary. "There's someone who cares for me. A Plain man. If there is such a thing as a calling for an Amish woman, it's to be a wife to a good husband and to be obedient to God."

Understanding spread across Nathan's face and, with it, chagrin. He smoothed the cap and slapped it on his head. "Leo."

She rubbed at the soot on her fingers, then forced herself to look up at Nathan and nod.

"Do you . . . care for him?"

"I do." Heat spread through her at such an admission to a man on the sidewalk in broad daylight in downtown Jamesport. "There's something about him that makes me feel brave."

"A person should shoot for more than caring. Shoot for the moon."

"I'll get there with time." She shooed away the desire to pat Nathan's arm, to give him comfort. He wouldn't want it from her. "He is patient."

Nathan sighed and slapped his hat on his head. "He's a lucky man."

"We don't believe in luck." Jennie kept her gaze on her hands in her lap. "I'll pray that you encounter someone in your travels who'll love you the way you deserve to be loved."

"Thank you." He stood. "I need all the help I can get."

Her curiosity got the better of her. "Does God talk aloud to you, then?"

Nathan looked back, his expression somber. "It's more that He shows me His will in everything that happens to me, in the people He places in my path and the words they speak to me. I only have to pay attention and have the courage to step out in faith."

Pay attention. For the first time in years, she too was paying attention. Leo stopped by the farm the night before. They had walked together and talked together for hours. About Matthew's newfound excitement over learning the trade of blacksmithing. About her budding friendship with Olive. About his shop. For a man who never talked, he suddenly had much to say. He hadn't spoken of the future, but everything about his face, his hands, his lips, his eyes, said he saw one future for them. Every kiss. Every touch.

Jennie smiled. "Blessed be, Nathan Walker."

"Godspeed, Jennie Troyer."

She sat still and watched him get into his car. He waved and drove away as Leo pulled up in his buggy. He tied the reins to the hitching post and strode toward her. "Nathan was here."

"Jah."

An uncertain look flitted across his face.

She stood and slipped closer. "He's gone to fetch his mother and father in Wichita. He's not coming back."

His expression lighter, Leo nodded. "Gut for him."

The warmth of his eyes and the line of his jaw and his lips mesmerized Jennie. "I hope Gott blesses him the way He has us."

His big hand squeezed hers. "Me too." He dropped her hand and his thumb wiped at her cheek. He grinned. "You have soot on your face. I smeared it."

"Now you have soot on your hands." Goose bumps prickled up her arms at his touch. Her breath caught. "I must look terrible."

"Not to me." He tugged her toward the buggy. "Come with me. I want to show you something."

"What?"

"You'll see."

Thirty minutes later they turned from the highway onto the dirt road that led to Leo's place. Instead of continuing on, Leo pulled off onto the shoulder and halted. Jennie surveyed the fence and the tree line. "What are we doing here?"

He grinned and hopped from the buggy. "Come on. You can help me."

She followed him to the back of the buggy where he pulled out a sign. A big, handmade, wooden sign that read *Handcrafted Amish Furniture For Sale.* He'd used a wood router to create the cursive letters and painted the background a deep blue. Underneath were an arrow and the smaller words *one mile down on the right.*

"You're inviting people to your shop to buy your furniture." Others might not understand the significance of this, but Jennie did. "I'm so happy for you."

"And for you too, I hope." He handed her the sign. She held it while he tugged a mallet from the buggy. Together, they carried the sign to the intersection, and he banged its poles into the ground until it was firmly entrenched. "Would you like to give it a whack?"

"I would." She took her turn and then stepped back to survey their work. "It's gut."

His hand slipped into hers. He faced her. "I'm starting my own business. I'm close to the road and only a few miles from town, no farther than some of the other Amish stores visited by the tourists. I've already talked to the Chamber about being added to the tourist map and their website."

"You've been hard at work."

"I was thinking we could make it a combination store."

"We?"

"You, Mary Kay, the others. We could sell your wares at the store too. We could even expand the space." His smile was tentative. His eyebrows lifted under a furrowed forehead. "If you wanted, I mean. If you think it's a good idea."

"I think it's wunderbarr." He believed in them. He saw a future for them. "Mary Kay will lieb it."

"I lieb you." His voice cracked and he studied the ground.

She swallowed back tears. "Leo—"

"I know. It's too soon. You've been through a lot. Things I wish I could have shielded you from. We have time. Lots of time."

"I don't know how much time it will take."

"Take all you need. You'll see the good I see in you and know the bad things Atlee said to you weren't true." His grip on her hand tightened. He took the other hand and held them both in his. "You're gut."

The terrible memories receded farther and farther, not gone, but with less power to hurt. "I can learn to see what you see."

"Gut. We'll work on the store together and we'll take our time and we'll see where we go."

"I have a feeling we'll go far."

He kept her waiting a few seconds as he studied her face, his gaze searching, asking. He surely found the answer he sought because he bent over and kissed her hard and long. She stood on tiptoes to return the favor.

When they finally broke apart, she put her hand on his chest and smiled up at him. "You bought the buggy, didn't you?"

"Melvin is letting Mary Kay and me make payments."

She tugged him down for another kiss, letting it linger, enjoying the feel of his lips on hers and his hands on her shoulders for as long as she could before her lungs demanded she breathe. They eased apart.

Fingers entwined, faces lifted to the warm summer sun, they strolled toward the buggy and a future full of promise.

DISCUSSION QUESTIONS

1. Jennie feels guilty because she wanted out of an abusive marriage and then her husband died in an accident, freeing her. Have you ever longed for a change in circumstances only to have something unexpected and equally difficult happen? What did you learn from it?

2. Blake reminds Nathan of Luke 14:26, which says "If anyone comes to me and does not hate father and mother, wife and children, brothers and sisters—yes, even their own life—such a person cannot be my disciple." What do you think Jesus meant when He said a person has to "hate" his loved ones in order to become a disciple? Why is it necessary? How did it apply to Nathan's situation?

3. Although the Amish are Christians and focus many of their beliefs on the New Testament Gospels, most do not believe in evangelizing because they choose to hold themselves apart from the world and show their faith by example. How do you feel about that? Is it possible to lead others to Christ through example?

4. Jennie is afraid to love again for fear of choosing badly a second time. Leo is afraid to love for fear of losing as he did with his father. They've both suffered loss and hurt. Some people think that when they become Christians their troubles are over. Scripture says we will have trouble in the world, but not to worry because Jesus has overcome the world. Why do you think God allows trouble or suffering in our lives?

5. What do you think this verse means: "See, I have refined you, though not as silver; I have tested you in the furnace of affliction" (Isaiah 48:10)? How does it apply to Jennie and Leo? How does it apply to your life experiences?

6. The Mennonites come from a splinter group of early Amish believers who broke off because they didn't agree with *Meidung* or shunning. How would you feel about no longer interacting with a family member who has left the faith? Do you agree with Jennie's assessment that it is not intended to be a punishment, but rather encouragement to return to the fold and follow the rules? Could you do it?

7. Jennie spent fifteen years in a marriage with a difficult, sometimes abusive, husband because she took her marital vows very seriously. The Amish do not divorce. How do you feel about that? Are there times when a situation cannot be tolerated, despite the nature of those vows? What would your advice to Jennie have been if you were her friend?

8. For Leo and Jennie both, loving each other represents taking a chance, relying on God, and having faith in the future despite the pain they've suffered. What events in your life have made you afraid or uncertain about taking chances? Have you overcome your fears? How did you do it?

9. Christians believe God has a plan for each one of His children. Jennie can't imagine how that plan could involve being married to a man like Atlee, his death, and her role as a single mother of seven children. Have you ever had experiences that made you wonder what God's plan is for you? How do you seek to know that plan and live it?

DOMESTIC VIOLENCE
RESOURCE

JENNIE'S STORY WAS A DIFFICULT ONE TO TELL and may be hard for some to read, but the sad fact is that relationship abuse—whether physical, emotional, or both—isn't fiction. It happens every day across the United States and around the world. If you are experiencing abuse, please know that people are standing by to help you. Call the National Domestic Violence Hotline, available 24/7, at 1-800-799-7233. Service is provided in two hundred languages. For TTY/Deaf/Hard of hearing, call 1-800-787-3224.

For more information about relationship abuse and resources, visit the website at www.thehotline.org.

ACKNOWLEDGMENTS

I AM DEEPLY THANKFUL FOR THE OPPORTUNITY to write these books. I treasure every minute of it, even when the words don't flow and the story disappears into a thick fog. It's a gift to be able to write full-time, and it wouldn't be possible if it weren't for my husband, Tim, and his support. I thank God for him every day.

My thanks to Susan Rohrer for the detailed explanation of laminitis for Leo's story. As always any mistakes are totally mine. Thanks to Eileen Key for taking the time to read the rough draft and save me from myself on a number of silly bloopers.

I continue to be blessed with a wonderful editor in Becky Monds, whose sense of story and character makes each book so much better. Thank you, Becky, for your hard work, thoughtful feedback, and dedication to the craft of writing and storytelling.

While this story takes place in Jamesport, Missouri, where there is a large Amish population, the characters in this book are figments of my imagination as are the businesses described, which have fictitious names. Some of the events, such as the Purple Martin Open House, are real, but the location, date, and characters are mine. I have used poetic license in my description of several places in my story, so please remember that, above all else, this is fiction.

As always, my deepest appreciation goes out to the readers who buy these books and make it possible for me to continue to write them. God bless you.

ABOUT THE AUTHOR

 KELLY IRVIN IS THE AUTHOR OF several Amish series including the Bliss Creek Amish series, the New Hope Amish series, and the Amish of Bee County series. She has also penned two romantic suspense novels, *A Deadly Wilderness* and *No Child of Mine*. The Kansas native is a graduate of the University of Kansas School of Journalism. She has been writing nonfiction professionally for more than thirty years, including ten years as a newspaper reporter, mostly in Texas-Mexico border towns. A retired public relations professional, Kelly has been married to photographer Tim Irvin for twenty-nine years. They have two children, two grandchildren, and two cats. In her spare time, she likes to write short stories and read books by her favorite authors.